DEMONS FROM HELL♨♨♨

Mike could feel the animosity from where he stood. He had never sensed such a mass of ugly emotion—hate, frustration, anger, a terrible longing for death, murder, and blood. And all that incredible malevolence was focused on Russo as he held them at bay with the cross.

The pigs blurred into motion, running at Russo. Mike raised the .45 and fired rapidly. *"Oh Christ."* One shot knocked aside a pig, stopping it with a squeal, but the others ran about Russo's legs, leaping at him. Mike saw a snout tear open Russo's leg and heard him scream. The cross flew skyward, metal flashing as it arced away into the snow.

Manfred and all the pigs fell upon Russo like the orange breath of a flamethrower. Grunting and screeching, the dog's snarls snuffed out Russo's dying screams. Black snouts and ears, fat bodies, the man's flailing arms and legs with his clothes and flesh being ripped away—all whirled about in a terrible blend of sound and shape.

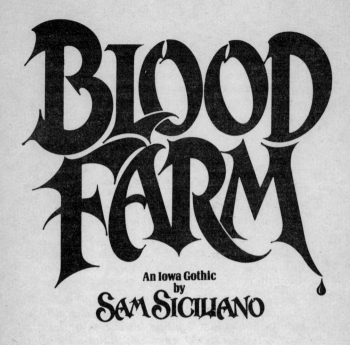

BLOOD FARM

An Iowa Gothic
by
Sam Siciliano

PAGEANT BOOKS

PAGEANT BOOKS
225 Park Avenue South
New York, New York 10003

Grateful acknowledgment is hereby given to the following for permission to reprint excerpted material in this book:

"Lullaby" by W. H. Auden. Copyright 1940 and © renewed 1968 by W. H. Auden. Reprinted from *W. H. Auden: Collected Poems* by W. H. Auden, edited by Edward Mendelson, by permission of Random House, Inc.

"Design" by Robert Frost. Copyright 1936 by Robert Frost, copyright © 1964 by Lesley Frost Ballantine, copyright © 1969 by Holt, Rinehart & Winston. Reprinted from *The Poetry of Robert Frost* edited by Edward Connery Lathem, by permission of Henry Holt & Company, Inc.

First Pageant Books printing: September, 1988

10 9 8 7 6 5 4 3 2 1

*To Professors Archibald Coolidge
and W. R. Irwin for all their
help and support from
1971 through 1975*

An Iowa Gothic

Iowa
February, 1972

CHAPTER ONE

◆

St. Agnes' Eve—Ah, bitter chill it was!
The owl, for all his feathers, was a-cold;
The hare limp'd trembling through the frozen
* grass,*
And silent was the flock in woolly fold . . .
              —Keats, The Eve of St. Agnes

SWATHS OF COLOR streaked the land's edge. Light blue, almost green, touched the black fields, then yellow faded to orange. Higher were wisps of crimson cloud, dark like veinous blood, and above all the deep blue rapidly emptying into night. Leafless branches clutched at the sky like fearful shadows, as if they too ached from the cold. Miles of rolling farmland, the ground everywhere ice-hard.

The sun had sunk slowly, the sphere of light

3

and fire reluctant to leave a few crazy men, dogs, and farm animals to darkness and greater cold. Night would eagerly freeze any living thing she could grasp, transforming the blood to black ice and the flesh to frozen meat. The sun had been a red disk, the sunset a cliché—overly dramatic, too red, a scene from numberless second-rate novels and movies. To heighten the drama, clouds gathered, swarmed gray and dark. Quickly they overran the departed sun's territory, devouring the evening star. The wind rose and fell, gusting like some pulsating organism. Down the road a dog barked, then howled.

Angela leaned back against the red-white-and-blue INTERSTATE 80 EAST sign. White vapor rushed from between her lips. "Shit." Her lips were chapped, but she licked them anyway. They were full, naturally red lips, matching her Italian name, the upper lip a Cupid's bow, warm and dark as the god himself.

She looked down again at her hiking boots. The scuffed, darkly oiled tops and the faded jeans contrasted with the dirty snow. She wiggled her toes, scrunching them down and backwards. The effort was unsuccessful, her toes stayed cold.

She had just about had it. A farmer on his way home had brought her this far and dropped her off about twenty minutes ago, but Iowa City was still a hundred and fifty miles away. She could only take about five more minutes of this. She didn't like hitching on the interstate because cars went too fast to stop, but at least there were cars there. One rotten truck and two cars had gone by, ignoring her and the minus-ten-degree temperature. And in spite of the balloonlike red down parka, a pair of thick wool socks, thermal underwear, bulky leather mittens, red wool ski hat, and in spite of her pounding down all the snow within a three-foot radius and waving her arms and shaking her hands and jumping—she was freezing. The wind picked up, its fingers caressing the flushed skin of her cheeks and lips. She wiggled her nose. It was going numb. She remembered skiing with Jane last week and watching the tip of Jane's nose go light grayish white.

"That's it." She grabbed her pack and started toward the on-ramp. A gust of wind, bigger than any before, confused her steps and swung the pack. Suddenly she heard the rumbling of a car, a big car and very noisy, the noise growing as it came nearer. She dropped the pack, put out her thumb, and looked down the road.

The double-eyed high beams of headlights jounced up and down as wheels spun and threw gravel. The lights touched her and leveled as the car moved from gravel onto asphalt. It was a huge car, black, and strangely shaped—a station wagon? Beetle black and scuttling down the road, moving fast, way faster than the speed limit, flying over chuckholes. Not a station wagon. Her eyebrows tightened, drew together, and she felt a flash of uneasiness low in the belly.

A hearse.

Stopped before her, noisy as hell (either a hole in the muffler or no muffler), she saw a Cadillac hearse, fins sprouting along the side below the dark vinyl box-shape where the coffin went. She leaned over to stare toward the back, ignoring the driver. Empty. She felt silly about being relieved.

The door boomed forth, locking wide open with a crunch and turning on the inside light to reveal Buffalo Bill Cody, cowboy hat and blond locks, sprawled across the front seat, one arm supporting him as he leaned toward her from the driver's seat. She felt the warmth, heard the heater belching forth baked air, and she smelled the sweeter-than-tobacco smell of marijuana. His right hand supported him on the seat, the left held the smoking joint, half-gone.

"Come on in. You're going to freeze your ass off out there."

She looked at Buffalo Bill, and his big grin widened another couple notches. The black battered cowboy hat with a flat brim was jammed low on his forehead. Blond hair varying from pale yellow to bright gold cascaded forth from under the hat and spilled onto the olive drab field jacket. The top of the grin was smothered in blond mustache. His eyes were light blue, and the smile put lines under them, accenting the pockets.

"And I'm going to freeze my ass off if I leave the door open much longer."

"Uh, I need a ride to Iowa City."

"*Great.*" He laughed too easily, probably because of the grass. "I'm on my way there. I can give you a ride. Please get in, my ass gets cold just thinking about your ass."

He looked at her more carefully and decided, strictly speaking, that wasn't true.

Angela stared at him, forehead tight, listening to the throbbing black machine. The heat and light from the car were warm and inviting, a refuge from the freezing nightscape. He looked fairly harmless. He was stoned, but that often made people drive more carefully. As for the hearse, he must just own it. He didn't look like a funeral director. And the alternative was standing on Eighty freezing to death. The wind gusted again, and she glanced up at the sky. An infinity of dark gray, complete cover with no stars. Snow was coming. She could always tell.

"You're going to Iowa City?"

"Yes, for Christ's sake. Don't I have a warm, friendly, open face? Think how much hot air you're wasting standing there."

She smiled and got into the car.

Sliding over to the driver's seat, he took another big draw from the joint, still grinning, but trying not to laugh and let the smoke out. With the door shut and the light out, the joint end glowed orange. Jesus Christ, things were looking up. He let the smoke out smoothly.

With a screeching noise the hearse leaped back to the road, the right wheels spinning momentarily in the snow along the road. The hearse went up to about forty, jerked back down to twenty-five as it screamed left to the freeway on-ramp. East on Eighty. Bringing his fist and the steering wheel around and up, he gunned the pedal and sent the quivering speedometer up to eighty. The exhaust coughed, wheezed, then settled to a comfortable but abnormally loud and throaty roar.

"That town back there is sure a lousy place to eat supper at. Do you go to school in Iowa City?"

"Yeah." She looked around for the seat belt. The left strap was buried under the seat.

"I live there most of the time."

"Oh."

"The Athens of America. Mecca of the Midwest. It's a crazy place."

His eyes drifted downward. Light jumped at him, the glowing green of the dash, like something you'd see in a View-Master, grotesquely three-dimensional. Definitely the dope was working. He remembered the joint in his hand and took another drag. Nontalkative girl. Fairly tasty looking from what he could see so far, probably another spoiled rich bitch, sorority type, Chi-something-or-other who prided herself on her Triumph and letting you put your hand down her pants but nothing more. He yawned. Probably his usual premature judgments.

"Hey, you want some of this? It's genuine Mexican dope."

Things couldn't get much weirder tonight. "Okay." She took the joint, drew in a long, deep breath, and felt the hot, unfamiliar smoke in her lungs. She held her breath, trying not to choke, but the smoke escaped in a sudden gag, followed by coughs. She extended her arm and offered him what remained of the joint.

"Have some more. I've got a head start."

She inhaled again, held the smoke longer before the coughs came. "God, it's hard when you don't smoke. Here."

He took the joint, one last long draw, then, still holding his breath, skillfully put it out and placed the roach in the field jacket pocket over his heart. Slowly the smoke came out of his mouth. He snapped the pocket shut. "I'll really miss this batch when it's gone."

"I'm getting hot. I think I'll take off my coat."

"All right." A burst of laughter and the grin reborn.

She stared at him, then unzipped her coat. He was easily pleased. She took off her hat carefully, not wanting to mess up the bundled hair, then removed her bulky parka and placed it between them. She looked over her shoulder. The piece of glass separating the driver's seat and the back was down. There was a long gray-carpeted expanse with leather straps to hold a coffin in place, a rolled-up sleeping bag, a rolled-up foam mattress, and a cardboard box of food and pans. She hoisted her pack over into the back.

The hearse approached a giant semi, a square of orange lights in back, then shot around it. The truck headlights cast a brief space of yellow-white light. He glanced at her. A profile: her nose dropping in a straight line from her forehead like a Greek statue; soft curve of the jaw from the earlobe; dark hair, bound up in back so a few wisps strayed down over her neck, other strands curling over her ear. The light caught the dark red of her turtleneck, bringing a brief flare of color into the cold night. She was small breasted, her body tall and slender. The hand lying on the seat was smooth, long fingers with trimmed nails. He looked at the road, swallowed.

Jesus the Christ Good Lord was she beautiful. Exactly the kind of woman he dreamed of, tall and on the thin side (he knew that wasn't fair since he had about fifteen pounds of beer gut, but he didn't care about being fair), with small breasts (others could slobber over the size of a woman's tits), dark hair and dark skin (Latin

looking, Greek, Italian, or Spanish, far removed
from his own Nordic blood, his bland blond
blood). And now the erotic thoughts buffalo-herd
stampeded across his brain, foaming, snorting,
bellowing with locked horns. Visions of her naked body—breasts, legs, feet, black hair curling
between the soft white thighs—her long body
clinging to his, fingers clutching, digging at his
back as she moaned softly.

He licked his lips, and the road flashed into his
eyes. Good thing he could drive automatically.
The grass and the woman did strange things to
his mind. Such women froze the habitual grin
and drove him, cowering, back to adolescent
terror. If she had blue eyes everything would be
over. He had always had a thing for blue-eyed,
black-haired women.

"You did say you were going to Iowa City?"
she asked. His sudden silence puzzled her.

"Yeah. After I stop someplace."

"Where do you have to stop?"

"Uh, some godforsaken little farm town about
fifty miles off the interstate. Udolph."

"I've never heard of it, but then I'm not from
Iowa."

"Well, I'm from Iowa and I haven't heard of it
either."

"What's in Udolph?"

"Nothing. Hey, what color eyes do you have?"

"What?"

"What color eyes do you have?"

"Blue."

"Jesus Christ," he groaned.

"Why do you ask?"

He grinned. She found herself smiling. "Jesus
Christ," he said, then laughed.

She laughed too. Must be the grass. "Do you have a Wild Bill Hickok complex?" That wasn't right.

"How come? I mean, as a matter of fact, I come from a long line of Hickoks."

"That wasn't right—I mean a Buffalo Bill Cody complex."

"I have a lot of problems with buffaloes. Some of my best friends are buffaloes. I knew a buffalo once—he was a great guy."

"But you wouldn't want your sister to marry one."

"No, no—wait, you've got it wrong—how did you know my sister was married to a buffalo?"

She tried to look serious. "Really?"

"Sure." Now he had her. "She met this buffalo out West one time in Wyoming, see? And this buffalo had this thing for her, and at first she could care less. This dude was always coming around and snorting and bellowing and shitting in front of the house, and my parents didn't like the guy too much, but gradually she saw this buffalo was okay. Really a warm, beautiful person inside. See?" He paused, and she nodded seriously. "This buffalo really loved her and she, she . . ."

"Realized it."

"Yeah! That's right. How did you know? Ever messed around with any buffalo? You don't know what you're missing—talk to my sister."

"So how long have they been married?"

"About twelve years. They have the cutest little pair of twin boys you've ever seen. Both have got their father's horns." She couldn't hold back her laughter. He liked the sound: she was neither a shrieker nor a giggler.

"Do we have to talk about buffaloes?"'

"You're one of those people who'd like to ignore the whole buffalo problem and pretend it'll go away, huh?"

"I only wanted to find out why you look like Buffalo Bill."

"Buffalo Bill had a goatee. I don't."

"Why the cowboy hat?"

"It's part of my self-image, see? An effort to assert my masculinity or some shit like that. Besides, my dad was a cowboy."

"Sure. Just like your sister is married to a buffalo. I suppose your mother was an Apache."

"Sioux. But really, my father was a cowboy, and we did live in Montana." The grin left his face. He stared off at the road. A couple of snowflakes splattered against the windshield. "We had a ranch in Wyoming. Thirty miles from the nearest town. Grazing land as far as the eye could see. Dad had about three hundred head of prime cattle."

"Isn't that a lot of cows?" She knew almost nothing about either ranches or farms.

"Yeah, but Dad could handle them. I can still see him sitting there in the saddle, kind of slouched, with a little thin ceegar clamped between his teeth, thin as a rail, lean in the saddle. 'Son,' he'd say, 'this is good land and those are damn fine cattle. Don't ever forget that.' He was a tough old son of a bitch, and could he ride— I've never seen anyone handle a horse like he could. Wouldn't carry a gun, but was he good with a bullwhip or knife."

"Oh, come on, you're joking."

"No—honest to God I'm not." He sounded somber.

"Is he still running the ranch?" she asked.

He sighed slowly. "No. No, I'm afraid not. He passed away just a little while back. About a year ago."

"Oh. I'm sorry."

Another sigh. "Yeah. Poor Dad. I remember him lying there in bed with a grizzled gray beard, same thin ceegar between his lips—he never gave a damn what the doctors said. 'Well, boys, it's all yours now. Told you some day it'd all be yours. Well, now that day's come. Take good care of it.' "

"What killed him?"

"Well . . ." He took another deep breath, trying to control something. "He went out to the west range to put in some fence when it hit." His voice quivered, he paused, and she thought of stampeding cattle, mountain lions, men with guns. "Pow—*hemorrhoids!*"

"Oh—no . . ." Her head fell onto the seat as she laughed.

"I really had you going there!" he gasped. "You should have seen the look on your face when I told you he was dead."

"You liar—horrible liar! I fell for the whole thing."

They gurgled words between fits of laughter.

"That's right." Tears flowed from his eyes. "Like you thought he was John—John Wayne— or Jimmy Stewart."

They howled like stoned hyenas. She could barely talk. "I thought of—of Henry Fonda." That set them both off again. It was a while before she could speak. "Where are you from, really?"

"Iowa, like I said earlier. Are *you* gullible!"

"I know. People are always fooling me like that. What does your father really do? Farm?"

"No. He's ..." His father's occupation suddenly seemed unbearably hilarious. "He's ..." Out it came, the laughter so hard he could barely see the road.

She was laughing so much it began to hurt, although she had no idea what was so funny. "What does ... ?"

"He's—he's—he's a *fuh*—feed salesman." Another laughter attack. "*Puh*—pig feed."

She saw a man going from door to door, the door answered by a pig in overalls with a straw between his teeth. He could only contrast the lean dying cattle baron with his portly father clad in dapper double knits, carrying leaflets about pig feed. Their laughter filled the black hearse as it hurtled along the freeway on the coldest night of the year, a few snowflakes drifting down from the dead gray sky. They laughed as if life was the funniest thing in the cosmos, existence one huge hilarity. Eventually the laughter faded into a comfortable silence.

She shook her head. "That story about your father was a terrible thing to do."

"It was the funniest goddamn thing I've seen in a long time."

She smiled again, feeling warm and comfortable. The heater blew air against her legs. Her hiking boots felt heavy. She had worn them since 6:00 A.M. Mountain Standard Time. The snow was increasing. He had turned on the windshield wipers. Their swish brushed aside splattered flakes, and the headlights made beams through falling snow. She bent over to unlace her boots.

The hearse went by another semi—long, dark, wooden beast stuffed with pigs. Inside the hearse they could not hear the ugly grunts and squeals of the cold pigs or see the snouts jammed against the wooden siding, trying to squeeze through narrow cracks. The pigs were on their way to Chicago.

"What's your name?" he asked.

"Angela. Angela Rosalba."

Sophia Loren. Claudia Cardinale. *La Dolce Vita.* Lasagna, spaghetti with Romano cheese, pizza, ravioli—goddamn, was he hungry. Must be the dope. "Ahhn-geh-la." They glanced at each other. "Rohhhhzzzz-aahhhl-ba. Angela . . . the angel?"

"Perhaps. What's your name?"

"Roy."

"Roy?"

The grin again. "Yeah, Roy. Rogers."

She laughed once, then groaned. "Don't start that again. What's your real name?"

"Mike."

"Mike what?"

"Michaels."

"You're joking again."

"No I'm not. Look on my field jacket if you don't believe me."

"Mike Michaels. Very alliterative."

"Huh?"

"Your name begins with the same consonants."

"Oh. Sophomore lit was a ways back. Are you an English major?"

"No, music, but I read a lot."

"Yeah?" Smart and sensitive besides beautiful? She became more and more threatening. "You must hang around the music building. Do you like organ music?"

"Very much. Do you play?"

"All the time, and not just the organ." His grin reappeared.

"What do you like to play?"

"Oh, uh, Bach, I suppose. I like the Toccata and Fugue in D Minor, even if it is an old warhorse."

Buffalo Bill, sitting before the double keyboard, fingers and feet finding those incredibly difficult polyphonic lines? "You're not putting me on again?"

"Hell, no! Listen—I'll hum it for you. *Duhh-DUM-del-luhdel-lum-DUM-DUMMM!*" His voice boomed the bass note.

"That's fine. I believe you." He did know the melody.

"No you don't, but the first time we happen across an organ I'll show you. What do you play?"

"The piano. And guitar or lute."

"The lute? For real? You and Julian Bream."

"Yeah. Where did you ever learn to play the organ?"

"I used to play around the church my parents dragged me to. Good Lutherans really dig organs, a Mighty Fortress and all that. My folks paid for lessons. And then I played the organ when I was in the army and when I worked for my uncle."

"Is your uncle a minister?"

"No."

"What does he do, then?"

His smile faded, only the corners of his mouth remaining uplifted. "It's really starting to come down." The lightly scattered flakes had multiplied, divided, expanded. The headlights caught them drifting down in their slow fall. The dark of the interstate had lightened under an inch of snow, and he slowed the hearse to sixty. She thought he was going to forget the question when he said, "Actually my uncle's a mortician."

"Then this hearse—"

"Is his. I like to take it on trips. It's great for sleeping in the back."

"Oh God."

He grinned. "Wide enough for two and plenty of length. I've been out West, got in some skiing and visiting with some old army friends."

"Hey, that's where I've been. I was skiing, too. My parents live in Boulder. Your uncle just lends you his hearse?"

"He has more than one. This is the old klunker, comes with the bargain basement deal. Stick the body in an orange crate and throw the crate in back. There was one catch in borrowing the hearse."

"Which is?"

"You know that stop I mentioned in Udolph? I have to pick up a body."

"Oh. How nice. Maybe I'll just get off now. It's been so nice meeting you."

"You *are* kidding?"

"Yes. I guess I am. But I'm sure something horrible is going to happen."

"Shit, no. When you stepped into this hearse it was the beginning of an incredible adventure. Full of thrills, chills, and excitement. See? Like when Fay Wray gets on the boat to go see King Kong, or when Dorothy gets blown away in the farmhouse."

"Which does that make you—King Kong or the Wicked Witch of the North? No, I'm sure something horrible is going to happen to me."

She was joking, but then she remembered horror stories about girls hitchhiking. A car going down back roads where the driver stopped, beat some sixteen-year-old, raped her, left her in a ditch with a broken nose, broken ribs, and missing teeth. The body of a young woman the police found in the Iowa River a week after she disappeared—naked, strangled, frozen. Last seen alive hitchhiking near Davenport on Interstate 80. In spite of the marijuana and fatigue, her eyes sharpened. She looked carefully at him. What if he was just trying to lull her into a sleepy comfort so he could strike? She was strong for a woman, but he was big, and if he had a gun or knife . . .

Noticing her silence, he looked over and grinned. She smiled back before she realized what she was doing. Somehow she already trusted Buffalo Bill. Besides, would a sneaky homicidal rapist drive a hearse and tell her he had to pick up a corpse? She sighed and relaxed, feeling foolish.

"Picking up a body is really no trouble. They're incredibly accommodating. This one will be all nicely pickled and packed away in its jar."

"Then why do you have to pick it up?"

"Some guy's brother wants to be buried in Chicago. My uncle's the closest big-time morti-cian around, so he's handling the whole deal. He called and asked if I'd stop in Udolph on my way back. I'll probably spend the night in Iowa City, then go on to Chicago."

"How far from the interstate did you say Udolph was?"

"About fifty miles. I figure we'll get into Iowa City around—seven-thirty now—around ten-thirty."

"I don't know about that. Look at it snow."

There were two inches of snow, and the flakes had metamorphosed from tiny sparkling diamonds to white-petaled flowers. The hearse had slowed to sixty but still moved faster than most traffic.

"Goddammit! It isn't suppose to snow. I listened to the forecast this afternoon, and the weather dude said clear and cold with less than ten percent precipitation probability. Good work, dumb shit weatherman."

"Do you have snow tires?"

"Sure. Watch."

His foot slammed onto the brake pedal, pitching them both forward. The hearse's rear end fishtailed, then recovered, as he steered madly. The view from the windshield lurched sideways, jerked back forward, lurched to the side again. Confused and mildly stoned, Angela was filled with fear. He was accelerating. She knew they were going off the road. A Volkswagen on the left honked as the hearse skidded by, barely missing the dwarfish car. Michaels used all three lanes to recover a straight course, leaving madly curving tracks in the fresh snow. Luckily the Volkswagen was the only other car around.

"Jesus fucking Christ, it's slipperier than I thought." They were in the center lane, once again roaring along smoothly.

"My God! Don't do that again."

"I only wanted to show you how well the snow tires work. Incredible, huh?"

"I thought you were going to kill us both. I was sure we were going off the road."

"Oh no, not with the snow tires. I've gone shooting around mountain roads in this coffin carrier at sixty-five, winding and skidding all over the place, but I never went off the road."

"I'm glad I wasn't with you. And there probably weren't cars in the other lanes. Don't do anything like that again. Please, Mike."

He heard the fear in her voice, a discordant note like she might want to cry. He felt like a fool. Sure, you big, cool, stupid *idiot*. He had thought he could handle dope and the two beers he'd had earlier, but he knew well enough what happened to people who got careless on the interstate. He'd been at his uncle's often enough when they brought them in.

He had a sudden vision of Angela's beautiful face hitting the windshield, the flesh shredding open on jagged glass. Then came the memories. The kid who'd had an M16 blow up in his face. The woman who had no face, only a lumpy mass of hamburger mixed with strips of skin. He swallowed and felt his fear. Every time he thought he had escaped death for a while, it snuck up behind him and screamed. The army hadn't helped, and he was in the wrong business now. Dope and beer usually soothed him, but other times they let the fear grow and swallow him, made the fear invulnerable to logic. He was angry with himself. Showing off like a goddamn high school kid with his girlfriend. You dumb, dumb fucker.

"I'm sorry. It was a dumb-ass thing to do. It's a good thing the hearse does have snow tires." He slowed down to fifty.

She knew he meant it. She let out a long sigh, trying to relax, still feeling her heart beat. "That's the last time I ask you anything about this car. I'd really like to get back to Iowa City alive, even it it takes longer."

"I'll get you back. I've also got chains if we need them. This thing will go anywhere with chains. Like a goddamn tank."

"I believe you—just don't demonstrate."

"Listen, I am sorry I scared you. It was stupid of me."

"That's okay. A little adrenaline cleans out the system. Maybe you're just trying to dig up business for the family."

His grin came back. "I value my own humble bod too much to donate it to my uncle. I've been around the receiving end too much. I know what kind of shit goes on. If anything ever happens to me, I want to be cremated. Bodies should decay in the earth and make good rich dirt or be burned. They shouldn't lie around in coffins. I don't want my blood replaced with embalming fluid."

"What kind of attitude is that for a promising young mortician?"

"Oh no, you've got me mixed up with good old Uncle Bill. I'm strictly part-time. I don't like the job, but the pay is good, and business always stays about the same."

"What do you do besides work for your uncle?"

"Smoke dope, drink beer, and when one's available, play the organ"—better not add 'fuck whenever possible'—"and read junky novels, sleep. Good stuff like that. I tried school for a while but got tired of it. I even took a music class and thought about being a music major. Basic Harmony. Turned out to be death."

"That shouldn't bother you."

"Ho, ho. I may go back some day when I get inspired. I should to get some nice GI bill. Working in a mortuary gets old fast."

"Do you—what kind of things do you do?" she asked. The subject had a grisly fascination.

"I stick needles in and out of people—out goes the blood, in goes the fluid—shave them, dress them. Uncle Bill does all the fancy work, restoring faces and that good shit."

"I don't think I'd like your job."

"You get used to it. You can get used to almost anything. The only thing that bothers me much anymore is little kids or people around my age. Especially chicks. Drives me up the fucking wall."

"Why should *women* bother you more?"

"Because there's this kind of horrible sexual attraction in a naked dead body if she's young and good-looking."

"Oh, come on."

"Attraction's the wrong word. There's something there, though, and it does bad things to my head. Somehow if they're really beautiful and really dead, see—I don't like it at all."

"I'm glad you don't. You'd be rather ghoulish if you did."

He didn't grin but almost smiled. "That reminds me of good old Cousin Chuck. He worked at the mortuary before I did, but Uncle Bill had to let him go."

"What for?"

"Do you know what necrophilia is?"

"God, yes."

"Cousin Chuck was into that. And into the bodies. Uncle Bill caught him in the act one night."

"Oh God, that's horrible."

"That reminds me of a super-sick joke."

"I don't want to hear it."

"Good. I don't really want to tell it. Maybe Cousin Chuck just liked super-passive chicks."

Again that word. She considered telling him she disliked such sexist, silly, stupid words. She didn't call men "roosters." But why risk alienating someone she hardly knew? He'd think she was a fanatic. "There must be other things we could talk about besides bodies and mortuaries, Boris."

"Uh-uh, Karloff's not my thing. Dracula, Prince of Darkness. Head honcho of the vampires. Look into my eyes. I usually carry my coffin in the back."

"So that's why you picked me up."

"Right. Bluhhh-d."

She yawned. "Maybe I'll just fall asleep and let you drink away. I'm so tired. It's been a long day."

"Go ahead and sleep if you want."

"You'll probably go for my throat or try testing the tires again."

"Nah, I'm turning over a new leaf. Sleep, Angela, guarded by your faithful friend and Indian companion."

"Sure thing, Dracula. Somehow you don't fit the vampire part. Your hair's the wrong color. And whoever heard of a cowboy vampire?"

"How can you say that of a true, pure-blooded

Transylvanian?" He sang, "Peg in my heart, you drove a peg in my heart."

Enough residual marijuana fumes drifted about her brain along with traces of their earlier hilarity so that she laughed. The laugh was closer to a moan. "That's awful."

Michaels grinned and drove. Outside the warm car the gentle snowfall was becoming a howling, snarling blizzard fit for wolves. The snow covering the highway drifted as the wind swirled dunes of strange, shifting patterns.

Angela slouched down, turning sideways so her back was on the seat, legs up, feet resting on the dashboard. Her left foot touched the windshield. Even through the thick wool she felt the cold permeating the glass. She watched the windshield wipers swish, swish, swish, valiantly pushing aside the myriad of splattered snowflakes. She yawned, which was difficult with her chin against her chest. The hearse passed another semi rumbling on its determined way. Her eyes closed.

Darkness.

She felt the hot air from the heater and the roar of the engine as vibrations through the seat. The radio made dim, distant hysterical sounds. Warm and nice. After all that time outside standing by roadsides, growing colder the closer she came to Iowa, as if some frozen center awaited her. And standing there at dusk before he picked her up, how horribly cold she was, with her toes and her nose going numb. How good this felt. Better than walking along the road, turning and putting out her thumb, no luck. Walking, her foot catching, tripping—she would fall. Her body jerked and her eyes opened.

"What's the matter? I thought you were asleep." His hands rested on the bottom of the steering wheel.

"I was. But I nearly tripped."

"Go back to sleep."

"Maybe I will. Oh, look at it snow."

"Yeah, goddammit. I'm going to have to put the chains on if this keeps up."

She watched as the snow fell into the beams and rushed at the car like stars at a spaceship. Rushing at the car and vanishing, more flakes appearing, coming, vanishing. The wind sent pale waves washing over the hearse. The snowy vision soothed.

"Where are we, anyway?"

"Near the turnoff. It should be coming up any minute now. We go north at the Smithsville exit. Jesus, look at this—a fucking blizzard. I'm tempted to bag the whole thing and just drive to Iowa City, forget the hundred-mile detour."

"That would be fine with me."

"Do you have to be back tomorrow? We may get stranded somewhere."

She was tempted to lie. "No, not really. As long as we get there tomorrow. I usually go to church around five on Sunday."

"Oh sure." He laughed. "You're joking."

"No I'm not. I usually go to five o'clock mass at Center East, you know, the Catholic student place. But it's not urgent."

"Oh."

Rosalba—sure, Italians were usually Catholics. Jesus Christ, so much for the sex fantasies. Roman Catholic virgins—*deadly*. What a waste. She was so beautiful. Everyone he knew in Iowa City was an atheist or agnostic. He *would* pick up a fucking Catholic. Or *non*fucking Catholic. Beware of patent leather shoes—petting and French kissing are mortal sins! Oh well, even if she were willing, he was hardly the world's greatest operator.

"There's your exit."

The headlights lit up the green-and-white sign, SMITHSVILLE ONE MILE.

"I suppose I'd better decide something." He'd be driving in a blizzard, and he'd have to lug out the chains, but if he didn't Uncle Bill would be pissed, and he'd have to come back this way soon. Besides, he'd have more time with her.

"Here goes nothing."

He slowed the car gradually, not wanting any more spectacular skids. The hearse swerved slightly as he braked. "Goddamn, there must be four or five inches on the road." He glanced over at her. She was falling asleep again. "Don't worry. I'll get you to Iowa City. It may take me awhile, but I'll get you there."

She smiled but didn't open her eyes. "I believe you."

He turned left at the stop sign, saw the other sign that said SMITHSVILLE 5, JENKIN'S CENTER 27, and UDOLPH 48. "Udolph, here we come." The hearse accelerated unevenly, wheels slipping, struggling to grip the snow-covered road. The wind gusted, howling, and dashed snow against the black vehicle. Michaels felt strange. The wind seemed enraged, but perhaps it was only amused, laughing at the pitiable hearse and its two occupants who could not know what they were caught up in.

CHAPTER TWO

◊

The sculptur'd dead, on each side, seem to freeze,
Emprison'd in black, purgatorial rails:
Knights, ladies, praying in dumb orat'ries,
He passeth by; and his weak spirit fails
To think how they may ache in icy hoods and
    mails.

> —Keats, The Eve of St. Agnes

MICHAELS SLOWED DOWN the hearse as he went through Jenkin's Center. Typical for a small Iowa town—three traffic lights, a hardware store, O'Donnel's Mortuary, a DX station, and a Polar Freezer. Everything was surfaced with snow, no one on the streets. Irene's Tavern was the only lit building, the window proclaiming HAMM's! in glowing blue neon.

Over the hill beyond a church was the town cemetery, small and forlorn in the blizzard. He might have missed it, but even through the storm he made out snow-covered crosses and statues. On a night like this he could feel sorry for the people in the graves, although he knew the icy dead felt nothing. Nothing. No more existence. Blackness. An odd sensation at the back of his neck—he shook his head abruptly.

He glanced at Angela. She'd been asleep for the hour it took the hearse to crawl from the Smithsville exit to Jenkin's Center. Her seat belt was on, extended to maximum length. She lay on her side, legs drawn up, her dark, loosely bundled hair touching his legs. The long, smooth fingers of her right hand lay before her lips and nose.

27

Michaels swallowed and sighed, feeling desire, but other feelings thrown in as well. He had visited prostitutes during his travels, picking up great locker-room stories for the boys, stories that didn't impress him. At least he'd missed the black clap in Nam. He had played around at school, too, before the army. Golden days in the joy of a happy youth, golden fraternity days, one hangover after another, when they pursued the sorority crown and slavered over morning-after stories. Didya score, Michaels?

He had fallen in love twice. The last time was about a year ago, when he'd tried school again. It ended when the law student's old boyfriend moved back in. Since then he had alternated between working for his uncle and wandering around the country. He was tired of that—of everything—of working, of living alone, of picking up occasional girls in bars. He wanted more than that. He liked waking up in the morning with someone warm, sleepy, and naked beside him. Shit, winters were deadly in Iowa City. But why torture himself with fantasies about this girl? He was always lusting and longing after women from afar, but nothing ever came of it. Besides, a girl as fantastic as this one always turned out to have been living with some dipshit for years. Not if she's Catholic. Even so, guys must be battling to take her out. No, he'd take her to Iowa City, she'd smile and thank him, and he'd never see her again.

She squirmed and shifted. He looked down at her and wished for more light. He liked looking at sleeping women. Their faces relaxed, all the tension went away, they looked comfortable, even childlike. Her falling asleep in the hearse showed some kind of trust.

A huge blast of wind hit the hearse. Eyes quickly shifting to the road, he steered nervously, causing a slight skidding motion. He resisted the urge to hit the brakes and steered out of the skid. All he needed was to lock the brakes. He had passed cars stuck alongside the highway and driven around others futilely spinning at hills. Now there was almost no traffic. The yellow headlights cut into the tempest, the shrieking wind tossing and swirling snow in the air and on the ground.

"Hell," Michaels murmured. He had never seen a storm this bad. He should definitely put the chains on, but he didn't want to go out in this mess and was afraid he'd never get moving again. He blinked his eyes, feeling sleepy, shook his head, and tried to be alert. He hunted around the dial until he found some music, horrible country-and-western crap. He turned down the volume, not wanting to wake Angela, and heard another warning about the surprise blizzard coming from nowhere, limited to central Iowa. Just his crazy luck.

He stared ahead, still trying to feel more awake, watching the windshield wipers swish and the snowflakes fall into the high beams. A black shape appeared against the gray-white, blurring with motion, and stopped. A deer, in Iowa? Jesus Christ, a giant black—dog? Strangely formless but huge and black and right before the car, head turning, amber circles in that dark mass of head glowing like cat eyes, glaring.

Michaels panicked; his foot stabbed for the brake, digging in. He realized too late it was the wrong thing to do. The car launched into a full skid, back end slamming around. The dog still came, yellow orbs growing. There was a loud *bam* as the hearse hit the dog, throwing Michaels forward, banging his head against the steering wheel. The hearse shuddered from the impact, and the long metal body went completely around in a 180-degree turn. He held the steering wheel, feeling it turn out of his control, too dazed for anything but fear.

Angela opened her eyes and felt the rush of frightening, uncontrolled motion. The rear wheels left the road, going down into the sloping shoulder. The hearse stopped, its engine dead, leaving only the growling wind. The headlight beams slanted upward, lighting the snowflakes' gentle fall.

Mike lay with his forehead throbbing against the steering wheel and thanked God he was alive. His hands gradually let go of the wheel. He heard Angela fumbling at her seat belt.

"Mike, are you all right?"

Her hands were in his hair, holding his head, and he opened his eyes to stare into her face. "I think so. Just slightly shaken up." He winced as her fingers touched a bump.

She shook her head, sighing, and lowered her hands. She held his arm below the shoulder. He did look shaken, the long blond hair tousled, his face pale even in the dim car. The grin seemed very far away. Completely awake now, she felt both afraid and relieved.

"What happened?—trying the brakes again?"

"Jesus, no! This time it wasn't my fault. A fucking dog ran right in front of the car."

"A dog?"

"Yes, a fucking black dog as big as a goddamn cow."

"Come on, I'll bet the dog wasn't that big, and I'll bet he wasn't fucking."

"A small cow anyway. It scared the shit out of me—ran right in front of the car. I locked the brakes, which was a pretty stupid thing to do."

"Did you hit the dog?"

"I sure did—maybe put a dent in the bumper."

"Oh no—do you think you killed it?"

"I must have. But it was a mean dog."

Her eyes were worried. She let go of his arm and reached for one of her boots. "We'd better go look for it."

"What the hell for? Stupid bastard dog." Remembering the black shape with the yellow eyes, he felt anger.

"Mike, that's cruel."

"Listen, I like dogs—I've owned dogs—but this didn't look like any dog I've ever seen. Jesus Christ, it was mean—it looked almost like it knew what it was doing."

"Come on, the whole thing happened so fast. How could you tell?"

"I don't know."

She finished lacing her boots and grabbed her parka. "Let's go look."

"Fucking dog," he mumbled, reaching back behind the seat to retrieve his cowboy hat.

She opened the door, stepped down and out. The blizzard hit full force, snow and icy wind striking her cheeks, cold surrounding her. She quickly pulled on her mittens. The wind couldn't get through the down parka, but she felt its frigid touch cut through her thighs. She realized now how truly warm and secure the hearse had been. Stumbling up the slippery slope she stepped onto the road.

Michaels shouted something from his side of the car, but she couldn't hear through the wind and snow. He walked over to her. The back half of the hearse was off the road, tipping slightly downward. They were at the summit of a small rolling hill.

He jammed his hat down further, wishing he hadn't left his gloves in the car. "We're going to have a hell of a time getting back on the road," he yelled.

"Let's look for the dog." She started forward in the direction of the headlights.

"Wait a minute, Angela." He caught her by the arm and pointed the other way. "Let's try following the tracks backwards before they disappear—you're headed the wrong way."

"Isn't Udolph that way?" She motioned ahead.

"No, it's back that way. We made a slight turn of one hundred eighty degrees or so. The car's pointed the wrong way."

"God, I'm glad I wasn't awake for the whole thing."

They walked around the hearse, saw tire tracks curving up onto the road. The tracks went backwards about twenty feet, then smeared and made an erratic curve around in the opposite direction.

"The dog should be around here. Here dog, nice dog, here son of a bitch."

He walked down the road to the place where he must have hit the animal, but there was no dog—no sign the dog had ever existed, no paw prints, no impression where its body would have fallen after being thrown. Nothing. Only the snow and the wailing wind that suddenly picked up his hat and tossed it away.

He quickly turned and saw the hat behind him. The frigid air played with his hair, interweaving the golden strands and powdering it with snow. He bent to pick up the hat, but the wind gave it another kick, flipping it over onto the crown. Michaels saw he had to be quick to outsmart the wind. He lunged suddenly, grabbing the black brim before the wind could blow the hat off the road into the ditch.

Distance seemed to have disappeared; he couldn't see the usual farm lights or the horizon. Instead, a white ocean swirled everywhere around him. Holding his hat down, he looked back toward the hearse. Angela was gone.

"Angela!" He ran up the hill. "Angela!"

She staggered up from the roadside where she'd been searching for the dog. "What?"

Michaels felt silly. You'd think there were werewolves in the woods. He grinned at the thought, but a strange uneasiness remained.

"Find anything?" he asked.

"Not a thing."

"Let's go back in the car and warm up."

She headed for the hearse, her eyes half-closed to keep out the bombardment of flakes. They flew at her face in bursts of differing intensity. She felt their tiny icy sting, individual pings, hitting her cheeks and especially her nose. She had seen absolutely nothing. Perhaps Mike had made up the story.

"Mike?" He bent toward her to hear better. "Are you sure you saw a dog?"

"Yes—goddammit. And it was huge."

"But in this storm . . ."

He laughed with a faintly indignant tone. "So you think I'm seeing things. Oh ye of little faith. Let's take a look at the car." They came to the hearse, its headlights still cutting into the sky. "Holy fuck. Uncle Bill will definitely be pissed."

"My God," she murmured.

Below the left light the immense bumper had been neatly pushed in. As if a giant finger had gently touched a metal-colored bumper made of butter. A smooth curve about a foot wide remained.

"I think I hit something quite solid."

"Good Lord, we're lucky we weren't killed."

Her eyes were apologetic and fearful. She looked small to him standing there by the whale-like hearse in the midst of a tempest. The ski hat was pulled below her ears and over her forehead. The balloonlike parka hid her shape, but her face with its straight Grecian nose and curving lips was a tiny shape of warmth and life. All around them, omnipresent, was storm—the earth underfoot, the sky above, everything between—all was gray-white howling chaos. Michaels felt fear coming from some deep and obscure source.

"Jesus Christ, let's go sit in the car and warm up."

He opened the door on the driver's side, let her in, got in, and slammed the door. He put one hand on the wheel. Her left shoulder and side pressed against him. "I wonder what happened to that dog. He should be very dead after doing what he did to the car."

"He might have managed to limp off somewhere."

"If he did, he must have been limping with every bone in his body broken into a million tiny pieces."

"We should look once more—he must be out there somewhere."

"What would we do if we found him."

"I don't know. But I'd feel better if we found him."

"I guess I would too." At least then he would know what that shadowy black shape was. "Let's warm up a little first. I'll get the heater going." He turned the key. A click, and nothing, no sound of any kind. "Oh, no." He turned the key off, waited, then clicked it again. "Oh Christ!—this is all we need. I don't get it. It sounds like the battery is dead."

"Could that happen from hitting a dog?"

Michaels grinned in spite of himself. "Not unless the dog totals the whole front end, including the battery."

"Then what's wrong?"

"I wish I knew. It should at least turn over. Hey, it's getting dark in here." The windshield and one side window were completely covered by snow. "I suppose I should go outside and have a look under the hood. Maybe the coil wire or the battery cable came off. The last thing I want to do is go back outside."

"And I can look for the dog. We must have just missed him in the storm."

"You and the damn dog. Wait a minute before you do."

He opened the door letting in white flakes and arctic air, and stepped out quickly. He used his forearm to clear the side window and part of the windshield. She pulled her zipper up tighter, then put her hands between her legs to warm them. The storm certainly wasn't abating. They would probably be stranded at least till morning, maybe later. Sitting alone in the darkened car, surrounded by storm, she became aware that the hearse was only a small fragile shell.

Why was he taking so long? She couldn't see him or hear anything behind the raised hood. What if he wasn't there anymore? What if he were to disappear, just disappear? She felt a knife twisting below her ribs.

"I'm going to go get him."

With a *bam* the hood came down. He got back in, letting in more snow and the cry of the storm. He blew on his hands, rubbed them together, clenched and unclenched his fingers.

"Jesus, is it cold out there. It's usually warmer when it snows."

"Did you find out what was wrong?"

"Everything looks perfectly normal. I'll try it again." He hesitated, then turned the key. Again a click and nothing. "Shit! I give up, I don't know what's wrong with this damn klunker. The battery's only six months old."

"Mike, let's look for the dog once more."

"You definitely have a thing for that dog."

"Just once. Then I won't bother you any more."

"Okay. And then we're going to have to enjoy being stranded. It would be crazy to walk off looking for help in this. We'd get lost and freeze to death. But we'll be okay in here. I've got my down bag and some blankets. And there's a jar of peanut butter and lots of crackers."

"Who gets the down bag?"

"Uh, I don't know."

"We can figure something out," she said. "But first let's look for the dog."

"Shit, you would say that. This time I'll wear my gloves."

He pulled them on, then stepped out, and the wind tried to blow off his hat again. Jamming the hat down, he waited for her. He used his hand to facilitate speaking, to shelter his voice. He noticed how really tall she was, her eyes only an inch or so below his, which made her around six feet. "Uh, you look one way, I'll look the other, but be careful not to go too far from the road."

"I won't. I don't want to get lost in this. That could prove rather fatal."

"Definitely. Maybe we should stick together. I don't want to get lost in this either."

She bit at her lower lip. "We can cover more ground faster if we're apart. Besides, being lost together wouldn't be much of an advantage."

"But it would be less spooky, and we could probably figure out some way to keep warm. Oh well, anything to get this over quicker. Here Fang, here boy."

Angela watched him walk down the road in the direction the hearse pointed, a tall dark figure in his field jacket, jeans, and black cowboy hat. A cowboy lost in the storm. She recalled a similar scene in some movie. What did happen? Wolves. A pack of wolves attacked and . . .

Come on! She shook herself awake and walked. She was getting wacky from lack of sleep, daydreaming about cowboys and wolves. The snow had nearly obliterated the hearse tracks, but she made out the spot where the hearse had skidded, where it must have struck the wolf—*dog*. She

shook her head, frowning, and looked around
her. The white ground and the gray-white sky
made the night lighter, but she saw no sign of a
dog anywhere, no paw prints, no indentation in
the snow. Nervously she licked her lips. There
were footprints around the spot, plain flat ones
and waffled ones, Mike's cowboy boots and her
hiking shoes.

She followed the gradually sloping road downhill, staring off along the sides. The shoulders
dropped, then rose to barbed wire and wooden
fence. There were long frozen fields on both sides
of the highway. She saw nothing alive and no
tracks. The wind screeched like a tortured animal and spat snow in her face. She stopped to
look back.

She had gone thirty or forty yards. The hearse
was on the hilltop, but she could no longer see it
through the storm, Being alone with nothing all
around made her uneasy. She would never have
thought she could miss the hearse. She would
feel better with Mike around. She sighed and
wiggled her numbed nose with her hand. God,
she was tired. Her calves and ankles ached from
the long day of standing. Ahead the road dipped,
then climbed sharply. She noticed a sign at the
bottom. Might as well go as far as the sign.

She walked along, aware how heavy her boots
were. She made a zigzag path, looking off the
road on both sides. No sign of anything. Mike
was right. This was a rather stupid, futile idea.

The NO PASSING sign was stuck in a little hill
alongside the road. Or was that a little hill? It
was shaped funny, not like a hill, not like there
was dirt underneath. Her feet stopped. She
stared and tried to quiet her fear. The wind

stung her face as she squinted, struggling to make out the thing under the sign. Could that be the dog?

She took a step, then another step, then another, and stopped, still fighting to calm herself. Why should she be so afraid? She realized her teeth were clenched, the muscles of her lower jaw rigid. She wanted badly to turn and run back up the hill and find Michaels. Not because he was a man but because he was another human being. Instead she took another step.

She guessed what might be under there but didn't want to think about that. She felt cold, very cold, even under the parka. She reached the thick square beam holding the sign and pulled off her right glove. Her hands trembled slightly. She bent over and made a quick pulling motion, a scrape at the snow.

God—*skin!*

She was up and back staring at the shape before she knew what had happened. Dear God, she had touched someone's flesh—there must be somebody under there—they must be dead. Someone had been sitting against the sign, they had slumped over and been buried under snow. She had touched it. She remembered once turning over an innocent-looking pan and discovering a four-inch cockroach, black antennae waving at her. She fought the urge to scream and made herself look more carefully.

She had pushed snow away from what must be the head. She bent over to pick up her mitten, hardly aware how cold her hand was. She blinked, shook her head—was she imagining things? *No*—the snow was quivering as if underneath something horrible were coming to life.

She turned and ran at the hill, running half-blind in the wind and snow. Her foot twisted, slipped, and she fell to one knee. She pushed herself up with both hands and ran. She reached the hearse. "Mike!" She ran down the other side of the hill and stopped, panting. "Mike! Where are you!" He probably couldn't hear in this, if he was—something touched her shoulder, making her head jerk around. Long hair and that familiar black cowboy hat.

"What's the matter?" His hand rested on her shoulder.

She turned, grabbing his arm. "I found a body down the hill—covered with snow."

Mike grinned, hiding the corners of his mouth in his snowy mustache. "Uncle Bill will like that." Then he saw the look on her face. "Hey, what's wrong?"

"At the bottom of the hill—by the sign. I thought it was dirt or something, but I touched it—touched skin. I thought it must be dead—but it shook." A glacial wave washed up her spine, making her teeth clench and her shoulders move upward in a shudder. "God, it really scared me."

"I'll go have a look."

"I'll come."

"I should hope so. I'm really pretty chicken shit."

"I know where it is."

They climbed back up the hill and passed the hearse. She hadn't let go of his arm. "Wouldn't someone freeze if they were buried under snow?"

"Not necessarily, unless they were there a while. As long as they had an air space to breathe, it might even help keep them warm on a night like this."

"I know they were shaking—the snow quivered."

He ran his lip between his teeth. "We'll see."

They were over the hill now. "There—see the sign." Through the gray-white sky and the white blips of snow, they saw the diamond-shaped sign. He felt her hand squeeze tighter as they descended.

Michaels took another chew at his lip. He felt the throng of ugly, familiar sensations that came with finding the dead or dying.

"Fuck," he whispered. They stood next to the sign and the snow-buried shape. "I suppose I'd better try to get the snow off. It's not shaking."

"No." She reluctantly let go of his arm as he squatted down. "Be careful."

"If someone's dead they can't hurt me."

"I hope not."

He brushed at the snow where the head should be, feeling something hard underneath. He used both hands, worked faster, tried to forget he was afraid. He uncovered the head lying on its side, a rubber hood over all but the face. "God," he murmured. He took off his gloves, quickly scraped the snow from the eyes, nose, and mouth. The nose was long, the cheekbones high, the features young and delicate. A thin mustache covered the cold lips, and the beard was snow-caked. Michaels put his fingers before the dark hole of the mouth, hoping to feel breath. Nothing. He slid his fingers along the bearded jaw down to the smooth neck, between cold rubber and cold skin, searching for the hollow space between the collarbones. Finding it, he pressed hard with two fingers and waited.

The snow blew in his eyes, stinging his face, and he did not like the feel of the man's cold flesh under his hand. Yes. Rapid and definite, the heartthrobs echoed under his fingertips.

"He's alive. We'd better get him back to the car."

"Oh Lord, I'm so glad he's not dead. I wonder how he got here."

They both worked to brush away snow and dig him out. He lay on his side wearing what Michaels recognized as a GI poncho. Mike freed one arm and used both hands to pull him out of the snow. Under the poncho the body had on a fatigue jacket, jeans and combat boots. Raising the poncho Mike examined the field jacket. The real thing, all right, U.S. ARMY in black letters over the right pocket, a Ranger patch on the shoulder, and the name RENWICK over the other pocket.

"We'll have to carry him back to the car," he said.

"Wait a minute." Angela dug around in the snow, pulled out a twelve-inch cardboard square, and brushed off the snow. Neatly written in large black capitals was UDOLPH.

"Christ, he couldn't have been hitching in this. How would he have gotten this far?"

"Someone might have dropped him off."

"On a night like this? They'd have to be a real bastard. I wonder if I could wake him up. Being unconscious in this weather isn't a good idea."

Mike raised him to a sitting position, grasped his shoulders with gloved hands, and shook him. The head rolled lifelessly. Mike gently slapped at his cheek. "Hey, come on—wake up." A low moan and mumbled words. "Did you understand that?"

"It sounded like 'Leave me alone.' "

"I doubt he's that far gone. We need to get him out of this storm, and I've got some booze in the car that might bring him around. Why don't you grab him by the ankles?" Mike hoisted him up, holding on under the armpits. Something was moving under his hands. "Hey—he *is* trembling."

"I know."

"At least he's light enough." The body was long but thin, almost skeletal.

They blundered up the hill carrying the body. The storm continued, vicious as ever, complicating their task. The heavy wind made carrying more difficult, and they waded through about nine inches of snow, deeper in places. The wind had built drifts, blowing white powder into the air, mixing fallen snow with falling snow.

Michaels opened the back door of the hearse, shoved aside the boxes and junk, and they put the body in.

"God, it's cold! We ought to try to get him out of here or at least warm the hearse up. Listen, Angela, kick over the key once more while I play doctor. It probably won't do any good, but we could give it a try."

"Sure."

He climbed in back beside the body and quickly shut the rear door. It was cold in the hearse, but some residual warmth was left, and at least he was sheltered. He straightened Renwick out, turned him onto his back, and brushed the snow off. He heard Angela get in and slam the door.

"It is so cold, Mike."

"I know."

"Here goes." She turned the key. A cough—
shudder—*ruhh!* The engine sprang alive, filling
the night with its rumbly roar.

Michaels's jaw dropped, and he stared at
Angela who was smiling. "Holy shit! How did
you manage that?"

"The magic touch. It likes me better."

"That's for sure. I don't understand this. It was
completely dead before. Remind me to take you
along when I'm worried about engine trouble—
you're better than jumper cables."

"Gee, thanks."

"I'd better look at our friend here." He began
pulling off the heavy poncho.

"Should I turn it off?"

"Christ, no! Don't touch it! I don't want to take
any chances. We've got plenty of gas. Let's let
her warm up. And why don't you turn on the
dome light so I can have a look at him."

He had the poncho off and shoved Renwick
toward the seat, nearer to the heater. He took a
heavy wool army blanket from a box and
wrapped it around the body, tucking it underneath. Angela had turned around to watch, her
elbows resting on the front seat. Removing the
poncho freed the man's hair, letting the long
strands fall onto the gray carpet. The hair was
longer than shoulder length, light brown and
very fine. The thin lips, high cheekbones, and
hollow cheeks gave him a gaunt, starved appearance.

The face was vaguely familiar to Michaels. Ah
yes, the guy looked like Jesus. Like those nause-
ating schmaltzy pictures on religious calendars

or in prayer books. Funny how so many freaks resembled Jesus. This guy looked like he'd been out in the desert without food—maybe John the Baptist was closer.

"He's stopped shivering." He put his hand on the forehead. "Pretty warm. I wonder if a shot would bring him around." He reached into a box, fumbled around, rattling metal, and pulled out a half-gone bottle of Old Crow. He uncorked and took a swig, felt the whiskey burn its way down. "Good. Want some?"

"No thanks. I can't stand it straight."

"Come on, it'll do you good, being cold and scared and all that shit."

She took the bottle, swallowed some, swallowed more, and tried not to cough as she handed it back. Michaels took another swig and felt the delightful burning. "How's it feel?"

"Good. Uh, why don't you give him some?"

"I was getting to that."

Michaels shook him, making him squirm and groan softly. He put the bottle end under his nose—the fumes caused more squirming—then poured into the parted lips. Renwick swallowed some, the rest ran down his face into his beard. Another groan, followed by painful inhalation. The lips opened slightly. Michaels poured more whiskey. Renwick moaned, his head jerking sideways. "Uh-uh . . . *no*."

Michaels shook him again, "Come on, wake up." Renwick began breathing faster. They heard him pant. His arms and legs twitched, his face tensed, contorted. A long, low moan as if he hurt badly inside.

"What's wrong with him?" Angela asked.

"I don't know."

"He looks like he's suffering from something more than exposure."

"Yeah, I'd say so." Michaels had guessed what that something was. He'd seen these symptoms before.

Renwick continued jerking, then began shivering. The trembling grew until the long form wrapped by the blankets quivered steadily. He breathed in huge, pained gasps.

"God—is he going to die?"

"Probably not, though he might want to."

The shivering stopped, the moaning went on. The thin hands tried to pull off the blanket. Michaels grabbed him by the shoulder. "Come on, take it easy."

A gurgling noise accompanied by a sick smell, and the whiskey came up, frothing around lips and beard, then a loud cough and choking sounds. "Jesus." Mike turned the head sideways so he couldn't swallow the thin vomit and choke to death. "He's definitely in bad shape. Hey—come on."

Renwick's eyes opened and he leaped for Michaels's throat. Even in the dim light Mike could see the eyes rage—they nearly glowed with their strange, sick intensity. Good God, the man was crazy. Regardless of what else was wrong, he was absolutely mad. Although Mike knew it would be hopeless, he tried to calm him. "Relax, it's okay now. It's warm in here. You'll be okay."

"*No.*" He sucked for air, gulping like a goldfish out of water, legs thrashing. "Why—why did you—I was—"

"Relax, man."

"No—*stupid fucking bastard!*" He spat the

words in a low whisper. "Why didn't you leave me there, warm and so fine—much better." Trembling, he closed his eyes. They jerked open. "Have you got any? Give me some."

"We don't have any."

"You mustn't! I mustn't—I—I mustn't. *He* gets me that way." He took a deep breath, shuddered, and was still. Michaels sat back on his heels, shaking his head. The eyes exploded open, raging as before, and the long, skeletal fingers struck at Michaels like a snake, gripping his arm with a strange power. "Give me some—give me some or we'll kill you."

Michaels glared back, sitting on his fear. "We don't have any—nothing. Now keep quiet. You'll feel better that way."

"Yeah. Yeah, you're right. Quiet. Huhhuh . . ." He lay still, breathing in rasps.

Angela looked shocked. "What's wrong with him?"

Mike took the left arm, rolled up the sleeve of the field jacket. The pale smooth skin had a strange tint, the veins knotty, raised rivers.

"No needle marks, but he has to have been on heroin."

"Heroin?"

"Yeah. Or some other opium derivative. I think he's having withdrawal symptoms. Some friends of mine in Vietnam got hooked on the stuff, and I worked with a lot of ex-addicts in the hospital over there."

"I thought people shot heroin."

"Nah, not if it's strong enough. You can smoke it or even eat it."

"Can he die from that?"

"Well, depends on how long he's been taking

it, how much, and what else is wrong with him. It's not that likely. But he will be pretty sick and pretty uncomfortable. He should be in a hospital. Hell, we're going to have to put on the chains and get out of here, and putting on chains in this shit is going to be a real pain in the ass. That's assuming we can get back on the road."

"We are on a hilltop."

Renwick turned his head and stared at Angela, aware of her for the first time. Michaels watched warily, but some of the crazy look had left his eyes.

"But you're beautiful."

She smiled nervously and touched his arm. "Stay quiet and rest. We'll try to get you out of this."

He closed his eyes and sighed, a long, tired sound flirting with hysteria. "You can't. No way. No one can. He's too strong." Eyes wide open: "But you must be careful—he'd like you—he'd like your—you . . ." His face twitched, and his body jerked. "For Christ's sake, be careful."

"We will," Mike said. "There must be a doctor in Udolph."

Renwick choked, then screamed—a high-pitched, ear-shattering scream, doubly effective in the small confines. His arms were out from under the blanket, hands fumbling, flopping about like dead fish. The bony fingers grabbed at Michaels's coat.

"Are we going to Udolph?"

"Well, uh, yeah."

"You mustn't—she mustn't—*her* especially. They are too strong. You mustn't take me to Udolph—anywhere else—anywhere but there."

"Uh, okay. We won't go there." Michaels decided to humor the madman.

Renwick blinked, then his eyes chiseled at Michaels's head. Slowly something evil crept back until the orange tongues of hate flickered in his eyes. A sharp ugly laugh, more like a pig's grunt.

"You dumb fucking fool. You don't even understand. Go to Udolph—let him have us—let him have me." His eyes closed as another huge groan seized him. His entire body went rigid, back arching, then he went slack. "Fucking moron. You'll enjoy dying, if you're lucky. And you—you—" Glaring at Angela, another spasm of pain came and went. "He'll enjoy you—he'll enjoy your—you—your dripping—" He giggled and more liquid came up.

Mike glanced at Angela, but she seemed to take the remark calmly. He wiped the liquid from Renwick's face with a rag. "Listen, my friend, it was not all that easy digging you out of a snowbank and carrying you back here, so you might try showing some small semblance of gratitude instead of badmouthing us both."

"*Fuck you.*" He closed his eyes and began trembling again. His breathing deepened, and he seemed to go into a trance.

Mike stuck his leg over the front seat. "Move over a bit." He climbed over, sat, and scratched his head. "Jesus, he's bad off. What a mess. You were really lucky to get a ride from me tonight, Angela."

She laughed once. "Yeah. I know."

He turned off the dome light, let his head fall back against the seat, and closed his eyes. The hearse idled quietly. "I'd like to forget where we are and our friend in the back and sleep." A low moan behind him.

"So would I. It's been a long day."

"What time is it, anyway?"

"Ten-forty."

"Oh, hell." He sat up. "I'd better get out and see how we're going to get out of here."

"I'll come too."

He opened the door and stepped out into snow, wind, and blizzard for what seemed like the millionth time. If anything, the storm had grown worse. Angela stood by him, and they looked at the giant hearse, tipped at an odd angle, half on the road, half off.

He bent over to her and said, "Forwards or backwards?"

"Forward. We should be able to get the car moving, and once it's going downhill it should be easy to steer back onto the road."

"Yeah, that's about the way I figure it. How would you like to wait here and watch while I try it?"

"I could try if you'd like. I've driven on snowy mountain roads a lot."

"Me, too, and it's Uncle Bill's car. Besides, I'd like to do something right tonight after nearly wiping us out a couple of times."

"Mike, what do you suppose happened to the dog?"

"I don't know. I'd almost forgotten about him. Myself, I'm wondering what that guy was doing with a sign with Udolph on it when he's scared shitless of the place."

"You wouldn't like having me in the car to cheer you on?"

"Not this trip. You can cheer from up here."

"How about our friend?"

"I don't want to try moving him. He's a real crazy, and very sick. Best leave him alone. I'll take a chance with him."

"But not with me?"

"But not with you."

"Be careful."

"I will. About the worst I can do—if she moves——is put her in the ditch at the bottom of this hill. Let's clear some space for the wheels."

Michaels got his GI entrenching tool and shoveled snow from in front of the rear wheels. Angela found some buried branches that she shook free of snow and placed before the tires. He used a scraper to clear the snow from the windows.

"That should do it." He got into the hearse and rolled down the window.

"Watch out, Mike. Straighten out the wheel and get some speed before you try steering onto the road." She looked worried and had put her hand on his shoulder.

"I will." They stared at each other while the wind and snow blew around them. "I'd better get going." He reached over from the wheel and gave her wrist a squeeze.

"I'll get in back and push." They were both aware of letting go of each other.

Michaels slipped the hearse into second. "Okay, son of bitch, let's go." Gingerly he applied gas and heard one wheel spin.

Angela saw the wheel spin and climbed onto the bumper, grasping the rear-door handle, the other arm awkwardly trying to hold the metal surface. The hearse began to move. She waited until it was going okay and jumped off, then watched the big black vehicle start downhill.

As the back went down he understood what she was doing. Good thinking. He straightened the wheels, accelerating gently. He felt her jump off. The hearse gained speed, up to twenty-five. He turned the wheel left and gave the car more gas. It started to skid. Ignoring the brakes, he steered wildly, forcing the car back onto the highway where it continued swerving.

Across from him in the other lane, through the snow, he saw two yellow lights. God, another car—the first car since—headed straight for him. He was halfway down the hill in the middle of the road, with the other car coming like a bat out of hell. Of all the goddamn luck—don't panic, dumb fucker—forget the brakes. Fear caught him, but he kept his foot off the brake and accelerated, cutting hard to the left. The lights rushed him and swerved by on the right, the big dark body swooshing by like a shark.

He skidded onto the other shoulder. It was much less steep than on the right side. He drove almost to the foot of the hill, skidded and veered back onto the road, hoping no more cars were coming. Finally he was in the right lane, headed uphill. The tires started to slip again. *Easy*— don't blow it now—don't hit the brakes. The car wheels spun slowly to a halt. Gently he pressed down on the brake pedal, then shifted into park. His mouth was dry, his heart still ricocheting around his chest. He put his head and arms down onto the wheel.

"Are you all right?" Angela was at the window, breathing fast from running.

"Yeah. But I think I'm going to give up winter driving."

"God, it looked like you were going to plow right into that bus."

"Bus?"

"Yeah, a black Volkswagen bus. It was really going fast, around fifty or sixty."

"Well, he certainly scared the shit out of me."

"Me, too. I thought you were crazy when you steered left, but he zoomed right around you."

"Angela, this has not been our night. These kinds of things don't usually happen to me. If I didn't have that guy in back, I swear to God I wouldn't go anywhere else tonight. Instead we get to put on chains." He jammed his hat down onto his head as he got out of the car and the wind attacked him. "Fucking storm—stop it!"

In answer the wind swelled into a gigantic blast of snow and frozen air. He turned sideways away from the wind, shielding her. She stumbled and grabbed at his back. He put his arm around her, steadied her. She put her other arm around him, resting her hands on the small of his back. They stared at each other. Michaels felt a fearful elation. She looked even more beautiful close up and the desire he had felt earlier surged back. In the space of frozen air between them they saw each other's steamy breath. Snowflakes stung their faces.

She knew they were standing in the middle of a blizzard, growing colder and being covered with snow, but she didn't move. The wind blew his long, light hair, and she sensed an uneasiness somewhere inside him. Drawing in her breath she pulled him toward her.

He immediately put his other arm around her, and they threw themselves at each other. His hat flew off. Her hands came up his back and gripped for his shoulder blades. They felt the awkward bulky clothing interfere, but they drew together, intensifying their embrace. They stood clinging to each other while the storm bayed anxiously about them. Gradually they loosened their hold. With his ear and cheek alongside her head, he could hear her breathing. He backed away so he could see her face.

She smiled. "You've lost your hat."

"I know," he said, tilting his head and angling for her lips.

Her lips found his, and her tongue was in his mouth. He had kissed many women, but she had an immediate passionate force that he found slightly intimidating. They enjoyed the kiss; their tongues and lips moving. When they were both out of breath, they stopped and hugged again.

The wind howled indignantly at such mockery of Chaos. How dare two useless specks of life and warmth scorn the powers of ice and storm? The snow swarmed angrily, a maelstrom of wind and white flakes screaming about them. Bodies pressed together, they clung to each other more tightly, and momentarily they forgot the storm, Renwick, the hearse, and the mess they were in.

CHAPTER THREE

◆

Seest thou yon dreary plain, forlorn and wild,
The seat of desolation, void of light,
Save what the glimmering of these livid
* flames*
Casts pale and dreadful? Thither let us tend
From off the tossing of these fiery waves;
There rest, if any rest can harbour there . . .
* —Milton,* Paradise Lost

IT TOOK TWENTY minutes to put on the chains and over an hour to drive the twenty miles to Udolph. Getting chains on in a blizzard on an incline was awkward, miserable, and the cold put Michaels's fingers to sleep. Back in the car they burned to life, hurting terribly. Cold and exhausted, Angela fell asleep almost immediately, slumping over onto her side. Mike was glad he'd slept till noon.

The hearse plowed toward Udolph, the chains making regular clunking noises. The tempest continued. Fat white flakes flew about the car— spinning, tumbling, gyrating—like a swarm of albino bees, and the wind alternately snarled with fury, and groaned with pain. Something new was added. Wispy vapor steamed from the ground, streamers shooting up from a monstrously fecund plant, clouds of pale smoke swallowing the hearse. Fog was everywhere.

Michaels cursed. A storm was bad enough, but whoever heard of a foggy blizzard? He had to slow down below twenty. Hard to tell where the road went, where road ended and ditch began. Everything was gray-white, and the yellow glare from the headlights hardly dented the mists. Like flying a plane in a storm: blind, no sense of direction, no reference points, no idea how high or low or where, beyond the touch of the earth, the security of ground beneath you. Only a hunk of metal floating, lost in the void. He nearly ran the car off the road twice but managed to recover. He didn't want to end up in a ditch again.

He yawned, blinked, decided it must be around twelve. He was sick of the monotony of the road and the furious storm, tired of crawling along staring into dimness. And the strange quality of this night worried him. Something nasty out there.

He blinked and caught a black shape out of the corner of his eye. Quickly turning he saw nothing, but the fear lurking about all evening throbbed into the foreground. A black shape like the dog he had seen earlier. Suppose it was running alongside the car? Maybe it was dead and wanted revenge. Goddammit, *stop that!*

Now what was that? A noise over the swish of wipers, the engine roar, and the clinking chains. Howling. He restrained the urge to stab into the brakes and slowly eased down his foot until the car stopped. The engine was noisy but at least the chains were silent. No howling, anyway. White void of shifting fog and snowflakes. Jesus, was he getting paranoid! So he had heard something. This was farm country. Dogs were everywhere.

Angela sat up suddenly. "Are we there?"

"Not yet, but we shouldn't be far."

"God, what *is* this—where are we?"

"It's fog. Nice, huh?"

"How can you drive in this?"

"With great difficulty." He accelerated slowly, and the hearse crept forward into the white mists and falling snow.

"Why did we stop?"

"Oh, uh, I thought I heard something." He was glad she was awake.

"How strange. I've never seen a snowstorm like this. It reminds me of those old movies where the ship gets lost in the fog." She raised her arms, stretched awkwardly because of the roof, stared out the front window. The yellow beams cast a feeble light onto the opaque vapors, spotlights on the madly dancing snowflakes. "How is the guy in the back?"

"Okay, I guess. He moans once in a while and thrashes around."

"I wonder where he got hooked on heroin."

"Probably the army. The army does wonderful things for people."

"You were in the army, weren't you?"

"Yeah, from May twentieth 1968 to May nineteenth 1970. Vietnam and the whole thing. Horrible, horrible shit."

"What did you do while you were in?"

"Oh, mutilated bodies, ran secret missions for the Green Berets, led John Wayne attacks against machine-gun nests."

"Okay, what did you really do?"

His grin returned, blond mustache scrunched around the smile corners. "You'd never guess."

"Didn't you say . . . wasn't playing the organ part of your duties?"

"Sometimes."

"You weren't a foot soldier or a medic? Well, were you in some kind of band?"

He laughed. "No."

"I give up. What were you?"

"A chaplain's assistant."

Buffalo Bill, a chaplain's assistant? She laughed, while he smiled and drove. Outside, the tenuous limbs of fog brushed along the black metal.

"You're trying to fool me again."

"Oh no. Cross my heart and hope to die. Stick a needle in my eye. Boil in oil and stew in lye. I'm really very devout. My family lived in the desert, and we dug flagellating each other."

"Don't start on your family again. How did you become a chaplain's assistant?"

"Well, like an idiot I let myself get drafted, see? But I decided I wasn't going to kill anybody, and I told them at Basic I wanted to file for conscientious objector. *Bad mistake.* I was at Fort Lewis, and when I could finally get off the fort I went to some Seattle draft-resistance people. This Lutheran minister, a real intelligent, pretty agnostic guy, decided I should try it as a devout Lutheran with scruples. He wrote letters about my deep faith and love of life. The love of life stuff was true, but the stuff about God and Jesus wasn't. Anyway, it worked. They gave me the kind of CO where you stay in but don't have to kill people. Unfortunately the first sergeant and the company commander still wanted to ship my ass to Vietnam as a combat medic."

"Why did they want to get you?"

"Gee, I don't know. I scored super-high on the PE-type test and the other competitive crap. Of course, some naughty dude was always smoking dope, sleeping on guard duty, even sabotaging trucks, that kind of stuff. When the company went out on bivouac he hid under a tree with a bunch of C rations and caught up on his sleep. He managed to escape and evade the whole company for three days, then told them he got lost in the woods. I did get a couple of Article Fifteens. That's where they fine you and make you do extra work. Luckily they never actually caught me with any dope. Before I left, though, I planted seeds everywhere around the fort I thought they might grow. Anyway, I didn't have many friends in high places. But the Lutheran minister knew a chaplain who was a full-bird colonel and told him what a devout, cool person I was. So I got sent to chaplain's school."

"What in the world did you do at chaplain's school?"

"Got to set up field altars and good shit like that. I spent most of my time in Vietnam as an assistant to the Catholic chaplain at Long Binh."

"They made a Lutheran assistant to the Catholic chaplain?"

"Yep. The army way. Unfortunately, every so often I had to go out to the field in goddamn helicopters. I saw some bad stuff. Lots of extreme unctions. Most of the priests were real assholes, soldiers first. Telling the poor dumb guys to get back in there and kill. Talk about hypocrisy. The only really sharp guy I ever ran across was a rabbi from New York City."

He stared ahead into the swirl of fog and snow, heard the wind screech over the engine's barrel-throated rumble. He could mock the army now, but at the time it hadn't been funny. Death everywhere. He blinked, forehead tensing as he tried to follow the curve of the road. The speedometer wavered around fifteen. Jesus, it was hard to see. He was sick of driving, felt the accumulated tension in his forehead, neck, and back.

"Do you know Pat Donahue?" she asked.

"No. Should I?"

"I guess not. He's a priest at Center East, but chaplains are a pet peeve of his. You sound just like him."

"Oh?" He wasn't particularly flattered at the comparison.

"He's read a lot of the Berrigans' writings. You'd like him, I think. He's not a very conventional priest. He doesn't believe in the Virgin Mary or hell." She laughed. "And he says he believes in celibacy but not chastity for priests."

"What's the difference?"

"Celibates don't marry, chaste people don't have sex."

"Oh. He doesn't sound like he'll last long as a priest."

"No. That's the sad part. The last two priests have run off to get married. Pat's already in disfavor with the local parish clergy. His sermons on Vietnam upset them, and they'd like to prove he's been sleeping with girls."

"Has he?"

"Oh, he's not a promiscuous lecher or anything, but he may have slept with someone. He's right, though. Surely you can love God and still love a person enough to sleep with them."

"I thought that was a mortal sin. You get chucked down the flaming tube." Michaels found this very interesting.

"I've never believed that, and no one I've ever respected very much believes it either."

"But didn't you get priests and nuns and your

parents feeding you that line? Most Catholics I know . . ."

"My mother went to parochial schools and hated it. She didn't want me to go through the same thing. She and my father taught me most of what I know about God."

"But didn't they tell you sex was filthy and dirty, and you'd get pregnant and. . . ?"

"No."

"Well, my parents didn't go to church *every* Sunday, but that's what they told me."

"What? That you'd get pregnant?" She laughed.

"No, but how wicked and—hey, your parents must be a couple of Commie perverts. What kind of degenerate attitude is that to give your kids? Not telling them sex is filthy. What does your father do?"

"He's a professor in the religion department at Boulder. My mother's a pianist."

"Christ." His father, the feed salesman, his mother the all-American housewife. She wasn't just beautiful, all right. "Goddamn Commie professors. I thought Italian parents were real protective."

"Well, usually they are, but my father came from a very liberal, intellectual family, and he's not that old, only forty-six. He met my mother when he was in graduate school at Columbia. She was from a rich, very conservative Italian family. My father jokes about how frustrated he got before they were finally married."

"How old are you, then?"

"Twenty. Hey Mike—look at the fog."

Huge tendrils of mist steamed skyward, growing thinner, then thicker, and finally fading away. The white fog rose, sucked into the void like the spray and foam of a wave retreating from the beach. With one final horrendous scream the wind slapped the hearse, then subsided to a moan, and the antic dance of the snowflakes slowed to a dying tempo. The space around the hearse seemed to expand, the constricting walls drawing back. The headlights shot forward unimpeded, and Michaels could make out fenceposts and trees along the roadside. The effect was magical, as if the tempest were vanquished. But this might be only the eye of the storm, and the night was still young.

"Holy shit, what lousy timing. We must be just about there. What time is it?"

"Twelve-thirty."

"Oh God. We can forget trying to make Iowa City tonight. We'll drop off our friend in back somewhere, and I'd better call the guy to tell him we won't be by until morning. Maybe there's a cheap motel in Udolph."

She raised her arms over her head, bent them to grasp her elbows with her hands, and yawned. "That's fine with me. This has been some drive." She lowered her arms, stretching them before her. The storm was ending, they were almost there, so why should she feel so . . ? She turned.

Renwick's eyes glared at her, ripped into her skull, burning with a sick intensity. He lay under the blanket, his head two feet away. With his long hair and beard he looked like a Christ possessed by demons he had meant to cast out.

"Oh my God." She shivered and turned away.

"What's wrong?" He started to slow down.

"Nothing—keep going." She slid closer to him.

"You're sure? What is it?"

"He's been staring at us, and he looks so—so evil. He's been listening. Spying."

Michaels quickly looked behind him. The blanket quivered, and Renwick's eyes were screwed shut from pain. "What can he do to us? We'll drop him off first thing."

But she couldn't relax. The loose, happy feeling of earlier in the evening was gone, and she knew it would not return. She laid her head against his shoulder and watched the road.

Road and farmland seemed to smoke: From frozen fire burned icy shreds, clouds of cold smoke. Only a few small flakes still fell. Snow covered everything as far as they could see, blurring sharp corners, the focus of things. The farmhouses they passed were strangely dark, missing the usual bright yard lights. The chains clunked regularly, and the engine made its throaty gurgle as the hearse rose and fell with the terrain. Finally the headlights illuminated the sign UDOLPH.

"Well, we made it," he said.

The town looked about the same as Jenkin's Center. All the ugly square-front buildings were unlighted. Surprisingly enough, the tavern looked permanently closed, boarded over. Mike stopped by a darkened gas station where he saw a phone booth's green glow.

"I wonder if there's a doctor in this town? I'd better call that guy first." He opened the glove compartment and fished around for a slip of paper. "Be right back."

"Good. I feel funny."

"Sick?" He stared at her, eyes worried.

She moistened her lips, then smiled hesitantly.

"No . . . It's just been weird. I feel strange. Like something's going to happen." A long blond strand of hair covered his face. She used her hand to brush it back. Her palm felt cool and smooth against his cheek.

"I know how you feel. Don't worry, though. All I need to do is drop him off, then we can find someplace to stay. We should be home free now."

He looked in back. Renwick still appeared unconscious. Michaels put his hand on the door handle, hesitated, staring at her. She put her hands on his face, the palms along his chin on either side, and their lips touched gently. When they were finished she sighed and let her hands drop, her fingers brushing against his legs.

Michaels stepped outside and closed the door. *Jesus* it was cold! The mild breeze ate right through clothes, flesh, muscle, bone, sucked greedily for marrow. He looked up at the sky. All the fog was gone, and even the clouds were breaking up, patches of black sky showing through. The full moon was a hazy circle of light behind gray cloud. The wind moaned.

He quickly walked to the phone, cursing the fact that the booth was more a stall coming only halfway to the ground. His fingers fumbled for the paper and a dime. He took off his gloves to dial, and the metal felt like ice. The holes didn't want to let go of his finger.

The phone rang six times. I hope I don't piss them off if I wake them up. Christ, what if they weren't home? "Come on, I'm freezing my ass off out here."

"Hello." A woman's voice.

"Uh, hello. Is, uh, Mister Blut there?"

"You mean Doctor Blut. No. He went out for a walk with the dog."

"You're kidding?"

"No." She sounded displeased. "I don't joke."

"Do you know when he'll be back?"

"No."

"Well, listen, you can tell him we'll be by to pick up the, uh, deceased in the morning."

"Deceased?"

"Isn't his brother dead?"

"Oh. Yes. You're the man from Iowa City?"

"Tell him I would have been here sooner but the roads were terrible and—"

"Wait."

He heard the phone put down. A big gust of wind hit and cut through his legs. He shivered. Of all the—*come on!*

"The doctor is back. He will speak to you."

"Hello, Mister Michaels, how are you? Did you have much trouble? I spoke to your uncle just today."

"It was pretty hard getting here, but we made it okay."

"Excellent. I'm glad you're all right."

"So am I."

A polite laugh, which was more than Michaels thought he deserved. The guy had a very smooth voice with a touch of some accent, so faint it was impossible to place.

"You must come here at once."

"Huh? We were going to find a motel."

"No, I insist. I have a large farmhouse with a great many vacant rooms. You may stay overnight and pick up my brother in the morning."

"You don't need to put us up. Besides, I've got a real crazy in the back."

"A what?"

"Some guy we found in the snow. He looks like he's coming down from some drug. Probably heroin."

"All the more reason you should come out here immediately. I'm the only doctor in town. There are no motels in Udolph. Let me give you directions."

"Oh—okay." It would have been nice to be alone with Angela. He jotted down directions, fingers shaking.

"All right then, Mister Michaels, I'll be looking forward to you and your friend. Good evening."

Mike hung up, wondered how the guy knew he had a "friend" with him. Oh sure, he'd said "we" several times. He quickly strode back toward the hearse, wind baying about him, and felt the shivering build up his spine. He opened the door. Angela smiling at him—and Renwick, caught unawares, his eyes half-open and blazing fear— scared to death. Mike swallowed and felt like completely panicking. Something was terribly wrong tonight. He sat and closed the door, smiling at Angela.

"Doctor Blut wants us to come out." A sound, half-moan, half-sob, from the back. "He'll put us up for the night."

"He's a doctor?"

"Apparently so. He's got a big house about five miles out. Go a mile out of town, turn left, go two miles on a curving gravel road, and turn left after the bridge, follow another curving gravel road over another bridge to the end."

"More driving. That must make you happy."

"Sure." He put the car in drive. "I'm ready to stop for the evening."

"What about . . ?" Her eyes motioned toward Renwick.

"He's a doctor. He said he could take care of him."

Michaels touched the accelerator, and the chains began their steady clatter. What a bleak, ugly town. Swallowed up in blackness, half the squat, square homes appearing deserted. Even the Dairy Queen was abandoned, the door torn off the hinges, the windows eyeless, all the glass out. They passed a courthouse of drab gray stone with what seemed the only light in town, a thirty-foot pole topped with a white Cyclops's orb, which threw an austere bluish radiance across the facade. Mike thought he saw something black flitter across the light, but when he looked more carefully there was nothing. He was glad to leave Udolph.

He drove a mile and made the left turn. The gravel road made no difference, lay buried under a foot of snow like everything else. The moon came out, creeping from behind a torn shred of cloud and flooding the landscape with cold brightness. The snow caught the light, scattered icy whiteness everywhere. They could not hear the wind because of the engine, but they saw the snow swirl and the trees bend. They passed a field where the wind created snow dunes, shaped and shifted them, playfully pawing the snow like a giant cat. Mike had thought he'd be relieved once out of Udolph, but the moonlit landscape was almost more oppressive.

"It certainly cleared up fast," she said.

"Yeah. Here's our bridge." He made another left turn. Darkened farmhouses had lined the other road, melancholy sentinels, but here were

only barren fields with scattered trees clawing at
the sky.

"Mike, is the heater on as far as it will go? I'm
freezing."

"Yeah, but I know what you mean. It must be
the cloud cover breaking up. I'd guess it's down
to twenty below."

"Well, it's sure getting cold." She slid closer to
him. He steered with one hand and put his right
arm around her. They both felt the sudden cold,
a diffuse chill that ignored the heater. Perhaps
the glacial atmosphere had oozed from deep
within the earth, or perhaps the cold was less a
presence than an absence, a hungry darkness
sucking away warmth like a leech.

She snuggled closer and tried not to shiver.
She closed her eyes. The dazzling light from the
moon and snow made her head hurt, and she
wanted to cry. She was as afraid as when she'd
been a child, and it worsened as the night wore
on. Abruptly, she wanted to tell him to turn
around and get away before—before—Oh *stop*.
She was tired out and upset by everything:
Renwick, the dog, the blizzard. Enough to upset
anyone. Mike would think she was a foolish
woman, and anyway, where for God's sake could
they go?

He sensed her uneasiness, a certain trembly
quality. He didn't feel so hot himself. He
squeezed her shoulder tightly and smiled. She
made herself smile back. Neither of them looked
convinced. He had to let go of her to use both
hands on the wheel.

"This road sure winds enough. My sense of
direction is gone. I don't even know which way
Udolph would be."

"It's so bright out there. There are no more clouds."

They were quiet. The road curved wildly, a serpent winding through empty fields. Angela shivered from the cold. Something rattled in the back. She turned. Renwick's eyes were open again, staring nowhere, his mouth gaping, and his body shook so hard she could hear it.

"Oh God, Mike, he's worse."

"Well, we're almost there." Another long sobbing moan.

The hearse came to a hilltop. The road dropped, curved, then rose again, and in the distance on a second hilltop they saw the house. White and cold like the snow, surrounded by a grove of trees, black, many-limbed forms squatting like goblin guardians. Angela felt herself trembling. The hearse started downhill.

A fence of broken, twisted wood and barbed wire ran along the road on either side; thin, weedy stalks and scraggly bush branches thrust from the snow like the feelers of hidden insects. The hearse crossed the small bridge. Beneath flowed dark water, strangely unfrozen, a black stream that cut in a jagged slash toward the trees. The oaks began at the bottom and silently followed the hearse uphill. Overhead a riot of black fingers strained and contorted, groping from opposite sides to form an archway. There was no snow on the dark branches. Mike decided some heavy blast must have blown it off. The hill was steep, slow going even with chains. The wind swept through the trees, making the branches shiver.

Michaels stopped the hearse by a wooden gate, which stood open. From a metal post hung the sign creaking in the wind. The sign was black and said BLUT FARM.

"This is it," Michaels said.

The hearse followed the curve of the road past the house, and Mike parked by the barn. He turned off the engine. The loud roar ceased, and the silence was shattering. Only the wind interrupted the quiet.

"Welcome to Doctor Blut's all-American farm." The attempt at humor fell flat.

"How lovely."

"Why don't we go see if the good doctor is in?"

Michaels stepped outside and put on his cowboy hat. Like stepping into a rather brisk Antarctic evening. The air was an ice-water bath. Everywhere glaring white snow and moonlight, sparkling and reflecting. Occasionally the wind stirred frozen clouds and blew into him, trying to replace life with its own icy breath. He quickly pulled on his gloves.

He glanced overhead and inhaled sharply. With no clouds and no outside lights, the sky was deep, deep black, the color of nothing, dotted by thousands of cold white points. On one side of the sky the moon was a sharp-edged circle, hard and white, somehow larger than normal. The vacuum, the eternal cold of space, seemed closer, another force drawing away warmth, sucking it skyward. He shivered. It must be at least twenty below.

Clang! Metal striking metal. Another clang. He turned toward the large fenced area before the barn. In the center of the yard sat a round metallic object that he recognized as a pig feeder. The animal could lift one of several metal doors with its snout. When it withdrew, the door slammed shut. Two large hogs ate eagerly, metal squares resting on their heads. Two more had just finished. The hogs were immense, unusually long but not very fat. Although Mike stood about thirty feet away, he heard snorty crunching noises. The creatures stood out against the snowy background, long black shapes on short legs. One pulled its head out—clang—and stared at Michaels. He thought it would run away, but it only stared. He never liked pigs, and this one seemed particularly repulsive, its snout longer than most, with a crooked mouth, a strange glint in the small eyes. Now all four pigs were staring at him. Probably more in the barn.

"My God, it's cold!" Angels hunched her shoulders.

"Did you see the pigs?"

"No—oh. What's that thing?"

"A feeder."

"Why are they looking at us?"

He laughed. "I don't know. Jesus, what an ugly hog." The big one still seemed particularly interested in them.

She laughed. "Are some cuter than others? What makes a beautiful pig?"

"Whatever it is, that one definitely does not have it."

"None of them look very good to me."

"Me neither." He made a sudden rushing movement as if he were about to charge the pigs. They didn't budge. "That's funny. That usually freaks them out. I know what . . ."

He bent over to get some snow, formed a good hard snowball, and threw it. A blur of black motion as the hog darted sideways, and a high squeal. The snowball splattered against the feeder, but the pigs didn't move. They were still staring at him. He remembered stories about farmers killed by pigs, eaten alive. Hell—all he needed now was to get paranoid about pigs. Impulsively he ran at the fence, yelling loudly and waving his arms.

The pigs hesitated, then ran for the barn. Michaels stopped at the fence, feeling slightly ridiculous. They stood at the doorway to the barn, four dark shadows, and watched him. He turned and walked back to Angela.

"Why did you do that?" she asked.

"I just wanted to see them run. Let's get inside—it's too goddamn cold out here."

They started for the house. "Did you see the stars?" he asked.

She looked upward, stopped. "Oh God—look at them." She shivered, and he rested his hand on her shoulder. "You could get lost out there so easy." She looked at him, wanting to kiss him, but realized they were both freezing. "Let's get inside before we both turn to ice."

There was no visible path, so they had to make their way through the snow to the porch. Closer up the house looked old and shabby, cracks splitting the white paint, scattered gray blemishes, spots like rotting sores, some window frames and the porch railing broken, other windows that looked warped or crooked. The house was immense, shapeless, a three-story mass of windows and odd little roofs and balconies jutting out here and there. No light or other sign of life showed from within.

Michaels stamped his feet on the porch, looked for a doorbell, and saw only a knocker. He rapped sharply. Nothing happened. He rapped again louder.

"Wouldn't it be funny if this was all a practical joke?" He was so cold he found it difficult to talk. His shoulders were raised, arms glued to his side, hands making fists.

The door opened, letting only an orange slash of light onto the porch. A very tall, thin man stood before them. With his back to the light and the porch shaded from the moon, they could not clearly see him, but his white hair and pale face stood out from the sea of shadow about him. "I am Doctor Blut. Welcome. Will you freely enter my house?"

The hint of a question mark in his last sentence made Angela hesitate, but Michaels, freezing, quickly stepped in and escaped an abrupt gust of chilling wind. He did wonder about Blut's peculiar phrasing and that mild but unusual accent. Angela followed.

Blut closed the thick, heavy door, turned, and smiled. Light from the far room fell across his face. Somewhat shocked, Mike tried not to stare. He had never seen a true albino before, but Dr. Blut had to be one. Long, thin face, well furrowed, prominent lines around and under his eyes, jutting nose like a hawk beak. The mouth was narrow, the lips thin and bloodless, like a seam cut in his face. But his striking characteristic was his color—or lack of it. He looked bleached. A few freckles sprinkled his pale cheeks, but even they looked anemic, and his hair, long for a man of his age, was dead white, matching his face. He had hardly any eyebrows, his eyes were pale, pale blue. The blue seemed weak, insubstantial, as if this color too might fade out of existence. His eyes were rather bloodshot; standing out against his general pallor, the red veins and blue irises made his eyes appear to jump from his face. He might be anywhere between forty and sixty.

"You must be Mister Michaels." He smiled and extended his hand.

Michaels shook hands. God, Blut was strong. The hand felt cold, damp, and oddly hairy.

"How are you both? You must be extremely tired. I can show you to your rooms if you wish."

"We are both pretty wiped out. This is Angela Rosalba. She's a—an old friend."

"How nice to meet you, Miss Rosalba." The vowels in "Rosalba" came out long and distinctive, the *r* immaculately rolled. Blut's teeth were perfect and sparkled like a Hollywood movie star's. "Would you like a drink before you retire?"

"Christ, yes."

"Mike, don't forget . . ." Angela began.

"Yeah. First you'd better take care of the guy in the hearse. We think his name is Renwick. He's having withdrawal symptoms. We'd better bring him in."

"Yes, of course." Blut turned the doorknob.

Mike stared. "You're not going out like that?"

Blut wore a black double-breasted suit, very stylish, with flared pants, tapered waist, and wide lapels. His shirt was white with a black knit tie. His apparel reminded Mike of Uncle Bill.

"I'll be perfectly all right."

"But it's twenty below out there—at least."

"Believe me, Mister Michaels, I will be all

right. Cold weather does not bother me." He smiled again at Angela. "We won't be long. Take off your coat and make yourself comfortable."

"Okay." She didn't care for him or his smile.

Blut opened the door and gestured for Michaels to go first. Mike hesitated, fastened the collar of his field jacket, and stepped out into the night. He hadn't had time to warm up, and the cold was every bit as bad as he remembered. They walked through the snow to the hearse. The wind whispered ominous threats, and the snow sparkled bits of moonlight. It was unnaturally bright, too white. Michaels didn't see how Dr. Blut could stand it. He didn't even have his hands in his pockets.

Clang. The pigs were still at it in the big barnyard. He opened the back door of the hearse. Rumpled blankets, a pack, boxes, and no Renwick.

"Oh shit—now where could he have gone? He must want to freeze to death."

"Don't worry, Mister Michaels, I think I know where he is. You will wait here, and I will return shortly."

"Are you kidding? You'll freeze, too. Besides, he's pretty crazy—he might be dangerous."

"Please, I insist. This will only take a minute. Wait here, and no harm will come to you."

"Me?" Michaels laughed. "You haven't seen the guy. He acts insane. I don't know what he'd do. If you think I'm going to wait while you—"

"Mister Michaels, I'm afraid I must insist." Blut's obsequious smile was gone, and the tone of his voice was discordant, threatening. The two men eyed each other. The staring contest made Mike extremely uncomfortable. The pale eyes, which seemed to leap from their sockets, grew at him.

"Jesus Christ, do what you want—I'm tired of playing guardian angel tonight. You can both freeze for all I care."

Blut looked amused, his voice had a restrained sarcastic quality. "I'm sorry, Mister Michaels, but believe me, I know Renwick and—"

"You know him?"

"He has been living in Udolph. This will only take a moment. Renwick is in that grove of trees downhill. The stream will have stopped him. You can see his tracks. Now *wait here.*"

Blut turned abruptly and flowed downhill, moving faster than a walk but not running. Mike saw Renwick's tracks swerve toward the dark grove. Blut quickened his stride, black shape gliding across white snow. His feet hardly touched the snow, seemed to skim along the top. He reached the trees, and the earth darkened.

Mike's eyes jerked upward. A single cloud, the only cloud in the sky, had covered the moon, obliterating the sphere like a feasting amoeba. The hard shadows cast by the moonlight vanished, the entire landscape blurred. Behind the wisp of cloud the moon became a fuzzy gray-white orb, and the trees were a meaningless dark mass. The wind made a long, low noise.

Michaels shivered, walked around the hearse trying to warm up. He had never felt this cold in his life. He stopped, eyes jerking toward the grove. A yell and a crashing noise. The sounds echoed through the gelid air, reverberated off the house, seeming louder because of the night's quiet. He took a step downhill and stopped, still shivering. Blut had told him to wait. Somehow he knew the doctor could take care of himself. And he didn't want to walk into the icy shade of the trees with that madman there—either madman.

Renwick stumbled out of the grove, fell onto his knees in the snow. Blut was over him at once, hovering above and yanking him to his feet. Renwick faltered, Blut pushed him forward, grabbed his arm and led him uphill. The doctor's path went sideways, away from the trees, and suddenly he seemed headless—a lean black shape without a head. With his dark form silhouetted against snowy fields, his white hair and face tended to vanish. The cloud drifted from the moon, and the snow was flooded with light. The wind cried out, swirled clouds of mist around Blut's legs.

"Are you okay?" Michaels shouted.

"Certainly."

Blut let go of Renwick, who walked submissively toward the hearse. Renwick's field jacket was powdered with snow, the same for his hair and beard. Totally listless, his eyes were barely open. His mustache had solidified from frozen mucus and blood. Blut appeared as dignified as ever. Mike couldn't understand how Blut could stand the cold. They had only been outside about five minutes, but his own thighs and toes were already going numb. He was glad to head back to the house.

"He'll be better as soon as I give him a mild injection. It should help him sleep and alleviate some of his symptoms. Rather a good thing you found him. He seems to be going into a mild catatonia."

Angela opened the door to let them in and smiled at Mike. She still had her coat on. She had gone into the huge living room, discovered a black coffin, removed her coat, and immediately put it back on. A bone-chilling draft blew through the house. A strange odor caressed her nostrils, seeping from the woodwork, an odor that made her want to open the windows despite the cold. Overhead she heard noises. The dull clump began on one side and crossed the room. Probably footsteps. She had returned to the doorway and watched Mike pace about the hearse.

"What took so long?" she asked.

"Renwick decided to go play hide-and-seek. Doctor Blut was it."

She stared at the doctor, eyes widening. "Aren't you cold?"

"No. I'm accustomed to it." He seemed completely undisturbed, not a white hair out of place. Mike looked really cold. Renwick just looked awful, cold, and as if someone had clubbed him, zombielike. Ice and snow covered his pale brown beard and hair. He was trembling again.

"You two may wait in the living room," Blut said. "There is some brandy there. Please help yourself. I will examine Mister Renwick."

The front door opened onto stairs leading to the second floor. To the left was the living room, to the right a door that Blut opened.

"You don't need any help with him?" Mike asked.

"No." Blut flicked on the light and pushed Renwick inside. They had a glimpse of white walls, jars and pill bottles, an examination table, before the door closed.

Michaels wandered into the front room, blowing on his fingers, clenching and unclenching them. He stopped to stare. A huge sable rectanguloid, seven feet long, of thick, cold, hard jet-black metal dominated the room, screaming for attention as it sat dead center on a large oaken table. The coffin's glossy finish reflected light from a small lamp, the yellow lights glimmering about the coffin edges. Probably a mixture of chrome and tungsten steel. Very expensive. Uncle Bill didn't unload many like that. Last for centuries, for an eternity, resisting fire, flood, earthquake, grave robbers. Molten lava might eventually melt it down, but even that wouldn't be a sure bet. And you wouldn't see five or six pallbearers carrying this—must be heavy as hell. In the dim light he made out the name on the side: BLUT. He examined the work, put his finger in the *B*. The letters appeared chiseled into the metal, set in about half an inch, but the coffin must have come from the factory that way. Most tools wouldn't even scratch the dark metal. That cost money; a name engraved in steel would cost way more than any lettering stuck on. Two handles grew out of the top half. Was it locked? He put his hands on the steel grips.

"God, Mike—don't open it."

He started wildly and turned. Angela looked worried. "Hey, don't do that," he said. "I already told you I was chicken shit."

"So am I. That's why I don't want you playing around with coffins."

"Only trying to get involved in the family business."

He walked away from the coffin. The room was

spacious, abundantly furnished in late Victorian: immense chairs of dark wood with swollen red velvet cushions, a similar sofa, yet deep purple. The carpet was thick, ancient, a pattern of red and black that brought to mind a bleeding animal. Slabs of dusky wood lined the walls, full of knotholes, the grain twisting wildly. The remnants of a fire died slowly in the stone fireplace, the coals red-orange. For a living room it was somber, and the thick scarlet curtains would keep it that way during the day. A tiny lamp with a green-and-red fringed shade threw out the only real light in the massive chamber, timidly orange under the shade.

Michaels tossed his hat on the sofa and unzipped his coat. "I wouldn't take that off if I were you," she said. "It's freezing in here."

"Yeah. It smells weird too."

"I noticed that before."

"A lot of old houses smell musty or something. Maybe it's the carpet. It smells vaguely familiar, but I can't place it."

She had collapsed into a chair, sat with her hands still in her pockets and her eyes closed. He walked over behind her and put his hands on her shoulders.

"How are you?"

"Fine." She opened her eyes and let her head fall back.

With her face staring up at him, he finally had a good look at her. They had been outside or in the dark for hours, but now, even though the room was dim, he saw her clearly. She was beautiful, and her eyes were an unusually dark shade of blue, very different from Blut's icy ocean-water orbs.

She shut her eyes, wishing he would kiss her. She heard him bend over, felt his long hair brush across her cheek, and his lips touched her face. They kissed, beginning slowly, gradually opening their mouths further. She thrust her tongue into his mouth and struggled to get her hands out of her pockets. His grip tightened on her shoulders.

"This is awkward," she said. She stood, got her hands out of her pockets, and put her arms around him. Her mouth found his again. Closing his eyes, his lips gently felt hers, exploring her mouth. He opened his eyes, saw the strange partial perspective of her face, one large dark eyebrow, her eye closed, some hair, and her nose. Shutting his eyes he held her tighter. Silence, except for their breathing and the low cry of the wind.

Clump. A muffled thud over them. Clump, clump. Off to the right. Clump, clump, clump . . . coming closer. He drew back, still holding her, and looked at the ceiling.

"What the hell is that?"

"I don't know. I heard something up there earlier."

The clumps stopped directly above them.

"There must be someone else in this house."

A sudden explosive snap. They looked at the fireplace. The embers glowed bright red.

"This place is scary," she said.

"It's better than being outside and freezing your ass off, anyway. I wonder what's keeping Blut." Reluctantly he let go of her and walked toward the doorway to the stairs. She sat down, yawning. She grabbed her elbows and rubbed her arms, still cold.

"As long as no one is screaming, I guess everything's okay. Ahh ... Here we are." He had discovered a bottle of brandy and some glasses. "You want a shot of brandy? Any man who drinks brandy can't be all bad. Hmm, this has just been opened. Good stuff. It tastes really aged. I don't recognize the label. Sure you don't want some?"

"Uh-uh."

He walked over to the fireplace, sipping the brandy, sloshing the liquid in the enormous glass between sips. Almost half the adjacent wall was bookshelves lined with volumes. "You are what you read," he muttered.

Fat brown tomes clustered on the top shelf: *Principles of Internal Medicine, Physicians Desk Reference;* at one end was a series of related titles like *Principles of Hematology, Fundamentals of the Chemistry of the Blood, The Cellular Structure of Human Blood,* and so on. Lower down were traditional novels, Dickens, the Brontës, Eliot. The backs looked ancient. He pulled out *Wuthering Heights.* The title page was dated 1847, the cover worn, the pages stiff and yellow. Jesus, it must be a first edition. Another shelf was devoted to books like *The Mysteries of Udolpho, Frankenstein, Great Horror Stories,* and *Poe: The Complete Works.*

Mike took a large swallow of brandy and strolled away from the books. "Are you awake, Angela Angel?" She nodded her head but didn't open her eyes. "Sure you are. Stay awake a little longer, just till Blut gets back."

He noticed a purple velvet curtain across a doorway. "I wonder where this goes?"

She yawned and struggled to open her eyes. "It's probably a closet."

"We'll see." He lifted the curtain and looked behind it. "Aha! Very interesting. If I'm not back by morning, call the highway patrol."

"Mike, I wouldn't go blundering around this house." But he had stepped behind the curtain.

Her lips drew tight, she shook her head and closed her eyes. Outside the wind howled continually. One of the windows rattled. "Mike?" She felt the fear beginning in her chest. "Mike, come on—come out." She turned to stare at the purple curtain. "Goddammit, Mike." She rose, still staring at the curtain. "Mike, please, if you're back there, come out—you're scaring me." She took a step toward the doorway.

With a tremendous swish, the curtain flew open. Michaels stood there, grinning.

"That's not funny!" She sounded ready to cry.

His smile fell away, and he walked toward her. "Hey, I'm sorry." He took her by the arms. She glared at him. "I'm sorry. I thought it might calm things down a bit. It's a good thing I didn't start making strangling noises."

"You asshole—you wouldn't have."

"I was going to do this." He grabbed his throat with both hands and went "aarggh," grimacing horribly and thrusting out his tongue.

She laughed. "That would have been it—you would have completely wiped me out."

"Well, I repented when I heard your plea. Come see what I found." He drew aside the curtain, revealing a small room completely filled by an organ. Different-size pipes covered one wall, below was the double keyboard. "I told you I'd play you some Bach, didn't I?"

"Maybe you should check with Doctor Blut first."

"Oh, I won't hurt it. This looks like a pretty good one. Electric with pipes."

He sat down on the bench, turned on a small light over the keyboard, and flicked a switch. There came a dull hum as pressure built up. He depressed one key, and the organ groaned forth the note. He pulled out various stops, pushed others in, searching for the right tone quality. He hit a few chords, going deep into the bass, then pulled out more stops.

"She sounds pretty good."

He pushed the bench back and eyed the wooden panels underneath. He played a quick scale using only his feet, cowboy boots dancing from pedal to pedal.

"It's easier with regular shoes. Well, here goes nothing. I'll try the Toccata and Fugue in D Minor. Great for horror movies—and for dark stormy nights."

His long fingers raced along the keyboard, and when he hit a long, sustained low note, he obviously enjoyed making the bass thunder. She could tell he was nervous, but he loosened up quickly. He played expressively and rather well. She watched his face. The long blond hair fell from his bent head, swishing slightly as he turned. Grin gone, his eyebrows crunched together in concentration, he paused at the end of the toccata, then launched aggressively into the fugue. The opening line required one hand, but the other voices soon had both hands and feet working hard.

Angela watched, fascinated. He played better the longer he played. Absorbed in the music, they forgot the cold dim house and Dr. Blut.

Bach's music, its intricate beauty, held them both.

The curtain opened with a loud swish, and Blut's bloodless face appeared, pale eyes glowing like two blue fuses. His lips rose into a polite but empty smile.

Michaels faltered, stopped. The music groaned and slowly expired.

"Hey, you're good," Angela said. "That was wonderful."

Mike grinned. The grin faded as he looked at Blut. "I should have asked your permission."

"That's perfectly all right."

"Do you play, Doctor?" Angela asked.

"Yes."

"Do you like Bach?"

"I must confess to a certain aversion for Bach."

"How could anyone not like Bach?" She sounded shocked.

"There is a certain spiritual aura about his music which I do not like."

"Which you *don't* like?"

"Yes. Especially his religious music. It has a somewhat facile quality. All those countless cantatas."

"How can you say that?" If she had mildly disliked him before, this clinched it.

Mike grinned at her righteous indignation. Her lower jaw thrust forward, emphasizing the curve of her lower lip, and her blue eyes were angry. He couldn't blame her.

"Who *do* you like, then?"

"I'm afraid my favorite composers are not very well known. There are certain erratic German and Italian schools which I enjoy. Perhaps you are familiar with the music of Teufelsmann? No? A pity. Perhaps I could play one of his fantasies."

Mike stood and turned to see a monstrous black head appear in the doorway. Pointed muzzle, sharp white teeth glimmering alongside the wet pink tongue, the small dark ears flattened against the giant head. The dog radiated menace like light, a halo of evil, and at the sight of Mike his eyes became amber flakes.

"Jesus." Mike reacted automatically, pushing Angela behind him. He and the dog eyed each other. Mike knew who would lose. The dog growled.

"Manfred—sit." Blut pointed a finger at the dog, his voice threatening. "*Sit.* Not now. *Sit.*" Angela noticed the long, yellowish nail of Blut's index finger.

Manfred sat.

Michaels straightened up slowly, not really convinced the dog would not fall upon him and rip him to pieces. "Jesus Christ."

"Manfred can be rather intimidating."

"Yeah, I'd say so."

"Manfred?" A woman's voice. The dog padded silently into the other room.

"This is my daughter, Ursula," Blut said.

Ursula appeared in the doorway, Manfred at her side. Michaels swallowed. Probably another albino, but how different, how attractive. A robe the color of blood dropped to her ankles, rose to her chin, covering her throat. Long curly, white-blond hair fell on either side of her face to her breasts, forming white ringlets that contrasted dramatically with the dark red robe, as did her white hands and feet. She had a turned-up nose, eyebrows so light they had to be searched for, and skin as colorless as Blut's. A few freckles spotted her cheeks and nose. Despite her bleached appearance, she was strikingly beautiful. A little weird though, Mike decided, especially her looking like she had no eyebrows. Her pale blue eyes fell on Michaels. She smiled.

"These are our guests, Ursula. Mister Michaels and his friend, Miss Rosalba."

"I think I spoke to you earlier," Ursula said, still watching Mike. "When you called from Udolph."

"Oh. Yeah."

"Manfred is Ursula's . . . pet."

"What breed is he?" Angela asked. "I know a lot about dogs, but I can't place him. He looks vaguely like a Doberman, but his features aren't quite right."

The two women stared at each other. The top of Ursula's head came to Angela's chin, and her white skin, pale eyes, and blond-white hair were antithetical to the brown skin, dark blue eyes, and raven hair. A tension crackled between the two women, matter and antimatter, ready to annihilate each other.

"Manfred is only a mongrel. He has a little of everything in him. Even some wolf, perhaps." She looked at Michaels again, her eyes listless.

"I thought you were asleep, my dear."

"I didn't mean to wake you up." Mike said.

"Oh, no, I was already awake." She ran her tongue across her lower lip. "I couldn't sleep. I heard someone playing and thought I would come down."

Blut raised the corners of his mouth, wan blue eyes staring playfully into wan blue eyes.

"Ursula and I are both troubled by insomnia."

Angela yawned. "I'm not.'"

"Ah, yes, you must be exhausted. It's after one. We must talk business for a moment, Mister Michaels, and then I will show you to your rooms."

"Weren't you going to play something, Doctor?" Angela asked.

"Ah, but no, you must be tired."

"Play us a few measures. I'm curious to hear whatever his name was."

"Herr Teufelsmann. Very well. I will play enough to give you the flavor of his music."

Blut sat down, extended forearms and fingers. He sat quietly for a moment, staring at the keyboard. His hatchet nose and big eyes made him a huge bird of prey, waiting. He pounced— his talons went for the keyboard and hit a rapid series of dissonant chords that filled the room with chaotic reverberations. Then his right hand began a cloying melody, while the left continued to add dissonant chords, and his feet brought in brief mad parodies of melody. It was a cynical mockery of conventional baroque, oddly form- less.

Michaels was fascinated yet repelled. He glanced at Angela. Her mouth was grim, her eyes worried. She took his hand and squeezed tightly. Ursula watched them, her face languid, mouth set in a frozen smile.

Blut's thin fingers scuttled along the keyboard like two albino tarantulas, all their legs working as they pursued their victims. His eyes glowed, seemed to swell with the music as it roared to its diabolical conclusion, a tangle of notes like a sinister web. The white fingers fell upon eight notes in the bass, a final dissonant chord. The chord was a long time dying. Even after the actual sound was gone the chord lingered in the mind, in the air. Blut flicked off the switch and smiled at Angela.

"What do you think of Herr Teufelsmann?"

"Weird stuff. Interesting, though," Mike said.

"And you, Miss Rosalba?"

She considered telling him his music was ugly, hideous, but she only said, "I'll stick with Bach." She was pale.

Blut laughed. "Each to his own taste. Come, then, it's late. I will show you to your rooms."

They followed him. Mike stayed as far as possible from the dog. Blut stopped before the oaken table, stood between the coffin and the lamp, and where his shadow fell the highlights on the black metal were annihilated. "One thing I must ask of you, Mister Michaels. You are to take the coffin in the morning. I will not be here, but I have made arrangements for some people from Udolph to assist you."

"Good. It looks heavy as hell."

"So it is. Truly. You are to deliver it. I must see some patients a great distance from here, which will require that I depart very early."

"When do you sleep?" Angela asked.

"I nap during the day." He smiled. "Remind your uncle to deliver my brother to the address I gave him in Chicago."

"Doesn't he need to be embalmed?" Michaels reached for the handle of the coffin. Blut's hand blurred and struck, grasping Mike's wrist instantly. The grip was incredibly strong, the fingers icy.

"That will not be necessary. He has already

been embalmed." He half-smiled at Michaels, the washed-out blue eyes amused. Mike felt the same uneasiness as earlier when Blut had insisted on going after Renwick. "Besides, the coffin is securely locked—as you may verify for yourself. We have mourned my dear brother long enough."

He let go. Michaels hesitated, then took the handles and pulled, but the coffin halves seemed fused together. "Okay, we'll take care of it. And I'll probably be the one driving to Chicago. By the way, that's some coffin."

"Only the best for my brother. We were very close."

"Did you have other brothers or sisters?" Angela asked.

"No." His eyes fell upon her. "Ours is a dying family. An ancient line which has known better times. We came here from across the waters when the country was young, when there were thirteen states and this land was all wilderness. When Iowa was covered with forests instead of farms, great dark woods. Even then the name of Blut was always . . . well known. And this farm has been ours for over a hundred years, though some fools have attempted to take it from us. Yes, an old but dying family."

"What about your daughter?"

Blut almost laughed. "Ah, yes, my daughter, my dear daughter. I had forgotten her." He smiled at Ursula, and the look that passed between them soured the air. "Enough of this. Now to your rooms. Goodnight, dear." He nodded at Ursula.

She had sat in a plush chair by the fireplace. Manfred crouched beside her, his eyes amber slits. The dying embers cast a fiery glow, bathing the black dog and the woman in red-orange light.

"Goodnight. Nice meeting you." She stared at Mike.

"Goodnight," he said. Angela nodded.

They followed Blut upstairs. The old stairway creaked, its ancient wood moaning under their feet. Outside they heard the dull cry of the wind. At the top they found themselves in the middle of a long hallway. Another flight of stairs led to the third floor.

"Your room is here, Mister Michaels." He opened the door across from the stairs and turned on the light. A small, dusty-looking room with a bed, gray rug, and a chest of drawers. "I hope this will do. This room has not been slept in for some time. It is difficult to keep up a large house like this."

"It's a big enough house," Michaels said. "How many rooms are there?"

"There are eight bedrooms on this floor. It is a grand old house. I myself have the three rooms on the top floor. Ursula, however, sleeps up here. Your room, Miss Rosalba, is the last one down the hall on the right. The bathroom is here." He struck the door next to Michael's room. "And now I must bid you goodnight. Sleep as late as you wish in the morning, but do not forget my coffin. Sleep well. I wish you pleasant dreams."

"Thanks," Mike said. Angela nodded, drawing closer to him and taking his hand. She ignored Blut's stare.

Blut smiled. His pale blue eyes gave off a strange luminescence. He turned and almost flowed up the stairs. From the back he was a white oval on a tapered black form, and his shoes made small clicking noises on the creaking stairs. Mike thought again of a bird of prey, a huge, dark hawk.

"Let's find your room," Mike said. She nodded, yawning, still holding onto him. He took a step and stopped. "Oh shit—I left my gym bag with all my crap in it in the hearse. I suppose I'd better get it. You want your pack?"

"Uh, I don't know. Maybe—oh, I suppose so." She squeezed his hand, then let go. "But hurry back."

He turned and sped down the stairs. Bracing himself, he jammed on his hat, opened the front door, and rushed out before he could worry about how cold it would be. Oh Christ—bad as he remembered. The icy air grabbed for him, but he ran to the car, his boots plunging deep into the snow. Overhead were the black sky with its white points and the giant eye of the moon scattering light on the surrounding fields. He got out the ancient canvas bag and the pack, then kicked the door shut.

Clang. The pigs were still at it. The big lean one stared at him. Fucking pigs. And dogs—especially big black ones. The house towered above him, reached out to enfold him, glad at his return. Blinded skull of many sockets. But one window was lit, his room on the second floor. The third story was utterly dark. He reached the front door and stepped back inside.

Ursula still sat by the fireplace, red woman and black dog. Why didn't she build up the fire, for God's sake? She smiled at him. She was beautiful. Her eyes had the same luminescence as Blut's, strange and blue. A barely discernible rumbling came from the dog's throat. Michaels smiled nervously and started up the stairs. He should find a tasty blond like her alluring. Instead she made him nervous.

"Angela?"

The room was empty. Cold and dusty. Fear tore a big bite from his heart, and he quickly walked down the dim hallway. A gruesome green wallpaper lined the hall, dark tendrils and olive vines all around him, a regular jungle. The last door stood open, light flooding into the hall. Angela lay on the bed with her eyes closed. Mike was incredibly relieved.

"Angela?"

She opened her eyes, smiled, and sat up. He put down the pack and his bag.

"Mike, this must be the coldest room in the house. God, it's freezing in here."

"Not like outside. Twenty-five below, I'd guess. It *is* cold in here, though. No drapes on the windows. The glass must be—ah, here's why." He pointed at one of the two windows. He put his hand by a crack across the bottom corner, felt the cold night breathe onto his skin and move the hairs. "God."

The room was small, twelve feet square, and bare, only the bed and a chair. Cracks groped their way up the yellow-gray walls, and hardwood strips covered the floor, almost worn through in spots. Overhead glared a bare light bulb. The room was situated at the corner of the house with two big windows on adjacent walls. The windows creaked and rattled as the wind hit them. Michaels sat down on the bed. An ancient four-poster with a spongy mattress, it too creaked, its ancient springs protesting.

"Gee, this is nice," he said.

"Sure. I suppose it's better than the back of a hearse."

They sat together on the bed and listened to the wind scream. A large gust hit the window, making it rattle, and even on the bed they felt the cold air leak in. Heads bent, they looked nowhere in particular and not at each other. Michaels saw her hand resting beside his leg, noticed how long and smooth her fingers were, the nails cut short. The longing he had felt at odd moments all night was returning. The wind crashed into the window, spewing in cold air. He shivered. Alongside the desire was the fear. Something touched his hand. Her fingers slid between his, and their fingers tightened about each other. He turned to look at her. She was slightly flushed, the half-open blue eyes both desirous and sleepy. He chewed at his lip.

Worry gnawed like an evil worm, lurked in the lines under his eyes. She sensed it. Without his grin he could look so serious. His lower face seemed very long. Bright gold dust was scattered along his jaw and chin, the light hitting his three-day beard.

He fell backward, drawing her to him, and they clung to each other. His fingers dug into her shoulder blades, her hair and ear pressed against his cheek, her face against the bed. The embrace lasted a long time.

She raised herself onto her elbows and looked down at him. He smoothed a strand of black hair out of her face. He put both hands alongside her face, stroked her cheeks, feeling how the skin was smooth and cool. She murmured "ohh" and went for his mouth. He played with her lower lip, then his tongue touched her lips. She thrust her tongue into his mouth, and their hands gripped, their bodies crushed hard together. She breathed awkwardly, a slight gasp as she forced her tongue deeper in. The kiss went on and on. Finally her head sagged onto his shoulder, and he felt her long body relax along him.

She rose again onto her elbows. She had the softened, yet intense look women got. "Oh Mike, I don't want to wait any longer."

He pulled her back down, and they kissed again.

CHAPTER FOUR

> *Lay your sleeping head, my love,*
> *Human on my faithless arm;*
> *Time and fevers burn away*
> *Individual beauty from*
> *Thoughtful children, and the grave*
> *Proves the child ephemeral:*
> *But in my arms till break of day*
> *Let the living creature lie,*
> *Mortal, guilty, but to me*
> *The entirely beautiful.*
>   —W. H. Auden, "Lullaby"

OUTSIDE, THE WIND ran around the old farm, baying at the moon. The cold orb bathed the snow with yellow-white light, making the night uncannily bright, the deformed twin of day. As if gleeful but wicked elves had scattered billions of tiny sparkles on the snow. The temperature had fallen to twenty-seven degrees below zero and the wind blew from five to twenty miles an hour, tracing dunes and swirls in the snowy fields. For miles around Blut Farm nothing truly alive moved, only white wasteland and the howl of the wind. Such a night might trouble the dreamless sleep of the trees, bringing horrible nightmares or desperate inconceivable actions—the stir of frozen branches and the flutter of pine boughs, snow and needles shaken off, then massive uprootings as the trunks tore themselves from the icy earth.

Clang.

The pigs were not asleep. Black shapes with curling tails massed about the metal hut, snouts burrowing into their strange repast, they fed. They consumed big mouthfuls, snorting. They did not eat corn or grain.

The only light for miles came from the second floor of the house. Inside, Michaels and Angela finished another kiss. He fumbled for his field jacket zipper. "Goddamn coats."

She laughed, then bent over to unlace the heavy hiking boots. He put his hand on her shoulder and ran it down her back, feeling the form under the dark red turtleneck. One long, smooth continuity, no bra. Mike pulled off a battered cowboy boot, one hand on the toe, one at the heel.

She watched. He had a hole in the toe of his sock. The other boot stuck. He cursed, then grinned nervously. His grin put crinkles on either side of his blue eyes. He wore a bright plaid shirt, orange, red, blue, and green. She brushed her fingers along the soft flannel, slipped her hand inside the shirt, touching his stomach. He shivered and drew in his breath.

She smiled. "Are you ticklish?"

"Not right now."

Still under the shirt, she shifted her hand around so she held his side. He pulled her toward him, and they kissed, going down onto the bed sideways. Her leg came up along his hip and thigh. He ran his hand down her back and slid it beneath her shirt, felt the smooth sloping on either side of the spine. She mumbled something, managed a jerky breath through her nose, and kissed harder.

He put his other hand under the turtleneck, then rolled over so he lay with her on top, his fingers feeling the skin over her shoulder blades. Her breasts were flattened onto him, and with his arms and torso he felt her chest move with her breathing. She went "ohh," and they kissed again. His hand went under her jeans and panties, following the rising curve of her buttocks. She shoved her belly against him, and they kissed more urgently. Awkwardly he brought his other hand around and grasped her breast, touching the nipple. She gasped, then raised herself onto her elbows and stared at him.

"Michael, you carry your bag everywhere, right?"

Puzzled, he breathed deeply. "Yeah." Her eyes avoided his. "Why?"

She hesitated. "Do you have condoms in there? Just in case?"

In spite of himself he felt the blood rush to his face. "Yeah." She could certainly see right through him. One dozen lubricated condoms with special receptacle ends neatly wrapped in foil lay securely at the bottom of the bag. Where they had been for six months. Just in case.

She squeezed him hard, then laughed. Her face was also flushed. "Good. I'm not on the pill, and I don't like living that dangerously."

"Now, how exactly did you know I would have some?"

"Oh . . . I just did. I'm awfully glad you do. Are you embarrassed?"

"No. Oh shit, yes I am, slightly."

"Me, too. Now there's nothing to stop us."

"No." An uneasy feeling tempered his elation, the same vague fearfulness that had pursued him all evening.

She lowered her head, and they began another kiss. Her hands held him under his shirt, her tongue and lips working wildly. Michaels found her eagerness amazing and slightly intimidating. Sex for him often became very cerebral, a continual monitoring to make sure he and his partner were doing okay. But Angela seemed to act intuitively, her entire body responding.

He kissed her by the earlobe, noticing the gold post through the lobe, and moved his lips along her neck. Beneath his shirt her hands stroked and squeezed at his sides. Awkwardly he managed to pull the red turtleneck up above her breast, took the nipple between his lips. She was still on top, and he held her along the rib cage. Her breast was small, the aureola a dusky pink, her skin a smooth light brown. She half rose, breasts still hanging over his face, and fumbled at his shirt buttons.

Suddenly she sat up and grabbed her turtleneck with both hands to pull it off. Michaels undid buttons. The turtleneck got stuck; she sat naked from the waist up with her head and hands caught. Grinning, he helped her pull it off.

She tossed her head, smiling, took out the crucial pin, and down came her hair—black waves cascading about her shoulders and covering her breasts, thick and curly, lustrous, gleaming in the overhead light. The wind snarled, buffeted the house, pawed at the window growling to get in. The cold air rushed through the crack, washing over the bed like spray from a dark icy wave. She used both hands to push her hair back behind her shoulders. "God, it's cold in here." His hand played about her back, and he could see goose pimples.

"Yeah."

He lay back on the bed, reached around from behind, and took her breasts in his hands. She inhaled sharply, lay back against him, and his mouth nuzzled at her shoulder. She put her hand between his legs, ran the fingers up along his thigh. He stroked her nipples with his fingertips. She twisted sideways, hunting frantically for his mouth, and they kissed. He slid his hand down across her belly, along the navel and surrounding flesh, then slipped his fingers under her pants. Her body tensed. His fingertips touched hair, then searched farther. She moaned and let her head fall back. "Oh God," she said and popped open the snap on her pants. The walls wailed, creaked, as the frozen wind hit like a battering ram.

While he kissed her back, her own hand slipped under his jeans and cupped the sensitive skin around his balls. Mouth opened wide, he jammed his lips and teeth against her shoulder.

Few woman had touched him there, and they had lacked her gentle confidence.

"Oh, Mike," she said, withdrawing her hand and turning over. They kissed, bare chests crushed together.

Finally she paused to catch her breath, laying with her head on his chest. Her fingertips played with the wrinkled lump of his nipple. A few golden hairs surrounded it, and his skin was pale with the pink tinge often found in extremely blond people. Somewhat soft about the waist, but his shoulders and back were hard, his upper arms solid. He was gentle and liked being tender. She didn't like the other kind—eager, but cold and rough. She heard the wind wail dully, the creakings of the house providing accompaniment. The wind reminded her of when she was a child. Afraid to go to bed, afraid of lying alone in the night, listening, while the mournful sound like the dirge of a black sea beat its way into her head. Her back was chilly except where his hands touched.

She snapped open the catch on his pants. He squirmed and reached for his zipper. She rolled off him. He stood to remove his jeans. She kissed his back, touched his bare hip with her hand, then lay back to shove down her own jeans. Off they came along with the heavy wool socks, leaving only her long underwear.

"God, it's cold," she said. He could see goose bumps again.

"You could always leave your long undies on."

She smiled. "No thanks."

He pulled aside the patchwork quilt and blankets. The hardwood floor was like ice to his bare feet. The sheets had a yellowish brown color and smelled musty. The bedsprings squeaked in mournful protest, mumbling threats of revenge. Its ancient frame had not been so violated in years.

Angela slid out of her long underwear, shivering, and quickly got her feet between the sheets. Michaels stood naked with the light bulb reflecting off his blond hair. Gold hair fell from his chest in a line and covered his thighs and forearms, but the hair curling around his phallus had a reddish tint.

She pressed her face against his belly, holding him by the buttocks, and hugged. Her mouth half-open, her lips slowly brushed across his skin making light kissing movements. Mike's breath drained out in a long sigh, and he ran his fingers through her thick hair. She drew back, caressed his penis, running her fingers up along the shaft, then touched the tip gently with her warm lips.

"Oh Christ." He knelt on the bed as she lay back, then kissed her on the navel, slid his face down to the tangle of black hair, kissed her inner thigh and between her legs. Her hands clutched at his sides. Finally he lay down beside her and she drew the covers over them.

All night they had struggled to embrace. They had struggled through layers of clothing at odd moments in the midst of cold and storm. Night, tempest, and the dark forces had done their best to keep them apart. Now they came together— pulled and clung, felt the naked warmth radiate all about them, arms, hands, and legs stroking, pressing as they tried to draw together—to melt into fiery unity. Outside the wind went mad, ran in circles around the farm, howling with rage. It paused a second, then smashed out at the house.

The tremendous slap sent a shudder through the ancient walls, a tremor felt deep in the foundations.

Angela heard nothing. She wanted everything between them to disappear. He ran one hand along her side, thrust the other between her thighs. She grabbed his head with both hands, drew him to her, kissing savagely. She brought one hand between his legs and again held him there.

Michaels closed his eyes, groaning. He hadn't had real sex in months, and now this. "Oh, Christ—enough with the preliminary stuff."

"Yes," she said.

He turned over, fumbled for the bag on the floor. He sat up, wrenched out the blue box, managed to tear off one foil-wrapped condom, then let the bag and the box fall. Throwing the foil aside, he unrolled the condom onto his hard flesh. He always felt slightly idiotic at this point. Her lips made soothing motions on his back.

He turned and looked at her. She lay on her back breathing deeply. Her face—dark blue eyes, Aphrodite's long straight nose and Cupid's lips— lay immersed in the waves of black hair. She was obviously flushed, even over the ski tan, the rosy hue most apparent at her throat below the collarbones. He touched her breasts with his face and, supporting himself with his arms, got his knees between her legs. With a long sigh, she spread her legs and used her hand to guide him in. He felt her back arch as she rose to meet him. She went, "Oh God," and clutched at his back, her legs curling about him. She was very strong.

A loud bang like a clap of thunder, and the wind backed off, screaming as if it had been stabbed, its airy essence slashed. The room flickered, then blackness fell upon them like a shroud, a part of night entering the room.

Power failure, Mike thought, or blown fuse. He pressed into her and realized he was afraid. Oh Christ, what was there to be afraid of? *Don't be— not now, with her.* But the fear blossomed inside like some cancerous growth he couldn't control, and being so much at the mercy of himself, his own fear, frightened him even more. He remembered a young girl with a beautiful body cut from cold white stone, her head crushed flat. The walls of Blood Farm creaked slowly, shuddering with satisfaction, and the wind gleefully licked its lips.

He became aware how cold his back was. Shreds of wind crawled through the crack, flittered to the bed where the icy legs scuttled along his naked back. He shivered. The fear grew— doubled, tripled, multiplied till he felt trapped in its sticky threads—everything else lost in this one, all-powerful anxiety. He could no longer see Angela. She was only a shape, a sweating form under him. Do I really want her? he wondered.

However, one fear was very specific—he was losing it. Oh you impotent fool, failing now with the most wonderful girl you've ever known. He tried to thrust rapidly and let the mechanics carry him through, but it was not enough. Although her warm hands clung to his back, the cold, dark, dead air was stronger, stroking him with hundreds of icy fingers. He felt the heat being sucked out, the fire in his loins swallowed by the void.

"Oh . . . *shit.*" He thrust limply and gave up, his head sagging. "God, I'm sorry." He wished he could see her face, her eyes, but the room was a black sea.

"Don't be. It's okay, really." Sensing his fear, she rubbed his back, trying to warm him, then pulled the covers up to his neck.

"Sure."

He was afraid in the night like a kid, but now there was no one to make it all right. Alone, and he'd always be that way. Sex was nothing, a game between adults—a stupid game he couldn't play. Angela could not know what he felt, could not help. He wished he were somewhere far away, alone with his fear and shame. And what if Angela were the talkative type? He didn't really think she was, but all kinds of strange fears sprang to life. Weary of supporting his weight on his elbows, he lay on his side. He was acutely aware of his small limp penis, the condom like a bad joke.

They heard the walls creak, the wind howl. With the sexual warmth gone they were cold under the blankets, even touching each other. The dark room grew more chill, as if night were determined to enter and extend its frozen domain. A huge eruption of wind smashed against the house, rattling windows, shaking walls, and with a splitting sound, another crack appeared in the window, growing from the other. Angela shivered and drew closer to Mike. A frigid breeze played across their faces. Overhead the ceiling squeaked, and a series of thuds crossed the room.

"Blut," Michaels murmured. "Doesn't he ever sleep?"

"God, Mike, it's so cold."

"Yeah. This goddamn house. I wish I'd never come here."

"What's wrong?"

"I don't know. It doesn't happen often—really, I don't make a habit of it."

"Oh God, I don't care about that. Did I do anything that .. ?"

"Christ, *no*." He hugged her, aware of her breasts pressing against him. He slid his leg between her legs, felt the smooth inner thighs and the stubbly feel of shaven calves. "You've been great—I really ... I got afraid, that's all. Really afraid."

"I know. I felt it, and I was afraid."

"I didn't want to scare you too."

"I don't think it was your fault. I've felt vaguely afraid all evening."

"Me, too. It's been weird."

"Yes," she said.

"I'm still glad I picked you up, but I sure wouldn't blame you for wishing you'd never seen me or that old black beast."

"Well, you are rather awful, and it has been a strange night, but I'm glad you did pick me up." She squeezed him tightly. "What were you afraid of?"

"All kinds of things." He paused. "It wasn't your fault, but I feel that way sometimes when ... Too many cheap scuzzy times. Then when you want it to be good, when you care about the other person ... There I was on top of you all turned on, and suddenly it's like I'm nothing—I can't really feel anything or really know anyone else. Sex is supposed to bring people closer than anything, and it becomes a big nothing. It makes me realize how alone I really am. How we're all dumb little specks who are going to die, and I feel trapped like I can't ever get outside myself."

"Mike, I've felt that way—I even started feeling it tonight—but it's not true! It's a temptation to believe that—something bad tempts us to believe that about ourselves. I don't know if the temptation comes from inside us or outside, but I do know it's a lie. And I do care about you. I know it's been fast and crazy, but I want to know you better when we get to Iowa City, when we'll have time. I like you so much."

"Oh, Angela." He hugged her, held her as tightly as possible.

They did not speak, but at Blut Farm a human presence in itself was reassuring. The wind snarled angrily. When their embrace finally slackened he was hard again. Relieved with him, she put her hand between his legs, wanting to help. He let out a long sigh.

She fumbled for his lips, and once more they were kissing. Michaels had a kind of achy desire, so strong it almost hurt. He rearranged the condom. Her mouth moved faster, their tongues churning about, fingers digging at backs. She brought her leg up along his side and again used her hands to guide him. He went in slowly, then pushed in as far as he could. She groaned, and he felt her contract around him. He rocked slightly—God, now he could go off any second. She found his lips and kissed fiercely. Hardly able to breathe, they clung to each other and began rocking in a wild rhythm. Their warmth had caught fire, consuming flames singed the night, and sensation washed over them with each thrust.

The wind screamed with fury. The old trees around the farm bent under the force, and clouds of snow flew from the dark pines. The pigs stopped feeding, gave a long shrill squeal in chorus. A small whirlwind coalesced out of night, corkscrewed insanely about the house, billowing snow like smoke. Blood Farm shuddered, the moan of the damned, its ancient timbers throbbing like an immense organism. Night was a poor loser.

Michaels rolled her over. "Oh God—God," she mumbled. They resumed the rhythm, panting in unison. The covers had been swirled aside, but the lovers were invulnerable to the cold. He felt her entire body contract, fingers digging in, legs curling around him, as she clamped down so hard it almost hurt him, and a long, low murmur flowed out from deep within her.

An explosive crackling like a tree riven by lightning, and the wind burst triumphantly into the room waving its limbs of icy air and snow. But the gloating triumph was premature. Michaels clutched, a spasm of release overwhelming him, and he pushed deep, deep into her. Their mouths opened wide, lips, teeth, tongues moving frantically. They felt the climax in their mouths—tasted it. They were warm now. They threw out heat like suns, colliding stars burning jointly, melting together and flaring to a nova— a fusion that radiated energy and could create life as the fires in the sun do. The cold and darkness receded, and night cowered in terror.

Then it was over. He lay above her breathing hard. He opened his eyes, kissed at her neck, wishing the light were on so he could see her face. He felt her breath coming and going. She mumbled his name, and they hugged.

Gradually he began to think pragmatically. Better withdraw before the erection went down and the condom leaked. And he was getting damn cold indeed. The blankets were almost off the bed, wind and snow flurrying about the room. Wind and snow? He used his right hand to withdraw, fingers securely holding the condom. She thought he might be tired of resting on his elbows, but he didn't want to move from her. Raising his head, he glanced at the window. A dim moonlit square, hazy snowflakes drifting, dancing in at the bottom. The corner, roughly a six-inch triangle, was completely gone. The groaning wind sounded louder, ominously so, and light snow sprinkled his back. He shivered.

"No wonder," he said.

"Huh?"

"Did you hear a noise like something breaking?"

"Uh . . . maybe."

"We lost part of the window."

Her head fell sideways, she saw the moonlit square minus a corner. "God, Mike, you must be freezing." Awkwardly, with him still on top, she reached for the covers, pulled them up to his neck and massaged his back.

"Not really, but I was getting there. I heard it crack out right after that big gust of wind."

"I don't think I was listening very well."

"No, you weren't."

They kissed slowly and gently. Michaels sighed, resting his head on her shoulder. She stroked him with both hands, beginning at the neck under his long hair and going all the way down along his spine. The wind had quieted, but seemed closer with the window broken, the breathing of some creature lurking just out of sight. They lay silently for a long time. Michaels almost dozed off, but couldn't sleep in that position, weight supported on his arms. He squirmed slightly.

"Are your arms getting tired?" She sounded asleep.

"Uh, yes." She moved sideways as he lifted his knees over her leg and collapsed onto his side. "Ahhuhh . . . Now I will go to sleep."

"Not me. It's too cold." Even under the blankets, holding each other, they felt night seep in.

"Yeah, I'm afraid you're right."

The light bulb went on, throwing a harsh glare across the room, blinding them both. He clamped his eyes shut, blinked. The bare room and cracked walls looked even dingier than he remembered, but her face surrounded by black hair, was beautiful and sleepy.

"What great timing," he said. "When I wouldn't have minded some light it goes out, and now when I'm sleepy . . ."

"It goes with the rest of the night."

"Yeah, definitely. Well, one of us is going to have to leave this warm secure bed, this super-nice womb surrogate, and run over to turn off the light switch. And they can also stuff something in the window to keep out the un-godly night air. Okay, men, who's going to volunteer?"

"You're the only man around, so you'll have to go."

"I was afraid you'd say that. Filthy sexist pig. Where's the light switch?"

"By the door."

He raised his head to look. "Jesus Christ! How *ugly*. That wallpaper—is it horrible!" He hadn't seen the wall around the door when entering the room, but it was covered with faded shredded wallpaper, a hideously pink floral pattern with huge, overly precious roses amidst leaves too green to seem real.

"All the more reason to turn off the light."

"Okay, okay." He sat up, grabbed his bag, and fumbled around for a dirty old T-shirt. "Here goes nothing."

He pushed aside the covers and stood. Despite his joking, he found the room unbelievably cold, hardly funny. The floor felt like a skating rink, and his body spawned goose bumps. As he headed for the window a gust of iced air spewed from the opening and rushed to meet him.

Angela had sat up, and watched with covers wrapped round her. "Mike, be careful—the glass."

He stopped dead, noticed the shards of glass scattered about. Staying a couple feet from the window, he bent over and used one hand to support himself against the wall. The wind shrieked, spit snowflakes mixed with frozen air through its ragged glass lips at his bare stomach and genitals. He quickly crammed the shirt in the hole, wadding it in tightly. The wind howled angrily but couldn't budge it. "Take that, you fucker." He noticed the crack and hoped the window would hold.

He ran to the light, flicked the switch, ran back to the bed in the dark, pausing just long enough to stub his toe on his bag. Cursing, he got under the covers. Angela felt warm and smooth and sleepy. She held him, rubbing at his back and sides.

"God, are you cold!"

"Listen, it's not exactly warm out there, no

balmy ocean breezes. I practically froze my ass off."

"Well now you won't have to go out in the big bad world anymore."

Michaels said nothing, but realized his bladder would soon necessitate another journey.

"Hey, I think your shirt is going to work. It already feels warmer in here."

"Good use for a far-gone shirt. Jesus, it must be cold out there."

"Poooor Michael."

She brushed aside the long hair, kissed him on the neck, ran her lips up to his mouth. As they kissed he felt her grow more excited, her mouth opening wider and her body clinging, curling about him. When they finally stopped, she squeezed him tightly.

"God, you are definitely a horny woman."

"Uh-huh. Is that bad?"

"Oh no. *No.*"

"You don't do so badly yourself."

"When I think about what I thought earlier, like when I first picked you up. That seems so far off."

"Yes. This has been such a long day. What did you think, anyway?"

"Well . . . when you said you were Catholic, I thought I'd had it. Guaranteed frustration."

She laughed. "Are you frustrated?"

"Christ, no." He hugged her again, then lay on his back, utterly relaxed. She was on her side, her head on his shoulder, his leg between her legs. He could feel the smooth thighs and the pubic hair. "Are you sure you're Catholic?"

"Yes, I'm sure."

"Where did you learn to like sex like that?"

"It's always seemed so natural to me, liking it, as long as the other person . . ." She sighed. "I've always liked it, even the first time. It hurt a little, but I was so much in love I wouldn't have minded if it had been really painful."

"How old were you? Uh, if you don't mind saying."

"Seventeen."

"Sweet seventeen. I hadn't even gone on my first date when I was seventeen."

"So?" She laughed, then kissed his neck. "Me neither."

"Sometimes I wonder. Maybe women have it a lot better than men in spite of everything. And I still don't think you're Catholic. You must be a pagan, maybe a Druid or something."

She laughed. "What do you have against Catholics?"

"You never met the Catholics in Morton, Iowa. Maybe it's your Italian blood."

"Sure. Everyone knows Italians are generally oversexed, unlike you blond Nordic types."

"I think I asked you this before, but didn't you have people telling you how wicked sex is?"

"No one that I believed."

"Your parents were definitely moral degenerates. You mean they didn't give you any good, old-fashioned American guilt feelings?"

"They told me if I had to sleep with someone, to make sure it was someone I cared for. And to take the usual precautions."

"What kind of filthy pragmatic attitude is that?"

"You're terrible, Michael. Now stop it. Just because I like sex. I've never slept with anyone I didn't care about. And I've never been picked up."

He grinned. "Except by me."

She smiled. "But I didn't meet you in a bar, and anyway, I feel like I've known you for a long, long time. I must admit I've never gone to bed with anyone this soon. It's been different with us."

"No one else has run you off the road and helped you find a body in the snow."

"You're hopeless." They went into a long slow kiss that left him wondering if they might do it again. "It *is* nice. Like this, anyway. I'm not really a nymphomaniac or anything. I can still count the men on one hand." He laughed, and she poked him in the ribs. "What's so funny, you? It's true. But I do fall in love rather easily. That's one good thing I got from my parents and being Catholic, a belief in love. I seem to fall in love with everybody I know for very long. Girlfriends, people I work with, teachers . . ."

"How lucky for your teachers."

"There you go—I don't mean *that* way. I just— well, never mind. And I cry at sad movies and become very gushy when I play the piano."

"Yeah, it must be from being Italian."

"Oh sure. It does have disadvantages. My feelings get hurt easily."

He hesitated. "Uh, did you mean what you said earlier about wanting to know me when we're back in Iowa City?"

"Of course not." She sensed his spirits tumbling into an abyss. "I just wanted to lure you on, wild, dark nymphomaniac that I am." She kissed him. "Certainly I meant it. I don't joke about things like that."

"Well, don't scare me that way."

She moved to kiss him but got blond hair in her mouth. "Yech. That doesn't taste so good."

"Look who's talking. I must have swallowed half a pound of black hair earlier, and at least I don't taste like a garlic-soaked Italian—*hey!*" She had poked him in the ribs. He used his fingers to push his hair away. "You didn't seem to mind a few hairs earlier. Now try."

She took his lower lip between her lips, then touched with her tongue while running the bottom of her foot along his leg. He thrust his tongue deep into her mouth. She turned her head, getting a good angle, and kissed furiously. When they finished she was breathing rapidly, and he was ready again. He put his hand on her breast, felt its smooth, round shape. She kissed at his neck and ear.

He liked the second time, no worries about holding back, slower and tenderer. Unfortunately his bladder demanded attention. "I think I'm going to have to run down the hall and visit the john. I'll be more responsive afterwards."

"I don't know if I can take much more responsiveness."

"Dammit, I do not want to get out of this bed. It's cold out there."

"I'll keep it warm for you," she said.

"Okay." She kissed his neck and caressed him again with her leg and the soft curve of her foot. He drew her to him as tightly as he could, and they held each other as if they would never let go, as if this were the last time. Within a vast, frigid sea of darkness, they were a pocket of warmth and life. The wind renewed its assault, rattling windows and creaking walls. Soon its anger would be stilled.

Angela sighed, feeling warm and safe. A muffled thud echoed above them. Something cold and fearful touched her spine. Michaels cursed under his breath, then said, "I don't want to leave you."

"Don't then."

"But nature calls. You wouldn't like me so much if I wet the bed."

She laughed once, snorting slightly. "No. I wouldn't."

He moved, and she let go reluctantly. The wind quieted. He sat up, one hand resting on her shoulder. "I suppose I'd better put something on in case Blut or his daughter or Fang is running around. I hope I don't run into that fucking dog. I can see him taking off my balls with one big bite. *Rowarrffff.*" He put on a terrycloth robe from his bag and sat back down on the bed.

He groped for her face in the dark. She took his forearm with both hands, kissed his wrist, leaving her mouth pressed against him.

"Angela, I . . ."

He bent over to kiss her. Her arms came out from the covers and drew him to her. She kissed, her mouth and tongue moving anxiously, wanting to make the kiss last forever, trying to lose her fear in him. Her fingers dug into his back, and she wished the robe, covers—everything between them—the house, the night, their own fears separating them—were gone. At last he drew away. Something trickled down one cheek and she was glad the darkness hid her foolish tears.

"Oh Mike, I like you so much." She wanted to say she loved him but was afraid to tell him.

He sat, a hand on each of her shoulders, his

fingers tightening slowly. "Oh God," he said, "you're—I . . ." His voice cracked, and she heard him swallow.

"I like you, too," he finally said. He felt terribly sad—which was stupid. He was only going to the john. He tried to grin, but it didn't help. He had never fallen for anyone like this. He took her hand, kissed her palm, then stood up and drew the covers over her shoulders.

"Hurry back," she said.

"Don't worry, Angela. Wild horses, or dogs, couldn't keep me away. Good Christ, this floor is cold!"

She heard the wind make a low raspy noise like the sound from deep in a cat's throat when it's watching a bird. The room filled with yellow light from the hallway, then went black as he closed the door and was gone. A chill like jellied essence of night seeped into the room. Shivering, she drew the covers about her.

Michaels blinked at the light and walked rapidly down the hall. Hard to say which was uglier, the rose wallpaper or this green crap. Like being in a jungle at night, creeping tendrils and vines crawling all around you. The floor squeaked under his feet, and the hallway was nearly as cold as the room. Blut certainly didn't care much about heating the place.

He stepped into the bathroom, fumbled at the condom, and pulled it off. Since he was rigid again the task was not easy. He threw it into the toilet and quickly began to urinate. Tension poured out with the liquid. He'd been holding it a long time. His eyes blinked sleepily. Thinking of Angela gave him a kind of glad, achy feeling.

Finished, he drew the robe about him. Maybe the condom would plug up Blut's septic system. He grinned and flushed the toilet.

He stepped out of the bathroom and noticed the door to his room was open. Something clunked. A weird sensation at the back of his neck. Fuck it—he'd forget he'd heard that.

"Michael." A female voice whispered his name.

He pushed open the door. She sat on the bed in the dark, a woman with white hair in a long robe. Blut's daughter, though it was hard to see. Thank God Fang wasn't with her.

"What do you want?"

"Where have you been?"

Question for question. He turned on the light. She shrank back like some albino cave creature nurtured in darkness. Her red robe screamed at him like a bright red gout of blood on a white sheet.

"Turn it off!"

The anger in her voice surprised him. He flicked off the light. Even in the darkened room he could feel, almost see, her pale blue eyes. They seemed larger in shadow.

"Now come here."

He walked slowly to the bed. Enough light came from the doorway so he could see her smile. "What do you want?" And what am I doing?

She grasped the zipper at her throat and pulled. Breasts appearing in the white V of flesh, two spheres coming to hard points, nearly glowing in the dark.

Oh Christ, this was like some weird crazy

fantasy coming true, but why now of all times? "What do you want?" The question did sound stupid, but he was so tired.

Her long white fingers undid the belt to his robe. God, her nails were long. She watched him, beautiful snowy face upturned, pale blue eyes staring. His robe opened and her hands touched him along the hips. He shuddered, wanting to draw away. Her fingers were icy things crawling on him. He was afraid, wanted to run back to Angela and forget this, but she was staring.

She stroked his penis, playing with him. He felt the stiffening as the blood poured into his groin. She gripped the shaft tightly, her thumb toying with the top. Her hand was cold, so cold, numbing. He didn't want her playing with him. He felt unable to move . . . as if he were falling asleep inside someone . . . someone very cold. Cousin Chuck. Was this what it felt like? He shivered, started to back away, but she held him firmly. Fear came, intense, an icy chill at his neck and back, but fading . . . floating away.

Why not? Never look a gift horse in the mouth. He could fuck her and anyone else, just keep fucking all night long, show the world how incredible he was. Jesus, where was that coming from? The thoughts seemed to have coalesced out of the air. He didn't believe sick shit like that, macho crap. This wasn't him . . . yet was. Stop—*stop*. He didn't want this. Again he tried to back away and realized she had him.

Slowly she raised and lowered her fist. Not only were her fingers cold, but she held him too hard, her grip almost painful. And she looked as if this disgusted her. She did not smile, but her lips had parted slightly. Her hand pulled him closer, and her face touched his belly. Her breath was like the cold of night. Her other hand came up under his robe and held his buttock. He thought of a small animal caught in a trap, frigid metal chewing at his leg. cold and storm all about him.

Her lips crawled along the tender skin of his belly and touched the pubic hair. He shivered again. Her hand slid down his penis, then something cold and wet closed around him, her tongue flickering across the tip. He jerked back automatically, but her hands held his buttocks. Christ, her mouth was cold, too. He felt goose bumps and an overwhelming chill building up his spine. He did not want this. She swallowed more penis, slowly, reluctantly, as if she might gag on him.

She paused, her mouth full. He could not see her eyes, but knew they were angry and eager, pale blue fires burning in the dark. She made a noise low in her throat, and he was again aware how she had him. First her lips, a moist sucker like on a giant leech, then her teeth, two rows of hard, sharp edge above and below him, then the long spongy wet tongue underneath, and his tip touching the back of her mouth. Moist, cold, strong—a trap, waiting for an unsuspecting prey like a fly-consuming plant or a jellyfish or . . . Good Christ, she was really going to—and he could not even get away. He felt the moist snare tighten, her nails digging in and the blood pulsating through his groin. If only—dear God, he belonged somewhere else—back with—back with Angela—*Angela*.

His hand exploded upward, palm hitting her along the jaw and knocking her backwards, as he wrenched away. He heard her teeth slam together, strike with a loud click, closing—thank God—on air. Her fingers raked at his hips, leaving scratches, and he cried out. She screamed, hissing like a snake. He backed away and turned on the light.

What he saw dried up his mouth and increased his fear. Her blue eyes burned with a reddish tinge, lips drawn back like a dog or wolf, teeth bared—huge canines, far larger than any normal human's. The robe was still open, and her breasts hung out as she crouched in a fighting stance, white fingers making claws. She hissed again, a supremely ugly sound.

"Good Christ, what are you?"

"You'll find out." The voice had a guttural quality.

Michaels glanced backward toward the door. He would find Angela and get out of here as fast as he could. He backed up slowly, watching her, whatever she was. She took off the red robe, almost rending it to pieces in her eagerness. A white corona of fire flamed round her head, blond-white hair, and her face radiated a chilling evil. But oh, how her body was white and beautiful, her arms and breasts and legs delicately chiseled marble, smooth and cool and white, so white, so horribly white, absolutely void of color.

He backed into the doorway and touched something. He turned. Jesus smiled at him, his face pale and serene with its long brown hair and full beard, but his blue eyes were deranged. Renwick's fist came at him, caught him dead center in the jaw, and he fell over. Something grabbed him, cruel sharp things digging in, picking him up off the floor. He opened his eyes, then realized tiny little Ursula had lifted him over her head and was about to throw him at the wall ten feet away. An instant of flying through space, body sprawled and twisting, then his head and arms smashed into the wall. He hit the ground and lay still.

Ursula ran for him, teeth bared, bent over, making hungry noises. Renwick watched dully. A swirl of black howled into the room, a hand grasped her hair, wrenched her up, and hurled her backward. Rage made Blut's eyes still paler.

"You silly fool—you slut."

"Don't call *me* a slut—I saw you look at her."

"*Idiot.* I see nothing in her except the promise of blood, and I found it amusing to trifle with her. But *this*—him. You should not have. It was imperative he leave Blut Farm with the coffin. My plans required it. Now all that is ruined."

"Then let me have him."

"No."

"And what of his little friend, the little Italian angel?"

"I will deal with her."

"Sure, you need her. And you called me a slut."

"You *are* a slut—as I remember, you were quite literally a whore when I found you."

"All that was long ago. I only want him for what he has in him."

"You, my dearest, will always be a slut. And she is worse than you. I sensed it in her—the lasciviousness, the love of the flesh. She revels in her sensuality, in 'love.' You are all sluts, all manipulative, hypocritical creatures craving one thing and one thing alone—not content until someone fills you."

Michaels understood he was lying on the floor, dimly heard the voices.

"And you—are you any better? What will you do to her?"

"I value her only for the strength she can give me."

Ugly laughter. "Oh sure, that's all. What you really want is to fuck her." A sound, someone being hit. "Go ahead, deny it then."

"I do deny it. Your mind is as foul as your body. What I will do, I do because I must, but there will be no pleasure in it. You and your sex disgust me. However, I must continue to exist."

"Do you think I' like you—or him—any better?"

"I don't care what or whom you like. But I do know that our ally created woman to bring about man's downfall. That much of the fairy story is true. I wish we were all one-celled beings who could feed at will on others and reproduce by ourselves. Then the strong and the hungry would rule. You are a weak fool, and you cannot even deal with him properly. He is waking up and listening. Renwick!"

Renwick kicked Michaels in the head with a combat boot.

CHAPTER FIVE

◆

O Rose, thou art sick!
The invisible worm
That flies in the night,
In the howling storm.

Has found out thy bed
Of crimson joy,
And his dark secret love
Does thy life destroy.
       —William Blake

WITH MIKE GONE the room continued to chill. The wind crouched on all fours, permeating the walls, readying itself for attack. There was another snapping sound as the crack in the window lengthened.

Angela lay wrapped in musty sheets and ancient blankets, trembling. Something wanted to freeze the life out of her, and she was too tired to resist. Sleepy yet cold, so cold. She remembered standing by the roadside hitchhiking. That was bad enough, but this was worse. She felt exposed to the night, naked. The blankets were nothing, mere air.

Where was he? He should be back by now. If something had happened to him . . . The fear grew, ripening toward a hellish fruition. She should get up . . . do something . . . look for him. But she was too tired, enwebbed in a cold, deadly sleepiness. Her mind floated, bobbing between consciousness and sleep but always aware of cold and fear. They followed her into sleep like two dark beasts, waiting.

She slept, but bad dreams came.

Michaels was impotent. He blamed her. His grin rotted away, rage deforming his face. He no longer looked like himself, long golden hair and mustache falling out. He screamed at her, and she knew he was right, knew she had wronged him. Slut. She was unclean, filthy—like sex itself. She despised him and herself. Beasts wallowing about—honeying and making love over the nasty sty—greased with sweat and her vagina oozing a foul, stinking liquid.

Oh God, how terrible—what had gone wrong? She tried to hold him, but he drew away, leaving her cold and alone. He returned. She pulled him close, but he was frigid—a man chiseled from ice. His embrace made her colder still, and he turned into a huge ice snake, frozen and invisible, hissing glacial air as he coiled about her and squeezed. Everywhere were pink roses. He would crush her. She fell into the crevasse, falling, tumbling into its black depths, and the walls were coming together, crushing. Still holding her, the thing slithered its scorpion's dart between her thighs, and the icy sting went off deep inside her.

Her eyes jerked open. God, she was scared. She remembered where she was, but reality was little better than the dream. The horror of the nightmare would not leave her. The wind howled triumphantly, a snowy puff of night's breath blowing into the room. Michaels's shirt lay on the ground, the hole in the window larger than before.

She shivered, pressing her hands together between her legs, vainly trying to warm them. In spite of the cold, a damp sweat covered her, and her mouth was dry. Something was going to happen. But *what?* If only Mike would come back—or if she could look for him. But she was too cold, too tired.

The moonlight gleaming in from the window hurt her eyes and she closed them, wishing the night, the moon, the room, the fear would go away and leave her in peace. Could she be sick? She felt so chilled. What strange sickness crawled around the house? Mike got her into this mess. But she remembered holding him, feeling him inside her, and being warm, warm all over. For a moment she was warm again, and her breathing grew more regular.

"Angela? Hey, Angela, are you okay?" Light from the hallway poured into the room.

"Mike?"

She jerked awake, staring at the doorway. He stood there in his robe, grinning, blond hair falling onto his shoulders. "Sorry I took so long. The bladder was pretty full, and something hairy came up."

"Oh God, Mike, I've been so scared—the nightmares . . ."

"Yeah? Tell me about it." He stepped toward her, still grinning. Then something happened—he began to blur, waver. Back in focus, his grin twisted slightly. "Hey, what's wrong?" His voice had a strange pitch.

"Mike—Mike?" Angela trembled.

"What's wrong?" He took another step.

"Stop—please *stop.*"

"Why? What's wrong? I want you, Angela." He pulled away the belt.

"Please stop—you're scaring me—don't."

"Don't you want me, Angela? Don't you love me?" The grin blurred into a leer. "I want to hold you."

"*No.*"

The robe dropped off like a shed skin. Underneath he was invisible, the icy worm. His yellow hair fell away, and he toppled to the floor, hissing. He slithered toward the bed, raising himself over her like a giant cobra, snake body swaying. She knew he would go for the throat. The white fangs dripped black venom. She lay amid the roses, a nest of pink and crimson petals, and waited for him to strike.

She opened her eyes. Oh dear Lord, no more dreams like that, please no more—better to stay awake and tremble than dream that way. The dreams were so real. She closed her eyes, then wrenched them open. *No*—no more sleep. But she couldn't really wake up, and the cold grew worse. The snowy breath of the wind hissed in steadily. God, she would freeze to death. She had never been so cold. Her eyes shut—somewhere *it* waited—jerked open. He looked exactly like Mike, but it wasn't him. She would never believe that.

Why not get up? That would keep her awake. But why—when—when the cold—oh God, my head hurts. She threw aside the covers and lay in the depression at the bed's center. Icy air flowed over her, caressing her breasts and throat, her thighs and belly. She sat up, shivering uncontrollably. A chill lurched up her back. Shuddering, she hunched her shoulders.

Get up. The window.

She walked across the cold floor. The window

grew, filling her vision, expanding into the outside. God, how bright. The moon, though lower in the sky, still flooded the snow with light. Snowy clouds rippled across the fields, dancing elfishly to the wind, wavering in strange patterns. A dull clang. The pigs still fed. A dark shape stared at her though she couldn't really see it. Pig—an ugly pig. The thought made her smile, she didn't know why, and the feeling disappeared immediately. The break in the window had grown. She felt the air's touch numbing the skin of her stomach and thighs, hurling powdery snowflakes into the black tangle of hair between her legs.

She stepped back and cried out as a sudden sharp bite stung her foot. Moonlight sparkled on fragments of shattered glass. Holding her ankle with her hand and balancing awkwardly on one leg, she managed to pull free the long sliver of glass lodged in the tender curve of her foot. Blood flowed, black under the moonlight. Moaning softly, she lowered her foot, being careful to avoid other pieces of glass.

She watched a whirlwind swirl snow in a tiny tornado. The whirlwind crossed the barnyard, sending the pigs squealing for shelter, and came through the wooden fence. It paused below her, whirling, growing, raising huge clouds of snow. It thickened, changing to mist, then dropping low onto the ground and spreading out, gray, darker than the snow. A shapeless mass drifted toward the house, disappearing from her view. Though she could not see below her she knew the mist was rising up the side of the house, crawling up the cracked white walls toward the hole in the window.

This was the thing—the fear—that had been pursuing her all night. The horror of it overwhelmed her, pulsing through every part of her body like blood. She shivered and realized she was standing naked before a window freezing to death, thirty-degree-below-zero air blowing onto her. She turned and ran to the bed, ignoring the pain in her foot. She fell onto the mattress, hiding her face in her arms, trembling violently, tears flowing freely. Get under the covers, for God's sake! But she couldn't move—too cold, too tired—and the dreams were coming again. So she lay with her face pressed into the bend of her right arm, her left hand gripping the sheet, the cold air flowing over her back and along the curve of her buttocks. Blood poured from the cut and stained her foot black.

Something gray slithered through the window, obscuring the moonlight. In a horrible parody of birth, the shadowy form's head appeared first, then its shoulders wiggled through, finally the arms were out and spread open slowly. The thing oozed into the room without a sound, even the wind was silent. It whirled slightly, darkening, solidifying into a human shape, the appearance of a man, a tall man in black with a white head and thin white hands.

Angela did not move, but she knew it was in the room.

"Angela."

She heard the hatred hiding behind the soft tones. She would not move. It came closer, a flowing black shape like a dark bird. The bed creaked as the thing leaned over her, one hand on the mattress.

"Angela." The threat sounded clearer.

She felt something cold between her legs—icy fingers roughly forcing themselves inside her. She cried out, groaning, her whole body tensing and her hands clutching at the sheets. The fingers probed deeply, cruelly, inside her. Her head and her back arched, her eyes clamped shut with pain, mouth open in a long, frightened "ohhh." For the first time she felt violated. The fingers inside her were a frigid obscenity.

"Don't you like it, Angela? Don't you like my fingers in there?"

She groaned, opening her eyes halfway. Blurry through tears she saw the moonlit wall, the giant roses. Roses. She closed her eyes. More icy fingers grabbed her shoulder. Roses. They swelled into an expanse of white, red, and pink, a soft and fragrant field of incredible beauty. A black splotch touched the edge, eating inward, devouring rose petals to bloat and swell itself. Almost instantly the canker destroyed the field of color and fragrance, turning it black and dead.

He wrenched his hand free, wiping it on the sheet, disgusted. She gasped and sank into the bed, hoping—futilely—that he was finished with her. He used both hands to turn her harshly. She opened her eyes and saw a white face, its wan blue eyes glowering angrily in the dark. Blut. About him swirled the blackness. He smiled, and the evil of the smile was more than she could bear. She closed her eyes.

Blut kept on smiling, bloodless lips drawn back. His fingernails punctured the skin of her shoulders as he flowed over her, black draping behind him. The black seemed too insubstantial to be a cape, more like the shadowy gray mist he could become. He crouched, a dark bird of prey about to feast.

Angela wished she were dreaming but knew she was not. A chilling weariness had her, a frozen opiate coursing through her veins. She could not move. The nightmare had trapped her.

Blut lowered himself, flopping onto her like a lizard, black tail curling between her legs and off the bed. He felt deadly cold. An icy something moved from her shoulder along her neck to her earlobe. Lips. His mouth half-open, she felt his moist tongue and the pressure of teeth. A cold limp thing touched her thigh. He clung to her, and his embrace was horrible, freezing, the grip of a huge leech.

She moaned, feeling suffocated, dreaming of Mike.

The lips fell on her mouth but she remained dormant. She would not kiss him. She did not want the coldness in her mouth, the touch of love profaned. The lips slid down to her neck, where they rested. She felt his mouth slowly open, his teeth touching the lightly throbbing skin of her throat.

She and Mike wandered through the roses, and there was no sky or grass, only roses and the two of them. The flowers pulsated like living, breathing beings. They came to the most beautiful bush of the garden, a plant of many blossoms, deep red roses glowing with a dark beauty like her own. Michaels would not harm the plant, but he broke a stem and gave her a rose. As she raised it to her face, it expanded to a red splendor. She saw the delicate layers of petals and took in its perfume.

She cried out and almost dropped the rose. Something had stung her throat, cutting into her. Thorns—she must have pressed the stem against her neck, forgetting the thorns. God, it hurt. Moaning she pulled away the rose, but it didn't help. Michaels watched, his eyes hurting with her, but he was unable to do anything. Oh God, it hurt. Somehow she managed to see her throat, vision leaving her body to zoom in from outside. A black worm (or was it a spider?) clung, sucking. It must have hidden in the roses. She knew the rose was sorry and realized the flower was dying. Its fragrance warped, exuding the sickly hint of decay. Red petals fell away, revealing a shriveled black core—the worm had eaten the rose's heart. Michaels disappeared, a snowy tempest howled into the garden, everywhere petals shriveled and lost color. The garden was dying. Including her. The pain in her throat increased, burning, and she felt the black rot seep into her as her life flowed away.

A new terror seized her. The shriveled thing against her thigh stiffened, swelling from the blood pouring into it—her blood. God, how cold—crawling along her—the worm, the icy worm feeding on her, growing.

Blut drew away, bloated, satiated for the moment, and blood ran from the wounds in her throat. His face seemed younger, his lips and hair suffused with color. He had a final task. Grimly he stared at her, night eyes seeing perfectly in the dark. Under her tan she was deadly pale. Her cupid lips had lost their warmth, and she breathed slowly, hoarsely, hurting deep inside.

He hovered over her, the darkness about him

like great black wings, then swooped and took her in his arms. Her heart throbbed under his icy chest; his own strange heart had not beat for centuries. Roughly he forced her legs apart. Her fingers could not push away the shadowy power from her loosening thighs.

Angela moaned. Dimly she knew what would happen. Something cold and horrible like a thick jagged icicle stabbed into her, tearing her. She screamed in agony. He was cold and formless, terrible to touch. Hands clawing at the sheet, she writhed and arched her back, trying to escape, to pull away, but he held her too tightly. She felt so weak.

She half opened her eyes, groaning, and saw Blut's face. He scowled angrily, his eyes terrible, pale blue flames of hate. "Please—oh God, you're hurting me." The hatred grew, the fire burning with a blue glare.

"Don't you like it, Angela? Don't you love me?"

"*No*—please . . ."

Blut clenched his teeth—black smeared their whiteness, black blood bubbled from his lips— and he thrust deep into her.

She was terrified, her vagina dry and sensitive, the icicle rasping. Like scraping jagged granite across skin. She screamed again. Blut rocked, forcing himself into her. The tears covered her face and she cried, hurting, wanting the icy violation out of her. She had to be bleeding— devil's rape.

Blut growled low and rocked faster. Her hands tore at the covers, legs kicking. She couldn't stand any more. And dear God—what would happen when?—Blut plunged his fangs into her throat, and his talons dug into her back. Angela's body went rigid, her mouth stretching in a soundless scream. The wind screeched with glee, playfully smashed the window and reached in, filling the room with cold air and snow. Blut scowled, a shudder in his groin engendering some nameless horror, and the icy worm spewed its frozen poison into her.

There was a new pain, a terrible cramping low in the belly, burning cold inside her. Distantly she heard gurgling sucking sounds. The dead thing remained inside her, but the stinging in her throat ceased. She felt something wet trickle down her neck. Blut went slack, a bloated corpse. Another spasm of cramping made her cry out. She sensed his ugly presence probing her mind, an evil intrusion.

What's the matter, Angela, wasn't I good?

Did she really hear him speak? It didn't matter.

You didn't like it? Wasn't I good?

The wind howled happily, and loud clangs came from the pig feeder. Night and night sounds had entered the room.

Wasn't I, Angela? Don't sleep—answer me.

God, *no.*

You didn't like it? But I thought you always liked it.

No.

You always liked it before, didn't you?

Yes. She began to dream of Michaels, but the black thing blotted him out.

Stop that and hear me. So you didn't like it. It was ugly, yes? It was filthy and degrading and obscene, something worthy of the gutter. I raped you, Angela. And it hurts, does it not?

Oh God. More cramping. How could it be so cold and burn too? He wiggled his hips, reminding her of the thing inside her.

Yes, it hurts. Now do you understand? Do you understand that it's nasty and wrong—that you've always been nothing more than a cheap little tramp.

Some terrible doubt from deep within her grew. The worm thing inside fed the doubt, nourishing it, and she was too tired to resist. Too cold. She was ready to die.

Blut pursued her eagerly. *Answer.* Do you understand? Do you understand that it is bestial and unclean and evil?

With you—oh God, yes.

With *anyone.* The act itself. It is intrinsically empty. Nothing. You have always used men to satisfy your own lust—you never truly cared for anyone—you only thought you did.

Leave me.

It's true—admit it. Admit it so I can finish you off, so I can drink all your blood and end your cheap, miserable existence. Then you will become like me. You will understand as we all do what an insignificant worm man is, how ridiculously petty his lust, how laughable his love. You will become part of the universal void like us, a fragment of its cold nothingness, and you will help to drain the insignificant warmth from the living, from lecherous fools like Michaels. My master is far stronger than yours. Choose the stronger side. You have no chance—Nothing matters. If you refuse you will still join us, only it will take longer and be far more painful. Answer *now.* Admit you are dirt, a fornicator who has never loved—admit the act is sinful, bestial, inhuman—admit you have damned yourself. *Answer.* Confess your sins and be damned like the rest of us.

She heard the quiet sound of the wind murmuring its approval. Over her hung the awesome weight of death, the cold of hell filling the room. How could she fight them? Oh dear God, help me! She was so cold and tired. All she could remember was the awful violation. And what if Blut were right? Then she remembered Mike and grabbed for the image wandering through her head. It was just tonight. She saw him. Buffalo Bill, yellow-haired and grinning.

Stop.

Ignore the blackness. Now she remembered. Ah God, how warm he was when they held each other—not like—how warm even with the wind and the night.

Stop.

The wind turned ugly, screaming, hurling snow into the room, shaking the walls and knocking over the chair. The pigs squealed.

He had been good to her, and she had been good for him. Angela wept. She dared not open her eyes.

No—you're wrong, *evil*—it's not true—not for me.

Blut howled, screaming with the wind. A high, inhuman cry, like a wolf but far more hideous. She felt him leap back from her, the evil flowing out of her mind and body while the wind thundered and smashed things. Blut kicked the bed in fury, knocking it against the wall eight feet away.

This is not the only test.

The black form swirled back into mist, whirling out the window along with the wind. Gradually the room grew quiet. Angela lay very still, breathing slowly, unconscious at last. She was on her stomach, head flopped sideways, one foot off the bed. Although the wind was gone, a draft of frozen air sighed across her body. The long, naked arms and legs sprawled limply, her face hidden by black curling hair. Blood stained her throat, a dark splotch soaking into the white sheet. The room grew lighter as the first pink tinge appeared in the east.

CHAPTER SIX

◊

> *Her lips were red, her looks were free,*
> *Her locks were yellow as gold:*
> *Her skin was white as leprosy,*
> *The Nightmare Life-in-death was she,*
> *Who thicks man's blood with cold.*
> > —*Coleridge,* The Rime of the
> > Ancient Mariner

MICHAELS CAME AWAKE slowly. Bad dreams: Angela, Ursula, Blut, him, all jumbled together, Blut and Ursula scuttling along—big hairy white tarantulas. Angela fading from his touch to reappear under Blut's cold white body, thin white hairy spider legs forcing apart her darker thighs—screaming as spider teeth bite.

Mike moaned and rolled over. Music, electric guitars, wailed in miniature. Maybe he should

sleep in. Then he remembered his dreams and
what had happened—Ursula's teeth slamming
together and the hungry rage in her eyes, that
crazy conversation between Blut and Ursula. His
eyes opened—white antiseptic light and white
walls—jerked shut. Wait and check this out. He
moved slowly. They hadn't tied him down. He
lay on his side on a long, narrow padded table,
his knees extending off the edge. The room
smelled funny, medicinal.

He cautiously opened his eyes. Blut's examination room. Renwick sat with his feet on one
table, cassette recorder and pistol on another.
His head lulled back, mouth slack, eyes half-shut,
feet bobbing to the music. Stoned, probably very
stoned. On the table were the cassette recorder,
then the black metal automatic, farther back
various jars and bottles, some of brown glass,
many full of pills.

Michaels shut his eyes, swallowed. He'd have
to rush him and grab the gun. Renwick looked
totally involved in the music. But Mike didn't
like B-movie heroics—they recalled times in
Vietnam. The side of his head throbbed where he
had been kicked. The alternative was waiting for
Blut or Ursula. Jesus. He repressed the shudder
trying to crawl up his spine. He opened his eyes.
Now—while Renwick was caught in the music.

He swung his legs down and leaped up. Renwick's head turned, eyes and mouth wide open, a
surprised Jesus whose hand knocked over the
recorder as he fumbled for the gun. Michaels hit
him in the shoulders with extended palms—the
chair crashed over, Renwick's hand raked at the
table, knocking over bottles. Michaels stepped
on him, reaching for the gun, and felt his legs

pulled out from under him, Renwick yanking at both ankles. Michaels grabbed for the tablecloth, bringing cloth and everything down with him. The gun hit with a dull thud; bottles crashed, broke, others spilling or rolling about the floor.

Michaels was on top. One hand went for Renwick's throat, the other held his wrist. They glared at each other, breathing hard. Renwick cursed steadily. His angry gray eyes were dulled with enormous pupils—obviously stoned. His thin arms and legs thrashed about, rage giving the skeletal limbs strength, but he was no match for Michaels, who outweighed him sixty pounds. The gun lay out of reach down near their feet.

Michaels smelled something strong, horribly sweet—chloroform. The broken brown bottle had emptied out its volatile liquid. He squirmed, half-rising, holding Renwick by the arm. Suddenly his hand lashed out, hitting the Christ face on the side of the jaw and knocking him toward the pool of chloroform. Renwick screamed and cursed. Michaels used his palm to force the face sideways, pushing with palm and extended arm, smashing Renwick against the stinking floor. Renwick shrieked, realizing what was happening, and hit him in the stomach. Mike bellowed but felt the thin limbs slow down, weakening. He pressed harder, covering mouth and nose with his hand, forcing Renwick to swallow chloroform. Renwick thrashed and grew still. Michaels kept pressing to make sure. Finally he let go, standing shakily, his legs weak.

Renwick lay sprawled out half onto his side, part of his face wet from the chloroform, the damp hair and beard darker. Fragments of-brown glass had scored his cheek, leaving red gashes. A skeleton dressed in old jeans and faded workshirt with the head of a calendar Christ.

Michaels shook his head. The guy was definitely stronger than he looked. Blut must have given him a nice jolt of smack, fixed him up real good. He breathed deeply, trying to relax. The room looked like a doctor's office. God, the chloroform stank. No doctor would have that lying around, a vet maybe. The tiny electric guitars wailed on, the cassette recorder oblivious to its fall. He bent over to turn the music off and thought better. Best leave it going. As for the gun . . .

He picked it up. Good Christ, a .45. Big, heavy, square thing of black oily metal. He remembered Captain Ruiz shooting a .45, holding it with both hands, big chunks flying from the target. Not likely it belonged to Renwick. Firing the pistol would probably shake loose one of those skinny arms. He pulled out the clip. Only three bullets? It would still come in handy, especially if Ursula or Blut . . . His fear was returning. He'd shoot them both if he had to. And if guns didn't work? Forget about that—he had to get Angela out of here. God, just let her be all right.

First he needed to attend to Renwick. Turning to a tall metal cabinet with glass doors, he took out two elastic bandages, turned Renwick over, pulling him away from the chloroform, and tied his hands tightly. Next he bound the ankles, then bent the legs, and tied hands and ankles together. How long would the chloroform last? Just to make sure he ripped off a big piece of three-inch-wide tape and covered Renwick's mouth. That would hurt coming off, especially on the mustache, but made yelling for help impossible.

Michaels fastened his bathrobe, which hung open and smelled of chloroform. He shivered. It would be nice to get his clothes on. He felt vulnerable enough in this house without being almost naked. His body ached with bruises from being bounced off a wall, kicked in the head, and that wrestling match just now. He opened the door, looked around, stepped out, and closed the door, diminishing the wailing guitars.

He took the stairs two at a time, his bare feet quietly moving from step to step, the ancient surfaces deadly cold. His heart beat rapidly, and his mouth was dry. The hallway at the top was still dimly lit, unchanged.

He would have to pass the room Ursula had been in. Oh God, how he hoped she was gone, that horrible—whatever she was. He gripped the .45 tightly, aware his palm was sweating. The door was open about an inch, a long black gap. He wasn't going to kick the fucking door in, that was for sure. Push it all the way open and make sure there's no one hiding behind it—*hurry*.

He crouched slightly, pushed hard, using his hand to make sure the door went all the way back to the wall, and stepped quickly into the room. Enough light came from the hall to show the room was empty.

He gave a long sigh, his fear abating somewhat. He stepped back into the hall. Careful now, lots of doors. Something nasty could be behind one of them. The floor creaked, and he tried to walk more quietly. Even in the hallway he could hear the wind moaning about the house.

At the end of the long hallway was the door to Angela's room, closed, a gray-white rectangle. Blut or Ursula could be in there. The wind rattled a window somewhere, and he felt a shudder building up. His shoulders rose, tensed, his teeth clenching as a cold chill swam up his back. What a god-awful, cold, horrible night. Please, Angela, be all right. He knew it was unlikely, illogical, that they would have left her untouched.

He turned the doorknob, pushing the door all the way open, and stepped into the room. Oh Jesus—no one but Angela lying naked and looking dead—the room total chaos like some dark maelstrom had howled through, whirling, crashing, and destroying—the window gone and so cold it—

Angela! He rushed to the bed, touched her shoulders—God, skin of ice. She lay on her stomach, face hidden in the mattress, arms and legs sprawling lifelessly, like a crumpled doll. Michaels turned her over very gently. What he saw made him wince, something lodged in his throat, and he wanted to cry.

She looked strangely thinner, cheeks gaunt, her color gone, and the long straight nose seemed bigger. There were dark circles under her eyes, bluish green, as if they had been blackened. Her face had a waxy look, her lips wan, with a gummy, sticky substance covering them, strung from lip to lip. Even the dark hair had lost its luster, gone flat. The long beautiful arms, legs, and torso had a pale marble quality, statuesque. And cold—she felt so god-awful cold. He knew his hands were trembling. She looked like—like something his uncle had prepared. He moaned and quickly laid his head between her breasts.

Low and far away he heard her heart beat.

Oh God, he mumbled. He put his arms around the limp body, pressed his chest against her, trying to warm her. He kissed her on the cheek, squeezed hard. She moaned and breathed noisily.

Michaels cursed Blut, Ursula, and the house. The wind screeched angrily, blew cold air and snow across his back. He turned toward the window. Finally some light out there, dawn was coming. Christ, no wonder she was half-dead with the window completely out. The room was like a meat locker. Or a mortuary.

He hugged her tightly, then stood and looked for the blankets. He turned on the light. Strange, the blankets were wadded up at the foot of the wall opposite the open window. Someone had also moved the bed. Oh God—now he could see the red—crimson splotches of blood all over the sheet. The sight twisted his stomach. Wrapping her in blankets, he found no obvious wounds, but her inner thighs were pinkish, bloody. An old patchwork quilt tore under his hands, dissolving like cobweb. Shivering, he grabbed his pants, stepped into them, put on his shirt and jacket. He still felt cold even with his field jacket zipped up.

He sat on the bed, lifted her with one arm. She moaned again. "Angela. Hey, Angela, come on, it's Mike. Wake up. It's okay now." He shook her slightly, and she sighed. "Come on, Angela. I won't hurt you." He began to feel choked up again. "Hey." He shook her. Her body jerked, and she went "ohhhh." "Honest, Angela, it's okay. It's Mike."

Her eyes opened, showing part of the dark blue irises. "Mike?" She didn't see him.

"Yeah."

"Mike?" She looked at him, blinked.

"Yeah. You remember." He grinned, even though he didn't feel like it.

"Mike." Her eyes suddenly filled with tears, and she began to cry. "Don't hurt me anymore—please. Don't be the worm."

"Huh? Oh Christ." He raised her, hugged her, then ran his fingers along her cheek and kissed her face. "I wouldn't hurt you."

"You are Mike. I'm so glad to see you."

"Who did you think I was?"

She closed her eyes. *"Him."*

She fumbled to free her arms from the blankets. He helped her, and she held him as tightly as she could. Something had drained the strength from her embrace.

"We're going to get out of here. Just as soon as you're dressed."

She sighed and closed her eyes again. Floating in blackness, she sensed Blut's presence, calling to her. A sudden cramp struck low in the belly. She groaned, remembering what had happened. She knew she would not leave Blood Farm.

"What's wrong? What is it?"

"Oh Mike." She clung to him, clung to the warmth he represented. She felt she would never be warm again.

"What did they do to you?"

She swallowed once. "He raped me."

Mike said nothing for several seconds, his face reddening. "Oh Christ. That fucker."

"But that's not the worst part—oh God, Mike,

he's so dirty—he's so totally filthy." She was crying.

He held her tightly, stroked her back, and made soothing noises. "Let's just get out of here. We can tell the cops. Just because he's a goddamn doctor . . ."

She drew back, staring, the blue eyes tired and sad, her face wan. Her eyes had a glassy overtone; something in her wanted to wrench her away. "You still don't understand, do you?"

They stared at each other. She took a deep breath, struggling with something. Suddenly she tensed, fingers digging into him as her eyes closed and she grit her teeth.

"Hey, what is it?"

Her body still rigid, she let her breath slide out between locked teeth. He felt like a helpless fool, unable to do anything. She finally went slack in his arms.

"What's wrong?"

She managed to smile through blurry eyes. "I'm just beginning to understand. Oh God, I can't take many cramps like that."

The long black hair came down over her shoulders and a few long strands had strayed into her eyes. Michaels brushed her hair aside, out of her face. She winced as his hand touched her neck. Puzzled, he gently pushed aside the hair on the right side. Below the earlobe four ugly wounds and bluish bruises marred the smooth skin— puncture wounds, jagged holes still bloody. The bruised indentations formed two half-circles.

He looked away, feeling the sudden shock right in the groin. "Good Christ, how . . ?"

"He's a vampire."

"What?"

"A vampire. You know, like in the movies."

"Oh Jesus, he can't be."

"But he is. You didn't—"

"I believe you. And he raped you?"

"Yes." She began to cry again. "He's so horrible, so evil. God, I could feel it—it seemed to ooze out of him—come out of his pores. I never really believed in the devil till now."

"Come on, we'll get out of here." He held her, caressed her, and tried to stifle his own fear. That explained the weird stuff all evening, the sense of something terrible about to happen. But what the hell were they going to do?

"Mike, you don't understand. He's in me now—part of him is *inside me*. And he doesn't want to let me go."

"What do you mean?"

"Do you know much about vampires?"

"No."

"I don't either, but I do know that if I die—if he took enough blood to kill me or if he does do that—then I'll become like him. Like Ursula."

"Oh good Lord—that can't be true."

"I wish to God it wasn't. He's hideous—he doesn't believe in love or sex or anything—he was like ice—like . . ." Another cramp tore into her with icy teeth of fire, making her cling to him. She groaned, her head falling back, tears pouring from her eyes. "Stop . . ." Michaels cursed, held her tightly, and felt completely helpless. At last she went limp in his arms, her head brushing against his shoulder. "Oh Lord, that hurt. I can still feel him inside. It feels bruised and sore, the cramps are cold and burn at the same time."

"Let's get out of here."

"I want to, but I don't know if I can." Another, smaller cramp came, contorting her face and further exhausting her. "Mike, I don't think I can." She knew she would not yet be allowed to leave Blood Farm, but she couldn't tell Mike that. He would want to know how she knew, and she didn't understand that herself.

"You've got to try."

Eyes closed, she sighed. "Yes."

"I'll help you get dressed. Can you walk?"

"I don't think so. I think I'll faint if I stand up."

"Then I'll carry you."

"Okay. We can try it."

"Good." He made himself smile, but the expression was far from his usual grin.

"Mike, one thing—if you get out of here and I don't, go to Iowa City and tell Pat Donahue and Tony Russo. Tony is a TA who knows a lot about Gothic novels, vampires and witches. Pat is a priest. They're my friends and can help you."

"I'm not leaving without you."

"But if you do, will you go to them? Promise me you will."

"Sure, I promise."

"Do you remember the names?"

"Uh, Tony Russo and Pat Donegal."

"*Donahue*—Pat Donahue."

"Okay. I've got it."

"You're sure?"

"Yeah." He was also sure he wouldn't leave without her.

She sighed and closed her eyes. Suddenly she jerked alert. "And don't tell anyone else— absolutely *no one*. Especially . . . okay?"

"Okay. Now let's get you dressed. If nothing else you'll feel warmer."

"Good. These blankets don't help. They feel cold. They're part of the house."

She swung her legs around, and he helped her sit up. The room went spotty, then gray, and Michaels disappeared. Somewhere far away she heard him asking if she was all right. His hands kept her from keeling over. The gray parted, became a design of spots superimposed over the room, things coming back into focus. Giant pink roses, gaudy things on green stems. Brown splotches ate at the pink petals, the canker of decay. She realized she was staring at the wallpaper, shivered, and looked away.

"Are you okay?"

"Just dizzy." She noticed the gun on the bed. "Where did that come from?"

"Renwick kindly lent it to me before I tied him up. Let me help you get your clothes on."

She made herself smile although she felt sick. "Okay, Mommy."

Michaels half-grinned, stood to gather the clothes that were scattered about the room. She sat on the bed watching, blue eyes half-open, looking woozy. He pulled a long-underwear leg over her foot. She bent over to help, and when she sat up the room grayed over again. She pulled the long underwear up above her knees. Michaels immediately began getting the jeans over her feet.

"You're going to have to stand up to get these on," he said. "Do you think you can?"

"I don't know. Let's try. I'll hold the pants, you hold me."

He stood, held her by the armpits. She rose and pulled simultaneously, bringing the underwear and pants up to her waist. The room went gray, then black. Michaels muttered "oh shit" and gently lowered her onto the mattress. He tugged at the elastic waistband on the long underwear, then adjusted the jeans, zipped them up, and fastened the snap. Christ, she was weak. There was no way she'd be able to walk to the hearse.

"Mike?" Fear in her voice.

"Yeah. It's okay. You done good. You've got your pants on." Sitting on the bed, he put his hand on her thigh and squeezed. Her eyes were not awake, but she smiled. Affection and sorrow spun around inside him; he bent over and kissed her on the lips. She touched his cheek with her hand, and her lips responded tenderly, her mouth opening wider. Suddenly she gagged, almost biting him, and clutched at her stomach. He jerked away. Eyes screwed shut, her mouth a black groaning hole in a pale oval, she brought her knees up toward her chest, fingers digging into her legs.

Michaels cursed, felt his own eyes filling with tears. He couldn't stand this—she hurt so bad. *"Goddamn you, Blut!"*

Her body relaxed. She was pale, and sweat highlighted her face, glistened on her forehead. He held her shoulder and squeezed gently, half-afraid what might happen. He picked up her socks and began to put them on her feet. Women's feet usually pleased him, but he was too upset now to notice.

"Mike, I don't think he's going to let me leave."

"The hell he isn't."

"I know something that might help. Would you get me my pack?" It was in a corner. He rose from the bed and carried back the pack by one nylon strap. "Open the bottom pocket on the right side and take out the box." She lay with her eyes closed.

He found a black cardboard box buried in white panties. She raised her elbow, tried to push herself up, but he had to help her. She clung to him, then took the box and opened it.

A radiant coruscation as light from the bare bulb overhead bounced off silvery metal. Michaels saw a cross attached to a strip of dark leather, the small silver beams widening at their ends, flaring outward. The slumbering wind suddenly sputtered awake and angrily doused them with cold snowy air. Mike glanced at the window. The gray-white square was clearly brighter. Dawn was coming. Angela stared at the cross, and he felt the tension stiffening her arms and shoulders, tightening her mouth. Her eyes opened wide, became very alert and the black pupils seemed to dilate.

He watched the light flicker over the cross, the metal shimmer, as he moved his head. "I don't usually like jewelry, but that's pretty."

"Someone made it for me. It's even been blessed. He kidded me about that because he wasn't sure about the value of blessing things." She took a deep breath. "I need you to help me put it on."

"Huh?"

"I want you to hold the cross—and don't let go of it until I say so, okay? Don't let go no matter what."

"Sure. I think I can handle that."

"Good. Take it out, then."

He took the thin metal between thumb and

forefinger and lifted the cross from the box. She flinched and jerked backwards. "Hey, I'm not going to hit you." He smiled, but her expression did not change. She stared at the cross, her beautiful face a grim mask, pale and thin, surrounded by black hair. "What are you scared of?"

"Just hold the cross, Mike." Her voice had a hard quality. "Keep holding the cross and don't let it touch me." Very slowly, using both hands, she put the leather strap over her head. The long fingers trembled, and she had closed her eyes. When the strap rested on the black hair at the base of her neck, she lowered her hands. He sensed her tension, felt it growing within him like a contagious disease. "Okay, Mike." Her voice shook. "Let go of the cross."

Goose bumps prickled the bare skin of her shoulders and chest. He opened his fingers, and the silver metal dropped between her breasts. Her head went back and she screamed, face twisting with pain, and the wind shrieked in reply, snarled, crashed into the room, hurled things about with icy fingers. The walls of Blood Farm creaked and shuddered.

Darkness and a white hot iron burning into her chest. Angela knew nothing of the wind. Dread boiled over the instant the metal touched her. All she could feel was fear and the pain of the fire in her heart. Despite the agony she must not remove the cross—she knew what that would mean. The unclean *it* wanted her to hurl the cross away. Her hand slammed flat against the fiery, searing metal, she fell backward onto the bed, and she pressed as hard as she could—as if she would drive the burning silver through the sternum into her heart.

Michaels tried to wrench her hand away but couldn't budge her. "Let go for Christ's sake—you're hurting yourself!" He could hear the *sss*—and smell the burning flesh.

She screamed *"no"* and rolled over onto her hand and the cross. Her face, lips, and teeth dug into the mattress, while her other hand clawed at the sheet, fingers tearing into the cotton.

Something ate at her, took huge bites from her heart. Not the cross—the worm. Blut's white corpse-face floated upon a dark sea, unable to speak in his fury—only the hiss of command. *Throw away the cross—slut, you cannot—fling it from your unclean flesh.* God help me, make the hurting stop. Blut angrily flowing away, leaving her with the pain and that finally subsided too.

Michaels gave up trying to turn her over. Fear had engulfed him, he wanted to cry. He lay over her, pressed his cheek against her back and held her shoulders. At least he could keep her warm. He felt her gradually go slack.

"Angela?"

No response. He squeezed her shoulders tightly. "Angela?" For an instant he was afraid she was dead but her back rose with her breathing. Gently he turned her. Her body moved easily, one arm flopping over. The tension was gone, her face peaceful. He winced at the burn, a charred red-black cross between her breasts. He took her hand, noticed a similar mark scorched into the palm. But the burning had stopped—the silver cross lay on her left breast over the nipple, harmless. What, for Christ's sake, was going on?

His mouth slowly opened and his eyes widened. The cross-shaped wound lost color, blurring, as the bright red faded. He watched it heal.

The mark almost vanished, leaving only a faint scar to show anything had ever happened.

"Oh God," he whispered. He had witnessed few miracles. Things made no sense tonight.

Angela opened her eyes. "Mike?"

"Are you all right?"

The burning pain was gone, and somehow she felt better, less shaky. A kind of cold localized ache above the groin, but she knew the bad cramping was over for now. The silver cross felt cool against her skin.

"I feel a lot better."

"What *is* going on?"

"Vampires hate crosses. I thought this would protect me."

"But why did it burn you?"

"Because of what Blut did to me. Part of him was in me—had infected me. He's still there, but not as bad. I can feel the difference."

"But isn't there any cure?"

"Yes." She sighed. "Killing Blut."

"Oh Christ! With the wooden stake and the whole bit?"

"That's one way."

"Let's get out of here."

She sat up slowly, swayed slightly as her vision grayed over, then smiled weakly. "I'm sorry, Mike, but I know I can't walk. I thought I might be able to now, but I'll just fall over."

"That's no surprise if you've lost blood. Here's your shirt—or it was here." He walked over to retrieve it. She pulled the turtleneck over her head, moving slowly, obviously not well. Mike chewed at his lip. If only he could get her away from here. "You want the cross under the shirt?"

"Yes. So it's touching me, and where it's

harder to take off." He used his fingers to stuff the leather strap underneath the turtleneck, and she reached underneath her shirt to pull down the cross. "I wish I had another cross."

"What for? Are two better than one?"

She smiled. "No. For *you*."

"Me? I'm hardly the type. But I'm beginning to wonder."

"You'll need protection too. Maybe . . ."

"But you're the one Blut—uh, got."

"I know—listen, there's another little box in that same pocket. Will you get it?"

He walked over to the pack, found another even smaller box buried amidst the panties. "Here you are." He grabbed her boots, put one on her foot and laced it. He watched her open the box, which was full of small shiny metal shapes. "More jewelry?"

"Earrings. Here we go." She pulled out two tiny crosses, three-quarters of an inch by a half-inch, gold with a squiggly design around the outside edge.

Michaels stared, forehead crinkling. Slowly his face relaxed into his grin, corners of his mouth disappearing under blond mustache. The blue eyes and yellow hair took her back to their first meeting, his face grinning up at her from the hearse.

"I refuse to have my ears pierced."

She laughed, and for a second or two they felt all right. "I don't want you to wear them in your ears, silly." She bent over, pulled out the pin, and fastened a cross to the collar of his field jacket. She pinned the other cross to the T-shirt he had on under the flannel shirt. "There, that may help."

Mike shook his head. "I feel like a chaplain wearing gold insignia. If anyone had told me yesterday morning that I'd let someone pin earrings on me for protection from vampires, I would've said they were out of their fucking mind. I would have laughed like hell. Now I'll try anything." He finished lacing her other boot and handed her the parka.

She quickly put it on, zipping it all the way up. "Uh . . . that feels better. This room is so cold." She put on her hat.

"Ready?"

"I suppose so."

"How much do you weigh, anyway?"

"A hndred and fifty pounds. Don't look at me like that. I *am* six feet tall."

"Oh God. I'll try the fireman's carry. That will leave one hand free for the gun." He picked up his hat, which was battered from being tossed around the room. "I guess I'd better leave this."

"Why?"

"I can't wear it and carry you. Too awkward."

"I'll carry it for you."

"If you want. You will have one hand free. But we'll have to leave the rest of our stuff. I don't want to risk coming back for it. Here goes nothing."

"Mike—are you sure you want to try carrying me? You'd do better alone."

"Uh-uh. It's not that hard using the fireman's carry."

"What's that?"

"Watch."

He turned sideways, grabbed her right wrist, and extended her arm. He bent and lifted simultaneously, pulling her onto him. Her torso was supported along his shoulders, her right arm coming down from his left shoulder, his hand gripping her wrist, her leg coming down from his right shoulder. He staggered slightly, shifting her to balance better.

"Mike, are you sure about this?"

"Yeah. How about you? How is it up there?"

"I'm okay. Dizzy, but not too bad."

"Good." He turned and picked up the gun with his free hand, turned again. Hard to see straight bent over. He had carried heavier people a long way in Nam.

"Wait," she said. He stopped; behind him she reached with her hand for the cowboy hat. "Okay, now we can go."

He opened the door clumsily and stepped into the hall sideways so he wouldn't bang her against the doorway. The hallway looked long, dim, and quiet; no windows to let the dawn enter, only the bare low-watt bulb. He flicked off the safety on the .45. He walked slowly, feeling extremely vulnerable. Carrying Angela he would be helpless, except for the gun, if anything rushed him. The floor creaked loudly under the feet supporting 340 pounds. The hallway seemed to stretch, to prolong itself, a dark tunnel of wallpaper green jungle that took forever. Finally he arrived at the stairs and looked down. Steep bastards. Don't trip, for God's sake—don't trip, that's all.

"You okay, Angela?"

"Uh-huh." She sounded only half-there.

He started down. Impossible not to make noise, so get down them as fast as possible—but don't trip. That'd be great—bang, crash—Blut finding them in a big heap at the bottom. He took the steps one foot at a time, aware of the girl's 150 pounds. Except for one frightening stagger, the going was smooth. What if Blut or Ursula—or Fang—was in the living room? His grip on the .45 handle tightened. The examining-room door was still shut, but the music had ceased. He stopped near the bottom, sucked in some air, took the last step down into the big open doorway, and quickly turned, sweeping the living room with the pistol.

Nobody. Big red plush chairs with no one in them, the black coffin dominating the room, the small lamp still on. He listened carefully. Only the wind low outside and the ancient walls groaning. The house might be empty. Where were they?

He went into the living room and bent over to put Angela down. She had to halfway stand to get off; she staggered, dropped his hat and went limp. He eased her into a chair where she sat breathing quietly.

His nose wrinkled, scrunched up. It still smelled funny in here. Weird. Then he recognized the smell. Flowers usually hid it, and his uncle used refrigerating units, but in Vietnam, in that hot heavy air, the smell came alive as quickly as men were blown apart. Death. The smell of death. Clinging like a gray ubiquitous parasite, like some dark moss, to the walls of Blood Farm. The house stank of death.

As usual the fear began at his neck, but it threatened this time to become total panic. Jesus, he wanted to get out of here. The more mysteries one untangled, the worse it became. But he had to keep hold of himself a little longer. Angela was too sick to do much. So by default,

goddammit, it was up to him. Do something
else—don't stand here until you totally freak
out.

He went to the nearest window and parted the
drapes to look out. The thick heavy material
blocked light like a protective shield. Outside he
saw a windblown snowscape under blue gray
illumination. The sun should rise soon.

And the hearse was gone.

The fear, the urge to panic, instantly returned,
and he felt sick to his stomach. Oh Christ, what
would they do? He couldn't carry her back to
Iowa City. He felt his heart beat against his rib
cage like it wanted out. The hearse may be out
there—it can't be far—can't be—you've got the
keys. But to go look for it he'd have to leave her.
Leave her alone with this darkness and the smell
of death.

"Mike?—*Mike.*"

"Yeah—I'm here." He turned to her.

"What's going on?"

"Uh, the hearse is gone. I'm going to have to go
look for it. You'll have to wait here. I could try to
carry you, but . . ."

She laughed weakly. "Don't be silly—it's cold
and it's blowing. You might slip, and then where
would we be? We'd both break something. I'll
wait here for you." But she knew he wouldn't be
able to come back.

"God, I hate to . . . I'll leave you the gun."

"No, you take it. It probably wouldn't help
anyway."

"Oh Jesus Christ." He sounded ready to cry.

"Go on, Mike. At least I've got the cross, and
it's almost day." Her eyes grew blurry. She felt
tired, sick, and the idea of being separated from

him for God knew how long made her want to weep. But he would never leave if she did. "You've got to go. It's the only chance." Her voice was hoarse.

"I know. Shit. Okay, I'll be right back—if I find the hearse, I'll drive to the door and run in for you." He clicked the safety on, put the gun in his pocket, and pulled on his gloves.

"Be careful."

"I will."

He leaned on the chair and saw the tears in her eyes. He didn't feel much better himself. She avoided looking at him. He bent over and gently kissed her. She responded, her lips moving slowly, and touched his cheek with her fingertips. He stood and they stared at each other. Seeing her in the red parka and the hat reminded him of last night, aeons ago.

"Don't forget your hat."

He picked up the black hat and dropped it on her lap. "You watch it for me. I don't feel much like wearing it just now. Besides, I'll be right back. I'd better get going."

She grabbed his forearm and squeezed. "Good luck." She knew he couldn't come back and tried not to cry. Losing him twice in one night just wasn't fair. "Don't forget those people in Iowa City."

He frowned, his face stubborn. "I'm not leaving this goddamn farm without you." Hard to talk. "I told you I'd get you to Iowa City by today, and I will. In time for five o'clock mass."

She laughed once and almost smiled. Hurry and leave—I can't bear this.

"I'll be back as soon as I can." He really did have no choice.

"Good-bye." She let go of his arm.

He knew it would be easier not looking back, but he turned at the doorway and attempted to smile. She smiled back, the tears starting. For the second time she watched him close the door behind him, shutting out light, leaving her alone in darkness. The dead, frigid darkness of Blood Farm. God help us, she prayed. The room grew colder, and she heard the low murmur of the wind.

Michaels stepped onto the porch and shivered. Good Christ, it was cold! The house was bad enough, but it must be about twenty-five below out here. Long white sloping fields stretched to the horizon; the sky was still colorless, a gray-white expanse overhead. Trees, fence posts, everything not covered by white was dark brown or black. The wind stirred the snow, sent thin mists running like herds of frightened rabbits, and the surface itself shifted. Wave after wave of cloudy snow unfurled across the abandoned fields. The wind made low contented sounds, playing with the snow. Its breath went right through his fatigue jacket and liner.

He glanced down the road past the barn— black beetle shape squatting by the roadside, squarish beetle with fins—*the hearse*. About twenty yards from where he'd parked. Someone must have released the brake and pushed it down the road. Now if it would only run. He grinned, took out the pistol, and quickly stepped off the porch.

Better stay close to the house, out of the open,

where they couldn't see him from the upstairs windows. He walked quickly along the house, stepping carefully because of the deep snow, two-foot drifts against the dirty paint-worn walls.

Clang, clang. Clang.

His friends the pigs were still at it. Black shapes clustered around the feeder, snorting eagerly, curly black tails pointed at him. The barnyard and the pigs lay between him and the hearse. They hadn't seen him yet. The big lean one was feeding, the ugly one. He remembered them making him paranoid earlier. *Paranoid* was not the right word—not at Blut Farm.

On an impulse he turned right, went around the house. Avoid the damn pigs. Just cut behind the barn, and you'll come out right near the hearse. He wasn't sure why he didn't want the pigs to see him, but there was something a little off about those pigs. And considering all that had happened . . . He shivered. God, the cold hurt.

He walked quietly, cowboy boots plunging into the snow. The pigs made noise, clanged, snorted, and the wind rose and fell. They still hadn't seen him. His ears felt frozen; his breath came in great clouds of white vapor; the subzero air froze-burnt his skin.

Now he was alongside the barn, clear of the pigs. He shifted the .45 to his left hand and pulled up his hood, wanting some cover for his ears. The barn wall was made of thick wooden planks, the dark red paint visible in the growing light.

He stepped around the barn, and the wind immediately jumped him with a great "haaa!" hurling snow to sting his eyes. Behind the barn an absolutely barren field—no trees, posts, nothing—seemed to unroll forever, providing a limitless playground for the wind. He walked faster but still quietly. You could never tell what might be in the barn.

He stopped at the end of the barn and took a careful look. A small shed, probably for tools, was about ten feet away. Beyond that were the hearse and the road curving into the trees. To his right lay the eastern horizon, where the long-backed field finally met the pale orange sky. A quick walk to the shed, then a run for the hearse. Christ, this was almost too easy—if Angela was all right. Blut could still be in the house. The thought contracted his stomach like a fist. Relax, you're safe now.

He stepped away from the barn and saw a black shape appear through the trees, come out of the grove onto the road—a huge black dog.

Michaels's forward momentum kept him going. The walk became a rush, feet bounding across the deep snow, and he flattened himself behind the shed. Then he had time to be afraid. His breath came out in a quiet shudder, and he felt himself tremble from cold and incredible fear.

Oh Christ—if he had come out from behind the barn ten seconds sooner he would have been caught in the open between the shed and the car. But had the dog seen him? He listened intently but heard nothing except wind and three clangs. Snow blew into his face, and his breath made white clouds. He was standing in two feet of snow. The dog had looked like the one that he hit last night—or was it Manfred?—or were . . . The .45 didn't seem worth much.

Jesus, he couldn't take this—standing here freezing to death and scared out of his head. The door to the shed was around the other side. Before he had time to ponder the risk, he was moving around the shed, pushing the door open with his shoulder—still no dog. Had it stopped by the grove? Inside was a small dark room littered with tools and junk, dirt floor, light coming from white cracks between black boards, a musty oily smell. He closed the door and paused to catch his breath.

Where was that fucking dog?

He walked over to the wall, pushed aside a rake, and put his eye against the long vertical crack. Through the bright split he saw the dog standing by the trees beyond the hearse. Black with yellow cat's eyes, amber flakes looking this way. Oh God, God. He clutched the gun tighter. Come on, it can't be staring at you. The dog gazed east, not at the shed, but further into the distance where the sun was about to rise. What was he doing?

The dog howled, a long mournful sound. Mike had heard recordings of wolf howls, and the dog sounded exactly like a wolf. From the direction of the house came an answering cry, followed by a chorus of pig squeals.

The wind screamed in reply, swirling about the dog, forming a white whirlwind. The dog seemed to stand, to rise on its hind legs and grow taller. The screams of the wind crescendoed, the snowy mist obscuring the black shape, blurring, then a pink tint appeared—as if drops of blood had been added—darkening, blooming to full crimson. The wind died down to reveal a new form, bright red in the dawning light. A blood-stain in the snow.

Ursula in her scarlet robe.

The black dog had changed into Ursula. No mistaking that red robe and pale blond hair, the horrible beauty. She stood out there in a foot of snow wearing a thin robe when the temperature was about twenty below. Smiling, her mouth smeared red, and her eyes languidly half-closed. She was probably barefoot. She glanced again off to the east, then started toward the house.

Mike was trembling. Ursula would walk inside and immediately find Angela. He was all that could stop her. Or try to stop her. Good Christ, an incredibly strong, dangerous, woman vampire. Good luck. Or he could stay hidden in the shack, wait for Ursula to leave, then get in the hearse, and drive off alone. And leave Angela to them. Oh God, he could never do that—even though that bloodhungry thing out there terrified him.

He turned and, needing some outlet for his fear, kicked open the door. He stepped out into the snow and the frozen morning, the blue-white dawn. *"Ursula!"* His voice had a high hysterical quality.

She stopped and jerked around. Seeing him, her eyes grew alert. Fresh meat, huh? he mumbled to himself. She smiled, showing teeth, then crouched low, long white fingers curling into claws. The movement reminded him of a cat flattening itself into the grass, and immediately she rushed him.

Michaels raised the pistol, gripped his wrist with his left hand for support, squeezed off a shot. The recoil jerked back his arm; the roar thundered off the barn wall, and echoed across the long barren fields. He saw the slug hit her in the chest—blood geysered out—like sticking a gorged leech. Probably not even her blood. A look of disbelief and a loud angry scream as the bullet knocked her over. He couldn't believe he had hit her, not at twenty feet with a pistol when he was the world's worst shot.

She raised her legs, those beautiful white legs, planting her feet in the snow and pushed herself up with her hands. God, she *was* barefoot. The smile was gone, the pale face contorted with anger, the blue eyes fixed on him. She bared her teeth—the upper canines were over an inch long—and he could hear the noise from low in her throat. She stepped toward him.

Oh Christ—what now? The gun wouldn't stop her, and he knew he couldn't outrun her—she would leap on him from behind and bury those fangs in the back of his neck. Another shot would give him time. Again the roar thundered over the morning stillness, the blood exploded from low in her belly, and she gave a loud scream as the bullet hurled her backward.

Michaels ran into the shed, shut the door, grabbed a pitchfork off the wall, and waited. Wouldn't it be nice if the last shot had killed her? But you can't kill a vampire—no, not that easy. He stood, legs planted, holding the pitchfork like a lance. It was a big hayfork, three long solid tines coming to wicked points. His hands began to tremble again. He heard nothing except wind. What was she doing?

The door burst inward, tearing the rusted hinges from rotting wood, and crashed onto the dirt floor. Furious, Ursula stood in the doorway, red robe and white hair. She smiled. He felt like she already had him by the throat, shaking him like a dog with a rat. Bloody silhouette against the rectangle of gray light, she watched him. Her blood-smeared mouth and teeth were horrible, but the pale blue eyes would not let him move—she had him.

With a loud, throaty laugh she stepped toward him, then stopped dead. For the first time he saw fear in her. She was staring at his neck or his coat. Angela had pinned the earring there.

He rushed forward and thrust the pitchfork like a rifle with a bayonet. The shock jarred his arms and the prongs slid through her. The pitchfork twisted slightly—one tine went through the rib cage below the right breast, the second dead center through the left breast, the last lodging under her left armpit. The curved metal head slammed against her chest, and his momentum knocked her out the doorway backward into the snow.

Screams, horrible screams. Feeling sick, Michaels hesitated, then stepped out of the shed. On her back in the snow, bare legs spread, she writhed, bloody mouth wide open, the long handle of the pitchfork flopping about. Like an insect freshly pinned. Blood all over the snow. Christ, her eyes were still open, the hate burning at him.

Good Lord—she's standing up. He grabbed the handle, pushed her over, let go. She growled and screamed, trying to stand again. His hands did not want to touch the pitchfork—too much like touching her—but he grabbed the handle again. This time she was ready, pushing forward, man-

aging to stand. Blood bleared her mouth and
frothed about her lips, dripping below the chin.
Those two huge teeth were unreal—so ugly. The
stolen blood that had become hers, seeped from
five wounds and smeared the white fingers clawing at the pitchfork handle. Only the piece of
wood separated them. Michaels held on for dear
life.

She gave up reaching for him, grasped the
handle with both hands, and attempted to
wrench the pitchfork out of her. Terrified, Michaels thrust hard, knocking her down into the
snow again. She made a snake hiss, struggling to
reach her feet. Christ, she's not weakening, but
you are—not enough sleep, and she's incredibly
strong. He could only hold her off so long.

Far beyond them on the horizon a flake of
red-orange appeared, turning the gray sky pink
and growing into a blurry orange circle. The sun
scattered light across the frozen fields, the miles
of snow-covered emptiness, bringing a hint of
warmth. Cold blue shadows grew out of buildings, trees, fence poles, and the long shade from
the shed covered Michaels and Ursula. She shuddered, and her efforts grew more desperate.

Michaels was sweating despite the cold. She
was still trying to remove the pitchfork, pushing
it away with both hands. He saw the dark bloody
steel slide out of the wounds, her face snarling
and not human. He panicked, and his strength
went into a tremendous lunge. The steel
slammed back into her, hurling her six feet
backward into the snow with another hissing
scream.

She shuddered, the pitchfork handle bobbing,
and her hands clawed at the snow's cold depths.

Her head arched back, the pale hair pushing, blending into the snow; her mouth made a wide O, a hoarse, slow gag with eyes welded shut. She raised her legs, opening the white thighs as the red nightgown slipped backward. She was naked beneath the robe, and her legs wiggled in a horrible parody of sexual invitation. Her upper body lay in the sunlight.

Michaels watched. Something was happening to her. She moved more slowly, and her face changed. As the tension drained away, wrinkles formed around the eyes and mouth, the pale blue eyes filming over, her hair fading from yellowish to pure white.

He breathed hard, making huge vapor clouds. Exhausted, he still felt sick. What was going on? Raising his eyes, he glanced east and saw the red-orange circle float above the white horizon. Now he understood. Sunlight. He looked at Ursula again. She was fast becoming a corpse, a dead thing pinned to the ground by the pitchfork. Even through icy air and wind, he smelled the stink of decay. Building up for God knew how long and emptied in an instant. He turned away, feeling himself tremble. Get the hearse and Angela and get away from this godforsaken place.

Eyes on him, watching. Where? The pigs. Black shapes at the fence, staring. Peering from between boards, little eyes set in their ugly pig faces, all leering snout and . . . Get away fast before—just turn around and—but they're only pigs. Only—Christ, get out of here—*run*.

He turned quickly, seeing the black blurs flow under and over the wooden fence like a swarm of rats. *Run*. His legs ate up ground in big strides, boots landing deep in the snow, arms moving with his legs. *Run*. The adrenaline obliterated cold and fatigue. The hearse bobbed up and down, jouncing to his steps, and grew. Behind he heard the high squeals of the pigs, dark Furies pursuing.

Almost to the hearse, something hit his leg and nearly knocked him over. His left hand shot out to grab the doorhandle, pushing in the button and wrenching open the door. He felt something under his leg and kicked down viciously with the boot heel. The loud angry squeal hurt his ears. He half-turned. The head pig, long and black, the other pigs fifteen feet away moving in fast.

The pig twisted its head, snorting, biting for Michaels's leg and seizing the denim. Michaels fumbled the .45 out of his pocket. Another loud roar crashed through the morning, the slug flipping the pig over. Michaels fell into the car and quickly squirmed around to slam the door shut.

Thunk—more thuds—pig bodies smashed against black metal, surrounding the hearse, squealing insanely. Michaels dropped the gun on the seat and searched his pocket for the keys. Thank God he hadn't shot himself in the leg. Never say you're paranoid—if he hadn't run— these pigs really wanted him. The car lurched continually as the pigs hit the sides. No telling what they could do, maybe eat through the tires. Swarming all over the place like big fucking rats. His hands quivered as he tried to start the car, his fingers freezing. The engine made a monotonous *uhrrr*—Christ, if it didn't start he was finished. A big pig crashed against the door right beside him. Another large dent—poor hearse!

With a loud cough the engine caught, and he made her roar. Give her plenty of gas so she won't stall. He wrenched the transmission into drive, pressed down the gas pedal, and the hearse jerked forward out of the snow. Rattling noise in back—thank God for the chains.

He took an instant to glance behind him in the mirror. The pigs were a scattering of black shapes against the snow. At their head was a huge thin one. Christ, bullets didn't stop anything around here.

How was he going to get back to the farm?— and into the house? He had to try. The road widened. Checking the mirror to make sure the pigs weren't in sight, he bore right, then cut hard to the left, stopped, shoved the car into reverse, and swung back around to face toward the farm. The chains rattled again as he accelerated.

The pigs were ahead, black shapes standing in the road. Off to the side more pigs sniffed and rooted around a shaft of wood swaying in the wind. Mike stabbed the gas pedal, and the car bounced wildly as the speedometer went past thirty, flying over the snowy road.

The pigs parted down the middle and fled squealing, but a couple weren't fast enough. The bumper knocked one sideways, another disappeared with a high shriek between the wheels.

Michaels kept going, watched the house grow, the many-eyed skull. How different by day—the decay was so much more obvious, the broken windows and blotchy paint. He glanced at the mirror and cursed. The pigs followed. And ahead, before the door to Blood Farm, stood a monstrous black statue.

Mike felt the fear clutch his lungs, his heart.

Oh God, Angela had been right, she had somehow known. The hearse slowed, then stopped, as
the pigs swerved sideways out of the rearview
mirror. They ran across the deep snow, the
smaller ones practically wading, and took up
positions before the house. On the porch was the
black dog Manfred.

Michaels cursed steadily, felt his eyes fill with
tears. Christ, to come this close and now to have
to leave her with these—things.

The pigs stared calmly, black statues with tiny
red eyes squatting in the snow. An immense dark
blue shadow came from the house, covering the
pigs and extending almost to the hearse. The dog
on the porch sat in the deepest shade,
half-hidden, motionless. A healthy living animal
would have had white highlights along his coat,
but this thing was utterly black, the blackness of
coal mined from deep within the earth. The
amber lights set in the head glowed at Michaels.
The latter-day Cerberus guarding the portal to
the dark kingdom.

Michaels's vision blurred over, and the tears
came out of his eyes. He hit the steering wheel
with both hands, muttering "fuck" between his
teeth. The second he stepped outside they'd be
on him, instant pig and dog food. He noticed the
.45 sitting on the seat. A lot of good that would
do, even if it were loaded. Angela was in the
house cold and sick, and he could do nothing.
And Blut must be in there. He remembered
holding Angela, the way she had felt, and the
way she had touched him, and her sitting beside
him laughing at buffalo stories. He moaned. This
wasn't helping. He blinked dully; his hands
trembled, still cold. Despite the heater he felt as

if he'd never warm up. The thing to do was find those two guys in Iowa City and get back here before dusk.

He looked at the house, white skull with square dark sockets set against the dawn-bright blue sky, and its black guardians squatting there. Crazy vision. *Pigs.* The whole thing suddenly seemed ludicrous, came out as a frustrated *"haaa."* God knew, the pigs were deadly enough, maybe next best after wolves. He had no doubts about what they would have done to him if they had caught him. Another frightened sick feeling, and he remembered the pitchfork slamming through Ursula's chest. "Oh, get out of here." Get away from this sick evil place. And Angela? Oh Christ.

He glared at Blood Farm and its sentinels, the angry, frightened tears wetting his face. "I'll come back—God, I promise I'll come back. I'll get you out no matter what." Worn out, he pressed down on the gas pedal. The hearse bounded off down the road and disappeared into the trees.

From behind the curtain, pale blue eyes watched. Blut exchanged looks with the dog and smiled, twisting his dead lips. In the chair beside him Angela breathed hoarsely, her eyes shut. More nightmares. Blut let the red curtain fall across the window and returned to the open coffin. The long night had ended, and day had come to Blood Farm.

Interlude in Iowa City

Sunlight worked at the few remaining clumps of snow, sparkled off chrome bumpers. Iowa City was quiet and unassuming on Sunday morning, most of the student population indoors sleeping something off. The temperature in the high twenties seemed a veritable heat wave to Michaels. The storm had somehow missed Iowa City, and the leftover snow was several days old.

He walked down Clinton Street past the fraternity and sorority houses, the dorms and churches. Parked cars, bumper to bumper, lined the streets. The frat dwellings were old two- or three-story houses, the dorms modern edifices of glass and gaudy orange brick. A few students wearing the habitual jeans and fatigue jacket or parka walked toward town to grab a paper at the Green Cross or a cup of coffee at Hamburger

Inn. Families strolled to church in their Sunday best. Everything was bright and sunny, reassuringly ordinary.

Mike glanced overhead, blinked at the sun's bright orange-yellow intensity, and felt its warmth on his face. The sun had never looked so good. If you were going to die, that would be the way to go—fall into the sun, like an errant comet, and let its fires consume you. Anything but dying cold, a chunk of ice lost in the void.

He shivered, remembering. He was morbid enough this morning. God, he should be. If only he were crazy or deluded. But the hearse was covered with dents, he was bruised and sore, and Angela was back there. The thought of her alone at Blut Farm made him sad and afraid. He was the one who had brought her there. He had to get her away, had to return before sunset. But first he must find the priest and the other guy.

He realized he had just passed someone he knew. He was exhausted—not sleepy but exhausted. Running on nerves, wound so tight he felt he might burst and scatter his parts all over the pavement.

The First Congregational Church towered over the neighborhood, the gray-brown building complete with ornate windows and a pointed steeple. People grouped about the entrance doors, mostly families. The couples wore fancy coats, legs of the men in bright double knits, the women in nylons. The kids ran continually, darting in and out of the crowd. A blond boy in a tiny overcoat chased a dark-haired girl, the red of her jacket radiant under the morning sun.

After-church crowds usually turned him off, but this morning he envied them the security of their faith and their families. They would not have to spend Sunday alone. They would have people and noise and warmth all about them.

Center East was across the street. The black metal of the fire escapes zigzagged back and forth, stuck to the flat wall of red brick. A former Catholic high school, the building recalled a prison or reform school with a cross on the roof. A large sign said CENTER EAST, THE CATHOLIC STUDENT CENTER. The second and third floor had supposedly been condemned, which left only the basement and first floor for use. Some environmental group had part of the basement, and Mike remembered draft counseling being available there at one time. He found the dingy ex-school more satisfying than First Congregational's pretentious exterior. At least the Catholics hadn't wasted money on a steeple.

He hesitated at the doorway. He hadn't been in a church for a long time, and in spite of the urgency he didn't want to go in. Everyone would be all dressed up, and with his hair and all he would stick out. Christ, though—what silly shit to start worrying about.

Inside he heard voices repeating something in unison, and a few latecomers stood on the stairway to the basement. Michaels murmured a tired oath and fought down another urge to flee. After his chaplain's assistant days he could at least fake his way through the mass.

The basement itself was roughly forty feet square and jammed with standing people. Thick pipes ran all around the ceiling. The garish yellow paint of the walls and pipes clashed horribly with the bright chartreuse of two supporting pillars and a small, set-in chamber behind the priest. Folding chairs served as pews, a folding table as altar. The crowd was mostly students, the youngest congregation Michaels had ever seen. Many of the pretty girls had long straight hair and wore jeans. Some of the men were straight, but others had reassuringly freaky sideburns, beards, mustaches, long hair. Noisy for a church service—families again, babies and kids cooing or bellowing.

Michaels felt better. It was unlike any church he'd ever seen. The priest wore a kind of linen robe, but nothing fancy. And unlike the skinhead chaplain with his major's oak leaf and his cross-shaped insignia, the priest had long white hair and a pink, healthy face. His voice was worthy of a preacher, deep and resonant. He raised a brown pottery chalice.

"When supper was ended, he took the cup. Again he gave you thanks and praise, gave the cup to his disciples, and said: 'Take this all of you, and drink from it: This is the cup of my blood, the blood of the new and everlasting covenant. It will be shed for you and for all men so that your sins may be forgiven. Do this in memory of me.' "

The priest drank. Next to him a trio began singing a jazzed-up version of the Our Father. People stood and walked down the center aisle. The priest handed them pieces of dark bread. Mike was surprised. He remembered a chaplains' school instructor warning them never to touch a consecrated host, those white tasteless wafers in a perfect circle. Communion came at the end, so he wouldn't have long to wait. He went down the stairs and found a vacant space of wall.

More singing, guitar twanging while the string bass provided a deep repeated note. "Love one another, love one another as I have loved you. And care for each other, care for each other, as I have cared for you."

"Body of Christ," said the priest, and the communicant responded, "amen."

"Body of Christ." "Amen." "Body of Christ." "Amen . . ."

Warm down here. Mike had closed his eyes. Warm, and the presence of people was comforting: voices, feet shuffling, babies gooing. And the continual refrain, "Love one another, love one another as I have loved you." He was finally relaxing, the sounds fading into the darkness.

Blackness, growing colder now, and the wind's insidious murmur beginning. White body out there, beautiful dead woman with bloody holes in her chest. Closing in—she wants him. Ah, but she can't. Angela must be singing. Clever of her. A hand touched him.

He flinched wildly, eyes snapping open. Realizing where he was, the fear left his face. He smiled weakly, an expression far from his usual grin.

The man still held his arm. "Why don't you sit down if you're tired? There are still some chairs."

"I wasn't sleeping."

"I didn't say you were." Roundish, pleasant face with short hair and red-brown beard. "You can sit in back and sleep through the whole thing if you wish. Lord knows, there have been times when I've wanted to." Very blue eyes, crinkled at the corners from his smile. "You don't look like you feel so well. Go ahead and sit down."

Mike sighed and nodded. He sat on a rickety old chair between a man with a baby and a young girl. The guy who had spoken was short, plump, and wore an old green sweater with patches at the elbows. Still smiling, he walked toward the altar. He was older than most of these kids, probably about thirty-five.

Mike closed his eyes and felt himself drifting away. Chairs shuffling, noise. He opened his eyes and stood along with the others.

"Go in peace." The priest's hand cut through the air twice, making the sign of the cross over the people.

"Okay, everyone," the trio leader said, "we'll end with 'Great to be Alive' on page thirty-two."

Pages turned as everyone flipped through the blue binders, then they sang loudly about being alive and feeling free, about sunshine and the darkness vanishing. Almost in spite of himself, Mike felt a thrill of emotion along his spine. The song was corny, but the enthusiastic singing was impressive. He was used to a bunch of lifeless soldiers, men afraid of dying or so well trained they came to church mindlessly. He had sat playing the organ and grinning inside while the chaplain's voice thundered over the feeble murmurings. But these people sounded good, genuinely strong and alive. Here in this basement what they represented seemed invincible. But could it beat what was out at Blut Farm?

The song ended, and people began talking and shuffling toward the back. Michaels spoke to the man beside him. "Uh, is that Father Donahue up there?"

The man glanced at the white-haired priest. "No, that's Father Johnson. Pat's to the left of the stairs. There. In the green sweater."

Mike looked past the crowd, the people laughing and putting on coats, and saw the priest talking with two girls. Green sweater and red-brown beard.

"Uh, thanks."

Donahue stood with his back to Mike, staring out the tall window. Beside him the old-fashioned radiator hissed steam into the office and clanked once. He turned back to Michaels, who had sagged into an old leather chair.

"This isn't some kind of joke?"

"No."

Mike felt the priest's eyes search him, trying to decide whether to believe him. Donahue brought his fingertips down through the red-brown beard to his chin. "She's out there alone at the farmhouse?"

"Yes, with Blut and his friends. I didn't have a chance of getting in the house. The pigs and the dog would have ripped me to bits."

"Did you think of searching for someone in Udolph to help?"

Driving into Udolph at dawn, tired, the hearse low on gas, the pink glow of dawn on the snow. Pink like the blood smearing Angela's thighs. The town had been even gloomier in the daylight, boarded-up buildings and broken-down homes, deserted streets. He had parked the hearse by the ancient gray courthouse and sat listening to the heater blow warm air against his legs. Finally he stepped into the icy morning, walking quickly to the tall wooden doors. Inside was a dim hallway with a high ceiling and an old hunchback in overalls monotonously mopping at the same spot of floor. Mike had to ask about the police several times before the hunchback showed any trace of comprehension. Flat, expressionless green eyes, something like Renwick's. He pointed and said, "Nex' door." The face was all pushed in, his hair white. He stuck the mop in the dirty gray water, then resumed pushing it around, hunched over the handle.

Feeling more and more uncomfortable, Mike had walked outside and crossed an alley, and then he saw the black Volkswagen bus. Parked right beside the black-and-white police car. Painted in red on the side was a strange emblem. A black bus had nearly run him off the road the night before. He felt a fresh chill slither up his back. Last night he had not trusted his fearful feelings. He was wiser now. He ran back to the hearse, heart throbbing, his breath making clouds of vapor.

"Things in Udolph convinced me to get away from there. The whole place gives off bad vibrations, the whole area for about a twenty-mile radius. Cold and ugly and dead. It makes sense, really. Blut must have some kind of control, or they would have driven him away long ago."

"Isn't much of what you say guesswork?"

"Yes, goddammit, but if you'd been in Udolph, you'd believe it too. It follows if you accept that Blut is a vampire."

"I suppose you're right. Did you consider the highway patrol?"

Mike made an exasperated noise. "To begin with, they'd think I was crazy. Even if I could get

them out there, Blut could hide Angela and talk
them out of anything. Who are the cops going to
believe—a respectable doctor or a long-haired,
freaky type like me? And anyway, guns are no
good—I found that out."

"So she's alone out there in the farmhouse."

"Yes, and we have to get out there before
dusk."

"Why?"

"Because vampires sleep during the day. Don't
you know anything about vampires?"

"No, I'm afraid not."

"Haven't you seen any movies?"

"Not that I remember."

"Christ. This is going to be great, stumbling
around there when neither of us knows anything.
I hope Russo knows something."

"Oh, he does. I've met Tony. I remember him
asking me about exorcisms."

"Do you know anything about exorcisms or
satanism?"

"Practically nothing."

Mike closed his eyes and cursed silently.
Priests were supposed to know about this kind of
stuff. Donahue looked apologetic.

"You've got to understand, the Catholic church
doesn't like to emphasize these things, at least not
in this part of the world. I've worked in a hospital
and taught in high school, hardly places where I
would be involved in anything like this. Frankly,
I've never believed in a real devil. God has always
been enough of a problem in belief."

"I don't think Angela did either. Until last
night. Until he raped her."

The radiator clunked again, hissed. Michaels
sighed and closed his eyes. "I wouldn't blame

you for not believing me. You haven't seen that god-awful farm, out there alone with snow and cold blowing everywhere, and those black pigs watching you and black dogs . . . And you didn't have to kill anyone or . . . or anything. You didn't see Angela after he was finished with her . . ." His voice grew hoarse, and he had to stop.

"I believe you," the priest said.

Mike opened his eyes, and the two men stared at each other. Closer up Mike noticed creases in the forehead, lines under the eyes, gray hairs mixed in with the brown, all of which pushed the priest's age closer to forty. His eyes were dark blue, the same color as Angela's, and right now they were equally sympathetic.

"Thank you," Mike murmured.

"Angela . . . she means a great deal to you?" Mike nodded, suddenly edgy.

"I . . . she is a very special person for me. I owe her more than I can ever repay." Now the priest would not look at him.

Mike wondered again about him and Angela. He thought of her body last night, those long arms and legs curling about him, gripping tightly, the small breasts, the creamy brown color of her skin. He thought of the same body curling around the priest. She must be taller than Donahue—but come on, what did that matter? The priest looked spongy about the waist, but then his own beer gut was hardly pure muscle. Still, his arms were strong. Strong enough to pulverize the priest if he wanted. Christ—stop that crap.

The silence grew uncomfortable. Pat finally said, "I will do all I can to help you."

"Thanks. I'll need all the help I can get."

"You look very tired. You can rest here if you wish."

"I'd like to, but I have a lot to do first."

"Would you like a cup of coffee before you leave?"

He smiled wearily. "No coffee—I'm hyper enough as it is."

"I don't usually offer anything stronger this early, but in your case I could make an exception."

"You're tempting me."

"I remember that being someone else's job."

"Thanks anyway." Mike sat up. "I'd better find Tony Russo. You don't happen to know where he'd be?"

"He has an office in the English Philosophy Building on the first floor. I'm sure he'd be there. He told me he did some of his best work Sunday mornings, although he refused to attribute this to divine intervention. Do you know where EPB is?"

"Yeah, I can find him easily enough." Mike stood and watched the room go gray, shimmery swirling gray. He was tired and had stood up too fast. He extended his hand and watched the priest's face come back into focus. "Thanks again."

"I wish I could do more." Donahue's grip was respectable.

"Well, if you know any good prayers that might work, I'm willing to try anything."

"I was never very good at prayers." The priest sighed. "Michael Michaels. There was an arch-angel named Michael. He fought rather well during the battle in heaven. He drove Satan and his angels into hell."

"No way am I the warrior type, angel or otherwise. We could use an archangel, though."

"Yes, we surely could." The priest pulled thoughtfully at his beard. "I always thought angels were mythical beings. Demons too."

"I wish that whole damned farm was a big myth, but it isn't."

"Call whenever you're ready to leave. You can use the Center East number. I'll wait here until I hear from you."

Mike started to go, then stopped. "Uh, do most people call you Father Donahue or . . ."

"No. Most people call me Pat."

"Good enough. I'll let you know when I'm ready to leave."

Dracula leaned forward, arms spread, his hands with their long pointed fingernails dangling from the wrists, a broad smile on his face. Lugosi wore the traditional white tie with tails and black cape. A different poster showed Dracula at the bottom of a stone staircase, his arms raised with cloak outspread, a giant bat form. Lugosi wasn't smiling in that one. His entranced, hypnotic look recalled a stunned cow. The Hollywood Hungarian just wasn't menacing. Perhaps if he had pale blue eyes. Fear breathed on the back of Michaels's neck.

Close by, the Wolfman glared down at you, and Frankenstein stood dumbly bound in his tight black coat with the sleeves that were too short for his long, stiffened arms. The mummy's wizened face (the ultimate dry skin problem) gave you the evil eye. Lugosi and Karloff glared at each other across a chessboard, while a different mummy strangled somebody in a pith helmet. The *Dracula Has Risen from the Grave* poster showed the count's most recent avatar clawing his way out of his coffin, a stake in his chest and blood running from his mouth. Strangest of all was a skeletal figure standing before a ship's mast and rigging. Its alien head seemed a skull, and its hands were outstretched scythes, the nails a foot long.

"What the hell is that?"

Russo looked up. "That's from a silent film, *Nosferatu,* a German impressionist treatment of the vampire theme."

"Those nails are incredible."

"Yeah, he's cute." Russo smiled dryly. He sat at his desk by the window, his feet up on another desk. The window overlooked the Iowa River and was a sunny square of light and color set against a wall covered by black-and-white horror photography.

Michaels could see Russo as a vampire, the cinematic kind. He had long curly black hair and flared sideburns dropping almost to his jaw, but his skin was pale. His face was thin with high cheekbones, dark thick lips, and a cleft chin, clean shaven but with a blue-gray shadow. The black nylon turtleneck was another Gothic touch. However, the long, tall body was sprawled comfortably in a very unvampirelike pose, and his smile wiped away the sinister lines and made him appear almost childish.

"A real vampire. God, it's still hard to believe. Doctor Blut. He must have a sense of irony. 'Blut' means 'blood' in German, you know."

Michaels sat quietly, his eyes half-closed. Russo had had less trouble with the story than the priest.

"When you read up on vampires, naturally you begin to wonder whether they do exist. The accounts are so detailed, occur and recur in so many cultures. Even ancient Egypt. Maybe now all the unusual knowledge I've accumulated will finally come in handy—for something besides trivia bowls. In Iowa—my God, in Iowa. Do you know anything about Udolph?"

"I've never heard of it before."

"I have, I think." He walked to a filing cabinet. "I cut out articles on the occult, horror films, that type of thing, and file them. I think this was about two years ago. Let's try 1970." He sat down with a thick blue canvas binder and began turning pages. "Ah, here we go. Take a look."

Michaels took the binder. "Grisly Tale Unfolds in Small Town." Written above the headline in ink was "*Des Moines Register*, February 1, 1970." "Authorities have pieced together a horrifying story of witchcraft and sadism in the small Iowa community of Udolph. Events began with the discovery of the body of Nancy Klein, age 17, two weeks ago. An autopsy revealed that the girl had been sexually assaulted and tortured. The girl's fifteen-year-old brother, Thomas Klein, confessed last week to murdering his sister during initiation rites for a diabolical society. The boy claimed that the devil had appeared to his father. Police are still searching for Harold Klein, the father. Teachers and friends of the girl, a bright pretty junior at . . ."

"Christ," Michaels said.

"They never did catch the boy's father. There was obviously a whole community of devil worshippers in Udolph."

Michaels felt fear waking him from his drowsiness. "In Udolph, Iowa? I thought that kind of thing just went on in California or . . ."

"Oh, no." Russo shook his head, smiling dryly again. "They're all over. Iowa is crawling with witches."

"Oh, come on!"

"They're not all involved in black magic, but the dorms are full of witches. A student in my freshman comp class gave a report on local witchcraft. He found several covens in the dorm and talked with lots of witches. They considered themselves white witches and were only playing at it, making love charms, using it on tests, petty things. The white witches knew about covens of black witches, but they were scared to death of the real thing. He couldn't find any of the black witches."

"I don't think I'll ever feel very secure in Iowa again."

"Oh, it's everywhere." Russo rubbed at his chin. "You did say the town looked strange?"

"Yeah. Deserted. Weird. Not even a bar open anywhere on a Saturday night. Like I said, I knew I couldn't trust the cops there."

"Wise of you. The whole town must be under his influence. Blut probably . . . they either brought him back, or he made a deal or . . ." Russo noticed his confusion. "Vampirism spreads like a disease, but something has to start it. Blut sounds like the source, not a victim. Like Dracula. He was an evil warrior who made a deal with the dark powers. But anyone who dies after being bitten also becomes a vampire."

"Then Angela was right . . . about what would happen."

"Yes, I'm afraid so. Luckily she knows a fair amount about vampires."

"She did put the cross on."

"That should help. *If* she can keep it on. Blut will do everything in his power to make her take it off. And if he has drunk her blood, she may find it impossible to resist. You're right—we must be there before dark. She's safe until then, as safe as she can be in that house. Vampires are dormant, immobile, during daylight."

"What are we going to do when we get to the house?"

"Destroy Blut."

Michaels stared at him. "Just like that? How? With a wooden stake?"

"That's one way. It can be risky if you do it wrong. Burning the body afterward is the best way to make sure."

"Don't they like fire? If he's a demon . . ."

"Oh, but he's not a demon. A vampire is no ghost or devil, even though they work with the other evil forces. A vampire is nothing but a corpse. Above all else, he is a corpse, a dead body that maintains a semblance of life by drinking living blood—but only a semblance of life. He's really dead, and the body will look and smell dead."

"God, the whole house stank."

"It fits. And sunlight on the woman vampire reactivated the process of decay and finished the dissolution. A really ancient vampire would probably flame up like a dried-up old log."

"So if we catch Blut . . ."

"In *Dracula* they recommend driving a stake

through the heart, cutting off the head, and stuffing it with garlic."

Mike burst into laughter with an undercurrent of hysteria. "Come on!"

Tony shook his head. "I'm not joking. That's how it's done, according to the ancient lore."

"Garlic? Why garlic?"

"Vampires are supposed to be repelled by garlic. And crucifixes—as you saw—and especially the host."

"The what?"

"The host, the consecrated host. The body of Christ from the mass. Pat can help us there. Maybe he knows something about satanism."

"No, he doesn't."

Russo smiled. "Ah yes, that's right. Still, I'll talk to him. We should bring along all the precautions we can."

Mike frowned slightly. The memory of last night was very near, and all of this ... this folklore sounded ridiculous. He could not see that thing he had stabbed and shot fleeing from a clove of garlic. "Do you really think these things will work?"

Tony grew thoughtful and stared out at the river. "I really don't know."

Michaels chewed at his lip. "If they don't, we're going to be in trouble. Really hairy trouble."

Russo scratched the cleft in his chin. "Well, we have no other choice. The Christian paraphernalia seems to have worked for you, but there are no guarantees. If they don't, I can't think what will."

"Guns are useless. I found that out."

"Still, it might be advisable to go armed. Blut does have his human helpers. I can borrow a couple of guns and get you some ammunition for your .45"

"God, I hate guns. They for sure won't hurt Blut, and I doubt they'll work on the dog. Maybe the pigs. What were those pigs and dogs, anyway? Ursula changed into a dog—I told you that, didn't I?"

"Yes. Did you see Ursula and Blut together along with the dog?"

"Yeah. Manfred, they called him."

Russo smiled. "How appropriate. Well, Manfred could be another vampire, or he could be a demon in dog form, or even a real dog. My guess would be that he is a demon, some evil spirit in animal form. Maybe the pigs are, too. You did say they were, uh, disturbing?"

"God, yes. Weird like the whole farm. How about the dog that hit the hearse?"

"I'd guess that was Blut. He was probably checking on you, and he did make you stop to find Renwick."

"That fucker—he had everything planned. Can he turn into a dog whenever he feels like it?"

"Yes. Or a wolf, a bat, an insect, a snake—even a mist, a kind of smoky cloud. That's why it's virtually impossible to trap a vampire at night. And they're strong, inhumanly strong, as you found out."

"But why did he want me there in the first place? Why the business with his brother?"

Russo stroked his chin. "You did see the coffin?"

"I'll say. It looked indestructible, solid steel with the name Blut on it."

"You must know by now that it's his *own* coffin."

"But why did he want to go to Chicago?"

Russo thought for a moment, his face twitched, and he gave a sudden sharp laugh. "No—no— that would be too close."

"What are you talking about?"

"Dracula in the novel wants to go to London. For new blood. A whole city teeming with unsuspecting victims."

"Hell, why not just fly there?—why hire me to—"

"Because he must return to his native soil during the day, some earth sprinkled in his coffin. Or coffins."

Michaels felt the chills starting again. That had to be it. Blut wanted to go to Chicago. Everything last night had been oh-so-carefully thought out. Except one small detail. His hands began to tremble. He tried to speak calmly.

"Just one thing. Why did he let me go?"

Russo frowned thoughtfully.

"He could have stopped me—killed me easily—any time before dawn. Why, for Christ's sake, did he let me go?"

Russo thought for a long while, then uncrossed his legs. "I don't know." The two men stared at each other. Russo stood. "Well, I'll call, and round up a few things, and talk to Pat. I should be ready to leave in a couple of hours, around two. You'll call me?"

"Yeah." Michaels sat slumped in the chair, thinking. The whole business was incomprehensible, horrible, and he was exhausted. "We might as well take the hearse. It's about a two-hour drive."

"You look like you could use some sleep, even an hour or two." Russo began flipping through the pages of the phone book. "Just don't forget to set the alarm. We need you to show us the way, and sunset is around six, six-thirty."

"I don't know if I can sleep. I'd like to." He stared at his knees, then looked up at Bela Lugosi. Garlic, crucifixes, hosts, a stake in the heart might work on him, but Blut and that farm were something else. "Tony, do you believe in God?"

He looked up from the phone book. "No. Not really."

"Me, neither. But I believe in vampires, in the devil, in evil—how can I believe in all these and not the other?"

"Oh, it's easy to believe in evil. Only a fool can pretend it doesn't exist. But whether a horned devil is responsible or other malevolent beings beyond our ordinary dimensions of existence doesn't really matter much."

"It does if you want some help, if you want to believe garlic will scare them off. I can't see it. I wonder if we can really fight them. How can he lose? How can he possibly lose?"

"Oh, there must be some force that repels them, something stronger."

"I hope so. Oh God, I hope so."

He stood groggily. Angela believed in God. There wasn't much evidence of God out at Blut Farm. He blinked, stared again at the vampires, mummies, and werewolves. Tony had jotted down some numbers from the phone book.

"Can I see that?"

Russo handed the book to him. Mike flipped through the pages to the Rs: Rosalba, Angela: 632 E. Bloomington, 351–7204. He stared at her name and thought about her. He felt himself getting tearful. He wished he could dial the number and talk to her. She lived only about four blocks from his place. He could walk by there on the way home.

Tony paused before dialing a number. "Are you okay?"

Mike closed the book. "Yeah. I'll call you."

"Don't worry—we'll get her out of there."

Oh, sure they would. He left the room with its black-and-white play monsters, hearing Russo ask someone about borrowing a pistol. The voice dwindled to nothing as he walked away.

Over the doorway were black metal numbers, 632. The house was one of many old homes in Iowa City, pseudo-Victorian with a tower, a big front porch, and tall windows. The place badly needed a paint job. The white had blotched gray or brown, peeled and blistered as if attacked by some strange disease. Overhead the black, pointed roofs sprouted T.V. antennae, and these antennae, befitting their name, were insectlike. On either side of the yard stood a stump six feet wide. The trees would have been victims of Dutch elm disease. Without them, the house seemed incomplete, an amputee.

Pretty rundown, Michaels thought. The sun felt warm on his face. It was at its highest point. Not a bad day for February, especially after last night.

The electric sign over the bank had flashed 34, then 11:27. Vaguely hungry, he'd stopped at Green Cross and bought two Almond Joys. The girl at the counter was a short, pretty blond Michaels had noticed before. She smiled and rang up twenty-one cents. Everything was so matter of fact, so terribly normal. But even now, in broad daylight, last night was very real.

He blinked again, realized he was on the point of falling asleep. The fear from the night remained, but he was exhausted enough that he hardly cared. The Almond Joys had been less than joyful and now sat in his stomach, smoldering.

Something was staring at him. Christ—pale blue eyes. It was only a cat. The big white cat jumped up on the porch railing and sank into a sphinx position to watch him. Michaels walked up the cracked, overgrown walkway to the porch. The cat had round blue eyes with thin black slits.

"Nice cat." He extended a gloved hand.

The cat hissed sharply, flattening its ears. It jumped off the railing and flowed away.

"Stupid cat." He glanced at the four brass mailboxes. On the one numbered 2 were the names Angela Rosalba and Diana Hawkins. Who was Diana Hawkins? Angela had said nothing about a roommate.

Something else was staring. The front door opened, and a tall girl stepped outside. Her blond hair was streaked with brown and cut in a long shag that just touched her red sweater. Above the gray-green eyes were pencil-thin eyebrows. Her face was narrow but attractive, the slight curve of the nose adding to her elegance. "Can I help you find someone?" She had a deep voice for a woman.

"Uh . . ." Michaels blinked. The woman looked like an apparition from *Vogue.* Over her eyes the skin was bluish green, and her lips were pale pink. Goddamn—Sunday morning, and she already had on lipstick and eye shadow. "I know someone here . . . Angela . . . and . . ."

"Oh—have you seen Angela? She's my roommate, and I've been worried sick. Do you know where she is?"

"Well . . . yes." He was too tired to pretend.

"Is she all right?"

"For now."

"Have you got a minute so you could come in and tell me about it?"

"Uh . . ."

"One second." She held open the door and called, "Here, Salome, here, Salome. Come on, kitty." The cat ran back up the stairs, a white blur that oozed around their ankles and vanished into the house. "I only wanted to get my cat. Come on in."

Michaels stepped into the small entranceway. The walnut door with a gold 2, the number twisted, was ajar. He followed her down a long steep stairway into the basement, dim and cavernous with a worn rug and old furniture. The floor around the edges looked like painted concrete, and the ceiling was so low he would have banged his head if he were even an inch taller. It smelled of cat shit and some antiseptic, perfumy odor, an awful combination. He noticed the litter box in the corner. He sagged down into an ancient stuffed chair that looked deceptively comfortable. A spring immediately gouged him in the back, and he squirmed about.

The girl kicked off her shoes and sat on the couch. "What about Angela?"

"She's in trouble?"

"Bad?"

"Uh . . . yeah."

"What is it?"

"Well . . . how long have you two been room-mates?"

"Two years."

"So you know her pretty well?"

"Yes, I think I do."

Mike could tell nothing from those green eyes. They were as expressionless as eyes in an ad for eye shadow, beautiful eyes in a beautiful face and nothing more. Angela had said nothing about a roommate. Find Tony and Pat, that was all. Had she deliberately left out Diana?

"What is it? What's happened?" Her pink lips formed a moue. "Please—tell me."

He was too tired to be very evasive. "You'd probably think I was crazy."

"Tell me and then see."

"Uh, do you believe in . . . oh, witches?" An easier place to start.

"Of course." Profound conviction.

"Oh. You do. Well, I picked up Angela, and we had to stop at a farm, and . . . something evil has her."

"A warlock?"

"No. Uh, oh hell—a vampire."

"A *vampire*." Her long lashes went farther apart, revealing the gray-green circles. She swallowed, and he saw the movement in her long, white throat. He wished he'd kept his mouth shut. The cat—she—it was staring. Crouched on the end table, white paws before her, white face sprouting long white and black whiskers, pale blue eyes with the black slits swollen to circles in the dim basement. "What are you going to do?"

"I'm going back there with two of her friends and try to get her out."

"I must come."

Mike blinked. "You're kidding?"

"Not at all."

"Oh no, listen—it's going to be super-dangerous out there, see? Very easy to get killed. This is no game—none of the nice, simple vampires like at the flicks. They play for keeps out there. One nearly killed me, and I—I had to destroy it."

"I'm not afraid. I've had some self-defense, and I can take care of myself. You don't need to worry about me. Besides, I'm very interested in the occult."

"No. Listen—I'm worried enough about myself. This is no gag, no sightseeing trip. I'd be more than happy to stay here myself if Angela weren't out there."

"You must let me come. Who else is coming?"

"Tony Russo and Pat Donahue." Did the priest's name bother her?

"I've met them both. Excellent choices. You have to let me come—what's your name?"

"Mike. Mike Michaels."

"I'm Diana Hawkins. Well, Mike, I simply must come. This is the chance of a lifetime."

Michaels sighed. "It's also a good way to shorten your lifetime."

"When are you leaving?"

"This afternoon."

"Good. I can definitely come."

Mike closed his eyes, tired of the girl and the cat staring at him. He squirmed in the chair and put his hands in his pockets. God, it was cold down here. He was glad he hadn't unzipped his field jacket. No wonder she had on that heavy red sweater. Something made a noise on the chair arm, and he opened his eyes.

God, what a monster—the cat must weigh fifteen pounds, but then she was super-furry, probably a Persian. Her face had the pushed-in look common to longhairs, as if someone had smashed in her nose. She was an immaculate white, color showing only in her blue eyes, pink nose, and a few black whiskers.

"I think Salome likes you. You'll let me come, won't you, Mike?"

"*No.*"

She sighed and began to undo the gold buttons to her sweater, the long cardigan of bright red wool. "Please, Mike, I must come." Taking off the sweater, she drew her bare feet up onto the sofa and wrapped her arms around her legs. "I've always known something like this would happen to me. I've always had strange visions, premonitions. Once I dreamed a friend of mine was calling to me, begging me to help her. I found out later she had fallen down some stairs and lain for hours with her back broken. I dreamed my grandmother came to say good-bye. The next morning they told me she had died in her sleep. And now I've been dreaming of Angela. I dreamed she was begging me for help. You must let me come."

Michaels chewed at his lip. He was a sucker for weird, scary stories like that. The girl's bare arms were slim, almost muscular. Her hands came together over her feet, blue veins trickling through them, long white fingers and long white toes. A glossy pink polish covered her toenails and fingernails. He glanced at her gray-green eyes.

"You'd be crazy to come," he said. "I'm crazy to go."

"I know it will be dangerous, but I can help, really. And I'm not squeamish. I'm in premed, and I've seen dead bodies before. I can fire a pistol." Her voice had a velvety eagerness.

In spite of himself, he was impressed. But he still didn't want her along.

"Let me come—for Angela's sake. She would want me there—I know she would. She's my roommate . . . and my friend, and she means a lot to me. Please let me come. For Angela." Now she was getting tearful.

He teetered, slipped. "Oh, well, let's see what Pat and Tony say."

"Oh—*great*. Thank you—thank you so much."

He was immediately sorry, but too tired to resist. If she really were Angela's friend. . . But then why hadn't Angela said something about her? *Why?* He squirmed in the chair.

"Mike, let me get you some coffee. You look so tired. And then you can tell me more about what happened."

"Okay, I guess I could use some."

She rose noiselessly and left. Christ, she even walked like a model. Somehow he couldn't see her and Angela . . . They seemed so different. The white Persian watched him carefully.

"Nice kitty." He scratched at her throat fur, but she seemed unimpressed. Mike liked alley cats but had always considered Persians rather silly, and their pushed-in faces ugly. Perhaps the cat sensed it. The blue orbs seemed cold, withdrawn into their distant cat world.

Something landed in his lap—the cat curled about his legs. Heavy son of a bitch. The loud steady purr rose and fell evenly. "Nice cat, you're not so bad after all." He petted her, but the constant purr seemed indifferent to his action.

He closed his eyes. "*UHHHuhrrUHHRHH-uhrr,*" like a lullaby in a beehive. Darkness. God, it was chilly down here, and damp, the bare concrete full of moisture. A groan and a clunk behind the wall as the furnace came alive. Now the wind begins again, swirling around the hearse, howling to break in, to get at them. Angela hugged and held him, while—swish, swish went the wipers, snowflakes rushing at the hearse through yellow beams. The lights caught a naked woman shaped from marble, snarling, pale blue eyes burning, and she spouted blood from her breasts, splattering the windshield with red. Christ, he couldn't see—he swerved out of control as she leaped at him, shrieking, clawing, ripping at his throat—red everywhere . . .

"Mike?"

He jerked violently and cried out as the cat departed his lap in a flurry of claws. Diana held a brown mug, and the steaming coffee gave off a rich, strong odor.

"What's wrong?"

"Oh . . . nothing. I fell asleep. Mild nightmares." He sipped the coffee. The taste was rather exotic. "Hey, this is good."

"It's Turkish, from a deli in Chicago. Are you hungry?"

He shook his head and drank more coffee. If that brief, living technicolor dream was a foretaste, he would rather stay awake. He didn't usually dream in color. Diana's bare feet were up on the edge of the sofa again. She sipped her coffee.

"What was it like out there at the farm?"

"Horrible. There aren't any other farms around, and it's cold and horrible."

"Is he alone out there?"

"No. There's a drug freak. And a bunch of hogs and a dog."

"Pigs?" She laughed.

"Where are you from?"

"Huh? Chicago. The suburbs."

"If you'd ever been around hogs you wouldn't laugh. They can easily kill a man. And these probably aren't ordinary animals. Did you ever read the part in the New Testament where Christ drove the demons out of man into a herd of swine? Then they all jumped off a cliff. I wish these pigs would do that."

"Then you think the devil is involved?"

"Yeah. Whatever you want to call it." His hands shook slightly as he sipped his coffee.

Her gray-green eyes seemed to have grown. "How exciting."

He made a short harsh "ha." "Exciting. I can do without that kind of excitement. Listen, this isn't any harmless Hollywood vampire or the kind of devil with horns and pitchfork. The things—whatever they are—are dangerous. And evil, terribly evil."

"Yes, I know you're right. It's just that, well, I've always been so interested in the occult and other ESP things." Michaels watched in drowsy fascination as her toes gripped at the sofa cushions. Such long toes, the second longest of all, with big knuckles so they looked more like fingers. The pink polish made her nails like glossy inlaid shells. "Did you say you killed one of the vampires?"

"Yes."

"How many are there?"

"I think, I hope, there's only one left."

"How did you kill him?"

"Her. It was a her."

"A woman? A woman vampire? How did you kill her?"

"Actually the sun killed her."

"How did she get in the sun?"

"I stuck her with a pitchfork and pushed her there—listen, I'd rather not go into it."

"Oh, I'm really sorry. I should have . . . really, I am sorry."

"That's okay." Again he found something about her vaguely offensive.

"It's just that I've never heard of a woman vampire before."

"From what Tony said I gather they're quite common."

She laughed, a tinkly sound. "Maybe there are some on campus."

"I doubt it. They have to return to their coffins during the day. They're helpless then."

She nodded and took a slow sip of coffee. He saw the motion in the long white expanse of her throat. She brushed a blond strand from her face and stared at him. God, she was beautiful, all that curling blond hair, the aquiline nose and big green eyes. He kept staring at her feet and hands. Somehow she attracted and repulsed him simultaneously. The repulsion came from the artificial aura, the creature from *Vogue* too special to touch.

With a single leap the cat returned to the chair arm and stared warily at Michaels. "This cat is a little weird."

"That's just the way she is. She's a silly Salome. Aren't you a silly Salome? Silly baby." The pink mouth made a kissing noise. Michaels could see a rosy stain on the white cup.

"Crazy cat," he mumbled. She jumped onto his lap, and he began petting her again. "She's certainly big enough."

"Eight months. She's only a kitten."

"Eight months? Christ, she's big as any tom. She must be something when she's in heat."

"Oh, she hasn't been in heat yet. She doesn't like males. You should see her go at the toms. They stay away from her."

"Well, one of these days she'll come around. Feline biology and all."

"I don't know about that. I have a feeling she never will." She sounded adamant.

Mike ruffled the cat's throat. "Hear that, Virgin Queen? Someday . . ." He yawned. The cat watched, its blue eyes unwavering. Green eyes were still staring, too.

"You look like you need more coffee or a nap."

"Oh. Yeah. Better be the coffee."

She stood. "I'll see if there's any left."

"Okay." He leaned back against the chair and closed his eyes. One hand was in his pocket, the other stroked the cat. No naps. He'd never get back out there in time. Twelvish now. Have to leave at two or three at the latest, take along this screwy girl so different from Angela. He tried to visualize Angela's face, but the purring distracted him. God, he was tired. But the nightmares. He had to have some rest, just close his eyes. He could tell Diana to wake him in an hour—if he could sleep in this icebox. Don't fall asleep, just rest a little.

How dark it was. The cat suddenly stopped purring, jumped down, and hissed at him, back arched, tail fluffing out as if an electric current were going through it. What a big cat, even bigger puffed up, expanding white thing of fur showing claws and teeth, pale blue eyes. Oh Christ—the eyes were changing and becoming more human. The pupils still had black slits—not human eyes—Blut's or Ursula's. The cat *was* Ursula. Marble woman with a corona of fire coming at him.

He tried to run up the stairs, but they were gone. Of course, at Blood Farm the stairs go *down*. He must find the stairs going down. And Angela—where was she?

Too late—he had waited too long. Ursula tripped him and leaped onto him. They wrestled. God, she was strong. She was naked. Her hands were hard like honed steel. The fingers tore, and he screamed, knowing he was doomed. He was also naked. With a swipe she ripped away everything between his legs. He screamed and screamed as she weasled her face over the wound and sucked greedily.

He wrenched around in the chair, realizing this was a dream. Wake up for God's sake. Like a drowning man he thrashed wildly, fighting for the surface, but he felt himself sink into the black depths.

"Here's your coffee." Smiling, Diana handed him the cup.

He ignored his dry mouth and the taste of the nightmare. The cat still sat purring on his lap.

He sipped the strong coffee, his hand trembling.

Diana popped open the snap of her jeans, undid the zipper, and let them collapse about her ankles. She stepped away from the wadded-up denim. Her legs were long, slim and firm like her arms. Smiling, she slipped the panties down. The thatch of brown hair was darker than her brown-blond curls. Nervously he continued to sip his coffee. Something strange happening here. She sat down on the couch, spreading her legs. He tried not to stare.

Suddenly he gagged, spitting madly, and hurled the coffee cup away. Oh *Christ*—still on his hand—the white tarantula thing clinging to the knuckles! He couldn't get it out of his mouth—he spit out half, but the rest crawled around inside his mouth—he could feel the hairy legs, taste them. He spit—retched—nothing would get it out.

Diana let her head fall back, and she laughed. Demurely she brought her knees together.

How—for God's sake—would he get the thing out of his mouth?

Wake up—please wake up!

No, he was sinking deeper. *Why?* You're supposed to wake up after nightmares—you have to—you're not supposed to be trapped.

RUHHRuhrrUHHRRuhrhh . . .

The cat, it was still going. Or was that the wind? It was the wind. He and Angela were in bed, warmth radiating from her, warming his chest and back, seeping into him. Warm and safe and indoors.

"Oh, Angela."

She stared at him, dark and beautiful with

black waves lapping gently against the beach
that was her face. She offered a refuge from the
nightmare, but her eyes were sad.

"Don't be sad."

He kissed her, and she responded slowly. Her
face and throat flushed as she became aroused,
and they writhed about each other breathing
hard. What if—if he couldn't? But she used her
hand to guide him in. He sighed softly and then
screamed, caught in an icy vise. Oh Lord—the
pain—crushing him, and the cold spreading
from his groin like frozen poison. Her fingers bit
into his back, drawing blood, and the black hair
fell away from her throat and revealed the ugly
wounds. Her dark lips parted, and he could see
the fangs—Ursula's teeth. An icy stench came
from her mouth.

"Please—you're hurting me!"

The wind howled, breaking in the windows,
covering them with snow, and out of the
whirlwind a giant snake formed. It towered
over them and smashed through the ceiling, a
cobra of ice. The pale blue serpent eyes glowed
with satisfaction.

Mike screamed again, screamed, screamed,
but nothing came out. Only Angela's eyes remained unchanged. I'm sorry, Mike. I'm sorry.
She tore open his throat and drank.

RUHHrruhrrRUHHRrr . . . went Blut.

Went the cat, only the stupid white cat, so why
not wake up? But his struggles drove him deeper
than ever before into the darkness, and the
nightmares went on until he was too weary to
dream.

Quiet. It's so quiet. The noise had stopped.

He opened his eyes. The cat regarded him from

the floor, and Diana sat on the couch reading a
magazine. She looked up and smiled.

"Feel better?"

"God." Despite a dry throat and mouth, a
sticky goo covered his lips. "I . . . Oh Christ, it's
good to be awake. What time is it?"

"Four-thirty."

"*Four-thirty!*" He leaped to his feet, making
the cat run into the other room. "Four-thirty!"

"Yes." She attempted to smile.

"Oh *goddammit—Jesus Christ.*" The fury
brought tears to his eyes. "Why the hell didn't
you wake me up?"

"You didn't say anything, and you looked so
peaceful asleep. I thought . . ."

"You fucking idiot! We should have left hours
ago—we'll never get there before sunset!"

"I'm sorry, Mike, you only said we'd leave this
afternoon, and I didn't know when. I was going
to wake you up soon, honest." Tears gathered in
her gray-green eyes.

"Look, I'm sorry—it just caught me by surprise, see? It was just important we get there
before sunset."

"Isn't there still time?"

"No. Get ready to leave. Where's the phone?"
She pointed out the phone and left the room.

Russo and Donahue must think he was out of
his mind. No time now to try to talk to his uncle,
to explain anything—load up and get the hell
out of here.

The road crews had worked all day to clear
Interstate 80. Only a slight spotty coating of
snow remained, and in the plowed lane cars had
worn two black strips through the snow. Along-

side the highway the fields rose and fell, vast expanses of snow sloping away to the horizon. The hearse had passed two snowplows.

Mike knew he was driving too fast. The visors were down, blocking off the pink-orange light of the setting sun. They were headed due west. Pat was beside him. Mike had put up the seats in back, and Diana and Tony sat there. Next to Tony was a leather bag full of equipment.

As they neared the Smithsville exit the wavery red disk slid beneath the horizon. Red-orange highlights shone on the black hood, the bloody glimmer cast by the dying sun. Slowly the wind began. It raised steaming clouds from the tall snowbanks along the road. Michaels cursed silently. He had known they were not going to make it by sunset, but that did not help now.

He remembered seeing the green-and-white Smithsville exit sign last night as he came from the other direction. Angela had been where the priest was, lying there asleep. He had almost gone straight on through to Iowa City. Oh dear God, if only he had—if only he had. He slowed down to take the curving off-ramp and soon pointed the hearse north.

Ahead the sky was dark blue fading into black, while to the left pink seeped from the heavens like life. Clouds massed in the north. Day, sunlight, Iowa City had become illusions. Night had returned.

PART II

Prologue to Part II

I found a dimpled spider, fat and white,
On a white heal-all, holding up a moth
Like a white piece of rigid satin cloth—
Assorted characters of death and blight
Mixed ready to begin the morning right,
Like the ingredients of a witches broth—
A snow-drop spider, a flower like a froth,
And dead wings carried like a paper kite.

What had that flower to do with being white,
The wayside blue and innocent heal-all?
What brought the kindred spider to that height,
Then steered the white moth thither in the night?
What but design of darkness to appall?—
If design govern in a thing so small.

                    —Robert Frost, "Design"

BLUT LAY WITHIN his steel cocoon. Darkness enshrouded him. The worm of death slept, awaiting his metamorphosis into the ravenous night moth. Continually reborn, this eerie phoenix was loosed on the world with an insatiable hunger.

Under him, above him, satiny fabric enclosed his dormant form as spun silk sheathed a larva; but rough particles disturbed the satin surfaces, grains of dirt from his native soil. The body lay motionless and silent. His heart did not beat; the lungs were still; what blood there was lay inert in the veins and arteries; also absent was the electrical complexity of millions of neurons firing over synapses. This was a stillness and silence only the dead attained. Yet thoughts drifted through the strange dark brain, wispy breaths of torn cobweb. His eyes were open and could see into the casket's night.

They were coming, he knew. The design of darkness, ingeniously patterned, the darkness controlling all. His mind wandered over Blood Farm, sniffing about like a black ferret. Tortured presences trapped in pig forms, wallowing in the shells of hogs, oh laughable torment—and one larger, more evil, shaped like a dog. Closer by, in this room near the coffin, was Angela, snared in the nightmares he created from the darkness within them both. Before the night had ended she would embrace the evil center.

Something inside the corpse quickened. Heart and lungs remained dead, but a perverse mockery of life animated Blut. As the power of movement came his lips formed a smile.

Night. Ah, night. He felt the power of night growing, spreading, bringing cold and darkness while the sun fled in terror. The icy blue of dusk shimmered on the snow, replacing the yellow tint of day, and the wind stirred eagerly.

He pressed a small stud in the coffin side, then extended his hand, palm first, and easily raised the lid. Two normal men would strain to open the casket. Michaels was correct about its value. The coffin was uniquely constructed, the sides six inches of steel alloy, an indestructible fortress more secure than most safes.

Blut rose, clenched his fists and felt a terrible strength permeate his dead body. Nothing could defeat him at night—*nothing*. Even during daylight the task would be most difficult, but at night it became truly impossible.

Inherently far more intelligent than most mortals, his long life in death had brought even greater knowledge. The centuries gave him an added edge, an inhuman cleverness. Human psychology and human minds had become ridiculously predictable, their baseness blatantly obvious. Rooted in sin, they played at the corruption he had embraced, and their ideals were a joke. He understood the controlling force in the universe—evil, death, chaos, greed, selfishness, Satan—all were aspects of the same thing, the unity which he served.

He stared at Angela. She sat in the red chair, sagged sideways, her head against the arm, black hair hiding her face. She moaned, shivering as he shaped dreams of violence and death. Blut smiled. He could finish her now, but he preferred to wait. The bloody rites of initiation would truly bring her into the fold, give her memories for an eternity. An appropriate punishment for so innately sinful a nature, for a fornicator who delighted in her

sensuality. When he finished ... And tonight
would be a night of great feasting, a night of
blood.

Angela groaned and turned her head, revealing
her face, the dark curving lips and Aphrodite
nose. Blut turned away. Her beauty disgusted
him. It would be better when she was dead.

His mouth moved woodenly, forming a rigid
smile. His eyes were blue-white fire. He saw the
outcome, bringing the vision of death alive inside
his dark brain. Michaels would bleed to death—
die, truly die. He was not worthy of the gift Blut
would give Angela and the priest. Blut would
again drink from Angela's throat, momentarily
satisfying his eternal thirst as he sucked forth
her young warm blood, this time draining all—
leaving the vessel cold and empty.

Angela moaned again.

"Rest, Angela, rest." His voice had a cloying
sweetness, honey laid out for flies. "Rest. You
will need all your energy for later." But the cold
fingers of his mind made rest impossible.

Now to arrange a spectacular welcome for his
guests, perhaps a trifle overtheatrical but spectacular all the same. He stepped to the window
and yanked it up all the way. Wind brushed
aside the scarlet curtains and screamed into the
room, scattering icy skimmings from the
snow-covered fields. Overhead clouds gathered
as the sky darkened. All color, the last pink flush,
had died in the west.

Blut stretched forth his arms and let his head
fall back, white talons clutching for the heavens.
The wind went insane, and blackness coalesced
around him as he called down the evil essence.
He felt his dead limbs melt, white face blurring

gray, his form whirling away. The night moth metamorphosed again, transition through nothingness. The gray smoke fell to the floor, outlining a new shape and growing darker.

The dog thing was huge, its coat far too black, an unearthly sable. The amber eyes stared at Angela, then the creature turned and glided across the threshold into the night. Like Milton's Satan, the black planet shot through the void toward a rendezvous with death and destruction.

CHAPTER SEVEN

ENOUGH LIGHT REMAINED in the west so that Mike could see the clouds gathering ahead. Despite his lack of sleep he didn't feel tired. He was too awake, hyper, one big nerve. He hadn't felt like this since the bad times in Vietnam. Next to him Pat stared ahead vacantly, not seeing the landscape. In back Diana hummed a strange tune. *Humming.* She and Russo acted like they were going on a picnic, fried chicken at Blood Farm. Russo read with a flashlight. Mike felt better with him along, but for a graduate student he sometimes seemed immature.

"I don't like that sky up ahead."

Mike glanced at the priest. "Me neither. I keep wondering what Blut has planned."

Diana leaned against the front seat. "How long before we get there?"

"About an hour. If things go smoothly."

"Do you think *he* will be waiting?"

"Shit, yes."

"What do you think he'll do to us?"

"Christ—how should I know?" Her questions seemed so incredibly stupid.

She turned to the priest. "Do you have some good prayers ready, Father?"

"Of course. I've memorized a lengthy Latin invocation against demons." He continued to stare out the window.

"Are demons scared of Latin?"

"Certainly."

"Weren't you supposed to say five o'clock mass? I remember that always being your time."

"That was last year."

"Last year? Has it been that long? Maybe I should try to get in a fast confession. Well, I'm glad you're along. Priests are nice to have around when you're threatened by vampires. But then you and Angela have always been close, haven't you?"

Donahue said nothing for several seconds, and Mike's suspicions about him and Angela came back.

"Angela is a friend, a very good friend. But I'm surprised you could find the time, Diana. Angela told me you'd been very busy with some new interests since you stopped coming to church."

"Things change, Father." She slid her elbows off the front seat and asked Russo what he was reading.

Mike chewed at his lip, staring out the window. The moon came up in a blue-gray halo, but the clouds threatened the sphere. The fields were a desert, its dunes of snow drifting to an icy sirocco. Michaels glanced again at Pat. The priest looked older, tired.

"Mike?" The word came out a whisper.

"Yeah?"

A sudden quiet enveloped the car, permeating even the engine roar. Pat pulled at his beard. His eyes jerked sideways, toward the back seat. "Never mind."

Like hell, Mike thought.

"The book is about vampires?" Diana asked.

"Yes. A genuine classic, ever since the twenties."

"Do you think you'll be able to handle a vampire?"

"If he plays by the book," Russo said. "There are rather surefire rituals for dealing with vampires, witches, and the demonic in general."

"Do you know a lot about witchcraft?"

"Yes."

"Wow, I've always found things like that fascinating—even though I don't really know much about them. Have you read the *Malleus Maleficarum*?"

Mike tasted the wrongness. The dark road was patched with ice and snow, and now the wind breathed steamy puffs that obscured the way. He braked gently, slowing down. Black as hell out there, the sun completely gone. Wrongness all over the place. What silly crap they talked about in the back seat. He didn't even know these people, and yet he was putting his life and Angela's in their trust. He had to be out of his mind. Blut would squash them all like annoying insects. Only the priest seemed to sense what they were in for.

He stared ahead out the windshield, and anxiety closed round him like a hand. Good Christ, it was dark out there. He felt like he couldn't breathe, and last night came back with a terrible immediacy—Blut, the power of evil. They were all crazy, all dead men.

"What's wrong?" the priest asked.

Mike swallowed, struggling for control. "Oh, I just . . . it's so dark and cold out there. It's hard to believe we can . . ."

Pat stared at the field. "Do children fear the dark because we teach them to, or because it *is* fearful? It's difficult to believe anything when you wake up alone in the night and are afraid. God, faith, love—in the dark they all seem to dissolve. The reality is nothing."

"Oh Christ, that's so true."

"Not necessarily. Just because love and faith are born from our own weaknesses does not make them untrue. The strongest people I've known have been the ones who best understood their weaknesses. Excuse my sermonizing, Mike. It becomes a habit in my profession."

"I don't mind. Not tonight."

"Living in Iowa City, being a priest at Center East, you forget about evil, the real thing. I always thought of evil in human terms. Stupidity, greed, the people who gave us napalm, the Vietnam War, and peace with honor, those who thought student rioters should be shot dead. But now there seems more to it."

There was a brief silence. Mike said, "But doesn't your faith . . . ?"

" 'Faith' would be putting it rather strongly. I have some love for certain people, but I can't even be sure how genuine that is."

"You seem pretty genuine to me."

"Thank you."

Mike looked at him and hoped the priest would get out of this alive. Ahead the sky lit up in a flash that revealed farm silhouettes against the horizon.

"What the hell?" Mike said. "Lightning?" The low, distant rumble was barely discernible over the engine.

Tony broke off his talk with Diana. "The vampire can control the weather over short distances. He can raise up storms, winds, and the like, as you discovered yesterday with that blizzard."

"But it just snowed yesterday. How can you have thunder in February?"

The horizon blinked light, and the rumbling followed more closely. "By now you should understand that he can bend the laws of nature."

"Hey, it seems to be getting warmer back here," Diana said.

"I don't think this will be his main attack," Russo said. "Merely a diversion to scare us, to show his power."

A shrieking gale swept out of the north, rushing at them like a tidal wave. The wind smashed against the hearse, raised tremendous clouds of snow, and bent the leafless black trees. Mike hit the brakes, skidded slightly, and jerked his foot away. Careful—still icy spots all over the road. He slowed down gradually.

The rumblings increased, the flashes taking up more sky. Ahead to the right a ragged white line flickered to the ground, darting quickly like a lizard's tongue. After a couple of heartbeats, the thunderclap sounded. More yellow-white charges crackled, lightning springing across the dark sky like white, roaring lions. The farmhouses and barren fields resembled scenes on film run through a primitive, hesitant projector, their very existence in question. The thunder seemed continuous. It reminded Mike of Vietnam, and he'd always freaked out when mortar fire started up. He saw a second wave coming.

The rain splattered onto the hood, cannonaded the roof, and flooded out the windshield. Mike grabbed for the wiper switch, knowing the brief terror of being blind to the road. The wipers lurched into action, cut windows into the night.

Rain poured all around them, wetting the snow and deluging the dark pavement. The lightning rippled and roared, the white strobes of fury set against black sky. The hearse drove through the strange realm that leaped between day and night.

"Christ," Mike murmured, "I don't believe this." The storm had the same fury, the same sense of elemental chaos unleashed, as the blizzard the night before. Even at high speed the wipers had a hard time keeping up with the torrents of rain.

Pat sat very erect and stared out into the night. "This reminds me of when I was a boy in Kansas. Tornado weather."

"I don't think he could create a tornado," Tony yelled over the thunder. "He only wants to show off, to frighten us."

"He's doing a pretty good job," Mike muttered. Only Pat heard him. Michaels glanced over his shoulder. A flash showed Diana's face, awe and exhilaration mixed, her green eyes wide open. God, the crazy chick was digging this.

"This will melt all the snow," Mike shouted.
"It'll cause floods." The sloping ditches between
the roads and the fields had already filled, and
there was an inch of water on the road. "Hell, at
this rate we'll get there about midnight. This
is—good Christ!"

The hearse reached the hilltop, and they saw
the final wave rushing them, a white wall obliterating everything in its pathway. Mike fought
to keep his foot off the brake and let it swallow
them.

Bam—bam—bam—bam—bam ... bouncing
off the hood, thudding over their heads. Michaels
fought the hearse out of skid, tried to keep them
on the highway as they careened to the bottom of
the hill. A shriek from the back—Diana's exhilaration was short-lived. Ahead was the green
JENKIN'S CENTER sign. Bam—bam—bam ... all
around them, pummeling their senses, bouncing
off the car, burying themselves in the snow,
rolling and swarming on the road like white rats.

"What is it?" Diana screamed.

"Hail." That was Pat. "The size of golf balls."

"Oh God," Mike said, "this poor hearse."
Buildings were coming up: Smithsville.

An especially loud bang right over his head. He
fought off the panic. Just like shells—he could
imagine them piercing the roof or perhaps they'd
simply pound the car flat with everyone inside.
Jenkin's Center Drive-In Bank was a dark brick
structure at the end of a parking lot. He swung the
car left. The black beast roared across the empty
lot, dancing across the myriad of hailstones, and
jerked to a stop by the teller's booth.

They all felt the relief. Lightning still came in
blinks, but the roof overhead protected them

from the storm's full fury. Michaels turned off the ignition and ran his hand through his hair. "It seems so quiet."

Pat took a deep breath. "I'm glad you noticed this place."

"Goddamn fast thinking." Tony sounded shaky. "Clever of Blut. I must admit I wasn't expecting that."

Diana squeezed Michaels's shoulder. "You were great, Mike. I was scared to death."

"Sure." Something about her put him off.

They watched the hail come down, but there were no people anywhere. Mike saw the hailstones fall through the yellow corona of a streetlight. He noticed all the dents on the hood.

"Shit, this poor klunker. My uncle will be pissed."

"It's stopping," Pat said. The hail and lightning were dwindling, but the rain continued.

"With my luck, as soon as we move, the shit will all start again."

"I don't think so," Tony said. "Blut wants to throw us off balance. He's also slowed us down."

A river of lightning split the sky with a deep, crackling boom. The hidden town sprang at them out of the shadows, its shapes exposed for an instant, then jumped back into night.

Mike heard Diana start. "That one was close," Pat said.

"Could he get us with lightning?" Mike asked.

"No." Tony shook his head. "He wants us alive, I'm sure."

"Well, we'd better get going. We've got to get out there soon. It must be after seven."

"Seven forty-eight," Russo said.

"*Shit.*" Michaels felt frustrated tears build up

in his eyes. This was hopeless. Angela was out there alone in that house. By now Blut might have . . . killed her. If it was possible to kill her. He shivered and wrenched the stick into drive.

A hard, steady rain fell, lashing the asphalt. The lightning had stopped. Everything looked wet and cold and miserable. The snow along the streets was dirty, soaked with rain, and riddled with hail. Scattered black pools reflected the yellow light of the street lamps, and the falling rain made tiny circles. The blue neon HAMM'S! sign was still on even though the tavern was closed.

Mike drove out of town. The others were quiet. They must finally be realizing what they had gotten into. They had seen a small sample of what Blut could do. The landscape of farmhouses and fields rose and fell with the road.

"God, it looks depressing out there." Mike was sick of desolation.

"You know," Tony said, "most vampire stories take place amid stupendous peaks in the Carpathian Mountains and thick, fearful forests, but somehow this ugly gray country works even better. Nothing seems more god-awful than Iowa in February, especially when the snow melts. Mile after mile of dead, gray-brown fields and bare trees."

Pat nodded. "You're right. And this same land turns a lush green in summer."

"Hot and green and humid, life and growing things, vegetation and fertility everywhere. The universe does like opposites. So during the winter we have this godforsaken emptiness. A rather nice setting for a vampire. Dracula amid the cornfields." A snorty "haa."

"I didn't see any corn growing around Blut Farm. Or anything else."

"Ah no. Pardon my ruminations, my chewings upon the intellectual cud."

Going down a steep hill the hearse picked up speed. Mike touched the brakes, felt the big hearse waver, skidding slightly. His brow tightened as he stared at the ribbon of black pavement. He touched the brakes and noticed more wavering.

"Oh Christ, this is just lovely—freezing rain. It's turning cold again. Soon there'll be a layer of ice on the road."

"Freezing rain's impossible to drive in," Russo said. "I was on my way to a farmhouse one time, but I turned back after making a one-hundred-eighty degree spin. It's far worse than snow driving."

Mike saw the ice form along the windshield where the defroster's hot breath didn't reach. He touched the brakes again, skidded slightly. Cursing, he carefully slowed the hearse. The wheels hesitated at the next hill, out of synchronization with the accelerator. "Hell, it's building up fast."

"The only way I made it back that time was by driving with one set of tires on the shoulder where the gravel and dirt provides something for them to hold on to. Unfortunately there's too much snow in this case." The wet dirty snow banked both sides of the highway.

The hearse cringed at another hill, wheels spinning, the back end swerving left. Michaels resisted the urge to gun it. "Come on, come on, you son of a bitch." They made the top, then gained momentum, quickly going downhill. "Well, we're sure as hell not going to make it much further. Dammit, we're only about thirty miles away. I could put on the chains, but there's hardly enough ice. It'd be super-hard on the chains and tires."

"Why not put on one chain and drive with that wheel in the snow?" Tony said.

"Good idea. But that means we'll have to do about twenty all the way—we won't get to Blut Farm until after ten."

"An hour or two won't make much difference now."

"I'll keep going till we have to stop."

"What are we going to do when we get there?" Diana asked Russo.

"Try to break into the house and get Angela out. I've brought enough equipment along that something should protect us"—the sound of his hand patting the leather bag.

"What's in there?"

"Diverse and sundry goods: a few crucifixes, pistols, garlic, wooden stakes, two vials of holy water, some holy oil, a steel mallet, a bayonet. And the good Father has provided us with consecrated hosts."

"My, how very thorough." Her voice sounded faintly ironic.

"If we can get inside the house we should be able to immobilize Doctor Blut—surround him with crucifixes and seal off the exits. Then we either wait for daylight or we immediately try the stake. Probably wiser to wait until day."

"How do you seal the doors?"

"Anointing them with holy oil in the shape of a cross."

"I'm sure glad you're along. You have it all planned out."

"As much as possible."

The hearse clawed at the hill, its tail swinging left. Michaels swore and eased up on the accelerator. "This is as far as we go." His foot shifted to the brake, the car jerked sideways, slipped downhill, and stopped. Mike glanced over his shoulder and let the hearse roll onto level ground. "Time to put on a chain."

The priest unlocked his door. "I'll help."

"Okay." He put the hearse in Park, glanced over the seat. Michaels again thought how much Russo resembled a cinematic vampire: the long black hair, the dark eyebrows arching in a solid line over large eyes, the thin face with shadow in the eye sockets and under the cheekbones. Next to him, legs demurely crossed, sat the girl from *Vogue*. "We'll be right back."

Diana's hand rested on Russo's wrist. "I have lots more questions about vampires."

Michaels turned the door handle, pushed, but it wouldn't budge. "Sticky son of a bitch." He used his shoulder, and the door opened with a loud crack as the ice broke. He zipped up his field jacket, stepped out, and nearly fell over. He caught himself by grabbing the door handle. "Jesus Christ!"

The highway surface glistened, the reflected light from the yellow beams creeping through the drizzle. A solid sheet of ice covered the hearse and the road. Up ahead a yellow yard light illuminated a house, an old Ford, and a mailbox.

Mike walked around the front of the hearse very slowly. Cowboy boots were hardly the thing for ice. The dirty, wet snow was easier going, and

Pat's feet had left black holes. The rain fell cold and monotonously steady.

Pat waited by the rear tire, his bearded face covered by a gray hood. He reminded Mike of one of Robin Hood's men or perhaps a wandering friar. The hood was part of an old gray coat that fell to the knees, six dark wooden buttons shaped like kegs on the right side. Mike opened the back and pulled a chain out of the box. Slamming the door nearly made him fall over. Stumbling slightly, Pat caught him and kept him up.

"Christ, it's slippery. Thanks."

The priest forced a smile. Lines crinkled his forehead. A solitary snowflake floated down, landed on his beard, and slowly disappeared.

"You've been quiet, Pat."

"I've been thinking. And I feel—it gets worse the closer we come."

A bitter laugh. "Yeah." He sighed, realizing how tired he was.

He knelt before the tire and began unraveling the chain. A snowflake landed on his wrist. He shivered. It was growing cold again. The drizzle made black stains of ice on his shoulders, and the cold seeped in. The priest knelt and helped straighten the chain in front of the tire.

"You'll have to drive forward, Pat, while I check to make sure it goes on okay."

The cry began low, so low it teetered about on the edge of perception, perhaps merely a nasty trick of the imagination, a childish attempt to scare the hell out of yourself, but then the sound pierced the brain, wounding body and soul.

Mike dropped the chain. "*Christ*—did you hear that?"

"Yes," the priest whispered. "What was it?"

"Wolf—dog—I don't know." He tried to control the fear, the quivering in his hands. Again the howl sliced open the night, releasing a long, flowing gout of sound. Michaels swallowed. He wanted desperately to get away. "We'd better hurry, Pat. Get inside and let her roll forward until you hear me yell to stop."

The window came down, and Russo's dark face appeared. "Was that something from the farm?"

"Yes."

"I knew it!"

Pat walked quickly around the car, got in, and started the engine. Mike watched the chain curl around the tire. Another howl swelled out of the night, reached a high, dissonant peak, and went on and on. Mike tried to concentrate on getting the chain on straight. His bare hands trembled from fear, cold, and the touch of frozen metal. "Whoa—that's good!" The hearse jerked to a stop. Mike fastened the opposite ends of the chain.

Another howl, the same long, wavering note dying so slowly. The sound glided up his spine like an icy hand and pinched his neck—his shoulders jerked upward, he shuddered through clenched teeth. The thing was coming closer. He smashed a finger against the metal. *Fucking chain!* His hands were trembling so hard he could barely use them. *There.* That would have to do.

He ran around the hearse and felt his feet slide out from under him as he fell on his ass. Christ, that hurt. His palms pressing against the rough, cold ice, he stood slowly and grasped the door handle for support. He struggled to get control of himself. Ahead the high beams reached for the rising road, illuminating the rain and snow-flakes. It was watching him, it was out there watching him—he felt its power. He knew with utter certainty that the thing was lurking out there, he could sense its presence.

"Mike?" Pat's voice.

Mike got inside, sat down, and covered his face with his hands. "Oh God."

The priest put his hand on his shoulder. "What is it?"

"Blut's out there—or the dog—waiting for us." Don't go to pieces before all these people. Crumbling, coming slowly apart, disintegrating little by little. If he drove any further it would leap out onto the road again, just like last night. He might still be able to go back, but he had to return to Angela, to the terrible house—he *must*.

The priest's hand tightened. "Mike, you're worn out. Let me drive for a while."

"All right." At least he wouldn't feel like he was driving himself to his own death. How crazy—it's all right if someone else drives you to your death.

The priest awkwardly slid under him as they switched places, then slowly started the hearse forward. The chain made a tremendous rattling. Pat steered to the right, putting the tire with the chain into the snowbank. The hearse easily climbed the hill where it had faltered before.

Mike closed his eyes, listened to the engine roar and Diana's siren voice. Still asking Tony dumb questions about vampires. He opened his eyes, focused on the raindrops and snowflakes splattering against the windshield. The proportion of snow had increased. The flakes smashed against the glass, and the wipers pushed them aside. But he didn't want to watch the road—that's where the dog would appear. He stared at Pat. The priest looked out into the night, his jaw locked, gaze fixed ahead. Mike closed his eyes. The chain went clunk, clunk.

He slipped somewhere between wakefulness and sleep, wandered in an anxious, half-conscious limbo, aware the nightmares would claim him if he slept. Occasionally he opened his eyes and stared at the priest. Much later he sat up and saw that the dark highway had vanished under the white.

"How far to go?" he asked.

"Udolph is about ten miles. There must be about six inches of snow out there."

"We'd better put on the other chain soon. It looks like it's working itself up to another blizzard." Staring at the white flakes swarming in the headlights, Michaels had an overwhelming sense of déjà vu. Exactly like last night. The wind howling, no sense of time or place—only nothing, nothing everywhere.

He wished he could sleep, really sleep. He thought again of Angela and felt sad. Last night while he drove, she lay curled beside him asleep. To find someone like her and then immediately lose her. He remembered how she had kissed him, her passion. How would it feel to kiss dead lips? Her mouth would be cold and horribly, utterly still. Oh God, how could Blut lose? But he still wanted to see her again, warm and alive, even if it could not last—even if they must all die.

"Mike, let's put on that other chain. It's difficult to drive."

Mike stretched, extending his arms before him. "Yeah."

The wind shrieked as they tried to straighten the chain and turned the metal to ice. The wind blew snow in their faces and made even gloved hands numb. Everywhere about them snowflakes tumbled, growing, mutating into giant, monstrous, white amoebas falling from nowhere. It was hard to stand. Underneath the fresh snow lay the ice sheet left by the freezing rain.

Michaels took the wheel again and drove through the storm toward Udolph. The hearse crawled along, chains rattling. The wind leaped, howling and screaming, and all around the hearse the fallen snow drifted, undulating in white waves. Russo's cheerful talk had ceased, and they all stared silently out into the night.

Mike would have liked to avoid Udolph after Tony's revelations about its satanism, but there was no other way. This time its underlying corruption seemed obvious. A withering shadow covered Udolph, the very foundations festering from within. A dead thing with only the semblance of life, a corpse like its master.

Where were the people, Michaels wondered, the ones left? Indoors watching, smiling because their master would be satisfied? God knew how many Blut and Ursula had infected. He remembered Ursula walking through the icy dawn, her mouth dripping blood. The whole place would be crawling with vampires, a breeding ground for the infection.

Ahead through the dark storm shone two small

red lights. Mike realized they belonged to a car parked by the last stretch of buildings in town. A black-and-white car—the police. Slowly they passed it. The back window of the hearse was covered with snow, but they all saw the pulsing red light and heard the siren start up.

"Oh Christ, we can't let them stop us—should I try to outrun him?" He jerked around and stared at Russo.

"We can't let them find these guns, and they probably are in with Blut. Stop, though, and let's see what they want. We can run if we must, but let's be sure first."

Michaels pulled over and stopped. He rolled down the window, letting in a rush of snowflakes and icy air, and watched the dark figure coming at them out of the storm.

The cop leaned against the window and surveyed them calmly. He chewed. A swollen face, very pale, and big shoulders under the blue jacket with the dark fur collar. Chewing, chewing, the big jaws and jowls monotonously moving. It didn't smell like gum. The cop had no hair over his ears, only the stubble outline of sideburns. The ears were huge, waiting outstretched like those of a cat for the slightest quiver of sound. His eyes were blanks, his face lacked expression.

"Leh me see your driver's license."

Michaels fumbled for his wallet and noticed the black leather holster. Probably a police .38, detective special.

The cop examined the license, chewing loosely. "All right, Mike, you know there's a bad storm around here."

"Yeah, I know."

"Good." The head bobbed, the jaws still working. "Well, you be mighty careful, or you'll never get where you're going. Even with those chains. Now I stopped you to suggest you clear off that back windshield."

"I'll take care of it." Pat opened the door and stepped outside.

Big head bobbing again. "Good, good. Some car you got here. Going to a funeral? Huh, huh, huh." Mike smiled weakly. "Hard to miss one like this." Pat got back in.

"Fine, fine, that's just fine. Be careful, I wouldn't want anything to happen to you." He backed off. The methodical chewing recalled an insect, the head of a grasshopper or praying mantis, the same large blank eyes, the jaws working inexorably. "No sir, I want you to get where you're going. Someone must be waiting for you." For an instant the facade collapsed, and the pale bloated face formed a smile, an expression of pure malice.

Mike jerked the car into drive, rattle-roared off without even closing the window.

"That was lucky," Diana said.

Mike shook his head. "He knew exactly where we were going."

"Yes," Russo said. "And he let us through."

Mike felt the fear in his belly. Pale bloated face like a drowned man, swollen all out of proportion. He had seen such faces at his uncle's.

The snow fell continually, but he easily found the turnoff. He had the heater on full blast, but he felt the cold oozing in. The night was a chilling parasite that wanted to wrap them in its frozen tendrils and drain their warm life. The growing aura of evil was impossible to ignore.

Mike sensed the anxiety of the others. And they didn't really understand—they hadn't been to Blut Farm and seen the essence.

"There is in the lore of haunted houses a phenomenon known as the cold spot." Russo's mock lecture voice had a nervous overtone. "That is, a spot in the house where the temperature is significantly lower. Such temperature discrepancies have actually been measured. Often the cold spot is associated with the evil center of the house. It is thought to be the heart, the core of evil. Standing on such a spot will make one feel terribly cold and depressed. A sense of dread overcomes you. We are obviously experiencing a similar phenomenon. Mike, do you have the heater as high as it will go?"

"Yeah. But even if it would go higher, it wouldn't help. It was the same last night."

"This farm, like a haunted house, must have its sphere of influence, quite large in this case. But the farm itself is the source of cold and fear."

"I know," Mike said.

"I'm not cold," Diana said.

Pat had his hands in his pockets. "I am."

The hearse rumbled across the wooden bridge and turned left. The road suddenly curved wildly, twisting and writhing as if insane. Like a great black beast the hearse plowed through the confusion of snow, its yellow eyes throwing forth beams of light, its voice a blend of roaring engine and rattling chains. The new snow drifted, exposing ridges of ice, yesterday's snow rained on and then refrozen.

The hearse climbed to the top of a hill. Below, the road fell, curving, then rose to Blood Farm. Mike stopped and turned out the lights. Through the lightly falling snow they saw the farm. The white building on the hill was surrounded by black trees, a skull perched on a bed of dark worms.

"That's it." Silence, except for the rumble of the engine and the swish of the wipers. "Now what do we do?"

Seeing Blut's stronghold, Michaels realized how utterly hopeless it all was. The best they could hope for was a quick death together, the worst, torture and dying alone. But he still wanted to see Angela one last time.

Russo broke the silence. "Might as well go from here. I rather doubt we can sneak up on anyone, but driving up to the farm would make little sense. Perhaps his power is weaker farther out. Anyway, we should arm ourselves, then cross the stream, and head for the house through the trees."

No one said anything. Mike doubted it would work, but what did it matter?

"One person should stay here and watch the hearse. Pat or Diana."

"Oh, I want to come!" Diana exclaimed.

Pat's bearded face had a quiet intensity. "I'm going with them. Angela is in there, and I can help her."

"But that's not fair." She turned to Russo. "You need someone that can shoot, right? You heard him before we left—he won't even *carry* a gun."

Russo had taken the .45 out of the bag. He slammed in the clip. The thin, dark face regarded the priest.

"There are some things I can't do. I will not carry a gun. It goes against everything I believe in, not just as a priest but as a man. You said yourself, Tony, guns are useless against vampires. You and Mike will be armed. And won't the person who stays need a gun for protection? Besides, I am a priest, whatever that means."

Russo finished loading a .22 revolver shaped like a Western six-shooter. He ran his forefinger along the barrel, musing. "Pat is right. Whoever stays behind should have a gun. They may be attacked by . . . well, animals under Blut's control. Mike has to come. I know the most about vampires. And Pat is a priest. Vampires are supposed to fear all that a priest represents. I'm sorry, Diana, but you must see the logic behind your staying."

"I suppose so." A sour look marred her decorous beauty.

"Good. Here's a .38. Be careful, the fellow I borrowed it from will kill me if anything happens to it. You know how to use a pistol, right?"

"Yes. My father and brothers are all hunters." She took the revolver in her hand, curling her long white forefinger with the enormous nail around the trigger. She pointed the gun out the window, sighting down the barrel.

"Mike has used the .45 before, so he gets it. I'll use this uninspiring .22. I also have a cross for each of us, and Father Pat will pass out some pieces of host."

The priest quietly withdrew a plastic bag from his coat pocket and handed Russo a cube of dark bread. Russo stared at the bread and smiled. "Somehow, it's not what I remember. I thought we weren't supposed to touch it?"

"Times change. But be careful with it. Don't throw it away, eat it when you have finished with it."

Diana's fingers quivered slightly, and she quickly put the bread in her pocket.

Russo zipped up his parka and pulled on black leather gloves. "Are we ready, then? Mike has chosen a good stopping place, Diana. You can see all around you. Stay here, no matter what, and be careful. If anything happens, the cross or the gun should protect you. Turn on the engine once in a while to warm up the car and clean off the windshield." The snow was increasing again, the car had darkened. "We may be gone a long time. If we're not back by dawn, then it should be safe to drive down and see what's happened." He opened the door.

Mike stepped outside, and the wind slapped his face, the snow stinging. Oh God, it was cold. He looked downhill at the stream, then his eyes rose to the dark trees and the house. Russo walked around the hearse, a tall bulky figure in the puffy parka. A sham Colt six-shooter dangled from his right hand, his left held the leather bag. Pat followed in his gray hooded coat.

The three grouped together. Wind howled around them, and the ground underfoot crunched. The wind had flayed off the outer layer of fresh snow, leaving ridges of bluish gray ice exposed. Russo spoke, and the night shrieked louder, whirling his words away. He pointed downhill, and they walked, their feet making hardly any impression in the frozen crust.

Mike could not keep his eyes off the farm. He jerked his head down and tried to hold the fear in check. The .45 in his field jacket jounced against his hip. His fingers were already cold, even with gloves, and his legs felt the wind worst of all. Night was a power, a presence, all around them.

Russo and Pat had stopped, and he almost bumped into them. They had walked about forty feet downhill where the wind seemed less powerful. Perched above them was the hearse. Russo opened his mouth to speak.

The beast coughed, roared alive. The headlights cut tunnels through the snowy sky above them. They turned to see the hearse hurtling down the hill, jouncing along the snowy road.

"Oh fuck," Mike groaned.

Russo dropped the bag and ran toward the road. *"Hey!"* The hearse rushed by, oblivious to the man or perhaps regretful he had not stepped into its path.

Mike watched the hearse's red taillights bouncing. It crossed the bridge and followed the road up into the trees. There could be no question where it was going. The skull would have a new visitor.

CHAPTER EIGHT

◊

Deux guerriers ont couru, l'un sur l'autre; leurs armes
Ont éclaboussé l'air de lueurs et de sang.
Ces jeux, ces cliquetis du fer sont les vacarmes
D'une jeunesse en proie à l'amour vagissant.

—O fureur des coeurs mûrs par par l'amour ulcérés!
Dans le ravin hanté des chats-pard et des onces

Nos héros, s'étreignant méchamment, ont roulé,
Et leur peau fleurira l'aridité des ronces.
—Ce gouffre, c'est l'enfer, de nos amis peuplé!
Roulons-y sans remords, amazone inhumaine,
Afin d'éterniser l'ardeur de notre haine!
    —Baudelaire, "Duellum," Les Fleurs du Mal

WHAT EXCITEMENT! THE hearse jounced and shook, bellowing in protest, gathering speed going downhill, weaving slightly and almost out of control—the speedometer past fifty despite the chains and snow. O'er the fields we go, laughing all the way.

Diana did not touch the brakes, knowing what would happen, and when the car reached the small bridge she accelerated, charging the hill. The bridge shuddered as the hearse passed over; black waters slicing through white snow on either side. The hearse still bounced madly. Its headlights formed a yellow-white pathway through the trees, carved a tunnel through the thick dark trunks and the gnarled branches arching overhead. Ice and snow hid the road, but she steered to stay in the clear space between the trees. She felt as if she could close her eyes and forget the wheels—just let go—and the hearse would still take her to the farm. Snowflakes flew at her through the yellow light, dashing themselves against the windshield as shadowy forms flickered amid the trees.

She smiled, recalling the expression on Russo's face as she hurtled by him. How simple. She had merely waited. The engine had started easily.

The hearse slowed as the hill steepened, clawing its way up the slope. Ahead the trees ended, opening into a snowy expanse, and she saw a monstrous white mansion with dark roofs and windows, and the ancient dwelling cried out to her. Voices without source or sound sang her name. Unearthly music, a tortured fugue veering toward chaos, chanted by a choir of dead spirits only she could hear. *Hear* them! They sang with the storm, with the wind and the snow. The moment of fulfillment drew near.

She saw the sign jangle in the wind, jangle welcome—BLUT FARM. The hearse rumbled through the wooden gate and stopped before the house. She jerked the stick into Park and turned off the key. The engine belched, then died. How wonderful to have that incessant roaring stopped. Now the music of night surrounded her, possessing her consciousness, shutting out all else. The wind hummed a high shrill note accompanied by sharp clangs. She sat listening while the hearse grew colder and darker, snow building up on the windows, burying her inside.

Snorting sounds interrupted her reverie. She slid across the seat and opened the window. Small eyes stared at her. It was a huge pig, sable colored, with leaflike ears flopping on either side of its head, the snout amazingly long. The hog blinked, turned, and waddled through the snow, hindquarters wobbling at her, curling tail and enormous testicles.

Her mouth crinkled in disgust. She shivered, noticing the cold. Snowflakes drifted through the open window. How ugly, how horrible to have to assume—she had sensed the presence in the pig. She might still get away. But the night music resumed, the house and voices welcoming her, and she forgot her fear.

She pressed down on the door handle, the lock disengaged with a crunch, and she pushed open the door. Night breathed upon her, a gentle puff of icy wind and snow. She stepped out and saw the house. More angular from here, sharp corners and edges, its black windows glaring angrily and the porch beckoning like a yawning mouth. Snowflake moths flittered about, landed on her cheeks, flying into her eyes and hair. The chanting voices blurred into something new.

Soon, she thought, *oh soon.*

She ran for the porch, her boots plunging deep into the snow, and raced up the steps. The hog watched from the shadows. She stumbled, her knee smashing into an icy step, but she felt no pain. She wrenched open the front door.

Organ music everywhere—so loud. Music conceived in hell. She walked slowly toward the source, passing Angela slumped in a chair. Self-righteous bitch. Red-orange light from the fire flickered over the large, dark room, setting aglow the plush furniture and the dusky wood, sparkling off the jet-black coffin.

Diana stopped before the coffin. Steel altar of death. She felt the fear and excitement prickle up her back. What unbelievable power. The music teetered toward its conclusion, a diabolical coda, a *prestissimo* nothing human could play. The final chord struck like a sonic boom, reverberating off the walls, echoing through the house out into the night. She turned from the coffin and waited breathlessly, her fists clenched, a sudden flush coloring her face.

He swept from the darkened square of doorway, a black form with white face and hands. The eyes fell upon her. Her body stiffened, and she felt her heart tremble like a dying animal.

"Welcome to my house." The thunder music reverberated in his voice.

"I've done everything like you and the master said. I've obeyed."

"Have you?"

"Yes. I kept him busy long enough so you could meet us in the night. I know what the men have planned. The members of the coven were honored that one of us was chosen. Now I've brought you the hearse. And myself."

"You have indeed done well." He smiled.

"Then—give me the knowledge—the secret. Make me one of the master's chosen ones. You . . . they promised."

His smile dispersed like mist, and the pale blue eyes devoured. "Do you know the price?"

"I . . . I thought . . ."

Do you know the price? The words throbbed straight into her mind, and as he stepped toward her the shadows accompanied him.

"I am . . . ready . . . to do what I must."

"Good, and . . ?" The inhuman face was almost eager.

She stiffened, drawing erect. "No one has ever violated me, though many have wanted to. I've saved myself. I've been . . . pure."

The bloodless lips rose, relishing the irony of the word. "Yes, you have done well, and you will receive what you deserve. You will see how our master rewards the faithful. The choice must truly be yours—*come to me.*" The power flowed from his eyes filling the room, swallowing her.

Afraid, she looked away, but he helped her to

conquer the fear. She unbuttoned the leather coat. The wind moved about her, growing colder and stronger. The front door was open, letting night and storm enter. She dropped her coat on the floor. Blut smiled. His eyes burned blue-white. She had on a white cardigan, gold corduroy slacks, and a gold turtleneck. Her hair fell about her long oval face in brown-blond ringlets, and even in the dim orangish light one could see the pink of her lips, the blue-green shadow on her eyelids, and the long eyelashes. The aquiline nose was part of an aristocratic, even austere, beauty. She unfastened the bottom button of the sweater. The fine lambswool was pure white. She took off the sweater and tossed it aside. It landed on the dirty, uncarpeted floor by the fireplace. An ember flew from the fire, smoldered on the wool, blackened.

She heard a moan behind her.

"Diana . . ? Oh God, Diana—what are you doing here?"

She turned and stared coldly. "I came to help rescue you."

Angela blinked. She tried to sit up but only half-succeeded. Surrounded by curling black hair, her face was pale, her blue eyes weary. She shivered and clutched at her arms, cold in spite of the down parka.

"You can't mean . . ?" She looked first at Diana, then at Blut. Her eyes fled the vampire. "Go, Diana—run—don't you see what he'll do to you?"

"Nothing I don't want him to."

"You can't mean that. Please—don't be crazy—get out of here."

"Oh no, dear roommate, I came here to help

save you. I told your big blond friend how much I cared about you, and of course he was glad to have me along."

Angela frowned, biting at her lip. "Mike—is here?"

"Of course. He and that priest you screwed and Tony Russo are all wandering around out there."

"You can't—how could you know about Pat and me?"

Diana laughed, a throaty haaa. "Don't look so shocked. I know all about it. That's a mortal sin, Angela. You can go to hell for that."

Angela seemed to stare through her. "There's no way you could know. Pat would never tell."

"Oh, there are ways, but they're not open to sweet little angels like you. Poor little roommate."

Angela refused to look at her. "I'm not your roommate. I moved out."

"Ah, don't you like me anymore, Angela? Just because I stopped going to church and started getting into the occult. Is that any reason to leave your old, best girlfriend?"

Angela took a deep breath. She looked tired and sick. "You changed, Diana. You didn't like me anymore. And I could see what those people were doing to you. You would look at me as if . . . I didn't like it." Tears ran down her cheeks.

"Ohh—she's crying. How sad. I thought you were so strong."

"I'm tired, and I don't feel good." Her eyes closed, shutting out the blond fury and the black thing whose presence dominated all.

Diana moved in on the chair, her beautiful face wrathful. "You dirty little hypocrite, you're the one who hated *me*! You thought you were so much better than me because you'd let anyone stick his thing in you. I was only a dumb virgin, and you were a woman of the world. And then you'd go running off to church and be all chummy with God. You hated me—*hated me!*—you *whore*!" Diana drew in her pink lips, then spit, spraying Angela's face. She wished it were acid or venom, something that would mar the beauty.

Angela stared sadly. "No. It's not true. I never hated you. You're sick."

Anger reddened Diana's face and twisted it ugly. "*I'm* sick! You still think you're better than I am. Jesus Christ, you are disgusting."

"Diana, I don't hate you, really I don't, and if you've ever cared about me or anything else at all, then get out of here. Leave this horrible place. Don't do what you're going to do. Oh God, fight him—at least fight him. You'll be so sorry if—"

An angry laugh. "So I'll be sorry. You have to keep your position of moral authority, don't you?"

The two women eyed each other. Angela's face was tired and drawn, her hair a mass of confused waves, her eyes half-closed. A pallor had replaced Diana's flush, the hard white features cut from marble, the hair like ringlets on a statue. Goose pimples blotched her pale arms, but she could not feel the cold. Angela was crying.

"*Please*," she whispered. "*Go.*"

"I think we have had enough of this amusing conversation."

Blut stepped forward; the shadows advanced, and the room darkened. Even while the two women spoke his silent presence was louder than their voices. His eyes fell upon Angela. Pale fire crackled from the corpse face, blackness swirling about him. Angela closed her eyes. "Oh God." She slumped in the chair.

"Now she will remain silent."

Worry touched Diana's face. "Have you killed her?"

Blut smiled slowly, then burst into laughter. His head fell back, and firelight sparkled off his teeth, exposing the pink curve of his tongue. "Of course not. I do not kill that way. There are more effective, more nourishing methods. I have in mind something special for her." His amusement vanished. "Now get on with it." The pale face and eyes filled her vision.

Diana moved her hair to unfasten the zipper in back, then pulled off the sleeveless turtleneck. Goose pimples sprouted along her arms, shoulders, and breasts, but she felt nothing, saw nothing except his blue eyes. She bent over to unlace her boots and kicked them off. Her long fingers fumbled at the snap of the corduroys. It opened with a pop. She hesitated, then pulled down the zipper. With a slight swish the pants crumpled around her ankles, and she stepped free of them.

Her body was tall and slender, her arms and legs firmly muscled, the outline of her ribcage prominent. Her brassiere, a transparent network of lace, cupped small breasts. Her belly was smooth and flat, a fleshy circle with her navel at the center. The bikini panties were cut very low, barely covering her pubic hair. The proud face with its gold-brown curls and beaked nose, the slim figure in bra and panties, recalled the long-limbed creatures of *Vogue* or *Cosmopolitan*. However, the wool socks spoiled the effect.

She pulled off the socks one by one. Her toes were long, big-jointed, more like fingers, and the bright pink toenails matched her fingernails. She withdrew her arms from the straps, then slid the bra around to unfasten the catch. The bra landed on her other clothes. Her breasts were slight, the nipples a faint pink, but the blue-black tattoo of a rune marred the white skin of her left breast. She paused, her rib cage slowly swelling. The long, sad sigh flattened her belly. Now she was afraid, a new and terrible fear.

"Get on with it!" Blut hissed. His eyes had followed each move with a voyeur's greedy intensity, wallowing in her body. His mouth was a disdainful twist, his face showing eagerness and disgust.

Diana swallowed. She must have the knowledge and become part of the elite. If only this awful fear would go away. She rested her hands against her flanks, pausing nervously, then hooked her thumbs under the elastic waistband and slid the panties down along her thighs. They fell to her ankles, and she stepped away.

A long moan came from behind her. Angela shifted restlessly in the chair.

Diana swallowed again. She felt an icy draft blow between her legs, nuzzling at her. Her legs came together, her shoulders jerking upward; she clenched her teeth and shuddered. She almost screamed, but the instant passed, leaving her vaguely embarrassed. The pale blue eyes sucked away the fear. In them lay some terrible truth. Her breathing quickened, and her breasts felt strange. Blut's smile blurred into a parody of desire, a mimicry of lust.

She had never stood naked before a man, never let a man touch her below the waist. At the sabbaths she had joined in the naked dances and the mutual stimulation, but her coven was made up entirely of women. As the black shape approached she heard her breathing grow louder. She did not know that Blut was not a man.

He charged, fingers clawing at her back while his frigid lips forced open her mouth, and his tongue slithered about inside her. She felt a rush of desire even though his embrace was deathly cold. He broke off the kiss and backed away, mouth wrinkling. Terrible anger burned from his pale eyes, his hair seemed white fire. "*Go on*—get down."

"Huh?"

"*Get down.*" His hands made a motion one might use to brush aside a fly. The blow knocked her over, and she landed near the fireplace. Only embers remained, a dying red glow.

He was on her at once, a black swirl, his face a scowling white oval. Sharp fingers pulled her against his cold naked skin, and his lips bit at her mouth. He felt cold, so cold, as his flesh touched her flesh. She returned the kiss ferociously. Something soft pressed against her thighs. His lips moved from her mouth to her throat, kissing harshly, then slid down to her breasts. She groaned, closing her eyes and twisting slowly. He took a nipple between his teeth and bit down too hard, sucking. Her fingers grasped his head, the white strands of hair like thin worms, and she drew him toward her.

His lips scuttled back up to her throat, his mouth widened, and she felt the moist tongue. A burning pain cut at her neck like ragged glass. She screamed, knowing pure fear. Then drowsiness came, an erotic stupor, and she lay moaning with satisfaction as he drained life from her.

The thing against her thigh stiffened, swelling with blood. His legs were clamped together, a great scaly tail flopping between her. Reluctantly he moved away from her throat, and the pale face glared down at her. She had a waxy look. Sweat glistened on her forehead and shoulders; a bright red flush covered her chest near the collarbones. Blut's lips pulled back into a smile that revealed blood-smeared teeth.

He thrust into her, stabbing deeply. Her head fell back, and she screamed. She felt the icicle tear at her, and her arms pulled the corpse closer. Pain and ecstasy. Her legs rose, curling about the serpentine form in an embrace with death.

Blut's smile disappeared, replaced by terrible anger. "You dirty, lying slut." His voice was guttural.

Diana opened her gray-green eyes and saw the white face floating against blackness. A dead man's face bobbing out of dark waters. The pain in her throat and groin drowned out all else. "What . . . are you saying?"

"*Slut*. You are no virgin."

Her eyes widened, then tried to escape Blut. "I—but I swear—no man has . . ."

"What was it then, a woman—or yourself?" Blut laughed once. "Yes, it was *you*. You defiled yourself." The thing's eyes saw her shame— nothing could hide from them. "Playing with yourself, sticking your dirty little fingers in there. That was it, was it not?" He thrust violently, as if he would rip open her womb and drive into the vital organs.

She screamed and screamed. "But it's not the same—I—"

"It *is*—it is the same, and you know it. Admit you know. Admit that you have committed a grave sin. You have defiled the temple of your body. Confess your damnation."

"I . . ." She felt his body crushing her, an inexorable weight, and that icy thing inside her. An awful dread blossomed, and she realized how weak she was. So cold and dark, and she was sinking, falling through dark waters, drowning in an icy stream.

Blut thrust again. "Confess, *damn you*!"

She screamed, aware of a cold agony seeping through her, black corruption spreading and rotting like gangrene. "*Yes*—it's true. I did—and I knew it was wrong—dirty." She had drawn her arms and legs away from him. The rough floor by the fireplace had scraped her upper back raw and soiled her hair.

Blut's smile returned, blue-white fires burned in her brain. "You have damned yourself. Now you may die."

He rammed into her and fell upon her throat, an icy horror ripping her, a leech sucking at her throat, gurgling down blood. She was falling through icy waters, life flowing away into the void. Cold, so cold, and no air, the surface a gray blur farther and farther away. Falling, dying, and nothing to be done. *Nothing*. Fear and water everywhere. There was no way out, no escape from the dank, muddy bottom. Thick, cold tendrils of weed tangled insidiously about her ankles, her thighs, between her legs, now at her breasts, corpse hands holding her. They pulled her down—deep, deeper, into that suffocating black mud.

Blut drank madly, his thirst insatiable, and thrust like a beast. With a shudder the icy worm discharged its venom, and Blut gasped, drawing in great gulps of blood. Diana wailed, a dying cry of despair. Her limbs twitched and were still.

Angela screamed and jerked open her eyes. Horrible, horrible dreams. White spiders crawling over her, worms eating at her heart, Mike melting into Blut. She realized where she was and shivered. Being awake was no better. Awake or asleep there was no respite.

She blinked, looking around the large dim room. The coffin called for attention, an incessant presence. The feeble orange light shimmered on the black metal.

"Oh God."

The dying embers were like bright eyes, the red-orange eyes of some sable-faced Argus who stared at the strange thing before the fireplace. It was black with white arms and legs, a gigantic black beetle with human limbs. Its arms and legs were long and well formed, and they lay very still. Angela heard slurping sounds, something feeding hungrily. She noticed the pile of clothes on the rug and understood.

She closed her eyes, shutting out the tears. Why wouldn't Diana listen? They had been friends once. She remembered Blut crawling over her, the frozen violation, the hate and violence. Her mouth and throat grew dry and she trembled. She was so thirsty.

Blut's lips broke their seal. Gorged, he withdrew from the body, and stood up. Or rather, he flowed upward like smoke. His hair had a yellow tint; the blood vessels flowed through the white eyes like red rivers, and his face seemed younger. Blood colored his lips. He smiled down at the corpse, then glanced at Angela.

"Open your eyes. Look at me."

Angela looked at him and moaned. She could feel his strength, along with cold and evil. Diana's body lay before the fireplace, a beautiful statue, the orange glow playing across the marble torso. Her legs were spread, her feet flopping sideways lifelessly. Light brown hair began below the belly and dropped between the legs.

"She was not truly a virgin, but she could still bleed. And hurt." The shadow fell as he thrust his head between the sprawled legs. Angela closed her eyes, trying to shut out the sounds.

"I said *open your eyes.*" He had risen again. "Your friend was not so passive. She actually enjoyed it at first, but I soon corrected that. She obviously had her foolish rape fantasies. All you women truly want is something rammed up inside you. Soon now I will teach you the disgusting sinfulness of the act. Then you may join her. My dear Renwick, I presume you enjoyed the spectacle?"

Angela turned. Renwick sat on the floor by the doorway, slumped over. Jesus wearing a field jacket, hands in his pockets, his benign face half-asleep, numbed. The wind moaned loudly, breathing cold air and snow into the room through the open front door.

"You enjoy watching, do you not? It gives you something to think about when you want to divert yourself." Blut smiled. Renwick's eyes blinked, showing a hint of anger. "You mortals are all alike. Death, if nothing else, frees one from the rule of the genitals." He prodded Diana with his foot. "As she has discovered."

Angela wished Blut would leave. She was so tired, and his interminable presence was more than she could take. She stared at Diana. "You've killed her."

Blut laughed. "Only in a manner of speaking. Surely you must know what has happened to her."

"Oh *God*."

Diana's right leg bent, her knee twisting out. Her eyes blinked rapidly, then remained open. Her chest was motionless, lungs and heart forever stilled. Slowly she rose up onto her elbows. Her face was a death mask, a pale beautiful death mask with green eyes that jerked rapidly about the room. Angela could see the terror and hate in her face. Life everlasting and the resurrection of the damned. Oh God, please help me—*please*.

The corpse saw Blut, and the lips drew back in hate. "You lied to me—you lying bloodsucking fucker."

"What's the matter, dearest? I thought you wanted knowledge, to become one of us?"

"Yes, but now I'm—dead." An overpowering emptiness echoed in her voice.

"Fool. That was part of the price. That, and your soul."

"*But*—but . . ." Diana's face showed a confused despair, and momentarily Angela saw her friend. "There is *nothing* . . . no knowledge . . . no . . . nothing. *Nothing*—everywhere!"

"That *is* the knowledge. That is all there is.

And you have died to discover it." Blut smiled, his eyes probing her wounds like gangrenous fingers. "You should be grateful. You have learned something few people ever learn."

"You *bastard*—you did this to me." Angela had to look away. The hate in Diana's face was incredible, beyond belief.

"You did it to yourself. *You*. No one else was responsible. And you will have eternity to think about that."

Diana covered her face with her hands, those long fingers with the pink nails. A shudder passed through her. She dropped her hands, green eyes searching, teeth bared. "I'm hungry—empty—so *hungry*—how . . ?"

Blut laughed. The laughter sounded like someone choking to death. "Feed yourself, find food." Diana glared at Renwick. "*Not* him, fool. He is useful to us. He can move about during the daylight when we must rest."

She turned her eyes upon Angela and smiled. "Angela, dear Angela. My friend, my old roommate."

Blut laughed again. "Unfortunately, I am saving her for myself. Her uniquely perverse nature merits something special, but first must come the joyful reunion with her friends. Amuse yourself if you wish. I doubt you can break her. That will require my male powers. But now I have other things to attend to."

Blut smiled at Angela, white face against darkness. His cheekbones melted away like wax, graying and dripping from the bone, mouth and nose blurring into smoke. He collapsed to the ground, gyrating into mist, and with a howl the wind swept him out into the night.

Angela gave a relieved sigh, then realized she was alone with Diana and Renwick. She held her arms with her hands, shivering. The house was so god-awful cold, with a chill that crept inside and wanted to freeze you dead. She could hear the steady cry of the wind and the night sounds entering through the open door. The cold did not bother Diana. She crept toward the chair, naked and white, so white her body seemed to glow fluorescently. Her face stared, thin with the green eyes and golden ringlets of hair, but not really Diana's face. Such hatred, and those long teeth. The eyes wanted to rip her apart, to hold her under the green waters until her lungs burst. Angela closed her eyes, still shivering. Not by her—dear God, *no*.

"What's wrong, Angela?" The voice had a harshness the sugar coating could not hide. "Look at me, Angela. *Look*."

Angela kept her eyes tightly closed and shook her head. The wounds in her neck throbbed painfully.

"I'm hungry, Angela, you've no idea how hungry, and you're going to help me. Look at me—*look*, damn you!"

Angela swallowed once and opened her eyes. Diana's face hovered over her, long white throat and bare breasts, the nipples pink and taut. The green eyes were hungry, greedy.

"Scared, Angela? *You* are scared? Come now, I can't be that bad."

"Oh Christ, you look awful."

Rage flowed into Diana's face. "Oh, I do? My body isn't so bad. I feel strong. I'll bet your friend Michael would like my body. Maybe I'll go find him when I'm done with you." She smiled at

Angela, but the smile disappeared when she got no reaction. "He was looking at me, lusting after my body. He wanted to fuck me. I could tell. I think I'll take him from you."

Angela's head ached, and the pain in her throat had worsened. "Don't hurt him."

Diana laughed. "You are stupid, aren't you? 'Don't hurt him.' I'll kill him, but first I'll play with him some, let him get turned on. Not that I like it." A shuddery hiss. "But you still don't understand. You still don't know what a curse it is, do you? Answer me!" She grabbed Angela's hair, making her cry out.

The vampire sat on the arm of the red chair, her naked white torso twisted slightly, her right hand grasping Angela's black hair above the forehead. Angela saw the green eyes, the mouth still faintly pink with lipstick. Currents of emotion crackled across the waxy face. The two women stared at each other. Angela's face was flushed, black hair curling about her, and the blue of her eyes recalled the sea, the source of life.

"I liked you once, Angela." The hand holding Angela's hair relaxed slightly; Diana's other hand slid along her own bare thigh and touched the curling hair between her legs. "You seemed so beautiful, with all your dark hair and dark skin, and you were so fun and alive. I liked you so much, Angela." Diana's fingers caressed the black hair, and she ran the inner curves of one foot along Angela's leg. The green eyes lost their terrible intensity, wandering in the past. "I loved you, Angela. I wanted you."

The wind filled the silence between them.

"I didn't know. You hid it."

"I had to."

"You were my friend, Diana. I would have understood."

"You would have hated me, and I knew it was wrong and hateful."

"I wouldn't have hated you—you can't help what you feel."

Diana yanked the black hair, jerking Angela's head so that she cried out. "Nothing is wrong for you, is it?!" The green fires burned again. "If that's so you can take off your clothes and we'll have some fun before I eat. You'll like it, Angela—I'm very good with my fingers." Still holding Angela's hair, she shook her head, pulling hard enough to fill her eyes with tears. "Take off your clothes."

"No."

"Take them off, whore—I want to see your thing."

Angela tried to close her eyes but could not. Tongues of flame ate at her throat and belly. Diana's face was a horrible mask, an evil mockery hammered out of flesh. Some demon must have forged it in hell. Thin and white with its high cheekbones and aquiline nose, with its penciled eyebrows and the bleared remnants of lipstick, her face still recalled the glamorous creatures from the world of fashion, but that expression would never appear in any magazine.

Angela heard the quiet *zzzzz* of a zipper and realized her own trembling fingers were undoing the parka. "Oh God, *no*. I *won't*."

"Don't fight me, Angela. You'll like it, I promise you." The voice dripped sweet, sticky honey, attempting to conceal the corruption.

Angela fought her fingers away from the zipper. Diana's eyes were horrible, but not so ghastly as Blut's, those blue-white essences of evil.

"Okay." Diana stood, furious. "I wanted it to be with your cooperation because it would have been worse for you afterward. But if you won't come willingly, I can still take you. I promise you it will hurt—maybe not like when *he* did it, but it will hurt."

Angela stared, feeling herself go cold all over. She scrunched back into the chair as Diana closed in. The pink lips drew back in a parody of a smile, revealing the long teeth. Hands reached for her, slender white fingers with the long nails glistening. The fire was nearly dead, the room only a flicker from utter darkness.

Angela knew she should fight or run or something. She could resist enough to avoid cooperating, but she could not strike back. Across the room, red light illuminated Jesus's face. What was Jesus doing here in hell? She looked desperately at Renwick but saw that he could not help.

A white blur as the hands struck, a tearing sound. Angela cried out, trying to shrink back and hide in the chair. The fingers ripped open the turtleneck and left scratches across her chest. The parka was more than half-open; shreds of the shirt fell to either side, leaving her throat and part of her breasts exposed. The scratches formed red droplets and began to bleed. Diana laughed.

"I'm strong now. Very strong. You will be too. Let me see more of your breasts, and then I'm going to eat. I can strip you down all the way later."

Angela tried to close her eyes, to shut out the

ravenous thing. Still smiling, Diana grabbed the shredded cloth and rent the shirt. The scream tore into Angela's skull, feeling as if it would blow open her head. Diana's hands touched white-hot steel—they jerked away, and she fell backwards.

Angela lowered her eyes, then moaned with relief. Lying between her breasts was Pat's cross. Cool silver throwing back the dying light.

Diana's hands trembled. Fear and rage made her face unrecognizable. She straightened up, fighting for resolution, and advanced her bare foot. Oh God, Angela begged—don't let her.

Resolution vanished. Diana screamed again, then with a snarl she turned and fled, a long lithe white animal, gliding over or around the furniture and through the doorway into the night. The wind howled angrily, sweeping a rush of cold snowy air into the room. The snowflakes danced and sparkled in the dim light.

Angela gave a great sigh and closed her eyes. How good to be alone. The house was hideous, an all encompassing obscenity, but it was better without *them*. Especially Blut. Diana still showed traces of humanity, but with Blut there was nothing. Absolutely nothing.

"That was pretty good."

Jesus smiled down upon her. A faintly cynical smile, his thin lips flaring out at the corners, his eyes only half-there. He stood beside the chair. Red scratches scarred the left side of his face.

"Are you . . ?"

"I'm not like Blut. Or her."

"Then why—what are you doing in this place?"

Renwick looked off into a corner and blinked.

"Uh, he gives me what I need—horse, smack, shit, whatever you wanta call it. Otherwise I go outa my fucking head. He wouldn't let me leave, anyhow. That's what I was trying yesterday, and he got me back. He likes you to think you've got him outsmarted, and then he grabs you by the balls and slams you around."

"I suppose you can't fight him."

"Fuck, no. He's too strong. You think I like this? I've tried to get away, tried real hard. Once he got angry and slapped me, just once, back-handed, light for him. My eye almost swelled shut, and the whole side of my face went black and blue. And I've seen him kill a lot of people. So I do what he says."

"How can you stand it?"

For a moment pain showed in his half-numbed eyes. "The shit helps. I can have all I want when I'm good, so I take a lot."

"But don't you—how can you stand watching him?"

"Ah, it's not so bad. Sometimes I . . ." A smile came to his face, reminding her where she was, reminding her that he only looked like Jesus. "I used to shoot people for a living. Ever see what fifty-caliber machine gun bullets will do to some-body? Or napalm? They run around frying like fucking shish kebabs. At least now I just watch instead of pressing the trigger and blowing peo-ple apart. I hit a pregnant woman once and —"

"*Don't.*"

The ugliness left his eyes, making him look mild and faintly sleepy. He sat down, itched at a scratch on his cheek, and winced. The fine brown hair fell below his shoulders, and she saw skin through the wispy beard.

"Someday I'll get tired of this and sneak an overdose."

"You'd kill yourself rather than try to escape?"

"Don't give me that crap! I said I've tried to get away—I've tried. Listen, when he really gets angry—I don't think he'd mind all that much if I killed myself. And like, when you've been around here a while, being dead, really dead, doesn't seem so bad anymore. At least I wouldn't be like him."

"Oh God, that's true. It must be so awful for you here." She felt her eyes filling with tears.

Renwick stared. His eyes didn't work right; they blinked at extraordinarily long intervals and seemed unwilling to move. "Shit . . . you are beautiful." He would not look away, but she did. "Why do you have to be so beautiful?" Another sigh. "Fuck."

Angela swallowed, noticing how dry her mouth and throat felt. Almost dark now, the bulky shadows around her filling the room. She heard the wind moaning, a continual whine like an animal with its foot caught in a trap.

"You know what he'll do to you?"

"No." The word came out hoarse.

"He's going to rape you again and drink all your blood like with the blond chick. He'll kill all your friends. He rapes women even though he hates fucking. I can't figure it out."

"I can." She was so afraid she felt sick. Low in the belly, intestines crawling around inside as if they had gained a life of their own.

"He's planning something big. I can always tell. He's going to rape you, and this time he'll let me watch."

"You—you like that?" The tears seeped out.

Renwick looked uncomfortable: Christ had his doubts. "I can't leave this farm, and I get awful horny. He likes young, beautiful girls. And afterwards they're like your friend. They come on real strong, practically shove their tits in your face, but I know what they want. Coupla times they've almost gotten me, but Blut came in and screamed at them." A bitter, jarring laugh. "He 'saved' me. I don't want to get near them. They scare me."

"But couldn't you—?"

"Don't ask me to help—I can't." A hysterical tremor entered his voice. "Even if I wanted to, I couldn't. Okay? I swear—I think he can read minds. He always knows exactly what you're doing. Like a cat with a mouse, he doesn't wanta kill you right away; he likes to paw at you. If I wanted to help you we couldn't talk about it or plan anything, because then he'd get us."

"So I have to sit here. And wait."

The long howl went from a low note to a high shrill one, wailing with the wind at a dissonant interval. The wolf cry.

"He's out there. Probably taking care of your friends."

"Oh my God." She thought of Mike outside in the storm and Pat and Tony wandering helplessly. Maybe they could fight Blut. Perhaps Tony with all his knowledge—but she knew it was hopeless. Blut had all the forces of night at his call, pigs and wolves and storm and God knew what else. She wept, the tears streaking her face. She didn't want to die—to become like *them*. And worse, she had brought three of her friends, two people she truly loved, here to die.

Renwick stared at her. His eyes were wide

open, angry, and confused, his skeletal fingers
dug into his knees. He muttered something.

She opened her eyes, staring at the Christ face.
She started to speak but choked on her words.
"I'm so thirsty."

Renwick rose noiselessly and left the room.
She watched through blurry eyes. If only he
could help, but that was foolish to expect. Living
in this house for any length of time would warp
anyone. She had been here only a day or so, and
already she could barely think straight. He must
be half-mad, badly wounded deep inside. She
closed her eyes, sensed the nightmares floating
out there in the dark sea of sleep.

"*Here.*"

Renwick stood before her glaring. He held a
plastic glass.

"What is it?"

"What do you think it is?—blood?—punch
spiked with acid? It's water. Drink it."

She took the glass and drank eagerly, spilling
some liquid. It had the faintly brackish, metallic
taste common to wells, but it was water and wet,
and she was so terribly thirsty. After she had
drunk it all she lowered the glass. The dryness
was gone; her words came easier.

"Thank you so much."

Renwick grabbed the glass. His face twitched,
the muscles becoming iron at intervals as if
someone were rhythmically shocking him. His
eyes were angry. "He'd punish me if he knew."
He stared at her, his thin chest moving rapidly,
his breathing louder than the wind. "You remind
me of someone—you remind me of someone I
knew." His eyes slammed shut, head falling
back, his teeth clenched. He whirled around and

threw the glass. The plastic struck the mantel above the fireplace, bounced.

"*Goddamn beautiful women*—why?" Jesus was going berserk, ready to smash something, his sad eyes about to cry. "I can't help you—I *can't*— *can't!*" He strode from the room.

Angela closed her eyes.

Alone with the wind and night, she felt like going hysterical, but she would not give Blut that satisfaction. She would not become one of those weak, tearful, absolutely helpless females. She would resist Blut and the farm as long as she possibly could. But when she thought about Mike, Pat, and Tony out there, she had to cry. If only there were some hope, any hope.

Sitting in the darkened room of that evil house, hearing the wind's constant howl—a moan that went on and on—she saw only death.

CHAPTER NINE

♦

J'implore ta pitié, toi, l'unique que j'aime,
Du fond du gouffre obscure ou mon coeur est
tombé.
C'est un univers morne a l'horizon plombé,
Où nagent dans la nuit l'horreur et le blasphème;
Un soleil sans chaleur plane au-dessus six mois,
Et les six autre mois la nuit couvre la terre;
C'est un pays plus nu que la terre polaire;
—Ni bêtes, ni ruisseaux, ni verdure, ni bois!
Or il n'est pas d'horreur au monde qui surpasse

> *La froide cruaté de ce soleil de glace*
> *Et cette immense nuit semblable au vieux*
> *Chaos. . . .*
> —Baudelaire, *"De Profundis Clamavi,"*
>   Fleurs du Mal

THEY WATCHED THE HEARSE cross the stream
and start uphill; then a gust of snowy wind
obscured their view. Mike shivered and raised
his hood. He squinted frequently trying to keep
snow out of his eyes. He felt tired and beyond
being surprised.

Russo grabbed his bag, strode over through
the snow. "What the hell is going on? If that's
her way of making sure she can participate . . ."

"I don't think that's why she drove away." The
priest looked worried.

"Why then?"

"I'm afraid she may be working for our oppo-
nent."

"*What?*" Snow flew about Russo's incredulous
face.

"Angela mentioned something to me a few
weeks back about Diana becoming involved with
an occult group, spiritualists of some sort.
Angela didn't like it, she even spoke about moving out. Diana had become very distant, unpleas-
ant to live with, and she was terribly secretive
about the whole matter."

Russo blinked, then spoke with unnerving
calm. "I suppose she's a witch."

"Oh Christ," went Michaels. "It all fits." Every
move he made drew the noose tighter. "She had
a huge white cat. I fell asleep in her apartment,
which conveniently delayed us from getting here
before dark. And I let her come along."

"Don't blame yourself. I should have said something sooner."

"Yes," Russo said. "Why the hell didn't you tell us?"

"I couldn't say anything in front of her, and it was only hearsay. But I did feel her animosity. We were never close, but we were on friendly terms. Tonight I could sense her hatred."

Mike nodded. "I knew I was picking up bad vibes between you. I should never have let her come. That's why Angela didn't mention her—she was the last person she wanted to come. I fell right into the trap."

"How could you avoid it?" Pat said. "The whole thing has been superbly planned."

Russo's lips formed a bitter smile. "And I practically gave her a discourse on vampires. Worthy of publication in the *Journal of Transylvanian Philology*. Well, let's assume she is a witch. She did know a lot about the subject for someone asking me questions. We have our work cut out for us. At least I didn't leave my bag of goodies in the car. We'd better hurry."

They spread out slightly and started downhill. Mike was in the middle, out front. Point man, the job no one wanted in Vietnam. He's the guy who got ambushed or hit the trip wire and had a claymore go off in his face or his balls.

The storm howled about them. Wind reached across the fresh snow, skimmed off clouds, steaming shreds, while new flakes fell slowly. Downhill the wind was light, the snow deeper, four or five inches over the frozen crust left from last night. Mike felt god-awful cold. He had been out long enough for the chill really to cut, but not long enough to dull the icy edge.

To his right Pat trudged through the snow, the short figure and the bearded face below the hood recalling a medieval pilgrim plodding toward a shrine. Pilgrim on his way to hell. Russo's orange parka had become a puffy colorless mass, his long arms swinging rhythmically, one hand holding the pistol, the other the bag. A black stocking hat hid his long hair, but below the wool his face, with its slanted sideburns and dark brows, appeared sinister. The hillside sprouted and shrank, the ground uneven, barren of bushes or trees. Mike sensed the night, a presence all around him. Gleeful loathing—fresh meat. He shivered and walked more quickly.

At the bottom of the hill dark lines of barbed wire cut across the gray-white storm, blocking their way, the wire unevenly strung on rotten logs. Mike went to the midpoint between posts. His gloved hands pushed down the wire, and he carefully swung a leg over. His legs were long enough that he could stand straddling the wire. He brought over the other leg, stepping into a snowdrift. Scraggly grasses, strawy tufts thrust themselves through the snow like hair growing along the fence line.

Russo crossed the same way, long legs swinging easily over the fence. Pat needed help. He almost snagged his pants, but with Mike and Tony both pushing down the wire, he managed to get his shorter legs over. He immediately stumbled and fell to his knees in the snowdrift. "Damn," he muttered.

Ten feet away the ground dropped sharply, and they heard the gurgle of water. A giant oak stood before the stream, its branches straining at the sky like human limbs. Beyond the stream the trees thickened, forming a grove of dark trunks that stretched up the hill.

They walked to the bank of the black stream and stood staring at the icy flow. A couple of feet below, the water gurgled and ran in a senseless serpentine, winding through the snowy land. The stream was roughly four feet wide, and the opposite bank rose sharply. Snowflakes, large white moths, flittered down, and the dark waters annihilated them, swallowing like a hungry maw. The stream's murmur had grown into a multitude of bubbling empty voices.

"This must be Acheron, and Charon will be waiting for us downstream," Russo said.

"Huh?" Michaels asked.

"Nothing. Mere literary ruminations. How are we going to get across? We could almost jump if the banks weren't so slippery. We could search for a log."

Mike had a vision of both feet slipping, plunging into that icy water. Instant frostbite in this weather. "We could try the bridge."

"Wouldn't it be guarded?"

"Why? Blut's expecting us. We could check it out."

The priest stared past them, his eyes fixed on the dark flowing waters and the gnarled roots that curled from the opposite bank like a nest of entwined serpents. "Why isn't the stream frozen? It's so terribly cold."

Mike felt a funny sensation at his neck. "Christ, I don't know. It's easily zero out here."

"Probably the movement," Russo said. "Let's go take a look at the bridge."

Mike turned to walk along the curving bank. The stream was a continual roar, hundreds of tinkly voices, devilish elves at work with tiny hammers. The heavy snow fell steadily, obscuring the landscape. Michaels felt as if something wanted to trap him under a gray-white bottle. The wind slapped at the snow, howling along with the waters. Mike stared across the stream into the grove of black trunks.

A shadow amid the grove came alive and flew toward him, blossoming teeth. The amber eyes flamed through the night, throwing a yellow gleam across the snarling face. Mike nearly ripped off his pocket getting out the .45. The thing crouched on the opposite bank, the muscles, like black metal, rippled as the dog-wolf sprang.

Michaels raised the .45, his left hand grasping his wrist for support, and fired before fear could give him the shakes. The *bam!* sliced open the night's belly, thundering and disappearing into the storm. The dog jerked as if he had been struck with a rolled newspaper, flipping backward, his leap broken off, then rose and slithered around. Christ, a direct hit in the chest did nothing.

The thing growled, its roar flowing out to join the void, and leaped over the stream. The black meteor with yellow eyes hurtled at him, its huge paws extended for a deadly embrace. The growl had become a funeral siren shrieking of damnation. Paralyzed, Mike waited for the dog to tear him apart.

The creature faltered in mid-air, landed, then whined as if it had struck something. It cowered in the snow and made a sound between a whimper and a snarl. Russo stepped past Mike toward the dog. Teeth bared, it oozed backwards kicking up snow, then turned to soar back across the stream and disappear amidst the dark trunks.

Russo sighed and let his arm sag. "Jesus God." He had held the crucifix as a knight would hold his inverted sword for protection against demons, arm thrust forward, fist clenched. "For a moment I didn't think it would work."

Michaels could barely speak. "Christ—thank you." He pocketed the .45, his hand still trembling.

The priest stared across the stream, his mouth half-open. "What in God's name was that?"

Russo glanced at Mike. "Manfred or Blut?"

"God, I don't know."

"I'd guess it was Manfred."

"But what *was* it?" the priest asked.

"A demon in the form of a dog. That's why the .45 hardly touched him. You can't harm such a creature with any normal weapon, but the cross or host terrify them. You saw the look in its eyes. It wanted to rip me into pieces but couldn't get close enough. The dogs and pigs are probably all demons in animal form."

Mike stared across the bank where the dog had disappeared. "Thank God for that. I really thought I'd had it. Good God, that dog scares me—even before I knew what he was last night. It's just so . . . Christ."

"Are you okay, Mike?" the priest asked.

"Sure. Scared shitless, but okay. It's when I think what would've happened . . ." He turned to Russo. "Hey, thanks, really. He would have killed me."

Russo smiled, snow flittering across his dark visage. "I'm just glad to know something will work. Well, we've made enough noise now that

every demon or vampire within the next several
counties must know we're here. I suppose they
probably knew beforehand anyway. We might as
well try crossing the bridge."

They followed the curving stream. Mike felt
himself trembling from fear and cold. His blue
jeans were like ice, and the skin of his wrists and
throat was numb where the cold grabbed. They
had been outside for more than a half hour. He
had never been so cold. Somehow in the morning, fleeing the house at dawn, it hadn't been so
bad.

The wind mauled the men, its incessant shriek
rising and falling, eagerly hurling snow at them,
and the tinkly voices of the stream joined the
confused din. Mike's cowboy boots stepped into
the snow, crushing a few scrawny stalks, and left
footprints the wind immediately obliterated.

They came to a narrow bridge. Russo looked
around, searching the nearby trees. They walked
onto the bridge. Beneath them the snow-covered
planks rattled, and the black water swept by, icy
blood flowing from a gash in the earth. They
stared ahead, blinking to keep snowflakes out of
their eyes. Snow covered the road, but they
could follow its outline curving into the tall
pines and twisted oaks. The tracks of the hearse,
half-hidden by now, also crept uphill.

Russo took the lead and strode boldly into the
trees. Pat and Mike followed silently. The
stream's mumble died away. It was colder and
darker amid the trees, the pines groaning with
the wind. Dark trunks rose on either side; overhead the branches met, strained, and clawed at
each other, drowning men who grasped at whatever they could. The wind was more noticeable

in the trees. They seemed almost alive, murmuring a warning from their troubled sleep. The woods were full of shadows, dark blurry places where night things hid.

Mike concentrated on the ground before him and tried not to think about where he was. It would drive you crazy. Close by he heard deep, awkward breathing. The priest stared ahead fiercely, trying to ignore being out of breath. Poor Pat, overweight and with shorter legs. Mike's own beer flab and lack of sleep were taking their toll. He slowed down.

Russo walked vigorously, leaving big gaps between the waffled footprints of his boots. He stopped, turned to see the others fifteen feet behind, waited impatiently for them to catch up, then strode off again.

Mike rounded a curve and almost walked into Russo, who had stopped to stare. They could make out a darker shape in the shadow. Two globular eyes, the body black with a large metal vw at the front, the bus sat parked along the roadside.

"What the hell is a Volkswagen bus doing here?" Russo asked.

Mike stared, feeling afraid. "It's Blut's, or someone that works for him." He watched Russo walk over to the bus and peer through the windows. He didn't want to get near it.

Pat opened the door and looked inside. "Hey, the keys are still here." He pulled them out and put them inside his bag. "Whoever it belongs to isn't going anywhere. If we can't find the hearse, we can leave in that."

Pat stared suspiciously at the black bus. "I wonder how long it's been there?"

"For a while. There's not a trace of any tracks in the snow. We'd better be moving." Russo again took the lead.

Mike breathed hard, feeling the heartthrobs echo through his body. The hill was quite steep. And soon, very soon now, the trees must end, and they would see the house. He tried to prepare himself, but when the dark trunks separated and revealed that skull on its devil perch, he felt a rush of pure fear. Wave after wave buffeted him, so bad he thought he would stumble to his knees and be sick in the snow.

The wind formed drifts in the clearing, dunes of a snowy Sahara, and momentarily the falling snow dwindled so they could see clearly. The house still recalled a bleached alien skull with its countless sockets. Some just God must have gouged out its eyes. Surrounded by a few stunted trees it sat there on its hilltop overlooking a frozen landscape light-years from the sun's warmth. Snowflakes whirled slowly through the blue-gray light . . . slowly, so slowly . . . as if, like everything else in this universe, they were dead. The wind raised clouds of snow, making the ground appear insubstantial, a hazy mist one might fall through. However, a familiar object sat before the house, a black square shape with fins—the hearse.

All three men looked at the house. Russo motioned them toward a large oak, and they left the road to gather behind the tree.

"What do we do now?" Mike asked.

Russo's gray eyes stared past him at the house. "We get inside."

"How? Do we just walk in?"

"That may be the easiest way."

Pat drew in his breath. "*Look*. We can't simply walk in."

The big hogs wandered around the house and stopped before the porch. Two smaller pigs joined them, waddling through the snow, their short legs completely hidden. The hogs turned to stare in the men's direction, and immediately the three tried to hide behind the oak. The largest pig raised its head, let out a shrill squeal. More pigs appeared and took up positions.

"Goddammit," Mike murmured. "Now how do we get in?" This was turning into a bad repeat of the morning. Morning: He realized Angela was in there, actually inside, and he wanted very badly to see her. With the fatigue and giant dogs, he had momentarily forgotten her.

Russo gazed at the house and pigs, his mouth a tight line. "We could fight our way in using guns and crucifixes, but that might take a while."

"God, that's putting it mildly."

Russo stared silently at the unearthly snow-scape. "Is that hearse insured?"

"Yeah."

"But it doesn't belong to you?"

"No. And my uncle is going to be pissed off when he sees what I've done to it."

"Would you consider writing it off as a total loss?"

"Listen, Tony, what are you getting at? I'm too tired for guessing games."

Russo's mouth twisted into a sardonic smile. "I'm thinking of using the hearse as a big battering ram. Even with the chains on you could get it up to forty. Run it straight into the side of the house."

"What's that suppose to do to the driver? Is he expendable too?"

"He weights down the gas pedal and jumps out at the last moment."

Mike shook his head. "That's crazy. You've been watching too many spy movies. How would we get away if we wrecked the car?"

"The VW bus. In fact, we could use that for the ramming job. Hardly strong enough, though. That hearse, on the other hand, could really do a job to the house. Smash a rather big hole. Which would divert the pigs. The other two could then get into the house."

"Suppose the farm has a concrete foundation."

"Very doubtful. No, not a house that old."

"There's a supergood chance the hearse would explode or catch fire."

"Now who's been watching spy movies? That could work to our advantage. In fact, even if the hearse doesn't explode, I'd suggest we set it on fire before we leave."

Pat listened attentively, watching the two men. Both heads rose about six inches above him. "What good would the fire do?" he asked.

"A purgation. Vampires can't stand—"

Mike shook his head again. "It's too crazy, too dangerous—and what makes you think Diana would have been nice enough to leave us the keys?"

Tony's bemused smile disappeared. "Oh hell, I didn't even think about that. Well, she might have. Definitely worth taking a look."

"The pigs would spot you if you got that close and—"

The priest slammed into them, shoving with both hands, and all three fell into the snow. Mike felt the hand hit his shoulder. He began to curse, then his mouth stayed open. Sailing over them, a great dark bird of prey, was Manfred. Mike squirmed desperately, felt the cold powder snow on his face and his side as he struggled to get his hand in his pocket and sit up before the dog could get him.

Manfred glared from the shadows, a black shape with yellow eyes, a low growl coming through the half-open mouth. The tiny ears had flattened against the black head, and the snarl revealed teeth. The amber eyes were ready to burn from the skull. Pat's quivering hand held a small piece of bread.

"Goddammit," Russo muttered. He stood up, holding the crucifix before him. Manfred flattened, drew back, growling louder. "The bag— get the bag." The priest grabbed the old leather bag.

Mike fumbled to his feet, tearing open the snap on his pocket. He stood staring at the dog, mouth dry, too frightened to decide whether to get the gun or the cross. The priest rose slowly, his eyes fixed on Manfred.

"Let's get out of here," Mike said. He wanted to scream.

Russo took a step toward the dog. It cringed and shrank back into the snow. "Start down the road. I'll keep him occupied for the moment."

Mike and the priest were both behind him. Overhead the black branches of the oak, mysteriously bare of snow, writhed and twisted like cracks in the sky, as though the vault of the heavens had shattered. The white flakes drifted down calmly and monotonously, oblivious to what passed with the men.

"*Go on,*" Russo said. His face seemed thinner, scared around the edges. His gray eyes and the demon's yellow orbs met in deadly battle. Mike and Pat stumbled back into the grove, and then Mike saw the pigs.

Like goddamn rats—a pack of rats—wading through the snow, coming across the clearing squealing, their eyes flaming red or yellow.

"Tony—watch out!" he screamed, pulling out both pistol and crucifix.

Russo half-turned and saw the dark furies swarming from the void. He backed toward Mike, nearly stumbling. The pigs stopped at the tree line and formed a ragged half-circle. The three large hogs joined Manfred. The dog rose from the snow, and slinked a step toward Russo. The tiny eyes of the three pigs were red coals smoldering in the great ugly heads, their snouts and the two nostril holes twitching with their grunts. The black forms wavered and flickered like a colorless fire, as if they were as insubstantial as the icy wind.

Mike could feel the animosity from where he stood. He had never sensed such a mass of ugly emotion—hate, frustration, anger, a terrible longing for death, murder, and blood. And all that incredible malevolence was focused on the person holding them at bay with the cross.

The small pigs blurred into motion, running at Russo. Mike raised the .45 and fired rapidly. "*Oh Christ.*" One shot knocked aside a pig, stopping it with a squeal, but the others ran about Russo's legs, leaping at him. Mike saw a snout tear open Russo's leg and heard him scream. The cross flew skyward, metal flashing as it arced away into the snow.

Manfred and all the pigs fell upon Russo like the orange breath of a flamethrower. The grunting and screeching, the dog's snarls, snuffed out Russo's dying screams. Black snouts and ears, fat bodies, the man's flailing arms and legs with his clothes and flesh being ripped away—all whirled about in a terrible blend of sound and shape. *Totentanz*, the dance of death.

The other two men drew back. Mike raised the gun. Darkness and the storm made it difficult to see, but he fired into the swirl of twisting black limbs, frustrated tears pouring from his eyes.

"You'll hit Tony!" Pat yelled.

Mike said nothing. He squeezed the trigger, heard the explosive *bam!* and felt the recoil jerk his arm, fired again and again without even aiming. It would be better if he did hit him. Smoke from the gun flurried with the snow, and he smelled burnt powder. The gun clicked. Empty, the barrel hot and empty. Mike cursed, threw the pistol and the crucifix at the pigs. Both landed several feet short in the snow.

"Goddammit—goddamn them."

"Mike, come on—we can do nothing." The priest yanked at his arm. They turned and fled the loud, groveling horror of the feeding pigs.

They stopped once to look back. Through the falling snow they saw the pigs and Manfred. A white shadow glided from the night. It stopped before the pigs, kicked and shrieked at them. The smaller pigs fled, squealing with fear, scuttling through the snow on their short legs. Manfred and the three hogs were more stubborn. They backed away slowly, sullenly, while she screamed and cursed them, kicking out with her bare feet. They flowed away into the shadows.

"Diana?" Pat asked.

Mike said nothing. Russo was only a dark shape, a stain in the snow, amorphous, and they could hardly see the woman.

Diana stared at the bloody remains, her lips drawing back hungrily. The wind moaned about her, reaching between the slender thighs, brushing its muzzle against her breasts, and ruffling her yellow-brown hair. But a part of the cold cannot feel cold. Snow covered her bare feet, rising halfway up her calves, and snowflakes flittered around her like white flies drawn to a carcass. She bent over in a single movement, her knees plunging into the snow. She pressed her mouth against the wounds, lapped and sucked frantically.

Michaels saw her kneel and could guess the rest. "Let's get out of here."

They ran—stumbling, fighting through snowdrifts, dark thick trunks jouncing, blurring past, the wind shrieking in agony, the white flakes everywhere, flying at their eyes, stinging. A gray-white universe of storm broken only by black trees, the sky had disappeared, faded into the earth, and the dark wood was all, went on forever. Mike leaped over a tree's frozen corpse, snagging his foot on a branch and falling. He caught himself with his hands, face and chest sinking into the snow. He shuddered, feeling cold swallow up his face, slide down his neck.

The priest stopped to help him up. "Are . . . all right?" He was breathing so hard he could hardly speak. Ice and snow covered his beard.

"Yeah." Mike staggered to his knees, shook the snow out of his face. Pat grabbed an arm and yanked him up. They stood panting, unable to speak. Next to Pat was the leather bag. The heavy snow fell ceaselessly and the dark oaks surrounded them. Nearby a pine moaned under the wind's obscene touch.

"That was Diana, wasn't it?"

"Yeah. Naked. She's a vampire. Like Ursula was." Motionless, Mike began to feel the awesome cold. He shivered. He remembered Russo, that tall figure, alive and well, swept under by all those black things. "He saved my life. Christ—poor guy."

"*Yes.*" Pat's voice was full of pain.

They stood silently, and soon the heart-pounding urgency of their fear faded. Mike felt a vast weariness, a frozen stupor, coming over him. "We'll freeze out here."

"I know. We cannot simply give up." The priest sounded angry. "What . . . I don't understand how those three pigs could rush him as they did."

Mike laughed harshly. "They could because they *were* pigs. Ordinary everyday barnyard pigs. My .45 worked fine on them. Only some of the pigs are demons, the others are only animals. A cross means nothing to a real pig. The big ones—those fuckers sent the little ones in to get rid of the cross so they could move in for the kill.

Pat's mouth slowly opened, then closed. He was still panting. Under the hood his face was pale, the brown hairs of his mustache coated with ice. "I wish I was in better shape. That last run nearly finished me."

"Yeah, me too." He felt nauseated and too tired to move. "What time is it?"

Pat had to stare a while before he could read the dial; he put the watch against his ear. "My watch stopped at one."

"What do we do now?"

Silence answered his question. Mike realized how much he'd counted on Russo for knowledge and direction. And now? Their weapons—guns, crosses, whatever—seemed futile, but they were all they had.

"We'd better find the house again," Pat said.

"Yeah. Christ, it's cold. At least you've still got the bag."

"I don't even remember picking it up."

"It may help if we ever get inside the house. I threw the .45 and a cross away back there. Guns are useless against vampires or demons, and there were too many ordinary pigs. God, are we ever lost. Which way do we go?"

"There, I think."

The two men walked slowly through the dark snowy woods. The wind had died down, and the snowflakes fell noiselessly all about them. Mike's knee hurt, and his hands were cold from the fall in the snow. He kept replaying Russo's death, seeing him go down under the black wave. The trees soon thinned, and they stopped behind a tall pine to stare at the house.

They were at the edge of the clearing left of the farm, closer to the hearse and the barn, about fifty feet from where they had come out before. Mike heard a clang, saw the metal feeder with pigs gathered around it. Several other pigs squatted before the house like sentinels. Mike glanced at the Cadillac hearse and felt afraid again, angry too.

"Oh hell," he murmured, "why don't we try Tony's plan?"

"All right. Suppose we do. We need to know if

the keys are there. I can run over and look. If they are I'll run the hearse into the house."

Mike stared, saw Pat was serious, then laughed weakly. "I do not believe this—we're both out of our fucking heads! It's my hearse, and I have more of a grudge against Doctor Blut and his pigs and lady friends. I get to play suicidal."

"Let me, Mike. I didn't believe any of this was possible. I've stood about and watched, I've been passive and frightened, now I want to do something."

"You did a pretty good job getting us out of the way of that dog. No, Pat. The hearse and I are old friends, see, and I'd rather wreck it. It's like a sentimental attachment. I'll do that, and you run in the house as soon as you get a chance. I'll try to jump out and join you."

"I can't change your mind?"

"No."

"You're sure?"

"Yeah."

They stared at each other. The wind moaned, accompanied by clangs. Then a new sound came to life: music, a fugue racing so diabolically fast it teetered forever between chaos and order.

"What in God's name is that?" Pat asked.

"Blut. Playing the organ. With all the stops out."

"It sounds horrible."

"Yeah. Probably another of his special favorite composers." The hellish music floated into the night merging with the powers of cold and storm. The pigs listened attentively. Orpheus, returned from Hades a convert, played music that brought death.

"Pat, if I get the car, I may have to drive away

to lose the pigs so I can get up some speed before I ram the house, but I'll be right back. After I hit the house try to sneak inside. Look for Angela. If we can get back to that VW and take off without meeting Blut, so much the better."

"All right. And what if the keys aren't there?"

"Start dreaming up some brilliant new plan. Here goes nothing."

"Wait a minute." The priest grabbed his arm. "Good luck."

Pat stared up at him, his face not so pleasant now, cold and tired, worried lines showing around the eyes. His grip was stronger than Mike would have expected. Michaels chewed at his lip. He could tell his mustache had frozen. "Pat . . ." He felt an urge to embrace the priest simply for being human, for being there and giving him support when he needed it so badly. "I'm glad you came along. I hope you get out of this."

"I hope we both get out of this. And Angela too."

Neither of them wanted to elaborate further. Against the odds they had come to like each other, and they both understood the hopelessness of their undertaking. Snow fell heavily about them.

"Well, here goes nothing."

Mike stepped quickly through the trees to his right. Wind howled in the branches and raised snowy clouds out in the clearing. He stopped when the hearse was directly ahead through the trees, the shortest distance from the grove. It lay between the barn and the house, hiding him from the pigs in the barnyard. If he ran fast enough the pigs by the house might not see him.

He peered carefully from behind an oak trunk.

Christ, he was cold. What if those little fuckers
swarmed all around him and tore him to bits
like they had Russo? Before he had time to think,
his cowboy boots were plunging into the deep
snow.

He leaped out into the swirling snow. The
wind shrieked, and the heavy snow hid him, but
the twenty-five feet was still an incredible
chasm. He ran crouched low, knees bent, and
ducked behind the hearse.

Staying scrunched down he listened carefully.
A few more clangs, the ubiquitous moan of wind,
and Blut's horrible fugue. Still crouching he
crept to the front door. Now came the fun part. If
the keys weren't there he was screwed. There
was so much snow on the hearse he'd have to
open the door to look inside and check. His hand
reached past a huge dent (some pig's work) and
seized the handle. He waited for another gust,
pressed in the button, opened the door a few
inches, and quickly thrust in his upper body.

Dark dim interior—God, the other door was
open, snow all over the front seat. He could
hardly see, but his cold fingers fumbled at the
dash, felt the thin metal in the slot—*keys!*

He quickly got inside, turned over the engine.
A shrill *eeeh* made his fingers shake. He stopped
to lock the door on the driver's side, then reached
across the seat. Black head with floppy ears,
small eyes, and snout coming for him. He
wrenched the door shut, nearly amputating the
pig snout, and locked it.

Ruhuhhh . . . Goddamn slow-starting car. The
hearse lurched and shuddered as pig bodies
thudded off its sides. Christ, this was getting old.
Start—goddammit! He floored the pedal as the

engine choked alive. He turned on the windshield wipers, but they would not budge under the heavy snow. If he went straight ahead he shouldn't hit anything. Driving blind was better than being bashed to pieces.

He touched the pedal, and the hearse lurched forward, chains clunking loudly. The thuds stopped. He rolled down the window and thrust out his head. Icy air and snow flew at his face, making him squint. Behind, dark blurs ran for the hearse. With his head out the window he followed the road, the car bouncing wildly, until the farm and the pigs were gone.

He jerked to a stop, stepped outside, and used his hands to brush the snow off the front and back windshields. He got back inside, yanked off his gloves and waited for feeling to burn back into his hands. Fresh snow splattered against the windshield.

All he had to do now was smash this several-ton beast into Blut Farm. Stuntmen did such things all the time. He could simply drive off and forget the whole business, leave Pat alone out there for the pigs and Angela for Blut. Angela. Oh God, he was already forgetting her dark beautiful face, forgetting how she had felt pressed to him. And he might never see her again. Might? The odds were excellent.

"Please . . ." he mumbled. His eyes grew foggy and he realized how terribly tired he was. Oh well, the chances were also excellent that he would die, so he wouldn't have to languish over her memory. He wanted the satisfaction of smashing the hearse through the rotting timbers of Blut Farm.

The snow was slowly burying him inside the

hearse, darkening everything. He turned on the wipers. *Swish, swish, swish* . . . Monotonous eternal snowstorm out there. Hell must be this way, not hot but cold and stormy. This was reality. He had been in this storm forever. Iowa City and the rest of his life were dreams. Get moving. You're fading out.

He went outside and took the cardboard box out of the back. The pots rattled noisily as he dropped the box on the seat. He could put the heavy box over the gas pedal and jam it down; as for the steering wheel, he'd just have to stay in until the last moment. Better not think this through too carefully. The insanity would become obvious.

He turned to the left, backing the car around so he faced the farm. The fear was getting to him, drying his mouth and throat. He accelerated and drove along the road, the headlights and windshield wipers vainly cutting at the storm. The hearse bounced and the chains rattled.

Rounding a curve he saw the house. As usual, the sight did bad things. The black eyeless sockets somehow saw him, or perhaps they were hungry mouths laughing. The pigs in the barnyard squealed and ran under the fence out onto the road; others ran from the house. They watched, shadows obscured by the slanting fall of snow.

"All right, you fuckers." He would head straight down the road and turn left slightly, which would let him hit the farmhouse broadside, kick a hole in its side.

Swallowing, he hefted the heavy box off the seat and awkwardly tried to get his arms between the wheel and the seat. A smaller box would help. Oh Jesus—a big black dog had walked around the house. He dropped the box, narrowly missing the brake. The hearse gave a hesitant gulp, then realized it was being fed gas. The beast lurched, shuddered, its wheels groaning, then drank greedily. With a furious roar it took off, struggling for a gallop.

Michaels stared at the jouncing swerving landscape, watched the pigs part like a black wave. The road sloped downhill, giving him added momentum. Testing, he let go of the wheel and felt the car start to swerve. He'd have to stay in until the last moment—it was going fast, the landscape blurring and shaking, him turning the wheel slightly to aim for that white side and its black windows.

God—the dog was right in front of him, all glaring amber eyes. He resisted the urge to swerve aside and held the wheel fiercely. Speedometer past forty, the dog still—with a noiseless howl it sprang at the hearse, flying over the hood all yellow eyes and teeth, smashing against the windshield, flipping up and over into the night. The windshield split with a loud crack, the hearse wobbled, shuddered. Mike's eyes had slammed shut, now he opened them to see the wall rushing at him through a web of cracked glass.

Out—now! Fingers clawing at the door handle, one hand still gripping the wheel, then both hands at the door—it opened, the hearse swerving as he slid out. The night air grabbed, yanked him out, his leg striking against the door. His face and forearms slammed into the snow, and he rolled and bounced—a tremendous crash, wood and metal impacting, warping each other—and he rolled over and stopped.

He lay quietly, only half-conscious, his face tasting snow. Darkness, ice on his skin, and quiet, so quiet. The wind blew snow over him, trying for a burial. Slowly he rose to his knees, shaking snow from his head. Realizing what had happened he jerked around.

All about him fragments—splinters of wood or glass—sprinkled the snow. The black projectile remained lodged in the thing's ancient side. The wound had splintered edges of wood, the wall pushed in as if an angry giant had struck. The hearse had penetrated almost halfway, the four-eyed head gone, only the finny tail showing. The rotten timbers had offered little resistance. The hearse had swerved only slightly and hit about five feet right of center.

Christ, everything happened so fast. Where were the pigs? He turned quickly and nearly fell over. Wind scraped the top layer off the snow and molded clouds, while more snow floated from the empty sky. The barren gray-white expanse stretched to the dark trees. The wind on his face made him shiver; his skin was cold and wet from his fall, and the air created frozen fire.

Hurry—get away before the pigs return. He staggered through the snow, running to the front of the house. He started up the steps and fell onto one knee. Pain twisted his face and he cursed. He felt sore all over.

The big wooden door was open. A red-orange glow showed through the gap, and snowflakes danced slowly in the light. He wrenched the door wide open, stepped inside, and stared about wildly. The wind slithered in alongside, howling its laughter. From the hallway he could see into the living room.

A huge fire burned, casting its flickering patterns of light and shadow. The coffin, that black bark from the underworld, sat in the center of the room, and the smell of death still permeated everything. All was the same—the dark wood, the plush furniture, the red-and-black carpet—except for one thing: The hearse's mutilated face leered at you. The twisted headlights rose a foot over the floor, the glass broken, and the front grillwork was pushed in, bent out of shape. Wind and snow drifted through the jagged wound. Plaster, dust, shattered glass, and splintered wood covered that side of the room. The red velvet chair where he had left Angela had fallen onto its side.

"*Angela!*" he yelled. He breathed deeply, hearing only silence answer. What a dumb thing to do. Now anyone else in the house would know he was here. Where the hell was Pat? And Angela? He stepped into the living room.

A white fury darted from the shadows and leaped on him, knocking him over. Sharp nails ripped open his field jacket. He turned onto his back, trying to fight off the thing.

Diana's *Vogue* face smiled down. New were the long canines and a lipstick of blood. The gray-green eyes beneath the pencil-thin brows were a coalescence of hate. She was naked, and her small breasts wobbled as they struggled. She seized his wrists, pulling his arms apart and pinning them to the ground.

Breathing deeply Mike went limp, giving her time to notice, then suddenly attempted to

wrench his hands free. He couldn't budge her.
The thin white face smiled, teeth still showing.
She crouched over him, legs straddling his waist.
The long arms, the torso with its small breasts
and flat belly, were pure white marble, marble
the fire tinted orange. A thatch of brown hair
curled in the shadow between her legs.

"What's the matter, big strong man? Can't you
throw a weak little woman aside?" Michaels
said nothing, avoiding her eyes. "I heard you call
for your little Angela, and I thought I'd see if I
couldn't cheer you up. What does Angela have
that I don't? Wouldn't you like to fuck me? I'm
almost a virgin. *Answer.*" Her hands squeezed
his wrists until they hurt, but he said nothing.
Her smile vanished. "When I finish with you, you
won't do anymore fucking at all. I think I'll make
you undress and have some fun with you. I'll
show you what agony sex can be. *Look at me!*"

She dropped his wrists, grabbing him by the
throat with one hand, while the other clawed
into his hair. She yanked the long hair, making
him wince and stare up at her. The green eyes
devoured, and she smiled. Mike felt a terrible
cold, an icy weariness seeping inside. Venom of a
white cobra. He had raised his arms, now they
slumped to the floor. Just like with Ursula. If
only he could close his eyes. Her tongue glided
quickly across her lips. *Move—get away*. But he
couldn't.

With a sharp hiss she leaped backwards, her
nails slashing open his neck. Nervously she
backed toward the wall, deeper into the shadows, the muscles in the white face tense with
hate.

Shaking his head, Michaels sat up and rubbed

at the scratches on his throat. Behind him in the doorway to the living room stood the priest. The cowl of his gray coat had fallen back, and in his right hand sparkled a silver cross.

"What's the matter, priest? Don't you want to watch? Afterwards I'll do it with you. I'd be a better fuck than Angela." Diana's words could not hide her fear.

"Mike, if you still have a host or cross, take one of them out." Michaels fumbled in his field jacket pocket and came up with a half-crumpled, frozen piece of bread. Diana hissed again. "Get on the other side of the room—*quickly.*"

He glanced at Diana and realized what the priest had planned. He lunged to his feet, or tried to, and staggered to the left before Diana could run past him. She backed off with a snarl. They had trapped her in a corner twelve feet from either man. She came forward.

"What's the matter with you? You'll fuck Angela but not me? How do you know she's any better than I am? Let me show you."

Mike stared at the priest. The two men walked slowly forward holding cross and host before them. Diana howled, retreating into the shadow.

"You fuckers! Hypocrites—liars! Kill one another—fight each other! I swear I'll tear your precious cocks off if you come any closer."

She tried to dart between them, but the priest jerked his hand sideways and drove her back. She snarled and spit, crouching low. Her body was long and slimly muscled like a great white panther. They stopped about five feet from the corner. Diana's green eyes flamed, her face twisted beyond recognition.

"Let me go, you *fuckers.* I'll let you have me—

you can satisfy your sick desires all you want—
but put those things away!"

Pat sighed wearily. He dropped the leather
bag, and his left hand pulled at the zipper while
he watched Diana.

Mike watched the vampire, his hand quivering. "What do we do now?"

"If we pour this around the corner it should
immobilize her." He took out a glass jar and
unscrewed the lid.

Diana sprang, hitting the priest and making
him drop the cross, but his other hand jerked
upward, the liquid spurting out and splashing
them both.

Diana screamed and fell to the floor writhing
desperately. The white legs kicked spasmodi-
cally like the dead limbs of a frog twitched by
electricity. The screaming grew louder, while
her long fingers with the pink nails clutched at
her face. Mike smelled burning flesh. Black
marks splotched her chest and arms, smoking, a
canker of decay that ate the deadly beauty. He
was glad he couldn't see her face.

Pat stared dumbly, holding the half-empty jar
of holy water. "I didn't . . . mean to."

"Just like acid. We should finish her off. For
her own good as well as ours." He felt the
weariness returning and a dread of what should
be done.

"How?" Pat had picked up the crucifix and
held it over the moaning writhing corpse.

Mike dug around in the bag. He withdrew the
stake. It was a couple of inches thick and so long
it barely fit. The pale hard wood was nearly
white, one end sawed off square, the other
carved to a fine point. Mike touched the point.

Sharp, deadly sharp. Doubtlessly it was the right length and thickness, the proper wood. There was also a heavy mallet in the bag. Russo had thought of everything. If only he were around to do it. Michaels felt sick. "I don't want to do this."

Pat looked tired. The snow had melted, leaving his beard soggy. His face had grown more lines as the night progressed. "I've never killed anything. Not even a squirrel or a bird."

"But it's not killing, see—she's already dead." His voice had a whine to it. The priest said nothing. "I know what you mean, though." Neither man would look at the other.

Diana had stopped screaming. She lay with one hand clutching her face and cursed them. A black steaming burn covered half her mouth, smaller burns spotted her throat and breasts. "You've blinded me. I'll tear off your balls and bleed you to death. *Fuckers*—you fuckers!" Her burnt mouth distorted the words.

Mike stared at the priest. "*I'll do it*," he whispered.

Pat quickly shook his head. "You don't have to." His voice quavered.

Mike swallowed, grabbed the stake in one hand, the mallet in the other, and rose to his knees. Her breast lay bare, a dead white mound, even the nipple almost colorless. He could see the outline of the rib cage and the shaven stubble in her armpit. The wooden point quivered over her chest. He tried to aim for the black splotch left of the sternum. He brought the point closer, felt the convulsive trembling coming. He hit the stake as hard as he could.

He felt the point penetrate the skin and drive

between the ribs into the chest cavity. Blood
splattered his field jacket and face—cold blood.
He hammered wildly, ignoring the white thing
writhing and shrieking and kicking, ignoring the
blood everywhere. He missed the stake and
smashed his knuckles with the mallet but felt no
pain. He hammered and hammered until he realized the wood would go no farther—the point
was merely being dulled on the hard floor. Diana
had stopped moving. Blood poured from her
mouth and nose, and her chest was a large red
stain. Black burnt cavities gaped upward where
her eyes had been. The *Vogue* face had vanished,
her beauty totally gone. She barely looked human. Four inches of bloody wood rose from her
chest.

Michaels dropped the hammer. Tears
streamed from his eyes and he wanted to throw
up. He slumped over and grabbed for the priest's
arm. Pat also had blood all over him, and his
eyes were wet.

Mike pressed his face against the gray wool
sleeve. He couldn't slow down his breathing. He
felt the priest's fingers slide into his tangled hair,
gently hold him by the side of the head. He
gripped the man's arm tightly. They could hear
the wind howl, its low dirge sweeping through
the wound in the wall, and the swirling fire
made the room tremble.

Mike sat up, and Pat let his hand drop. The
fingers he had smashed hurt, throbbed painfully.
He looked down at Diana. "Oh good Christ."

Her face had relaxed, and the burns, the black
pockmarks scarring her throat, face, and chest,
had disappeared. Her gray-green eyes stared

lifelessly at the ceiling. Pat reached down and closed each eye with his forefinger.

"Requiescat in *pace*," he whispered. "Dear God, in *peace*."

"How touching. What courage, what bravado."

The two men jerked around.

Blut's white face smiled, smiled from the darkness that surrounded him. Beside him stood a black dog with yellow eyes and a tall girl with a face like a Greek statue. Mike shivered, feeling fear drain him like a leech.

CHAPTER TEN

◊

And they are gone—ay, ages long ago
These lovers fled away into the storm.
That night the Baron dreamt of many a woe,
And all his warrior-guests, with shade and form
Of witch, and demon, and large coffin-worm,
Were long be-nightmared. . . .

      —Keats, The Eve of St. Agnes

"ANGELA," MIKE SAID. She stared at him, her face listless. Blut must have—but no, her lips made a tired smile, and her eyes were sad but okay.

Her smile was hesitant because of Blut's presence but genuine. Mike and Pat looked so good to her; human, truly human, not nightmare creatures or demonic beings. Mike was a mess, his long blond hair scattered about, his field jacket bloody. And Pat, wearing that ageless gray coat with the wooden buttons, his gentle bearded face so serious. She stared at Diana and wondered if someone would have to do that to her. Diana hadn't deserved that—or Tony. Blut enjoyed telling her about Tony. Her eyes filled with tears. She was so tired of all this and afraid, afraid for everyone.

"I would not attempt anything, my dear Father Donahue. Manfred, though a rather petty demon, is extremely quick. He will rip out your throat before you can reach the bag, and even if you did, I assure you, there is nothing in it which will frighten me."

Pat said nothing but stared longingly at the leather bag two feet away. Jesus appeared in the doorway, his eyes sunken shadows, hands in his pockets.

"Renwick, relieve the good Father of his bag. It is worrying him."

Renwick's long thin legs stepped neatly over Diana's body. He took the bag, walked over, and leaned against the bookshelves. Blut stared at the white corpse covered with blood.

"Very amusing. This is the second of my females you have destroyed, Mister Michaels. And the last. Diana and Ursula were both fools, but then most women suffer from similar defects. Perhaps Angela will prove more long-lived. Or rather, she will exist longer than her predecessors." Angela tried not to show her fear.

Michaels swallowed. He could not ignore the dog staring at him, those amber eyes of hate set in the black head. He was trembling. Blut would turn the dog on him.

"Relax, Mister Michaels. I will not let Manfred harm you. Not that he doesn't deserve it. He has been frustrated twice this evening. First Mister Russo with the cross, then your running over him with the hearse." He glanced at the big hole in the wall, the crumpled black metal, and broken wood. "Not only my women but my home—the Blut Farm." His eyes whooshed aflame but he put the anger into a smile. "You will be punished, though not by Manfred. He is a rather minor devil, utterly lacking any subtlety or attention to detail. He would love to simply tear you and the good Father to pieces, rending the flesh from your bones as with your friend Mister Russo. But I assure you, I have something more aesthetically appropriate planned. Manfred will have to content himself with watching, though he can clean up the leftovers. Manfred, of course, is not his real name. I assume he was some trivial fertility demon, the type who enjoyed frightening savages."

The dog growled deep in his throat, yellow eyes turning on Blut, small black ears flattening against the head. Red-orange light flickered across the shadowy form. Mike realized the creature hated Blut, hated him as only the damned could hate. Blut's watery blue eyes glared back at the dog. He made a guttural laughing noise.

"I prefer servants who hate me. Hate is a stronger, more genuine emotion than love. Is it not, Manfred?"

Man-thing and dog-thing eyed each other, fury crackling about them, yellow and blue fire set in black silhouettes. Michaels watched intently. *Clunk* beside him. Renwick had dropped the leather bag practically in Pat's lap. The priest's hand fumbled madly inside.

Manfred growled, the roar echoing off the ancient walls, and he rushed toward them like a black wave. Thick fingers clenched into a fist holding the cross, the silver reflecting the firelight. Manfred stopped, snarled, and slunk backward, his tail curling between his legs. He glared at the priest, then at Blut, his eyes the essence of hate.

Blut's dead face twisted, the yellow-white brows merging over the terrible eyes, his lips scowling. "You stupid fool—put that away—*now.*"

Pat licked his lips. He stood slowly, holding the cross before him. Instinctively Michaels and Renwick got behind him.

"Angela." The priest beckoned to her, his head moving while his eyes stayed on Blut.

She hesitated, wondering if she could break the vampire's hold. She stepped forward, and Blut pushed her aside. She fell backwards, slamming against the bookshelf, knocking over several books. Stunned, the dim room wobbling about her, she tried to rise. Blut growled, and the room grayed over. She moaned and her head slumped.

Blut's eyes were the maws of volcanoes, blue lava bubbling within. "Do you want something, priest? Let me see if I can't help you." He stepped forward. His form wavered; the blackness around him, the blackness which *was* him, seemed insubstantial—a dark whirlpool, the center dead white with two pale blue eyes. Manfred lurked behind him, pacing the floor, growling continually.

The priest stepped back twice and stopped. His arm was rigid, locked ahead in a challenge. His eyes focused past the cross on Blut's dead face. With his gray coat and his full beard Pat recalled some medieval monk confronting Satan himself. The wind rose, howling in through the open front door and the wound in the house. Snow floated in the frozen air, flakes of blood in the firelight.

Blut advanced until he was only a foot from the cross, then stopped. Mike sighed and felt Pat and Renwick relax. For a while he wondered if anything could stop Blut. The vampire stared, the narrow jaw thrust forward, the irises like ragged pieces torn from the sky. He was close enough for Mike to see the tiny red network of blood vessels set against the white.

"So you think to defy me, to frighten me with empty symbols and destroy me with stakes." His voice was a file scraping across flesh. "Haaaa— You think you can destroy *me*!" His lips tortured themselves into a smile. "I, who have killed thousands of worms like yourselves—many far better than you. A renegade priest who copulates with willing trash, and a worthless fool who works with the dead and still fears them. Do you think you can match wits with me? Among the greatest of the undead, a warrior aristocrat who has lived centuries—who was alive when you and your parents and grandparents were not even conceived—were sperm crawling greedily about a few eggs. I have planned every moment of this evening, foreseen all that will occur. I knew Renwick would betray me, and I let that foolish piece of dead flesh on the floor delay you. And who do you think let you leave Blood Farm,

Mister Michaels? Did you think it was your amazing courage and ingenuity? I could have destroyed you at any time, crushed you with my bare hands. I *wanted* you to leave. I was tired of Ursula, and that slut there promised to be equally idiotic. I let you harm my house because I no longer need it. Enough of these ridiculous theatrics—I would instruct you, Priest, to lower the cross because of its uselessness, but I know you would not believe me."

His fingers struck, curling about the priest's wrist like a snake. Pat sucked in his breath. "My fingers are cold, are they not? Let me give you a demonstration of my strength." Very slowly he drew the priest's hand and the cross closer. His arrogance faltered, face stiffening, but as the cross came closer his smile intensified. With the silver metal an inch from his face, he broke into laughter, a loud noise like someone choking to death.

"Oh Christ," Mike murmured. Fear, a chilling shiver, washed up his spine. They were dead. They were all dead.

"See, my good Father. You can frighten children like that slut on the floor or imbeciles like Manfred, primitive malevolence without intelligence, but you cannot touch me. You cannot touch the essence. I know the truth, the power of evil. But this, this hunk of metal—symbolic nonsense. You might as well threaten me with garlic cloves. And now you will drop your toy."

Smiling, he applied pressure, the skeletal hand tightening. Pat drew in his breath, wincing, and tried to pull his wrist free. Blut said nothing, smiling, smiling, always smiling like some lifeless image in a photograph. Pat went pale, breathing faster. Michaels could see the tendons, cords of white metal, stand out in Blut's hand. Pat closed his eyes and gritted his teeth. Sweat droplets appeared on his forehead.

"Oh, you are a brave priest, brave not to cry out. But we can fix that." He raised his white hand and the man's wrist, angrily gritting his own sharp white teeth.

Pat groaned, tears seeping from his eyes. The cross slipped from his fingers and clattered onto the floor. He squirmed wildly and cried out, a long moaning ohhhh.

"Stop it!" Angela screamed.

Michaels rushed at Blut. "You fucking bastard!" Blut brushed him aside with his free hand, virtually ignoring him. The blow knocked him backwards into the wall.

Blut snarled, eyes blue-white coals, and brought his fingers together, popping both bones in the priest's wrist. Pat yelled, a high, pained shriek. Blut let go. The priest fell to his knees, groaning and weeping. He clutched his forearm with his other hand and tried to control himself.

"Maybe now you will listen, Priest, when I command you to do something. We are hardly finished, you and I. And Mister Michaels, you are becoming a definite annoyance. As for this . . ."

He bent over and after hesitating an instant, picked up the cross. The dead fingers held the sparkling silver metal. Blut smiled. "Would you like this, my dear pet?" He whirled, thrusting the crucifix toward Manfred. The dog growled, leaping back and crouching down.

Blut laughed. "Silly idiot. This is only a piece of metal, only junk." Lips wrinkling inward, he spit on the cross. Fingers blurred, a jumble of motion, crumpling the crucifix beyond recognition, and with both hands he forced the metal into a ball. With a final laugh he threw it aside. "Now we may proceed. You—Renwick."

Renwick kept his head bowed, not looking up. Michaels saw his hands tremble.

"How would you like to die? I knew, of course, that you would betray me. Was it your hatred for me, or Miss Rosalba's charm?"

Angela stared at the thin, tired figure, the face hidden by the long brown hair and beard. She realized her talk with Renwick had condemned him to death. "Don't hurt him." She was immediately sorry she had spoken.

Blut gurgled up laughter. "Hurt him? I won't 'hurt him.' I will kill him—truly kill him. He does not deserve to join the undead. At heart he is another romantic idiot like Mister Michaels. Look at me, Renwick."

Blut glared, a dark-winged bird of prey, waiting. His bloodless lips made a straight line, the blue whirlpools of his eyes pulling at them all. He advanced toward Renwick. The others watched silently, while Manfred crouched down by the fire. Renwick backed away, reached the wall, and stopped. His eyes showed a sleepy terror, and his hands shook. Blut moved in.

"Undo your jacket."

Renwick's thin hands fumbled at the field jacket, his eyes open wide. Angela thought of Christ at Gesthemane confronting his death. Or perhaps this came later—Christ in hell, face to face with Satan and the eternal darkness. But Renwick looked so human—and afraid, afraid deep in his half-dead mind.

Blut's voice was a malevolent whisper. "Customarily the penalty for traitors is hanging." His hands reached forth and seized Renwick's neck. "The hanging man rarely has time to appreciate the sensations of gradual suffocation. I will let you savor them fully." Slowly he squeezed.

Renwick's face went red, his mouth open. The cords in Blut's hands stood out, and he lifted Renwick effortlessly, letting him dangle a couple inches above the floor. The thin legs, the combat boots kicked futilely at air. Renwick's face darkened.

Michaels murmured, "You fucker." He glanced about desperately, knowing that if he rushed Blut he'd merely be knocked aside again. His eyes fell on the leather bag beside him.

Renwick's face was a reddish purple mask forged of pain, and his legs had stopped moving. Blut let the boots touch the floor. "We will allow you to recover slightly. No—you must not breathe too much." Renwick choked as the hands tightened, his eyes bulging. "This will take time. You will almost catch your breath, then you will dangle and choke for a while. Finally I will tire of trifling, your tongue will come out, your face will go black, you will die. Was your glorious attempt at rebellion worthwhile?" Laughing, he lifted the man, and the thin legs began their senseless dance.

Angela looked away, weeping steadily. She had challenged Renwick to help, and now Blut was torturing him to death.

Michaels took a long bayonet knife from the bag, stood quickly, and thrust the blade into Renwick's back on the left side. Renwick gave a convulsive jerk, eyes opening wide for the last time. Blood soaked a dark circle into the field jacket. His struggles stopped and he went limp.

Angela was shocked, then understood. Renwick was already a dead man, like them all. Mike had prevented Blut from playing with him, tormenting Renwick like a cat with a half-dead bird. Mike himself looked sick, his eyes full of tears.

With a frustrated growl Blut broke Renwick's neck and tossed him aside. Rage blocking his speech, he bared his teeth at Michaels. *"How dare you?"*

His right hand lashed out, a slap from the wrist that caught Michaels along the side of the head. The hand felt like a metal club. The blow knocked him backward over a chair. Groggily he watched Blut sweep toward him, a dark rage about to strike, but the white face hovered above him, the eyes spewing hatred.

"You almost made me forget myself. I was about to kill you. I contemplated crushing in your skull. But I will wait. My congratulations. You have actually frustrated me. That I did not foresee. But your own death, its agony and slowness, will make up for what you have cheated me of."

Michaels swallowed. He felt his pulse throb monotonously in his head and knew that side of his face would swell and turn blue. Oh God, Blut was so strong, so unbelievably strong. What was the use?

Recovering, the vampire forced a smile and looked around the room. He was the only one standing. Michaels sat up slowly. Pat was on his knees, white-faced, still clutching his forearm.

Angela sat slumped against the bookshelves. Tongues of flame, orange, red, yellow, cavorted in the fireplace, their light flickering across the large dim room. Outside the wind moaned, renegade snowflakes creeping inside along with gusts of frigid air. The twisted face of the hearse stared blindly from the wall. Manfred stood before the crackling fire like Cerberus at the gate of Hell. And the true dead were silent as only they can be. Renwick was a mass of sprawling limbs, while Diana lay decorously even in death, on her back with the stake protruding from her chest.

"What a charming domestic scene: my faithful dog before the fire, my guests lying at ease on the floor. Now let me tell you my plans for the evening. You, Miss Rosalba, and your priest friend, will become as I am. You merit joining the undead. The thought of a vampire priest especially amuses me. I do hope he will retain his priestly powers, the ability to do magic tricks with bread and wine. We can use someone who can change wine into blood." Blut laughed once, then stared down at Angela, smiling.

"Angela, my dearest Angel—a rather dark angel—you will be the means of my disposing of both gentlemen. When I have drunk your blood, then I will let you feast on the priest. As for Mister Michaels, we will have his blood also, every drop, but he will not join us. He is a fool who does not deserve the gift of immortality." The blue-white eyes fell on Michaels. "You will die slowly. You will feel life ooze from you drop by drop. And you will know that your beloved Angela has killed you. We will have the blood, but Manfred and the pigs may finish you, clean you to the bone as they did with the unfortunate Mister Russo."

Michaels tried to avoid the trap, to avoid creating visions of his own death. Blut seemed oblivious to the positive side of the death sentence: Mike would not become like them. He had always feared death, but dying seemed less horrible after seeing the alternatives. He glanced over at Diana and shivered. Better than that. In death he would be free of the vampire. A scream of wind slid through the splintered gap in the wall. Cold, so cold, and that smell of death everywhere, a stench soaked into the pores of the house. Already he sensed what death would be. At least then the fear would end.

Angela glared at Blut, her eyes full of tears. "You're horrible—totally horrible." She couldn't stand the icy contempt, the smugness.

Blut laughed. "Thank you."

"What—what you're doing isn't clever or superb, it's sick and trivial. What do you expect from us? How can we fight you? You brag about your centuries of knowledge and your victories, but you've never met anyone who could really oppose you. So you've killed a lot of weak, sad little humans like us—so what? Fight Manfred and his friends if you want to show how wonderful you are."

Blut continued smiling, but her words had their effect. If only she could get him really angry. He would have killed Mike if he hadn't caught himself. Perhaps she could turn that anger on herself.

"You have a nimble tongue, Miss Rosalba, but it will not save you. Don't you see the exquisite fitness of having you dispose of two old lovers?"

She drew in her breath, trying to ignore her tears. "I *won't*. You can't make me."

The eyes grew, blue ice-water holes in that frozen face. "I can. You know I can. And we will drink their blood together. You and I, savor the thick taste on our tongues."

Angela shut her eyes. "Oh God. *No*." But she knew he would make her.

"You will be an excellent vampire, dear Angela. Though you are a whore, you have an impressive intelligence. Especially considering that you are a woman. First, however, we shall have a group confession. I prefer that you all acknowledge your sinfulness, your lowly natures. I prefer that you damn yourselves."

Pat stared at the vampire, his face clammy, white, and his eyes full of pain. He licked his lips. "How can we damn ourselves with a creature like you nearby?" He swallowed, trembling.

"Are you going to teach *me* theology, Priest? I know more about damnation than you ever will. But perhaps I should begin with you. Who better to begin confession with?" Blut walked over to the priest. "Get up." Pat staggered to his feet, swayed, and nearly fell over. He stared at Blut, his face terribly pale. One hand still clutched his forearm above the break. As Blut glared his eyes seemed to dilate, opening deep black pits. "You know you have sinned, do you not?"

"Liar."

Blut snarled, holding back a blow. "I do not remember it being permissible for priests to copulate with young girls. Does Mother Church condone such practices? The name for that particular sin is fornication, Priest."

Pat's mouth formed a weary smile, and he shook his head with a brief laugh like a sob. "I can hardly believe this. You—*you*—are lecturing me on morality. I don't remember rape and murder being permissible."

Blut smiled. "Oh, they are not, but then, I have accepted my damnation, my evil center. You have not. You persist in seeing yourself as a moral, ethical being, despite the fact it is obviously not true. Before you join the dark world I would prefer that you acknowledge your guilt, that you admit you have failed as priest and man. You do not truly believe in God, and you have copulated with our little friend and not even acknowledged the petty sinfulness of the act."

Pat stared at the vampire. Blut's mouth twitched, holding an uneasy smile. "I'm not sorry about what I did. There was nothing sinful about it."

The smile vanished. "And you call yourself a priest? You, a man, are no better than her."

Pat laughed again, a tired "huh." "I know that. She's a remarkable person, surpassing me in many respects."

"*You disgust me.*" The malevolent voice suddenly assumed a cloying sweetness, honey for the flies. "Does your arm hurt, Priest?"

Pat swallowed. "Yes."

Vampire hand blurred white, seized and shook the man's wrist. The priest jerked, unable to hold back the yell. He groaned and tried to fight off the tears.

"You bastard," Angela screamed. "Leave him alone!"

"He's trying to show us how brave he is," Mike said.

Blut ignored them, concentrating his energies on the priest. His hand struck again, seizing Pat's left wrist, wrenching it into the air. Pat winced. His right arm hung limply at his side, the swelling at his wrist obvious. They stared at each other. Blut's thin profile dominated by the hawk nose, dead white with equally colorless hair, rose above the man's bearded face. Sweat showed on the priest's forehead, the thick reddish mustache and beard were damp.

"How would you like your wrists to match perfectly?"

Pat said nothing. Angela started to crawl on her knees across the floor. With Blut's aid she had walked into the room, but she knew she would faint if she tried to stand now. Mike watched her, considered trying another suicidal rush at Blut, then noticed Manfred. The amber eyes stared hungrily.

"That's right, Mister Michaels, stay exactly where you are. Manfred, kill him if he moves. Isn't this touching, Priest? Your beloved is coming."

Angela sat, panting, at their feet. She looked up at them, her face an island in its sea of black hair. "Let him go—stop playing with him." She held Pat's leg, pressing her face against him.

"*Don't touch him.*" Blut's foot shot out, striking her square in the breast. She gasped, choking for breath. Despite her parka, the pain was overwhelming.

Michaels jumped up but stopped when he heard Manfred growl. Pat glared at the vampire, but Blut held his wrist tighter. "Do not think, Angela, that you are any more exempt from pain or death than these two. I don't want you pawing at him with your dirty fingers." His eyes shimmered, boring at Pat, hungry worms eating at the skull. "Now, Priest, tell me about how the two of you met, tell me this tender love story."

Pat breathed hoarsely. "No."

"*Tell me.*" The pale eyes were enormous suckers drawing everything from the skull.

"I was lonely. I had never been sexually intimate with anyone. I knew I wasn't tall or handsome. I was a short, fat man who—that's wrong—no, most people saw me only as a priest. Father, guide, counselor, spiritual adviser and comforter, but no one thought of me as a man. I had been a priest for ten years, and it had gone stale. I was weary of pretending to counsel people when I suffered from the same problems. God seemed to have fled the universe. Not that I could blame him.

"Angela would come see me to talk. She was friendly, very young and alive and beautiful, and she seemed to respond to me. One day I looked at her and wanted very badly to . . . touch her, hold her. We both felt it that day. She had broken up with someone and been hurt; she felt empty too. I held her very tightly. But she had touched me first. She put her hand on mine, and when she stared at me I knew."

Blut hissed "ha," his eyes still fixed on the priest. "But it didn't end there—come to the point, Father Donahue. You had to get your eager fingers down her pants—the story does not end with this touching embrace."

"No. I told her all the doubts about myself and the longing I had for her. And—"

"And so you fucked her." Blut's face had an obscene glee, a voyeur's insistence.

"No—it wasn't like that, not the way you say." He thrust forward his jaw. "You dirty everything. I was clumsy . . . frightened. She helped me, and we did love each other. But I knew later that must be the only time. We both understood that. She was a young beautiful girl—I couldn't bind her with my own problems. I had to decide about being a priest alone." Pat swallowed and closed his eyes. "But now I know someone can love me, and I can love."

"How admirable! How full of self-sacrifice and passion! Don't stop, Priest—tell us about those valiant first efforts at love. Were you a miserable failure, a trifle impotent like our blond friend here?"

"Oh shut up."

Blut squeezed the man's wrist. "Oh no, we want to hear the details about how the little Italian whore deflowered the virgin priest."

"You think I'll tell you about that? *You*? Not for anything."

Blut's eyes grew angry, his fingers tightening. "Oh no? Perhaps that's because you realize what you have done—you have made a mockery of your priesthood, your vows, and committed a grave sin."

"*No.*"

"You felt no guilt, no sense of wrong?"

"Some, but I believe—I know there was nothing wrong in what we did. It was good for us both."

Pat stood with his eyes closed, breathing loudly, the sweat shining on his forehead. Angela stared up at him, wanting to reach out to him, but she was afraid of what Blut would do. The fire snapped, spitting forth an ember. Mike watched the red flake smolder on the carpet. Slumped against a chair beside Diana's body, he realized he liked Pat even better than before. After all the priest had done—God, if he could only do something! A whole bag of crucifixes, garlic, and shit next to him, but they were all worthless. All they could do now was try to die well. Across the room Manfred's eyes were two more embers smoldering.

The wind screamed and screamed, a tortured creature condemned to life. A breath of frozen air hissed through the jagged mouth, the wound torn open in the farm, and careened off the dark walls. Night raced toward its unseen fruition. The black cloak-shape about Blut swirled, and the tendons in his hand swelled like white-hot metal. Pat groaned.

"It was not good, Priest. It was evil. Fornication is a mortal sin. Mother Church teaches that. And in your case, sacrilege was added."

"I don't care," Pat gasped.

"Oh, you don't? It is nothing to you that you wallowed about like a greasy pig in his sty with a piece of trash? With someone who meant nothing to you?"

"Oh you liar! Liar. I love Angela."

Blut's lips pulled back, baring the white teeth, and the wet pink tongue showed in the dark cavern. "You petty dirt. You piece of insignificant scum. So you 'love' her." The word is a curse on his lips. "You are the liar—confess she means nothing to you."

Pat shook his head, screamed, and fell to his knees. Blut's white hand constricted inexorably, like a metal claw or some circular wrench slowly tightening. "Confess," Blut whispered. Pat shook his head, unable to speak.

"Stop it—you can't—not both!" begged Angela.

With a growl Blut snapped the two bones in the forearm, tossing the wrist aside. Pat screamed and sagged. He tried to catch himself with his broken right arm, screamed again, and yanked his arm away so that he fell on his side. His face was bloodless, almost gray.

"Goddamn you—goddamn you!" Mike yelled.

Tears running down her cheeks, Angela tried to help Pat, to soothe him, her hands fumbling at the gray coat. This time Blut's black oxford slammed into her stomach. She sucked in her breath, gagging, and fell on top of Pat. She hit his arm and he cried out. Doubled over, she struggled to breathe, to see.

Mike was up on his knees cursing steadily, exhausting his vocabulary on Blut. For the moment rage had replaced fear—he wanted to kill the vampire—to try to even though Blut would break him in two. But Manfred held him immobile. The dog crouched behind a chair, shadow within shadow. Mike could hear the low growl, a rumble like a distorted purr. The demon would love an excuse to rip him apart.

Angela felt herself being lifted; a hand grabbed her parka at the neck and hoisted her high into the air. She opened her eyes, but the universe was a gray whirlpool, a blankness dissolving into a white oval with giant blue eyes but no eyebrows, hair and lips that melted into the pallor of a corpse. The rest of the room came into focus, all dark shadows and orange firelight, a strange world hovering and flickering with the flames.

"Now, Angela, it is your turn." He lowered her, letting her feet touch the ground. She sagged, swaying dizzily, but his hand held her up. "We have some unfinished business, you and I."

"Oh God," she murmured. The pain had diminished enough so that she understood the full significance of his words.

"I warned you last night that I was not through. I presume you will insist that you love your wormlike friend?" Pat lay on the floor writhing slightly, both arms useless, his eyes shut.

Angela looked at the priest. "Yes."

"And I suppose you will tell me you love that other fool?"

"I don't know. Yes."

Blut made an exasperated noise, a blend of growl and laugh. "And you see no inconsistency to that? What will you do, share your body with them?"

"*No*—it doesn't have to be that kind of love."

Blut pushed her hard backward against the books. It hurt. She gave out a tired moan. Blue fire burning from his skull held her up. "Take off your coat." The vampire burned like a black star, a fragment of dark energy ripped from the cosmos.

Angela watched her fingers rise, vanishing beneath her chin. The zipper opened with a slight, ragged sound. The wind murmured happily, slipping inside, its icy fingers fondling her breasts, fluffing open the parks. The red turtleneck shredded by Diana left her throat and chest exposed. Firelight flashed off the silver metal dangling between her breasts.

For an instant Blut seemed frightened, then angrily he grabbed the cross and wrenched it away, snapping the thin chain. He crumpled the cross in one hand, then flung the twisted metal into the fire.

Mike groaned. Behind the chair, a crouching darkness, Manfred waited. God, if only he could do something—*move.* He felt like a fly stuck to a flypaper strip, hanging and buzzing helplessly.

Angela drew in her breath. With the cross gone she felt totally vulnerable. Pain burned at her throat and low in her belly, the places where Blut had infected her, and fear seeped through her like the cold, a slow poison lying heavy on the bone.

"Take off the coat."

Angela breathed slowly, her blue eyes half-open. Her head pulsed with each heartbeat. Part of her wanted to close her eyes, part wanted to take off her coat. The white face floated before her, an ugliness that would not go away.

Blut made an angry noise; his thin hands nearly ripped the parka pulling it off. He seized the remnants of the turtleneck and tore them apart. The rags landed on Renwick, scarlet shards like dried blood falling on the real thing.

She felt the wind touch her back, slide through her hair, and stroke the nape of her neck. She shuddered, convulsively raising her shoulders. Her bare skin prickled. Blut stepped back and smiled at her nakedness. She swallowed, feeling how dry her throat was. Fear touched her naked skin, and she trembled. She glanced at Mike and Pat, resisting the urge to give up. Blut would kill her, take her, but she would give him as little satisfaction as possible.

His dead mouth split open in a grin. "Still fighting me, Angela? I thought you liked it. Do you know what I'm going to do to you?"

She said nothing, afraid of the answer.

"First we will mingle blood, a rather ancient ceremony of the undead, which should make you more compliant. Then you will cut Mister Michaels, and he may bleed to death and watch me rape you. After I have drained you we will feast together on his blood. Finally, I will reward you with a first victim, the priest."

Blut's hands parted the darkness below his face, revealing the white gash of his dead man's chest. He made a fist, leaving only the forefinger extended, skin-covered bone. Angela saw the thin phalanges, the thicker joints, and the long jagged nail curving from the end. Still smiling he plunged the nail into his chest, jerking the finger to open a wound. Blood gathered and reddened the cut but did not flow.

His other hand seized her arm. The closer Blut came, the more her stomach and the marks in her throat hurt. Scratches made by Diana crisscrossed her breasts. His finger punctured the skin of her left breast just over the heart.

She started, tried to pull away, but his icy fingers held her arm. The fingernail opened a small cut, blood trickling down her dark skin. She clenched her teeth and squirmed, tears coming to her eyes. The pain was insignificant, but Blut's presence, his eyes, the wind and storm screaming, amplified everything. The face wavered, a white pool in the darkness, and his words seemed to sound in her head without passing through her ears.

"Now embrace me—let our bloods mingle."

Plunge into the abyss, the frozen stream—let the icy jaws have you. The urge lasted an instant, then she shut her eyes, fleeing into the darkness.

Waves of blackness washed about her, eddies of polar water pulling her down. Blut drew her close, forcing his grim caricature of an embrace. Icy chest, dead flesh burning her—venom poured from his wound into hers, and blood, warm and vital, went into him. Oh God—he was inside her again, crawling around in her head—there was no place left to hide. She groaned.

"Angela!" Mike's voice came from a distance, above water. Blut clung to her, trying to drag her down. "No, Angela—*don't.*"

She sensed Blut's terrible anger, his hatred for Mike and the priest. Worm thing gnawing at her, eating out her head, chewing up brain and blood to empty her skull. God help me . . . I can't take much . . . Blut was falling away, leaving only a weak residual force. She opened her eyes and saw the angry white face.

"You are annoying, Mister Michaels." His eyes returned to Angela. "We are not finished yet, though now you belong to me. First we must drink."

He gripped her arms below the shoulders and

she understood how he could break bones with his hands. "Thus did the king of vampires." Corpse face dropping out of sight, then the cold lips fastened themselves on her skin and sucked greedily. She heard the sounds. A horrible parody of a baby nursing, this great black monstrosity slurping at her breast. The room disappeared.

Michaels grew frantic. Her face was a battleground reflecting the opposing forces. "Oh Christ." He clenched his fists, and his eyes shifted from Blut to the yellow-eyed demon. *"Angela."*

She tried to hear him. Then the white face rose before her. The vampire recalled a clumsy child who had played with lipstick, a red circle about his mouth. The painted lips moved. "Now it is your turn." Her eyes fell, staring at the hole in his chest. "Drink." His voice dropped to a whisper. *"Drink."*

Nausea rose in her throat. She shook her head. Blut was surprised, then angry. *"Drink."* His hands tightened; she felt him reach toward her, trying to crawl his way back inside her.

She could not withstand another full-scale intrusion. The wounds in her throat and chest burned, her belly was ready to cramp. The vampire thought he had her under control, which gave her a kind of advantage. She could drink and pretend her resistance was gone. But staring at that gouged chest, that strip of dead yellow-white flesh, made her want to vomit.

"Drink!" Blut hissed the command through clenched teeth, growing angry. She sensed the dark energy gathering about him. The wind swept through the room, moaning hollowly. The

icy worm chewed at her skull, seeking a place to feed, to nest, to grow. She would not kill for Blut, not yet, but anything was better than letting him into her mind again.

The white gap of flesh expanded, filling her vision. She closed her eyes, the sickness in her throat and stomach overwhelming. Her lips touched his chest and she gagged. A corpse's skin: smelling faintly rotten, dead fish or frog belly smooth, slightly damp and so cold. Blood on her lips, some in her mouth—a taste like when she has a nosebleed—but this blood, like everything else about him, was cold.

"*Ah!*" His hand clutched her hair, crushing her face against him, and she felt a shudder of excitement pass through him. She swallowed blood, choked, swallowed more blood, more— he would suffocate her—she would drown in blood.

He pulled her head back. She choked, coughed wildly, while he watched smiling. If she had had food in her stomach she would throw up. Only his power kept her standing.

"It becomes simpler after you are dead."

"Goddamn you, Blut—Goddamn you."

"And now, Mister Michaels, at last it is your turn."

His hands drew the blackness together, covering his white chest, and from somewhere he produced a long ivory handle. Always smiling, he pulled out the blade. The firelight turned the ivory orange and glimmered on the steel. Angela shuddered. Sharp knives had always disturbed her.

"Do you know what this is, Mister Michaels?"

"Of course I do, you fucking bastard. I'm not quite as stupid as you think."

"Ah, but you are. If you had any real intelligence you would have never returned here, not for her or any woman. But I digress. I was about to tell you about this razor. It is over three hundred years old, a genuine heirloom constructed of the finest ivory and steel. I still use it."

"*You*?"

"Yes. I do shave occasionally." He smiled. "The hair and fingernails continue to grow for some time after death. This is a beautiful piece of steel, incredibly sharp. Would you like a demonstration?"

"No thank you."

"Regardless, you shall have one. Angela is going to cut open your wrist so you may bleed to death."

Angela trembled, feeling the icy wind on her bare skin, chill after chill slithering up her back. She stared into space, eyes half-closed. She tried to ignore the taste in her mouth. If she looked at Mike she would give herself away. She saw the razor, licked her lips, and tasted blood. Steel and Blut's blood. The hint of an idea drifted by.

"You realize, of course, this means you will truly die. You are not worthy to join the undead."

"Ah, isn't that too bad." The sarcasm was forced, his mouth dry. He tried to ignore the razor.

"I imagine it will take some time for you to bleed to death. We will let your blood collect in the log bucket." Blut walked toward the fireplace, lifted the ancient gray bucket, staying well back, and threw the contents, old logs and dried boards, into the flames. He stepped away quickly, almost fearfully. The fire had died down but now roared back alive, flames devouring the old wood, the bright orange lighting up the room. Angela felt a touch of warmth.

Blut went to the center of the room before the coffin. His blackness, his dark limbs and flowing cape, differed from the metal. The man-shape hungrily swallowed light, creating an utter darkness, while the coffin reflected the firelight, its corners and edges gleaming red-orange.

"Mister Michaels, do you know why I wanted my coffin transported to Chicago?"

"So you could get started there. Plenty of unsuspecting people."

"Very good. So good Mister Russo doubtlessly thought of it. A pity about him. As I said, you are stupid. Did he tell you why I need my coffin?"

"Yeah. I just wish there was some way I could destroy that stinking hunk of steel."

Blut laughed. "Do you think this is my only coffin? I have another hidden in the house, another hidden in the land, two in Udolph, and all are virtually indestructible. When I returned to existence this time, I determined to make myself absolutely secure. And believe me, I will have my way. I will go to Chicago. Perhaps more slowly than I intended, but five victims are well worth the delay. Besides, when you have lived for hundreds of years, minor delays seem insignificant. But enough of this." The pale eyes expanded into blue vortexes. "Come here."

Angela watched Mike. He stood slowly. He looked scared and utterly exhausted, running on

nerve alone. Red-brown splotches covered his
field jacket, Diana's blood. The long blond hair
was woven into tangles, and the five-day growth
of beard added to his scraggly, worn out appearance. The side of his face was swelling and
changing color where Blut had hit him. She
wanted to hug Mike but knew Blut would retal-
iate instantly. Pat looked even worse—shivering,
both arms lying swollen at his sides, his face a
white pasty color. He must be in mild shock.
Both forearms broken, all four bones. God, that
must hurt. She was aware of the tears in her
eyes.

Why had they come? Because she was stupid
enough to want them to come. Tony and Diana
were already dead. And Renwick. Pat and Mike
. . . Five deaths because of her, when she might
have been the only one. If she started crying Blut
would become suspicious. She must wait and
watch for . . . *what*? She would not give up. She
would not lie back passively like some stupid
blond heroine in the movies and expose her
throat, letting the vampire finish her.

"Come on, Mister Michaels. Or would you
prefer that Manfred drag you over here?"

Mike stared at the dog, a black shape with
yellow eyes crouching in the shadow. He drew in
his breath. He was tired and ached all over.
Christ, he didn't want to die. And Angela would
do it. She stood there shivering, looking thin,
sick, and very cold. Blut Farm had dulled her
beauty. She was gaunt now, her black hair
straight and lifeless, scratches covering her
chest, the cut on her breast dripping blood, her
skin prickly and tight. He tried to remember her
last night. He would never hold her again.

"*Manfred.*" The dog growled and stood.

•Michaels swallowed once, then stepped over Pat. Christ, bodies all over the place—Diana and Renwick, their blood soaking into the damned house, greedy leech like its master. Walking felt stiff. It hurt to move. He stopped before the coffin. Warmth reached him from the fireplace, from the rippling orange flames.

"Very good, Mister Michaels."

Mike stared at his feet, the damp pointed toes of his cowboy boots against the red-and-black rug.

"*Angela.*"

Michaels watched her walk, Blut's gaze buoying her up. She would not look at him, her blue eyes staring vacantly at nothing.

"Now we are ready."

The vampire stood before the couple, a dark form about to enfold man and woman within its black wings, and behind them glistened his bark from the underworld. A satanic priest preparing the obscene, bloody caricature of a sacrament before his altar of death. Blut smiled and raised the razor, his face shining with evil joy. The pale blue eyes drew them toward the icy depths. Before the three figures the fire raged, a riot of orange and yellow.

"Take the razor, Angela."

She did not move. Her eyes blinked.

"*Take it.*"

Blut held out the razor, the back of the blade between thumb and forefinger, leaving the edge untouched. The perfect sharpness must not be dulled. Angela grasped the milky handle. Smooth. Cold. Blut's touch made the ivory cold.

"No, Angela—throw it into the fire." Pat had

managed to sit up, breathing hard with both arms dangling.

"Be silent, Priest, and wait. Your turn comes next. You should be happy to see your rival eliminated." His eyes fell on Michaels. "If you resist, if you struggle, I will let Manfred have you. He will maul you sufficiently to keep you quiet." His hand struck like a white snake, seizing Michael's wrist.

Mike shivered. God the fingers were cold—and hard, like metal. Fear throbbed through him. Blut tore off the leather glove, pulled down the field jacket sleeve, then held up the wrist. His grip was tight enough to hurt. Mike felt his own quick pulse under the dead fingers. An inch of skin below his palm was exposed.

"Would you like to confess your sinfulness, Mister Michaels? Your stupidity?"

He shook his head.

"I doubted you would. You should enjoy watching Angela admit she felt nothing for you. Last night she was troublesome, but before I finish with her she will acknowledge her own worthlessness. Now, my dear Angela, you will make the incision perpendicular to the arm. You will cut him to the bone. Another type of incision might kill him faster, but this will be slow and painful. As he bleeds to death he may watch me rape you. Go on, cut him."

"Throw it away, Angela—in the fire." Pat's voice resounded with pain.

"Shut up, Priest. Go on, Angela."

Her lips moved, mouthing the word "fire."

She and Michaels stared at each other. Her blue eyes were sad but compassionate. He could see the tension, the trembling in the arm and hand holding the razor, but he could not tell what she would do.

"Angela, look at me," Blut said.

She raised her eyes, shuddered. Bottomless blue pools, crevasses in the glacier that go on forever. God, he's trying to get inside again, and she can't . . . not with him staring. Maybe if she moved? She lifted her hand, holding the razor like a hatchet. Blut smiled, baring his teeth, then turned to show Michaels his satisfaction.

Mike saw the gloating face, felt the eyes stake him down. He saw the razor go back, firelight sparkling on the blade, Angela's scared face tensing for the blow. She was really going to do it, and he realized he had never been so afraid. "Angela . . !"

She struck, hitting as hard as she could in a whack that sent forth a tremendous spurt of blood.

Blut had turned to look, but too late. That beautiful edge of perfectly honed steel cut easily through the dead flesh, opening his entire throat in a deep gash from under the left ear to a point to the right of his larynx. He screamed, a horrible cry that made his earlier rages nothing.

His jaw fell open, revealing the large white teeth discolored by a bloody foam, and his eyes clawed for Angela. He tried to growl but could only gurgle. She threw away the razor as if she had discovered some venomous insect crawling from the ivory onto her hand.

"The fire, Mike—*fire!*" she shouted.

Michaels stared dumbly, too surprised to move. *Fire?* Blut was choking, clawing at his severed throat, his borrowed blood all over—but he was by no means destroyed, only hurt, turning now on Angela. She screamed and fell to the floor, agony in her chest and belly.

Michaels understood. He hesitated, then rushed at Blut, catching him totally unaware and knocking the vampire backwards. Claws ripped at his shoulders, but Mike hit him again in a tackle that sent them both flying toward the fireplace. Flaming red mouths rushed forth to meet them.

Blut shrieked and caught fire like a dry leaf. Michaels felt his own hands burn, flame eating at the bare skin and singeing the arms of his field jacket. He let go of Blut, squirmed madly, and fell backward out of the fire. Before him Blut lay outstretched on the wood, howling, howling, flaming like some great misshapen black log. Michaels felt the heat radiate forth and begin to burn his face. He turned, staggering away on his knees.

A black fury with yellow eyes roared out of the shadows straight at him. He covered his face with one arm and desperately rolled sideways. The dog hurtled past. With a shock he realized Manfred did not want him.

Blut had managed to stand, a black silhouette with a corona of yellow-white fire, screaming and waving its arms. The dog hit him square in the chest, knocking him back into the flames, where the two dark forms merged, melted, and burned together. The demon's snarl became another howling, and the cries of the dog and the dying dead man slit open the belly of night.

Mike turned, stumbled toward Angela. She did

not see him. She lay on the floor rolling in pain, her eyes fused shut. Everywhere Blut had touched her burned, blood and semen turning to liquid fire, a jellied napalm with delayed action. The venom blood filled her rib cage with a fiery whirlwind, devouring heart and lungs. The remnants of his seed tried to eat out her womb, wanting to leave her as barren and sterile as its source.

"Angela—Angela." Mike tried to hold her.

The night, rent open and mortally wounded, echoed the death cry of the vampire. Tremendous winds hurtled through the room, screaming in at the front door and the punctured wall, bringing a swirl of frozen air and snow. The wind fed the fire, swelling the flames. The house creaked, an awesome shudder. The wind continued to grow and buffeted the windows. Shrill squeals joined the din, pig cries with an unearthly quality.

Michaels bent over Angela trying to discover what was wrong. Blut hadn't touched her, but she lay clutching her stomach and moaning, her eyes shut. The priest staggered toward them on his knees, face still white.

"We must leave this place." He could hardly be heard through the noise.

Mike nodded. "I know."

The terrible stiffness flowed out of Angela's face. Eyes, lips relaxed; her body straightened, her hands going slack. Mike realized she was trembling. God, she must be freezing. He grabbed her coat, wrapped it around her, and hugged her at the same time. Her eyes half-opened, and she stared at him.

"He's dying," she said quietly. "For real this time."

Dog and man rolled about on the fiery bed, locked in a deadly embrace like two mad lovers, their dark bodies wrestling, twisting, amidst the orange holocaust. Embers and bits of logs flew from the fireplace and smoldered on the rug. The screaming, whirling wind breathed upon them; the embers glowed white-orange and flared alive. The rug began to burn. The house quivered, groaning deep within the foundations.

Angela stared into the flames. "Fire. Fire destroys vampires. Better than anything. Tony said so."

Mike watched the flames grow. Orange tendrils eagerly crawled along the rug, leaping up the blood-colored curtains and throwing forth creepers. As the fire consumed, the room finally warmed up.

With a crash a window exploded inward—the red curtain puffed open as the head appeared, thick snout first, black hog head with its tiny eyes, the short legs and trotters extended—ice-like shards of glass showered the floor. The long dark body flowed through, slicing itself open on the glass. A tortured squeal blended with the wind's shriek as the demon plunged into the fire, joining the writhing figures.

The wind screamed louder in reply, screamed through the broken window, a new mouth for its icy breath. A second demon soared through the window and rushed into the fire; then another followed, and another. Their form, their shape, seemed to waver, to change. Drapes of red-orange flame twisted about the shattered window, then the fire ate the dark wood. Fire-light glowed red on the dark hides and lit up the terrified faces of the damned before they were lost forever. Blut and Manfred were gone. Perhaps they lay beneath the other black forms, perhaps they were already falling toward hell. The stench of burning hair and flesh filled the room, and the noise was deafening. The cry of the wind blowing up the flames, the shrieks of the damned—a sound like an animal being slaughtered but with a diabolical edge, the crackling roaring fire—all merged in an over-whelming dissonance, the death song of Blood Farm.

Michaels saw the red-orange tongues reach for the hearse's mutilated face. "Angela," he yelled, "we've got to get out before the hearse catches fire—can you walk?"

She sat up, breathing deeply, and pushed her hair back out of her face. He noticed the smooth expanse of her throat—the wounds had van-ished. "Yes, now I can." He couldn't hear, but understood her nod. She began pulling on her coat.

Mike glanced at Pat, coughed, and blinked. Christ, the smoke was getting bad. "How about you, can you walk?"

The priest nodded, but his face was pale, and his eyes showed the hurt. Both arms hung at his side, swollen and useless.

Mike helped Angela stand. She swayed slightly, then smiled. "It's okay. It's gone."

He couldn't hear her. The din was incredible. He grabbed Pat's arm above the elbow and helped him up. He stepped over Renwick's long

thin body and had a last look at the dead Christ
face. Flames had reached Diana's feet, tickling
the soles and curling toward the pink toenails.

They stumbled into the hallway. Wind and
snow charged them through the front door, hitting them in the face, but the cold fresh air felt
good after the fiery heat and the thick, dark
smoke. Mike turned for a last look. Thick smoke
obscured the room, but the conflagration threw
a hellish red glow over everything. Flames
touched the wall of books, and the dusty brown
volumes caught fire with a whoosh. He turned to
follow Angela through the front door, still holding onto Pat. A blast of wind hit them, slapped at
the front porch blowing snow up the steps in
white clouds. The snow-covered ice on the porch
was slippery. Angela paused to yank at her parka
zipper.

"Hurry!" Mike yelled, grabbing her with his
free arm.

They stepped off the porch onto the icy steps.
Pat almost fell, but Mike held him up. They
waded through a foot of snow while the wind
undulated the surface of the land about them,
blurring the boundary between ground and air.
Giant flakes swarmed about like fuzzy white
insects. The wind gave out a terrible cry, a
death rattle, and whirled round the house. The
gale nearly knocked them over, but Michaels
closed his eyes to shut out the stinging snow
and concentrated on pulling Pat and Angela
forward.

The hearse exploded, and although the sound
was muffled by the house and wind, its sudden-
ness made Michaels lunge forward wildly and
his right foot slipped out from under him. They

all went down. He lay still for a few seconds, tasting the snow in his mouth. He rose, brushing off his face and coat. He saw the house, a white skull with fire pouring from its sockets. Christ, what an incredible relief.

Angela sat up, the white snow in her black hair and all over her face. Another time he would have laughed because she looked funny, a little girl some mean kid had shoved into the snow.

"Pat?" She and Mike gently pulled the priest out of the snow. She brushed off his face, the thick beard. He looked cold and sick.

"I'm all right." He stared at the burning house. "It has been worth it. Only I don't want to fall over again."

"Christ, look at it burn," Mike said.

The priest nodded. "Fire cleanses. Purifies." He sighed, then closed his eyes, searching wearily for the words. " 'For behold the day cometh that shall burn as an oven, and all the proud and all that do wickedly shall be stubble, and the day that cometh shall burn them up that it shall leave them neither root nor branch.' That's not quite right, but it's close."

Mike suddenly realized how quiet it was. *No wind.* Overhead the sky was blue-gray, the flakes dwindling to nothing. "Let's get out of here," he said.

Pat watched the fire intently. With a sigh an entire section of the farm gave way, walls and roof caving in with a gush of orange flame. "All right." They turned from the house.

In the east the sky had a pink tinge; overhead the clouds drifted back to the nothingness from which they had come, leaving gaps of sky and stars. Behind, the crackling murmur of the dying house grew fainter. Dawn, cold and clear.

Off in the west a reddish glow lit up the sky. "What's that?" Angela asked.

"Udolph is burning. Dying with its master. Neither root nor branch." Pat looked haggard, his eyes feverish with circles beneath them, the bearded face of some saintly hermit tested in the wilderness. He walked drunkenly but was careful not to let his wrists touch his sides. They entered the grove of trees and saw the black bus with its large metal vw on the front.

Michaels slid open the second door and looked in back. "Pat, you can lie down here."

Angela looked at the priest. "I'd like to give you a hug, but that might hurt you."

"I certainly couldn't reciprocate."

She smiled, then put her arms around his shoulders and squeezed very carefully. She pressed her cheek against his face, feeling the long soft beard, faintly damp and still cold from the snow, and she kissed him lightly on the lips. He raised the corners of his mouth, smiling wearily, even though his eyes still showed pain. They stared at each other.

Mike grasped the man's shoulder. "We'll stop the first place we can for a doctor. Not Udolph, though. We may go further north."

They helped him in. One arm hit the door frame, and he groaned. His wrists were big, awkward burdens. The back was empty except for an old tarp he sagged down onto. Michaels jumped out of the van into the snow and nearly fell over. God, was he stiff and tired.

Angela grabbed his arm. In the soft dawn light

the blue of her eyes showed beneath the dark brows, and he remembered seeing her for the first time, that face with the long straight nose and Cupid lips surrounded by black hair.

"Now it's your turn." She put her arms around him, and despite their weariness they hugged as hard as they could, feeling strength and life.

"Oh God," she said. "I thought I was going to kill you."

"So did I. You scared the shit out of me."

She laughed. His grin was coming back, the blond mustache hiding the corners of his mouth, crinkles forming at his blue eyes, the long yellow hair a tangled mess. She thought of the freaky stranger grinning at her from the hearse and realized that the black hat was lost forever in the house. She went for his mouth, felt his lips touch hers, move slowly. She thought of the agony doubling her over yesterday morning when they had tried to kiss. She opened her mouth wider, and they sensed each other's desire, muted though it was, the fire in the blood which is so much a part of being alive. The kiss was a promise between them.

As he drew away he noticed the cold air around them and how the sky had grown lighter, faintly blue. He stared at her, and the words rolled out: "Oh Christ, Angela."

"It's good not to be afraid anymore. For now."

"Yeah. We'd better get moving." But he didn't want to let go of her, to risk losing her again.

She smiled, aware of his emotion and her own.

"This place will leave scars."

She nodded, remembering her nightmares in

that horrible room, Blut coalescing out of the darkness, the icy worm coming for her. She held Mike tightly.

He sighed again. "It's been a long night."

"Yes," she said softly.

A Message To Our Readers...

As a person who reads books, you have access to countless possibilities for information and delight.

The world at your fingertips.

Millions of kids don't.

They don't because they can't read. Or won't. They've never found out how much fun reading can be. Many young people never open a book outside of school, much less finish one.

Think of what they're missing—all the books you loved as a child, all those you've enjoyed and learned from as an adult.

That's why there's RIF. For twenty years, Reading is Fundamental (RIF) has been helping community organizations help kids discover the fun of reading.

RIF's nationwide program of local projects makes it possible for young people to choose books that become theirs to keep. And, RIF activities motivate kids, so that they *want* to read.

To find out how RIF can help in your community or even in your own home, write to:

RIF
Dept. BK-2
Box 23444
Washington, D.C.
20026

Founded in 1966, RIF is a national nonprofit organization with local projects run by volunteers in every state of the union.

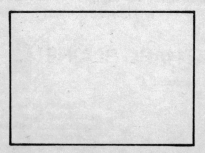